Please turn to the back of the book
for an interview with Anne Perry

"FASCINATING."
—*San Francisco Examiner*

"An Anne Perry novel is a delight to read as much for its Victorian-era details as for the mystery it unfolds. . . . [She] captivates readers with her vivid descriptions of a time that often has been thought virtuous but in reality was plagued with problems and scandals. She intertwines characters and their lives—their daily routines, hardships and emotions—into a suspenseful tale that always tackles a social issue."

—*Chicago Tribune*

"Anne Perry is deliciously at it again. . . . Perry's style is expressly gracious and fluid, as impeccable as Victorian manners. And she will keep you guessing right up until the final pages, when everything suddenly, violently, falls into place, revealing yet again the depths to which people will sink in order to keep their proprieties and public facades intact. Perry's seamless surface reveals a seamy underside, and the shock is swift and sure."

—*The Providence Sunday Journal*

Please turn the page for more reviews. . . .

"A RIVETING READ YOU DON'T WANT TO PUT DOWN."
—JILL JACKSON
Hollywood

"Perry, as always, excels at portraying the richness, poverty, and class distinctions of Victorian England. However, she achieves brilliance in palming the ace which would give the whole game away to a reader alert enough to spot it."
—*Chicago Sun-Times*

"History, social commentary, and suspense blend artfully . . . [The] reader . . . will be swept along by the narrative's rush and engaged by its attention to period detail. Aiding Pitt is a cast of smart, well-drawn female characters. . . . Yet again, Perry delivers an astute and gripping examination of life behind Victorian England's virtuous facade."
—*Publishers Weekly* (starred review)

"Anne Perry, who critics and fans agree writes Victorian mysteries better than anyone else, explores high and low London society in Bedford Square."
—*St. Paul Pioneer Press* (Pick of the Week)

By Anne Perry
Published by The Ballantine Publishing Group:

Featuring Thomas and Charlotte Pitt:
THE CATER STREET HANGMAN
CALLANDER SQUARE
PARAGON WALK
RESURRECTION ROW
BLUEGATE FIELDS
RUTLAND PLACE
DEATH IN THE DEVIL'S ACRE
CARDINGTON CRESCENT
SILENCE IN HANOVER CLOSE
BETHLEHEM ROAD
HIGHGATE RISE
BELGRAVE SQUARE
FARRIERS' LANE
THE HYDE PARK HEADSMAN
TRAITORS GATE
PENTECOST ALLEY
ASHWORTH HALL
BRUNSWICK GARDENS
BEDFORD SQUARE

Featuring William Monk:
THE FACE OF A STRANGER
A DANGEROUS MOURNING
DEFEND AND BETRAY
A SUDDEN, FEARFUL DEATH
THE SINS OF THE WOLF
CAIN HIS BROTHER
WEIGHED IN THE BALANCE
THE SILENT CRY
A BREACH OF PROMISE

BEDFORD SQUARE

Anne Perry

BALLANTINE BOOKS • NEW YORK

FOR MY MOTHER

A Ballantine Book
Published by The Ballantine Publishing Group
Copyright © 1999 by Anne Perry

www.randomhouse.com/BB/

ISBN 0-449-00582-8

Manufactured in the United States of America

First Ballantine Books Hardcover Edition: April 1999
First Ballantine Books International Edition: January 2000
First Ballantine Books Domestic Mass Market Edition: April 2000

10 9 8 7 6 5 4 3 2 1

1

P_{ITT} _LEANED OUT_ of the bedroom window in his nightshirt and looked down into the street below. The police constable was standing on the pavement staring up at him. The constable's face, yellow in the gaslight from the street lamps, was tense and unhappy, and it was for more reason than simply having woken the commander of the Bow Street police station at four o'clock in the morning.

"Dead, sir," he answered Pitt's question. "An' I can't see as 'ow it could a' bin an accident, not 'ow 'e is, an' w'ere I found 'im. An' I oughta be gettin' back, sir. I darsen't leave 'im there by 'isself, sir. Someone might move 'im, like . . . mess wif evidence."

"Yes, of course," Pitt agreed. "Go back, Constable. You did the right thing. I'll get dressed and I'll be there. I presume you haven't had a chance to call the surgeon or the mortuary van?"

"No sir, I come straight 'ere, seein' as w'ere 'e is."

"I'll call them. You go back and stand guard."

"Yes sir. I'm sorry, sir."

"Don't be. You did the right thing," Pitt repeated, pulling his head in and shivering involuntarily. It was June—at least nominally summer—but in London the nights were still chilly, and there was a faint mist hanging over the city.

"What is it?" Charlotte sat up in bed and fumbled for a match. He heard it scrape and then saw the flame as it caught the wick of the candle. It lit her face softly, gleaming on the

1

warm, dark color of her hair, which was falling out of its long braid. She looked worried.

"They've found a body in Bedford Square," he answered. "It seems as if he was murdered."

"Do they really need you for that?" she protested. "Is it somebody important?"

Since his promotion Pitt had been asked to concentrate on those cases which were of political significance or threatened scandal.

"Maybe not," he replied, closing the window and walking over to where his clothes were hanging across the back of the chair. He took off his nightshirt and began to dress, not bothering with collar or cravat. There was water in the ewer, and he poured it into the basin. It was cold, but there was certainly no time to light the kitchen stove and heat it so he could shave. Unfortunately, there was also no time for a cup of tea, which he would have liked even more. He splashed his face and felt the sharp tingle of coldness, then with his eyes shut, felt for the towel.

"Thank you." He took it from Charlotte's outstretched hand. He rubbed his face vigorously, feeling the rough cotton stir the blood and warm him. "Because apparently he was on the front doorstep of one of the big houses," he replied.

"Oh." She understood the implications. London was peculiarly sensitive to scandal just now. In the previous year, 1890, a scandal had occurred at Tranby Croft. Now the trial was rocking the entire country. It was all very regrettable, a matter of gambling at a country house party, an accusation of cheating at baccarat, an illegal game, and of course an indignant denial. But what could not be hidden or excused was that the Prince of Wales had been involved and was now to be called to the witness stand to give evidence. Half of London opened the daily newspapers with bated breath.

Pitt finished dressing. He put his arms around Charlotte and kissed her, feeling the warmth of her skin and pushing back the heavy hair with his fingers, enjoying its softness with an all-too-fleeting pleasure.

"Go back to bed," he said gently. "I'll be home when I can,

but I doubt it'll be for breakfast." He tiptoed across the floor and opened the door quietly, not to waken the children and Gracie, the maid, asleep up on the top floor. The landing gaslight was always left on very low, and it was sufficient for him to see his way downstairs. In the hall he picked up the telephone—a fairly recent acquisition in his home—and asked the operator to connect him with the Bow Street Station. When the sergeant answered, Pitt instructed him to send the police surgeon and mortuary van to Bedford Square. He replaced the receiver, put on his boots and took his jacket from the hook by the front door. He slid back the latch and stepped outside.

The air was damp and chilly but it was already beginning to get light, and he walked quickly along the glistening pavement towards the corner of Gower Street and turned left. It was only a few yards into Bedford Square, and even from that distance he saw the unhappy figure of the constable standing alone about halfway along the pavement. He looked immensely relieved to see Pitt striding towards him out of the gloom. His expression brightened visibly and he waved his bull's-eye lantern.

"Over 'ere, sir!" he called out.

Pitt neared him and glanced where he was pointing. The dark figure was easy to see lying sprawled on the front steps of the large house immediately to their left. It seemed almost as if he must have been reaching for the doorbell when he fell. The cause of death was apparent. There was a deep and bloody wound on the side of his head. It was difficult to imagine how he could have come by it in any accident. Nothing that could have occurred in the roadway would have thrown him so far, nor was there another wound visible.

"Hold the light for me," Pitt requested, kneeling down beside the body and looking at it more closely. He touched his hand gently to the man's throat. There was no pulse, but the flesh was still just warm. "What time did you find him?" he asked.

"Sixteen minutes afore four, sir."

3

Pitt glanced at his pocket watch. It was now thirteen minutes past. "What time did you come this way before that?"

"Abaht quarter afore three, sir. 'E weren't 'ere then."

Pitt turned around to look up at the street lamps. They were off. "Find the lamplighter," he ordered. "He can't have been here long ago. They're still lit on Keppel Street, and it's barely daylight enough to see anywhere. He's a bit sharp as it is."

"Yessir!" the constable agreed with alacrity.

"Anyone else?" Pitt asked as the constable took a step away.

"No sir. Too early for deliveries. They don' start till five at the soonest. No maids up yet. 'Nother 'alf hour at least. Bit late fer partyers. Most o' them's 'ome by three. Though yer never know yer chances, like. Yer could ask. . . ."

Pitt smiled wryly. He noticed that the constable had abandoned doing it himself and considered Pitt the one to work the gentry of Bedford Square and ask them if they had happened to notice a corpse on the doorstep, or even a fight in the street, as they returned from their revels.

"If I have to," Pitt said dourly. "Did you look in his pockets?"

"No sir. I left that fer you, sir."

"I don't suppose you have any idea who he is? Not a local servant or tradesman, suitor to one of the maids around here?"

"No sir, I in't never seen 'im afore. I don't reckon as 'e belongs 'ere. Shall I go an' find the lamplighter, sir, afore 'e goes too far?"

"Yes, go and find him. Bring him back here."

"Yessir!" And before Pitt could think of any more questions for him, he put his bull's-eye down on the step, turned on his heel and strode off into the broadening dawn light.

Pitt picked up the lantern and examined the dead man. His face was lean, the skin weathered, as if he spent much of his time outside. There was a faint stubble of beard across his cheeks. His hair had little color, a dark mousy brown that had probably been fair in his youth. His features were pleasant enough, a trifle pinched, upper lip too short, eyebrows wispy, the left one with a pronounced break in it as if from an old

4

scar. It was a face easy to see and forget, like thousands of others. Pitt used his finger to ease the collarless shirt back an inch or two. The skin under it was fair, almost white.

Next he looked at the man's hands. They were strong, lean, with fingernails chipped and far from clean, but they did not look like the hands of a manual worker. There were no calluses. The knuckles were torn as if he had been in a hard fight very recently, perhaps only moments before his death. The bleeding was slight in spite of the ripped skin, and there had not been time for bruising.

Pitt slipped his hand into a jacket pocket and was startled to close his fingers over a small metal box. He pulled it out and turned it over under the light. It was exquisite. He could not tell at a glance whether it was gold-plated or solid, or possibly even pinchbeck, that brilliant imitation of gold, but it was intricately modeled like a tiny cathedral reliquary, the sort used to house the bones of saints. The top was decorated with a tiny reclining figure, relaxed in death and wearing long clerical robes and a bishop's mitre. Pitt opened the box and sniffed gently. Yes, it was what he had supposed, a snuffbox. It could hardly have belonged to the man who lay dead at his feet. Even if it were pinchbeck it would be worth more than he had seen in a month, perhaps in a year.

But if he had been caught stealing it, why was he left here on the doorstep, and above all, why had whoever killed him not retrieved the box?

Pitt felt to see if there was anything else in the pocket, and found only a short length of string and a pair of bootlaces, apparently unused. In the man's other pockets he found a key, a piece of rag for a handkerchief, three shillings and four pence in small change, and several pieces of paper, one of which was a receipt for three pairs of socks purchased only two days before from a shop in Red Lion Square. That, if diligently followed, might possibly tell them who he was. There was nothing else to indicate his name or where he lived.

Of course, there were thousands of people who had no homes and simply slept in doorways or under railway arches and bridges, or at this time of the year in the open, if tolerant police did not disturb them. But looking at this man, Pitt deduced that if such misfortune had happened to him, it must have been recent. His clothes were all hard worn; there were holes in his socks—these were not the new ones! The soles of his boots were paper-thin in places, but he was dry. He had not the inlaid grime or the musty, moldy smell of someone who lived outside.

Pitt stood up as he heard footsteps along the pavement and saw the familiar, awkward, angular figure of Sergeant Tellman approaching him from the Charlotte Street direction. He would not have mistaken Tellman even in the lamplight, but the dawn was now whitening the eastern sky.

Tellman reached him and stopped. He was hastily dressed, but it was noticeable only in his jacket, buttoned one hole crooked. His collar was as tight and straight as usual, his cravat as plain and neat, his hair wet, combed back from his lantern-jawed face. He looked dour also, as usual.

"Some gentleman too drunk to avoid being run down by a hansom?" he asked.

Pitt was used to Tellman's opinion of the privileged.

"If he was a gentleman he was on extremely hard times," he replied, glancing down at the body. "And he wasn't hit by a vehicle. There isn't a mark on his clothes other than where he fell, but his knuckles are grazed as if he put up quite a fight. Look at him yourself."

Tellman eyed Pitt sharply, then bent as he was told and examined the dead man. When he stood up again, Pitt held out his hand with the snuffbox in it.

Tellman's eyebrows shot up. "He had that?"

"Yes."

"Then he was a thief. . . ."

"So who killed him, and why here on the front doorstep? He didn't go in or out that way!"

"Don't reckon as he was killed here either," Tellman said with a hint of satisfaction. "That wound on his head must have bled a good bit . . . heads do. Cut yourself and you'll soon see. But there's not much on the step around him. I'd say he was killed somewhere else and put here."

6

"Because he was a thief?"

"Seems a good reason."

"Then why leave the snuffbox? Apart from its value, it's the one thing that could trace him back to the house he stole it from. There can't be many like it."

"Don't know," Tellman admitted, biting his lips. "Doesn't make sense. I suppose we'll have to start asking all 'round the square." His face reflected vividly his distaste at the prospect.

They both heard the clatter of hooves at the same time as a hansom came from the Caroline Street corner of the square at a brisk clip, followed immediately by the mortuary van. The van stopped a dozen yards along the curb and the hansom drew level with them. The frock-coated figure of the surgeon climbed out, straightened his collar and walked over to them. He nodded greeting, then regarded the dead man with resignation. He hitched the knees of his trousers slightly, to avoid stretching the fabric, and squatted down to begin his examination.

Pitt turned as he heard more footsteps, and saw the constable coming with a highly nervous lamplighter, a thin, fair-haired man dwarfed by his pole. In the dawn light through the trees he looked like some outlandish knight-at-arms with a jousting lance beyond his strength to wield.

"I din't see nuffink," he said before Pitt could ask him.

"You passed this way," Pitt reaffirmed. "This is your patch?"

There was no escaping that. "Yeah . . ."

"When?"

"S'mornin'," he replied as if it should have been obvious. " 'Bout first light. Like I always do."

"Do you know what time that was?" Pitt said patiently.

"First light . . . like I said!" He sent a nervous, sideways look at the body, half obscured by the surgeon as he bent over it. " 'E weren't 'ere then. I din't see 'im!"

"Do you have a watch?" Pitt pursued, with little hope.

"Wo'for? Gets light different time every day," the lamplighter said reasonably.

Pitt realized he was not going to get more exact than that.

7

The answer, from the lamplighter's point of view, was sensible enough.

"Did you see anyone else in the square?" he said instead.

"Not this side." The lamplighter shook his head. "There were an 'ansom on t'other side, takin' a gennelman 'ome. Bit the worse fer wear, 'e were, but not fallin' down, like. Din't come 'round 'ere."

"No one else?"

"No. Too late fer most folks from parties, an' too early fer maids an' deliveries an' like."

That was true. At least it narrowed it down a little more. It had been dark when the constable had been on his previous round, and barely light when he had found the body. The lamplighter could not have been around long before. Which meant the body had been put there within the space of fifteen or twenty minutes. It was just possible, if they were very lucky, that someone had awoken in one of the houses on this side and heard footsteps or shouting, even a single cry. It was a forlorn hope.

"Thank you," Pitt accepted. The sky was pale now beyond the heavy trees in the center of the square, the light shining on the far rooftops and reflecting mirrorlike in the top-story windows above them. He turned to the surgeon, who seemed to have completed at least his superficial examination.

"A fight," he pronounced. "Short one, I'd guess. Know more when I see him without his clothes. Could be other abrasions, but his coat isn't torn or stained. Ground was dry, if he fell over or was knocked. Wasn't on the street, anyway. There's no mud on him that I can see. No trace of manure or anything else. And the gutters are pretty wet." He glanced around. "Rained yesterday evening."

"I know," Pitt retorted, looking at the glistening cobbles.

" 'Course you do," the surgeon agreed, nodding at him. "Don't suppose I can tell you anything you don't! Have to try. What I'm paid for. One very heavy blow to the side of the head. Killed him. Probably a length of lead pipe or a candlestick or a poker. Something of that sort. I'd guess metal rather than wood to do that much damage. Heavy."

"Likely to be marks on the person who did it?" Pitt asked.

The surgeon pursed his lips thoughtfully. "A few bruises. Perhaps where the fist connected. Judging by the splits on his knuckles, most likely a jaw or head. Clothes or soft flesh wouldn't do that. Face would be bruised, hand wouldn't show. Other fellow had a weapon, this one didn't, or he wouldn't have had to use his fists. Nasty."

"I'm not arguing," Pitt said dryly. He shivered. He was getting cold. "Can you say anything about time?"

"Nothing you can't deduce for yourself," the surgeon replied. "Or about the poor devil here," he added. "If I can improve on that, I'll send you a message. Bow Street good enough?"

"Certainly. Thank you."

The surgeon shrugged slightly, inclined his head in a salute and went back to the mortuary wagon to instruct his men in the removal of the body.

Pitt looked at his pocket watch again. It was just after quarter to five.

"I suppose it is time we started waking people," he said to Tellman. "Come on."

Tellman sighed heavily, but he had no option but to obey. Together they walked up the steps of the house where the body had been found, and Pitt pulled the brass doorbell. Tellman rather liked Pitt's refusal to go to the tradesmen's entrance, as someone of the social order of policemen should do, but while he approved the principle, he also loathed the practice. Let Pitt do it when Tellman was not with him.

It was several long, uncomfortable minutes before they heard the bolts slide and the lock turn. The door swung inward and an extremely hastily dressed footman, not in livery but in ordinary dark trousers and jacket, stood blinking at them.

"Yes sir?" he said with alarm. He was not yet practiced enough to have the really superior footman's supercilious air.

"Good morning," Pitt replied. "I am sorry to disturb the household so early, but I am afraid there has been an incident which necessitates my making enquiries of both the staff and the family." He held out his card. "Superintendent Pitt, of the

Bow Street Station. Would you present it to your master and ask him if he will spare me a few moments of his time. I am afraid it concerns a very serious crime, and I cannot afford the pleasantries of waiting until a more civilized hour."

"A crime?" The footman looked startled. "We haven't been burgled, sir. There's been no crime here. You must have made a mistake." He started to close the door again, relieved to shut the whole matter outside on the street. It was somebody else's problem after all.

Tellman moved forward as if to put his foot in the doorway, then resisted. It was undignified. He hated this. Give him ordinary people to deal with any day. The whole notion of being in service to someone else was abomination to him. It was no way for a decent man, or woman, to make a living.

"The burglary is incidental, if indeed there was one," Pitt said firmly. "The murder is my concern."

That stopped the footman as if frozen. The blood fled from his face.

"The . . . the what?"

"Murder," Pitt repeated quietly. "Unfortunately, we found the body of a man on your doorstep about an hour ago. Now, would you please be good enough to waken your master and inform him that I need to speak to everyone in the house, and I would like his permission to do so."

The footman swallowed, his throat jerking. "Yes . . . yes sir. If . . . I mean . . ." His voice trailed off. He had no idea where one left policemen to wait at five o'clock in the morning. Normally one would not permit them on the premises at all. If one had to, it would be the local constable, perhaps for a hot cup of tea on a cold day, and that in the kitchen, where such people belonged.

"I'll wait in the morning room," Pitt said to assist him, and because he had no intention of being left shivering on the step.

"Yes sir . . . I'll tell the General." The footman backed in, and Pitt and Tellman followed him.

"General?" Pitt asked.

"Yes sir. This is General Brandon Balantyne's home."

The name was familiar. It took Pitt a moment to place it. It

10

must be the same General Balantyne who had previously lived in Callander Square when Pitt was investigating the deaths of the babies, nearly a decade before, and who had also been involved in the tragedies in the Devil's Acre three to four years later.

"I didn't know that." It was a foolish remark, and he realized it the moment it had crossed his lips. He saw Tellman turn to look at him with surprise. He would have preferred not to discuss the past with Tellman. If he did not have to, he would let it lie. He walked smartly across the hall after the footman and followed him into the morning room, leaving the door open for Tellman.

Inside was so exactly what Pitt expected it jerked him back sharply, and for a moment the intervening years disappeared. The shelf of books was the same, as in the previous house, the dark brown and green-leather furniture, polished with use. On the mellow wood of the small table was the brass replica of the cannon at Waterloo, gleaming in the gaslight the footman had lit and turned up for them. On the wall over the mantelpiece hung the picture Pitt remembered of the charge of the Royal Scots Greys, again from Waterloo. The Zulu assegai was on the wall next to the fireplace and the paintings of the African veld, pale colors bleached by sun, red earth, flat-topped acacia trees.

He had not meant to look at Tellman, but he turned and caught the sergeant's eye accidentally. Tellman was staring, his face a mask of disapproval. Tellman had not even met the man, but he knew he was a general, he knew that at the time of his service officers had purchased their commissions rather than earned them. They came from a few wealthy military families, all educated at the best schools, Eton, Rugby, Harrow, and then possibly a year or two at Oxford or Cambridge, more probably straight into the army and at a rank no working-class man could hope to achieve even after a lifetime's service, risking his life on the battlefield and his health in foreign climes for no more recompense than the king's shilling.

Pitt knew Balantyne, and liked him, but there was no point

11

in saying that to Tellman. Tellman had seen too much injustice and had felt it too keenly among his own people to hear anything Pitt would say. So he kept silence, and waited, standing by the window watching the light broaden across the square outside and the shade deepen under the trees in the center. The birds were loud, starlings and sparrows. A delivery cart rattled by, stopping regularly. An errand boy on a bicycle came around the corner rather too sharply and steadied himself with an effort, his cap falling over his ears.

The morning room door opened, and Pitt and Tellman both turned to face it. In the entranceway stood a tall man with broad shoulders. His fair brown hair was graying at the temples and beginning to thin. His features were powerful, with an aquiline nose, high cheekbones and a broad mouth. He was leaner than when Pitt had last seen him, as if time and grief had worn down the reserves of his strength, but he still stood very upright—in fact, stiffly, his shoulders squared. He was wearing a white shirt and a plain, dark smoking jacket, but it was easy for the mind's eye to see him in uniform.

"Good morning, Pitt," he said quietly. "Should I congratulate you on your promotion? My footman said you are now in charge of the Bow Street Station."

"Thank you, General Balantyne," Pitt acknowledged, feeling a faintly self-conscious flush in his cheeks. "This is Sergeant Tellman. I am sorry to disturb you so early, sir, but I am afraid the beat constable found a dead body in the square at about quarter to four this morning. He was on the doorstep just outside this house." He saw the distaste on Balantyne's face, and perhaps shock, although of course the footman had told him, so he was not taken by surprise now.

"Who is it?" Balantyne asked, closing the door behind him.

"We don't know yet," Pitt replied. "But he had papers and other belongings on him, so we shall almost certainly be able to identify him quite soon." He watched Balantyne's face but saw no discernible change, certainly no tightening of lips or shadow across the eyes.

"Do you know how he died?" Balantyne asked. He waved

12

one hand at the chairs to invite Pitt to be seated, and included Tellman in a general way.

"Thank you, sir," Pitt accepted. "But I should like your permission for Sergeant Tellman to speak to your household staff. Someone may have heard an altercation or disturbance."

Balantyne's face was bleak. "I understand that the man did not meet a natural death?"

"I am afraid so. He was struck across the head, most likely after a fight, not long, but very fierce."

Balantyne's eyes widened. "And you think it happened on my doorstep?"

"That I don't yet know."

"By all means have the sergeant speak to my staff."

Pitt nodded at Tellman, who left eagerly, closing the door behind him. Pitt sat down in one of the large, green-leather-covered armchairs, and Balantyne sat a little stiffly in the one opposite.

"There is nothing I can tell you," Balantyne went on. "My bedroom is at the front of the house, but I heard nothing. A street robbery of such violence would be extraordinary in this area." A fleeting anxiety puckered his face, a sadness.

"He wasn't robbed," Pitt answered, disliking what he must do next. "At least not in any usual sense. He still had money." He saw Balantyne's surprise. "And this." He pulled the snuffbox out of his pocket and held it out in the palm of his hand.

Balantyne's expression did not change. His face was unnaturally motionless; there was no admiration for the beauty of the piece, no amazement that a murdered man involved in a fight should be in possession of such a thing. But all the self-mastery in the world could not control the blood draining from his skin and leaving him ashen.

"Extraordinary . . ." He breathed out very slowly. "One would think . . ." He swallowed. "One would think a thief could hardly miss such a thing." Pitt knew he was speaking to fill the emptiness of the moments between them while he decided whether to admit owning it or not. What explanation could he give?

Pitt stared at him, holding his eyes in an unwavering gaze.

13

"It raises many questions," he agreed aloud. "Have you seen it before, General?"

Balantyne's voice was a little husky, as if his mouth were dry. "Yes . . . yes, it is mine." He seemed to be about to add something, then changed his mind.

Pitt asked the question he had to. "When did you last see it?"

"I . . . don't think I remember. One gets used to seeing things. I'm not sure I would have noticed its absence." He looked profoundly uncomfortable, but he did not evade Pitt's eyes. He anticipated the next question. "It's kept in a cabinet in the library."

Was there any point in pursuing it? Not yet.

"Have you missed anything else, General Balantyne?"

"Not so far as I am aware."

"Perhaps you would be good enough to check, sir? And I'll see if any of the servants have noticed anything moved, signs of a burglar in the house."

"Of course."

"It sometimes happens that burglars have called at the house earlier, to make an assessment or to—"

"I understand," Balantyne cut across him. "You think one of us may recognize him."

"Yes. If you, and perhaps your butler and one of your footmen, would come to the mortuary and see if he is known to you, it may help."

"If you wish," Balantyne agreed. He obviously disliked the idea, but he accepted the inevitability of it.

There was a sharp knock on the door, and before Balantyne could answer, it opened and a woman came in. Pitt remembered her immediately. Lady Augusta Balantyne was handsome in a dark, cold way. There was strength in her face, but it was inward, self-contained. She, too, must have remembered him, because there was instantly a chill in her when she saw him, more than could be accounted for by the fact that he had disturbed the household so early in the morning. But then, after their two previous encounters she could hardly think of him with any memory except that of pain.

She was dressed in a dark silk gown of formal cut, suitable for making morning calls, fashionable but subdued, as befitted her age and dignity. Her dark hair was streaked with white at the temples, and grief had faded her skin but not the intelligence or the iron will in her eyes.

Pitt rose to his feet. "I apologize for waking you so early, Lady Augusta," he said quietly. "Unfortunately, there has been a death in the street outside your home, and it is necessary that I enquire if anyone here was aware of the disturbance." He wished to spare her feelings as much as possible. He did not like her, and it made him even more careful than he would have been otherwise.

"I assumed it was some such duty that brought you, Inspector," she answered, at once dismissing any possible social contact between them. This was her home. He could only have come in the course of his trade.

Ridiculously, he found himself clenching inside, as aware of an insult as if she had slapped him. And he should have expected it. After all that had passed between them, the tragedy and the guilt, what would he have presumed differently? He tried to make himself relax his body, and failed.

Balantyne was on his feet also, looking from one to the other of them, as if he, too, should apologize—to Pitt for his wife's condescension, to her for Pitt's presence and for another tragedy.

"Some unfortunate man was attacked and killed," he said bluntly.

She took a deep breath, but her composure did not crack.

"Was it someone we knew?"

"No," Balantyne said immediately. "At least . . ." He turned to Pitt.

"It is most unlikely." Pitt looked at Augusta. "He appeared to have fallen on hard times and to have been involved in a fight. He was not apparently robbed."

The tension slipped away from her.

"Then I suggest, Inspector, that you question the servants to see if they heard anything, and if they did not, then I regret

15

we cannot assist you. Good day." She did not move. She was dismissing him, not herself leaving.

Balantyne looked uncomfortable. He had no desire whatever to prolong the interview, but then neither did he wish to avail himself of a rescue by his wife. He had never retreated from battle. He was not about to do so now. He stood his ground painfully.

"If you would inform me when it would be convenient to go to the mortuary, I shall do so," he said to Pitt. "In the meantime, Blisset will show you whatever you wish to see, and no doubt he will know if anything has been moved or is missing."

"Missing?" Augusta queried.

Balantyne's face tightened. "The man may have been a thief," he said curtly, without explaining further.

"I suppose so." She lifted one shoulder slightly. "It would account for his presence in the square." She stood back into the hallway to allow Pitt to leave, and waited silently until he should pass.

The butler, Blisset, a middle-aged man of stiff-backed, military bearing, was standing at the foot of the stairs. Very probably he was an old soldier Balantyne had employed, knowing his service. Indeed, when he moved he did so with a pronounced limp, and Pitt guessed it was a battle injury which had caused it.

"If you will come with me, sir," he said gravely, and as soon as he was sure Pitt was behind him, he went across the hallway to the baize door and through to the servants' quarters.

Tellman was standing by the long table in the dining hall where the servants took their meals. It was laid for breakfast, but obviously no one had yet eaten. A housemaid was standing in a gray stuff dress, white apron crisp and clean, lace cap a trifle crooked on her head as if she had placed it there hastily. She was looking at Tellman with considerable dislike. A footman of about nineteen or twenty was standing by the door to the kitchen, and the bootboy was staring round-eyed at Pitt.

"Nothing so far," Tellman said, biting his lip. He had a

16

pencil and an open notebook in his hands, but there was very little written on the page. "Lot of very sound sleepers here." His tone was bordering on the sarcastic.

Pitt thought that if he had to get up at five in the morning as a matter of habit, and work with little respite until nine or ten in the evening, he would probably be tired enough to sleep soundly too, but he did not bother to say so.

"I'd like to speak to the housemaids," he said to Blisset. "May I use the housekeeper's sitting room?"

The butler agreed reluctantly and insisted on remaining present, to protect his staff, as was his responsibility.

But two hours' diligent enquiry and a thorough search of the main part of the house produced nothing of value. The housemaids had both seen the snuffbox but could not remember how recently. Nothing else was missing. There was quite definitely no sign whatever of a break-in or of any unauthorized person in any room upstairs or downstairs.

No one had heard anything in the street outside.

There had been no caller or tradesman other than those who had dealt with the household for years, no vagrants, no followers after the female servants that anyone would acknowledge, no beggars, peddlers or new deliverymen.

Pitt and Tellman left Bedford Square at half past nine and caught a hansom back towards the Bow Street Station, stopping just short of it to buy a hot cup of tea and a ham sandwich from a stall on the pavement.

"Separate bedrooms," Tellman said with his mouth full.

"People of that social status usually have," Pitt replied, sipping his tea and finding it too hot.

"Hardly seems worth it." Tellman's face was eloquent of his opinion of them. "But it means no one in the house is accounted for. Could have been any of them, if the fellow did get in and was caught stealing." He took another mouthful of his sandwich. "One of the maids could have let him in. It happens. Anyone could have heard him and got into a fight . . . even the General himself, come to that."

Pitt would have liked to dismiss that suggestion, but the

17

expression in Balantyne's eyes when he had seen the snuff-box was too sharp in his mind to allow it.

Tellman was watching him, waiting.

"Early to speculate," Pitt answered. "Get a little more evidence first. Go 'round the rest of the square, see if any of the other houses were broken into, anything moved, any disturbance."

"Why would he move something rather than take it?" Tellman argued.

"He wouldn't." Pitt looked at him coolly. "If he were caught in the act and killed, presumably whoever killed him would take back what belonged to that house, but not the snuffbox, because it wasn't theirs and would require some explanation. And we'll see what the surgeon can tell us when he's looked more closely. And there's the bill for the socks." He sipped his tea now it was cooler. "Although putting a name to him may not help a great deal."

But diligent enquiry all around Bedford Square and the immediate neighborhood elicited nothing whatever of use. No one had heard anything, nothing was moved or missing. Everyone claimed to have slept through the night.

In the late afternoon General Balantyne and his butler, Blisset, fulfilled their duty by going to the mortuary to look at the dead man, but neither knew him. Pitt watched Balantyne's expression as the face was uncovered and saw the momentary flicker of surprise, almost as if Balantyne had expected to see someone else, possibly someone familiar.

"No," he said quietly. "I have not seen him before."

Pitt arrived home late, and a small domestic crisis kept Charlotte too occupied for there to be time to discuss the case with her more than briefly. He did not yet want to tell her of General Balantyne's involvement. He remembered that she had liked him. She had actually spent some time in his house, helping him with something or other. Better to see if a simpler explanation appeared before he distressed her, perhaps unnecessarily. Last thing at night was not an appropriate time.

18

In the morning Pitt went to inform Assistant Commissioner Cornwallis of the case, simply because it had occurred in a part of the City where such an event was remarkable. The crime itself might not have concerned any of the residents or their households, but they would certainly be inconvenienced by it.

Cornwallis was fairly new to his position. He had spent most of his career in the navy and was well accustomed to command, but the natures of crime and of politics were both new to him, and politics in particular he found at times beyond his comprehension. There was no deviousness to his mind. He was unaccustomed to vanity and circular thinking. The sea did not permit such indulgences. It sorted the skilled from the clumsy, the coward from the brave, with a ruthlessness quite different from the impulses of ambition in the worlds of government and society.

Cornwallis was of no more than average height, lean, as if physical occupation were more natural to him than sitting behind a desk. When he moved it was with grace and control. He was not handsome—his nose was too long, too prominent—but there was balance in his face, and an honesty. The fact that he was entirely bald became him. Pitt found it difficult to think of him any other way.

"What is it?" He looked up from his desk as Pitt came into his room. It was a sultry day outside, and the windows were open, allowing in the noise of traffic from the street below, the rattle of carriage wheels, the occasional cry of a coachman or hansom driver, the heavy rumble of brewers' drays, the sharper treble of crossing sweepers hoping for a penny, peddlers calling their wares: bootlaces, flowers, sandwiches, matches.

Pitt closed the door behind him.

"Found a body in Bedford Square early yesterday morning," he answered. "Hoped it might be nothing to do with any of the houses there, but he had a snuffbox in his hand which belonged to General Brandon Balantyne, and it was actually on Balantyne's doorstep that he was lying."

"Burglary?" Cornwallis asked, the assumption in his voice.

There was a slight pucker between his brows, as if he were waiting for Pitt to explain why he had bothered to mention it, let alone to come in person.

"Possibly he was burgling one of the houses and was caught in the act by a servant or the owner, there was a fight, and the thief was killed," Pitt said. "Then, in fear of the consequences, they put him outside Balantyne's door instead of leaving him where he was and sending for the police."

"All right." Cornwallis bit his lip. "I take your point, Pitt. Not the actions of innocent people, even in panic. How was he killed?"

"A blow to the head with a poker, or something like it, but there was a fight beforehand, to judge by his knuckles." Pitt sat down in the chair opposite Cornwallis's desk. He was comfortable in this room with its watercolor seascapes on the walls, the polished brass sextant on the shelf next to the books, not only on police matters but also a Jane Austen novel and a copy of the Bible, and several volumes of poetry: Shelley, Keats and Tennyson.

"Do you know who he is?" Cornwallis asked, placing his elbows on the desk and making a steeple of his fingers.

"Not yet, but Tellman is working on it," Pitt answered. "There was a receipt for three pair of socks in his pocket. There's a chance it might help. They were bought only two days before he was killed."

"Good." Cornwallis seemed to be unconcerned over the matter, or perhaps he was occupied with something else.

"The snuffbox in his pocket belonged to General Balantyne," Pitt repeated.

Cornwallis frowned. "Presumably he stole it. Doesn't mean he met his death in Balantyne's home. I imagine—" He stopped. "Yes, I see what you mean. Unpleasant . . . and puzzling. I . . . know Balantyne, slightly. A good man. Can't imagine him doing anything so . . . stupid."

Pitt had a strong sense of Cornwallis's anxiety, but it seemed to have been present since before Pitt had come in, as if something else held his attention so strongly he was unable to put his mind fully to what Pitt was saying.

"Nor I," Pitt agreed.

Cornwallis jerked his head up. "What?"

"I can't imagine General Balantyne doing anything so stupid as putting a corpse outside his own front door rather than simply calling the police," Pitt said patiently.

"Do you know him?" Cornwallis looked at Pitt as if he had walked into the middle of a conversation and was aware he had missed the beginning.

"Yes. I investigated two previous cases in which he was concerned . . . indirectly. As a witness."

"Oh. I didn't know that."

"Is there something troubling you?" Pitt liked Cornwallis, and while aware of his lack of political knowledge, he had a profound respect for his honesty and his moral courage. "It's not this Tranby Croft business, is it?"

"What? Good heavens, no!" For the first time since Pitt had come in, Cornwallis relaxed, on the verge of outright laughter. "I'm sorry for them all. I've no idea whether Gordon-Cumming was cheating or not, but the poor devil will be ruined now, either way. And my opinion of the Prince of Wales, or anyone else who spends his time drifting from one house party to another, doing nothing more useful than playing cards, is better unexpressed, even in private."

Pitt was uncertain whether to ask again, or if that had been a polite way of evading the issue. Yet he was certain that Cornwallis was worried to a degree that it intruded into his thoughts even when he wished to put his entire mind to a present issue.

Cornwallis pushed back his chair and stood up. He walked over to the window and pulled it closed sharply.

"Terrible noise out there!" he said with irritation. "Keep me informed how you progress with this Bedford Square case."

It was dismissal. Pitt stood up. "Yes sir." He walked towards the door.

Cornwallis cleared his throat.

Pitt stopped.

"I . . ." Cornwallis began, then hesitated.

21

Pitt turned around to look at him.

There was a faint flush of color in Cornwallis's lean cheeks. He was profoundly unhappy. He made the decision.

"I've . . . I've received a blackmail letter. . . ."

Pitt was astonished. Of all the possibilities that had come to his mind, this seemed the most outlandish.

"Words cut out from the *Times*," Cornwallis went on in the prickling silence. "Pasted on a piece of paper."

Pitt scrambled his thoughts together with difficulty.

"What do they want?"

"That's it." Cornwallis's body was rigid, his muscles locked. He stared at Pitt. "Nothing! They don't ask for anything at all! Just the threat."

Pitt loathed asking, but not to would be to walk away from a man whose friendship he valued and who was obviously in profound need of uncritical help.

"Do you have the letter?"

Cornwallis took it out of his pocket and passed it over. Pitt read the pasted-on letters, most of them cut out singly, some in twos and threes or where a whole word had been found as the writer wished to use it.

I know all about you, Captain Cornwallis. Others think you are a hero, but I know differently. It was not you who was so brave on the HMS Venture, it was Able Seaman Beckwith, but you took the credit. He's dead now and he cannot tell the truth. That is all wrong. People should know. I know.

Pitt read it again. There was no explicit threat, no request for money or any other form of payment. And yet the sense of power was so strong it leapt off the creased paper as if the thing had a malign life of its own.

He looked across at Cornwallis's pale face and saw the muscles clenched in his jaw and the faint, visible pulse in his temple.

"I suppose you have no idea who it is?"

"None at all," Cornwallis replied. "I lay awake half last

night trying to think." His voice was dry, as if he had held himself rigid so long his throat ached. He breathed in deeply. His eyes did not waver from Pitt's. "I've gone over and over the incident I think he's referring to, to remember who was there, who could have misinterpreted it to believe it that way, and I don't know the answer." He hesitated, acute embarrassment naked in his face. He was a private man who found emotion difficult to express; he vastly preferred the tacit understanding of action. He bit his lip. He wanted to look away, so he forced himself not to. He was obviously sensitive to Pitt's discomfort and unintentionally made it worse. He was aware of foundering, of being indecisive, the very sorts of things he had meant to avoid.

"Perhaps you had better tell me about the incident," Pitt said quietly. He moved to sit down, indicating his intention to stay.

"Yes," Cornwallis agreed. "Oh . . . yes, of course." He turned away at last, his face towards the window. The sharp daylight emphasized the depth of the lines about his eyes and mouth. "It happened eighteen years ago . . . eighteen and a half. It was winter. Bay of Biscay. Weather was appalling. I was a second lieutenant then. Man went up to shorten the mizzen royal—"

"The what?" Pitt interrupted. He needed to understand.

Cornwallis glanced at him. "Oh . . . three-masted ship." He moved his arms to illustrate what he was saying. "Middle mast, middle sail . . . square-rigger, of course. Injured by a loose rope. His hand. Got it jammed somehow." He frowned, turning towards the window again, away from Pitt. "I went up after him. Should have sent a seaman, of course, but the only man near me was Beckwith, and he froze. Happens sometimes." He spoke jerkily. "No time to look for someone else. Weather was getting worse. Ship pitching around. Afraid the injured man up on the mast would lose his grasp, tear his arm out of its socket. Heights never bothered me in particular. Didn't really think about it. Been up often enough as a midshipman." His mouth tightened. "Got him free. Had to cut the line. He was almost dead weight. Managed to get him back

23

along the yard as far as the mast, but he was damn heavy and the wind was rising all the time, ship pitching around like a mad thing."

Pitt tried to imagine it, Cornwallis desperate, frozen, trying to hang on to a swaying mast forty or fifty feet over a wild sea, one minute above the heaving deck, the next, as the ship keeled, out over the water, and carrying another man's helpless body. He found his own hands were knotted and he was holding his breath.

"I was trying to readjust his weight to start down the mast," Cornwallis went on, "when Beckwith must have unfrozen and I found him just below me. He helped take the man's weight, and we got down together.

"By that time there were half a dozen other men on deck, including the captain, and it must have looked to them as if Beckwith had rescued me. The captain said as much, but Beckwith was an honest man, and he told the truth." He turned back to meet Pitt's eyes, the light behind him now. "But I can't prove it. Beckwith died a few years after that, and the man up the mast hadn't the faintest idea who else was there, let alone what happened."

"I see," Pitt said quietly. Cornwallis was staring at him, and in the misery that was in his face Pitt glimpsed some perception of fear that he was trying to hold inside himself. He had lived a life of discipline against an element that gave no quarter, no mercy to man or ship. He had obeyed its rules and seen the deaths of those who had not, or whom misfortune had overtaken. He knew as few men can, who spend their lives in the safety of the land, the value of loyalty, honor and sheer, overwhelming physical courage, instant and absolute obedience, and total trust in those with whom you serve. The hierarchy within a ship was absolute. To have taken credit for another man's act of courage was unforgivable.

In what Pitt knew of Cornwallis, it was also unthinkable. He smiled at him, meeting his gaze frankly. "I'll look into it. We need to know who is doing this, and most of all what he wants. Once there is a specific demand, then there's a crime."

Cornwallis hesitated, still keeping his hand on the letter, as if already he feared the result of any action. Then suddenly he realized what he was doing. He thrust the paper at Pitt.

Pitt took it and put it in his pocket without looking at it again.

"I'll be discreet," he promised.

"Yes," Cornwallis said with an effort. "Yes, of course."

Pitt took his leave and went out of the room, along the corridor, downstairs and out onto the pavement. He had gone barely a dozen yards, his mind consumed with Cornwallis's distress, when he was forcibly stopped by almost colliding with a man who moved across in front of him.

"Mr. Pitt, sir . . . ?" he said, looking up at him, but although his words were framed as a question, there was a certainty in his face.

"Yes?" Pitt replied a trifle sharply. He did not like being accosted so physically, and he was too concerned about the ugliness of Cornwallis's situation to wish interruption in his thought. He felt frustrated and helpless to protect a man he cared about from a danger he feared was very real.

"My name is Lyndon Remus, from the *Times*," the man said quickly, still standing directly in front of Pitt. He produced a card out of his inside coat pocket and held it out.

Pitt ignored it. "What is it, Mr. Remus?"

"What can you tell me about the dead man found in Bedford Square yesterday morning?"

"Nothing, except what you already know," Pitt replied.

"Then you are baffled?" Remus concluded without hesitation.

"That is not what I said!" Pitt was annoyed. The man presumed without justification, and Pitt hated trickery with words. "I said I can tell you nothing beyond what you know . . . that he is dead and where he was found."

"On the front doorstep of General Brandon Balantyne's house," Remus said. "Then there is something you know but cannot tell us. Is General Balantyne involved, or someone in his household?"

Pitt realized, now with considerable anger, that he must be a good deal more careful how he phrased his replies.

"Mr. Remus, a body was found in Bedford Square," he said grimly. "We do not yet know who he was or how he died, except that it seems extremely unlikely it was an accident. Speculation would be irresponsible and might severely damage the reputation of an innocent person. When we know something for certain, the press will be told. Now, will you please get out of my way, sir, and allow me to go about my business!"

Remus did not move. "Will you be investigating General Balantyne, Mr. Pitt?"

He was caught. He could not say no without both lying and appearing to be prejudiced or inefficient, and if he said yes, then Remus would take it to imply suspicion of Balantyne. If he evaded the question Remus could put any complexion on it that he wished.

Remus smiled. "Mr. Pitt?"

"I shall begin by investigating the dead man," Pitt replied awkwardly, aware of inadequacy in the face of questions he should have foreseen. He took a breath. "Then, of course, I shall follow that lead wherever it takes me."

Remus smiled bleakly. "Isn't this the same General Balantyne whose daughter, Christina, was involved in the murders in the Devil's Acre in about '87?"

"Don't expect me to do your work for you, Mr. Remus!" Pitt snapped, and slipped around him smartly. "Good day." He strode off, leaving Remus looking satisfied.

Pitt arrived home at the end of the day tired and unhappy. They had the full information about the death of the man in Bedford Square. The written report added nothing to what the surgeon had told him in the beginning. Tellman was busy pursuing the bill for the socks and further questioning all the residents around the square. Nobody had seen or heard anything of value.

Actually, Pitt was more troubled over the letter Cornwallis had received. Although the two matters were not dissimilar, insofar as each could cause harm to the reputation of a good man by whisper, suspicion and innuendo before any facts were known. Suggestions could ruin a person if they were believed even by a few. Both men were vulnerable, but Pitt knew and liked Cornwallis, and he believed him totally innocent. It was odd that he had received what was clearly a threatening letter, yet with no request or demand. Presumably it would follow soon.

He went in through the front door, hung up his coat, then bent and unlaced his boots and took them off. He walked in stocking feet along to the kitchen, where he guessed Charlotte would be. They had an excellent maid, Gracie, but Charlotte still did most of the cooking herself. A maid-of-all-work came in four days a week to do the heavy linen laundry, scrubbing and so on. At least that was what he thought. It was not his concern.

Charlotte was at the stove, as he had expected, and there was a savory aroma coming from the oven. Everything was clean, smelling of scrubbed wood and fresh linen. He glanced up and saw sheets hanging on the airing rail across the ceiling, ropes to the winch that held it up on the wall. Blue-and-white china on the dresser gleamed in the sun from the windows. Charlotte had flour on the front of her dress, her apron was caught up at the corner and her hair was coming out of its pins.

He put his arms around her and kissed her, ignoring the long spoon in her hand which trailed egg yolk across the top of the stove and onto the floor.

She kissed him back with considerable enthusiasm, then told him off.

"Look what you have made me do!" She indicated the egg. "It's all over the place!" She went to the sink, wrung out a cloth and came back and wiped it up. On the stove it was burnt and smelling slightly.

He stood still, Cornwallis's face sharp in his mind's eye. Cornwallis had none of Pitt's safety protecting him; no one Cornwallis knew would believe in him regardless of what anyone said, not even someone with whom he could share the tension of waiting for the next letter to come or explain why it mattered so much.

"What is it?" Charlotte asked, watching him more closely now. Automatically, she pulled the dish with the egg away from the heat. "Is it the body in Bedford Square? Is it going to involve one of the houses there?"

"I don't know," he answered, sitting down on one of the hard-backed chairs by the kitchen table. "It's possible. I was stopped by a newspaper writer this afternoon. He wanted to know if I was going to investigate General Balantyne."

She stiffened. "Balantyne? He lives in Callander Square. Why would you investigate him?"

"He must have moved," he replied, still unable to rid himself of his fear for Cornwallis. "I'm sorry . . . it was on his doorstep that the body was found. I don't suppose it was more than mischance."

It was only towards the end of dinner, when he was eating the baked egg custard, that he even thought of the snuffbox and realized that he had told her a good deal less than the truth. But there was no point in distressing her by adding that now. It would worry her for nothing. She could not help.

He was too absorbed in his own thoughts to notice her silence as anything but companionable. Where should he begin with Cornwallis's letter? How could he protect him?

2

CHARLOTTE HAD BEEN distressed to learn that the tragedy of murder had again overtaken General Balantyne, even if only in that the dead man had been found on his doorstep. But it was a public place. Certainly anyone at all might have come to it without his knowledge or any acquaintance with him.

The following morning when Pitt had gone, she left Gracie to clean away the breakfast dishes while she saw nine-year-old Jemima and seven-year-old Daniel off to school, then returned to the kitchen with the daily newspaper, brought to the step as a kindness by Mr. Williamson along the street. The first thing that leapt to her eye was the latest report on the Tranby Croft affair. Speculation was running riot as to whether the Prince of Wales would actually be called to the witness stand—and of course, what he would say. Having the heir to the throne appearing in court like a common man had never even been imagined before, much less had it happened. The room would be jammed with people curious just to stare at him, to hear him speak and have to answer questions put to him by counsel. Admission to the court was by ticket only.

Sir William Gordon-Cumming was represented by Sir Edward Clarke; for the other side, Sir Charles Russell. Present, according to the newspaper, were Lord Edward Somerset, the Earl of Coventry and Mrs. Lycett-Green, among many others.

Baccarat was an illegal game. Gambling in any form was

frowned upon by many. Cards were viewed as a waste of precious time. Everyone knew that thousands of people played, of course, but there was a world of difference between knowing and seeing. It was said that the Queen was beside herself with anger. But then she was rather a straitlaced and forbidding woman even at the best of times. Ever since Prince Albert had died of typhoid fever, nearly thirty years before, she seemed to have lost all pleasure in life and was fairly well determined to see that everyone else did too. At least that was what Charlotte had heard said, and the Queen's rare public appearances did nothing to disprove it.

The Prince of Wales was a spendthrift, self-indulgent, gluttonous; and wildly and regularly unfaithful to his wife, the long-suffering Princess Alexandra, most particularly with Lady Frances Brooke, who was also intimately admired by Sir William Gordon-Cumming. Until this point Charlotte had had a very slight sympathy with him. Facing the court, Sir Edward Clarke and the public would be nothing compared with facing his mother.

Then, farther down on the same page, she saw an article by one Lyndon Remus about the corpse found in Bedford Square.

The identity of the dead man on the front doorstep of the house of General Brandon Balantyne two mornings ago remains a mystery. Superintendent Thomas Pitt of Bow Street informs this writer that as yet the police have no idea as to his identity. Indeed he went so far as to say that he knew no more of it than any member of the general public.

When pressed he refused to say whether or not he intended to investigate General Balantyne, who as readers will remember, was the father of the infamous Christina Balantyne of what came to be known as the Devil's Acre Murders which scandalised London in 1887.

There then followed a brief but lurid outline of that terrible and tragic case, with which Charlotte was all too familiar, remembering it now with a profound sense of sorrow. She

30

could see Balantyne's face as it had been when he had learned the truth, and everyone was powerless to help or comfort.

Now another wretchedness threatened him, and all the misery and grief of the past were resurrected again. She was furious with Lyndon Remus, whoever he might be, and her mind was filled with anxiety for Balantyne.

"Yer all right, ma'am?" Gracie's voice cut across Charlotte's thoughts. The little maid picked up the smoothing iron and automatically shooed Archie, the marmalade-and-white cat, from his nest on top of the laundry. He uncurled and moved away lazily, knowing full well that she would not hurt him.

Charlotte looked up. "No," she replied. "The body that Mr. Pitt found the other night was on the doorstep of an old friend of mine, and the newspapers are suggesting that he may somehow involved. There was an appalling crime in his family a few years ago, and they have raked that up again as well, reminding everybody of it just when he and his wife might be beginning to forget a little and feel normal again."

"Some o' them people wot writes for the newspapers is downright wicked," Gracie said angrily, gripping the iron like a weapon. She knew precisely where her loyalties lay: with friends; with the hurt, the weak, the underdog, whoever he was. Sometimes, with a lot of reason and persuasion, she could change her mind, but not often and not easily. "Yer goin' ter 'elp?" she said, looking narrowly at Charlotte. "In't nuffin' yer needs ter do 'ere. I can manage ev'rythink."

Charlotte smiled in spite of herself. Gracie was a born crusader. She had come to the Pitts nearly seven years before, small and thin, in clothes too big for her and boots with holes in them. She had filled out only a little. All her dresses still had to be taken in and taken up. But she was not only an accomplished maid who knew all the duties in the house; with Charlotte's help, she had learned to read and write. She had always been able to count. Above all, from being a waif that nobody wanted, she had turned into a young woman who was very proud of working for quite the best policeman in London, which meant anywhere. She would tell everyone so, if they appeared to be ignorant of that fact.

"Thank you," Charlotte said with sudden decision. She closed the newspaper and stood up. She jammed it savagely into the coal scuttle and went to the door. "I shall go and visit the General and see if I can be of any help, even if it is only to let him know that I am still his friend."

"Good," Gracie agreed. "Mebbe we can do summink as can 'elp." She included herself with both pride and determination. She regarded herself as part of the detective work. She had contributed significantly in the past and had every hope and intention of doing so in the future.

Charlotte went upstairs and changed out of her plain summer day dress of blue muslin and put on a very flattering gown of soft yellow, which complemented her complexion and the auburn tones of her hair. It was also cut to a very becoming shape, tight-waisted, full-sleeved at the shoulder, with a sweeping skirt and a very small bustle, as was the current fashion. It had been her one recent extravagance. Mostly she had to make do with what was serviceable and could last several seasons, with minor changes. Of course her sister, Emily, who had married very well indeed the first time and then been widowed, and was now married again, was generous with castoffs and mistakes. But Charlotte was loath to accept too much, in case it made Thomas feel more acutely aware of her step down in circumstances by marrying a policeman. And anyway, Parliament was in recess at the moment, and Emily and Jack were away in the country, on this occasion taking Grandmama with them. Even Caroline, Charlotte's mother, was away; in Edinburgh with her husband Joshua's new play.

But there was no questioning that this particular gown was as successful as anything she had ever worn, either owned or borrowed.

She left the house and went out into the sunshine of Keppel Street. There was no need to think of transport, as she had no more than a few hundred yards to go. It was odd to think of General Balantyne's having moved to live so close by, and she had never encountered him. But then there must be scores of her neighbors she had not seen. And in spite of their proximity to each other, Bedford Square and Keppel Street were socially of a very considerable difference.

She nodded to two young ladies walking side by side, and they nodded back to her politely, then immediately fell into animated conversation. An open brougham clattered past, its occupants surveying the world with superior interest. A man walked by swiftly, looking to neither side of him.

Charlotte did not know which house was the Balantynes'. Pitt had simply said "in the center of the north side." She gritted her teeth and rang the bell of the one that seemed most likely. It was answered by a handsome parlormaid who informed her that she was mistaken and that General Balantyne lived two doors farther along.

Charlotte thanked her with as much aplomb as possible and retreated. She would have liked to abandon the whole thing at this point. She had not even any coherent plan as to what she would say if he were in and would receive her. She had come entirely on impulse. He might have changed completely since they had last met. It had been four years. Tragedy did change people.

This was a ridiculous idea, quixotic and open to the ugliest misinterpretations. Why was she still walking forward instead of turning on her heel and going home?

Because she had told Gracie she was going to see a friend who had been visited by misfortune and assure him of her loyalty. She could hardly go back home and admit that her nerve had failed her and she was afraid of making a fool of herself. Gracie would despise her for that. She would despise herself.

She strode up the steps, seized the doorbell and pulled it firmly before she could have time to think better of it.

She stood with her heart pounding, as if when the door opened she could be facing mortal danger. She had visions of Max, the footman the Balantynes had had years before, and all the tragedy and violence that had followed, and Christina . . . how that would have hurt the General. She had been his only daughter.

This was absurd. She was grossly intrusive! Why on earth

should she imagine he wished to see her now, after all that Pitt had been forced to do to their family, and Charlotte had helped. She was practically the last person on earth he would have any kindness for. He certainly would not care for her friendship. It was tasteless of her to have come . . . and hopelessly conceited.

She stepped back and had half turned away to leave when the door opened and a footman asked her very distinctly, "Good morning, ma'am, may I help you?"

"Oh . . . good morning." She could ask for directions somewhere. Pretend to be looking for some fictitious person. She did not have to say she had called here. "I . . . I wonder if . . ."

"Miss Ellison! I mean . . . I beg your pardon, ma'am, Mrs. Pitt, isn't it?"

She stared at him. She could not remember him. How could he possibly have remembered her?

"Yes . . ."

"If you'd like to come in, Mrs. Pitt, I shall see if Lady Augusta or General Balantyne is at home." He stepped back to allow her to accept.

She had no choice.

"Thank you." She found she was shaking. If Lady Augusta was in, what could Charlotte possibly say to her? They had disliked each other before Christina. Now it would be even worse. What on earth could she say? What excuse was there for her presence?

She was shown into the morning room and recognized the model of the brass gun carriage from Waterloo on the table. It was as if the years had telescoped into each other and vanished. She felt the horror of the Devil's Acre murders as if they were still happening, all the pain and injustice raw.

She paced back and forth. Once she actually went as far as the door into the hall and opened it. But there was a housemaid on the stairs. If she left now she would be seen. She would look even more absurd than if she stayed.

She closed the door again and waited, facing it as if she expected an attack.

It opened and General Balantyne stood there. He was

older. Tragedy had marked his face; there was a knowledge of pain in his eyes and his mouth which had not been there when they had first met. But his back was as straight, his shoulders as square, and he looked as directly as he always had.

"Mrs. Pitt?" There was surprise in his face, and a softness which was almost certainly pleasure.

She remembered how very much she had liked him.

"General Balantyne." Without thinking, she stepped forward. "I really don't know why I have come, except to say how sorry I am that you should have the misfortune of some miserable man choosing your doorstep on which to die. I hope they can clear it up rapidly and you ——" She stopped. He did not deserve platitudes. Lyndon Remus had already done the harm by resurrecting the Devil's Acre case. No solution to this new murder would undo that.

"I'm sorry," she said sincerely. "I suppose that was all I wanted to say. I could have written a letter, couldn't I?"

He smiled very slightly. "A beautifully phrased, most tactful one, which would not have meant much and not sounded like you at all," he answered. "And I should think you had changed, which I should regret." Then he colored faintly, as if he were aware of having been too outspoken.

"I hope I've learned a little," she said. "Even if I sometimes fail to put it into practice." She wanted to remain at least a few minutes longer. Perhaps there was something she could do to help, if only she could think of it. But it would be horribly intrusive to ask questions, and Pitt would already have done so anyway. Why did she imagine she could do anything more?

He broke the silence. "How are you? How is your family?"

"Very well. My children are growing up. Jemima is quite tall. . . ."

"Ah, yes . . . Jemima." A smile touched his mouth again. No doubt, like her, he was thinking of Jemima Waggoner, who had married his only son, and after whom Charlotte had named her daughter. "They returned the compliment, you know?"

"The compliment?" she asked.

"Yes. They called their second son Thomas."

"Oh!" She smiled back. "No. I didn't know. I shall tell him. He'll be very pleased. Are they well?"

"Very. Brandy is posted in Madrid now. We don't see them very often."

"You must miss them."

"Yes." There was a moment of deep loneliness in his eyes. He looked away, staring out of the window into the quiet summer garden, roses lush and heavy in the morning sun, the dew already evaporated from them.

The clock ticked on the mantelshelf.

"My mother remarried," Charlotte said awkwardly.

He dragged himself to the present and turned back to face her.

"Oh? I . . . hope she is happy." It was not a question; one did not ask about such things, it was far too personal and intrusive. One did not even speak about happiness or unhappiness; it would be indelicate.

She smiled at him, meeting his eyes. "Oh, yes. She married an actor."

He looked mystified. "I beg your pardon?"

Had she gone too far? She had meant to lighten the tension, and perhaps he had taken it for levity. She could not go back, so she plunged on. "She married an actor, rather younger than she is." Would he be scandalized? She felt the heat burn up her cheeks. "He has a great deal of courage . . . and charm. Moral courage, I mean . . . to remain loyal to friends in difficulty and to fight for what he believes to be right."

His expression eased, the lines around his mouth softening. "I am glad." For an instant, almost too short to be certain she saw it, there was passionate regret in his eyes. Then he took a breath. "I gather that you like him?"

"Yes, I do, and Mama is very happy, although she has changed a good deal. She has the acquaintance now of people she would never have imagined knowing a few years ago. And I am afraid some of her earlier friends no longer call, and even turn the other way if they encounter her in the street."

36

A flicker of amusement touched his mouth. "I can imagine it."

The door opened and Lady Augusta Balantyne stood in the entrance. She looked magnificent, her dark hair piled in a great swirl on her head, the silver streaks making it look even more dramatic. She was dressed in lilac and gray in the height of fashion and wore a very fine amethyst necklace and earrings. She regarded Charlotte with cold distaste.

"Good morning, Mrs. Pitt. I assume I am addressing you correctly?" This was a sarcastic reminder that when Charlotte had first entered their house it had been ostensibly to assist the General with some clerical work on his memoirs, and she had used her maiden name to disguise her connection with Pitt and the police.

Again Charlotte felt the blush warm her cheeks. "Good morning, Lady Augusta. How are you?"

"I am perfectly well, thank you," Augusta replied, coming farther into the room. "I presume it is not mere civility which brings you here to enquire after our well-being?"

This was an icy impasse. There was nothing to do but brazen it out. There was little room to make it any worse.

Charlotte smiled brightly. "Yes, it is." Everyone would know that was a lie, but no one could call it so. "It was only yesterday I realized that we were near neighbors."

"Ah . . . the newspapers," Augusta said with immeasurable contempt. Ladies of breeding or gentility did not read the newspapers except for the society pages and the advertisements. And Charlotte might once have had an element of breeding, but she had married a policeman, and that had disposed of any pretensions to gentility now.

Charlotte raised her eyebrows very high. "Was your address in the newspapers?" she said innocently.

"Of course it was!" Augusta said. "As you know perfectly well, some unfortunate wretch was murdered on our doorstep. Don't be disingenuous, Mrs. Pitt. It ill becomes you."

Balantyne flushed hotly. Like most men, he loathed emotional confrontations, and those between women most of all. But he had never flinched from his duty.

"Augusta! Mrs. Pitt came to express her sympathy for our misfortune in that issue," he said critically. "I assume she knew of it from Superintendent Pitt, not from the newspapers."

"Do you!" Augusta retorted with equal chill towards him. "Then you are very naive, Brandon. But that is your own affair. I am going to call upon Lady Evesham." She turned to Charlotte. "I am sure you will be gone when I return, so I shall wish you good day, Mrs. Pitt." And she turned with a swirl of skirts and went out of the door, leaving it open behind her.

Balantyne went over and closed it with a sharp snap, to the obvious surprise of the footman standing in the foyer and holding Augusta's cape.

"I'm sorry," Balantyne said with profound embarrassment. He did not offer any explanation or attempt to make better of it. Any candor between them would be shattered by such a denial of the truth. "It was . . ."

"Probably well deserved," she finished for him ruefully. "It was rather clumsy of me to have come at all, and I had no idea what I was going to say, except that I feel for you, and I hope you will consider me as your friend, regardless of what should transpire."

He looked thoroughly taken aback by such frankness, and acutely pleased. "Thank you . . . of course I shall." He seemed about to add something more, then changed his mind. He was still deeply troubled, and there was another emotion more powerful beneath the surface anger or shame for Augusta's behavior or for his own discomfort in the face of candor.

"Actually, I did read the newspaper," she admitted.

"I assumed you did," he said with the ghost of a smile.

"It was a shameful piece! Completely irresponsible. That was what prompted me to come—outrage . . . and to let you know I am on your side."

He looked away from her. "You speak blindly, Mrs. Pitt. You cannot have any idea what may transpire."

He was not uttering some platitude. She was quite sure—from the stiffness in his body, the unhappiness in his face and the way he glanced away from her—that he feared something

38

specific, and the anxiety of it underlay everything else he was able to think of.

It frightened her for him, and her response was to defend him, instantly and without thought.

"Of course not!" she agreed. "What kind of friend makes their support conditional upon knowing everything that will happen, and that there will be no unpleasant surprises and absolutely no inconvenience, embarrassment or cost?"

"A great many friends," he said quietly. "But none of the best. But this loyalty must run both ways. One does not allow friends to walk unknowingly into danger or unpleasantness, nor require of them a pledge, even unspoken, whose costs you know and they do not." He realized he had overstated what she had offered, and looked deeply uncomfortable. "I mean . . ."

She walked to the door, then turned and met his eyes. "There is no need to explain. Time has passed since we last met, but not so much as all that. We do not misunderstand one another. My friendship is yours, for what that may be worth. Good day."

"Good day . . . Mrs. Pitt."

Charlotte went straight home, walking so briskly she passed by two people she knew without even noticing them. She went in her own front door and straight through to the kitchen without bothering to take off her hat.

The ironing was finished, and Archie was asleep in the empty basket.

Gracie looked up from the potatoes she was peeling, the knife still in her hand, her face full of anxiety.

"Put on the kettle," Charlotte requested, sitting down in the nearest chair. She would have done it herself, but one did not go near even the cleanest stove when wearing a yellow gown.

Gracie obeyed instantly, then got out the teapot and the cups and saucers. She fetched milk from the larder. She set the blue-and-white jug on the table and removed the muslin cover, weighted down all around with glass beads to keep it from blowing off.

" 'Ow was the General?" she asked, getting the tin of biscuits off the dresser. She still had to stretch to do it, standing on tiptoe, but she refused to put them on a lower shelf. That would be acknowledging defeat.

"Very distressed," Charlotte answered.

"Did 'e know the man wot was killed?" Gracie asked, putting the biscuits on the kitchen table.

"I didn't ask him." Charlotte sighed. "But I am afraid that he might. He was extremely worried about something."

"But 'e din't say, I suppose."

"No."

The kettle began to hiss as steam blew out of the spout, and Gracie took the holder for it to pick it up, poured a little hot water into the teapot, swilled it out and threw it away down the sink. She put three spoonfuls of tea leaves into the pot and carried it back to the stove, then poured the rest of the water on. She filled up the kettle again as a matter of habit. One should always have a kettle of hot water, even in June.

"Are we goin' ter do summink about it?" she asked, carrying the teapot over and sitting down opposite Charlotte. The potatoes could wait. This was important.

"I don't know what we can do." Charlotte looked across at her. Absentmindedly, she took off her hat.

"Are you scared as mebbe 'e did do summink?" Gracie screwed up her face.

"No!"

Gracie bit her lip. "Aren't yer?"

Charlotte hesitated. What was Balantyne afraid of? He was certainly afraid of something. Was it simply more pain, more public exposure of his personal and family affairs? Every family has grief, embarrassments, quarrels or mistakes they prefer to keep unknown from the public in general and from their own circle of acquaintances in particular . . . just as one does not undress in the street.

"I'm not really sure," she said aloud, setting the hat on the table. "I believe he is a totally honorable man, but all of us can make errors of judgment, and many of us do foolish or rash things to protect those we love or feel responsible for."

Gracie poured the tea. " 'Oo's 'e responsible fer, the General?"

"I don't know. His wife, maybe any of the servants, perhaps a friend."

Gracie thought for several minutes. "Wot's 'is wife like?" she said at length.

Charlotte sipped her tea and tried to be fair. "Very handsome, very cold."

"Wouldn't a' bin 'er lover, would 'e, this corpse?"

"No." Charlotte could not imagine Augusta dissembling sufficiently to have a lover, let alone one who would be found dead on a doorstep.

Gracie was watching her anxiously. "You don' like 'er a lot, do yer?"

Charlotte sighed. "No, not a lot. But I don't think she would attack anyone without extraordinarily good reason, and I can't think of anything that would make her kill someone and then not be perfectly prepared to call the police and explain herself—if, for example, she had caught him in the house attempting to steal, and he had turned on her."

"Wot if the General caught 'im?" Gracie asked, taking a biscuit.

"The same. Why not call the police?"

"I dunno." Gracie sipped her tea also. "Yer sure 'e were upset about the body, not summink else?"

"I think so."

"Then I s'pose as we'd better keep up wif everythink as the Master finds out," Gracie said seriously.

"Yes," Charlotte agreed, wishing they could know at least some of it before Pitt found out.

Gracie was watching her, waiting for her to take the lead with some practical and clever plan.

There were only two things in her mind: the sense of fear she had drawn from General Balantyne as he stood by the window in his morning room; and her sharp awareness that Sergeant Tellman, very much against his will and judgment, was attracted to Gracie. It was against his judgment because they disagreed about almost everything. Gracie considered

41

herself to be very fortunate to work in Pitt's house, to have a roof over her head, a warm bed every night and good food every day. She had not always had these things, or expected to. She also considered that she was doing a very important and useful job, and was appropriately proud of it.

Tellman had profound feelings regarding the innate social evil of any person's being servant to another. From that basic difference sprang a host of others on every subject of social justice and personal judgment. And Gracie was cheerful and outgoing by nature, while he was dour and pessimistic. They had neither of them yet realized that they shared a passionate sense of justice, a hatred of hypocrisy and a willingness to work and to risk their own safety to fight for what they believed in.

"Sergeant Tellman is on the case," Charlotte said aloud.

"I don't see as 'avin' 'im 'elps," Gracie replied, wrinkling her nose a little. "I s'pose 'e's quite clever, in 'is own fashion." This last was added half grudgingly. "But 'e won't 'old no favors for generals an' the like."

"I know he won't," Charlotte admitted, thinking of Tellman's opinion of all inherited privilege. No doubt he was fully aware that in Balantyne's time of office commissions were purchased. "But at least we have him."

"Yer mean like ter speak to?" Gracie was puzzled.

"Yes." A plan was rapidly forming in Charlotte's mind, not a very good one so far. "He might be persuaded to tell us what information he has learned."

Gracie brightened. "Yer reckon? If yer asked 'im, like?"

"I was thinking more if you asked him."

"Me? 'E wouldn't tell me nuffink! 'E'd say sharpish as it were none o' my business. I can see 'is face now if I started meddlin' wif questions about 'is work. Tell me right w'ere to put meself, 'e would."

Charlotte took a deep breath and plunged in.

"I had in mind more if he were to make his reports to Mr. Pitt at home, instead of at Bow Street, and perhaps when Mr. Pitt happened to be out."

" 'Ow are we goin' ter manage that?" Gracie was non-plussed.

Charlotte thought of Tellman's face as he had looked at Gracie the last time she had observed them together.

"I think that could be arranged, if you were to be very nice to him."

Gracie opened her mouth to argue, then colored very pink.

"I s'pose I could be, if it was important. . . ."

Charlotte beamed at her. "Thank you. I should be very grateful. Mind, I do appreciate it will take a great deal of careful planning, and it may not work every time. A little sub-terfuge may be necessary."

"A little what?" Gracie frowned.

"A little more or less than the truth, now and again."

"Oh, yeah . . . I see. O' course." Gracie smiled back and took another sip of her tea, reaching for a second biscuit. In the laundry basket, Archie woke up, stretched and started to purr.

When Sergeant Tellman had begun to work on identifying the body found on General Balantyne's step he had naturally started at the mortuary. Looking at corpses was part of his duty, but something he disliked intensely. For a start, they were naked, and it was an intrusion into a man's decent pri-vacy he was helpless to prevent. Tellman found it offensive, even though he completely understood the necessity. Sec-ondly, the smell of dead flesh, formaldehyde and carbolic turned his stomach, and no matter what time of the year it was, the place always seemed cold. He found himself both sweating and shivering. But he was conscientious. The more he disliked a job, the less would he stint in doing it.

However, even the most diligent examination taught him nothing he had not observed in the first few moments by lantern light in Bedford Square. The dead man was lean to thin, wiry, pale skinned where his clothes covered him, weathered where they did not, as if he spent much time in the open. His hands were not those of a laborer. He had several scrapes, as if he had fought hard to save himself, especially

43

across his knuckles. He had been hit extremely hard on the head, killed with one blow.

He looked, as nearly as Tellman could judge, to be in his fifties. There were half a dozen old scars of varying sizes. None of them looked to be from major injuries, just the sort of thing any man might collect if he had been involved in dangerous work or lived largely on the streets. There was one exception: a long, thin scar across the left side of his ribs, as though from a knife slash.

Tellman replaced the sheet gratefully and moved to the clothes. They were well worn, rather grubby and uncared for. The soles of the boots were in need of repair. They were exactly what he would have expected of a poor man who had spent the day outside, and possibly the night before as well. They told him nothing.

But the contents of the pockets were a different matter. Of course, the most interesting thing was the snuffbox, now in Pitt's keeping. He was puzzled as to its meaning; it could be any of a dozen things, all more or less implicating General Balantyne. But Pitt had said he would look into that himself. A year before, Tellman would not have believed him, expecting him to protect the gentry from the just desserts for their own deeds. Now he knew better, but it still rankled.

The only other thing that seemed relevant to the search for either his identity or that of the person who had killed him seemed to be the receipt for the three pairs of socks. Actually, he was surprised that a man in such circumstances should purchase socks from a shop which had its name on the paper. He would have expected him to buy them from a peddler or market stall. Still, the receipt was there, so he should follow it.

He was relieved to be able to go out into the sun again, and the relatively fresh air of the street with its smell of smoke, horse dung and dry gutters, and the sound of hooves on the cobbles, peddlers' cries, the clatter of wheels, and somewhere in the distance a barrel organ and an errand boy whistling off-key.

He caught a horse-drawn omnibus, running after it the last few paces as it drew away from the curb and swinging himself onto the step to the great disapproval of a fat woman in gray bombazine.

"Yer'll get yerself killed like that, young man!" she said critically.

"I hope not, but thank you for the warning," he replied with politeness, which surprised both of them. He paid his fare to the conductor and looked without success for a seat, being obliged to remain standing, holding on to the post in the center of the aisle.

He got off again at High Holborn and walked the two blocks to Red Lion Square. He found the haberdasher's shop easily and went inside with the receipt in his hand.

"Mornin', sir," the young man behind the counter said helpfully. "Can I show you anything? We have excellent gentlemen's shirts at very agreeable prices."

"Socks," Tellman answered, wondering if he could afford a new shirt. Those on display looked very clean and crisp.

"Yes sir. What color, sir? We have 'em all."

Tellman remembered the socks the dead man had been wearing. "Gray," he answered.

"Certainly, sir. What size would you be requiring?"

"Nine." If the dead man could afford socks, so could he.

The young man bent to a drawer behind him and produced three different pairs of gray socks in size nine.

Tellman selected the pair he liked best, glanced quickly at the price, and produced the money, leaving himself sufficient for his bus fare back to Bow Street but unfortunately not enough for lunch.

"Thank you, sir. Will that be all?"

"No." Tellman held out the receipt. "I'm a policeman. Can you tell me who bought these gray socks five days ago?"

The man took the receipt. "Oh, dear. We sell a lot of socks, sir. And gray is a popular color this time o' year. Lighter than black, you see, and better looking than brown. Always look a bit country, brown, if you know what I mean?"

"Yes. Think hard, if you please. It's very important."

"Done something wrong, has he? They were paid for, that I can swear to."

45

"I can see that. Don't know what he did, but he's dead."

The young man paled. Perhaps it had been a tactical error to have told him that.

"Gray socks," Tellman repeated grimly.

"Yes sir. What did he look like, do you know?"

"About my height," Tellman said, thinking with an unpleasant chill how much he resembled the man on the step. "Thin, wiry, fairish hair receding a little." That at least was different. Tellman had dark hair, straight and still thick. "And mid-fifties, I would guess. Lived or worked outdoors, but not with his hands."

"Sounds like two or three what come here often enough," the young man said thoughtfully. "Could be George Mason or Willie Strong, or could be someone as never came but the once. Don't know everybody's name. Can't you tell me anything else about him?"

Tellman thought hard. This might be their only chance to identify him.

"He had a long knife or bayonet scar on his chest." He indicated on himself the place where it had been, then realized the futility of telling the salesman such a thing. "Could have been a soldier," he added, more to defend his remark than anything else.

The salesman's face brightened. "There was one gentleman come in, and I think he did buy several pairs, thinking on it. Had a bit of a conversation, 'cos he spoke about being a soldier, and how important it was to keep your feet right. I remember he said, 'Soldier with sore feet is use to neither man nor beast.' That's why he sold bootlaces himself, now he's fallen on hard times. But I can't tell you his name or where he lives. Don't recall as I ever saw him before. An' didn't see him that well this time. It were a fine evenin', but he was muffled up, said he had a chill. But he was thinnish and about your height. Couldn't say dark or fair."

"Where did he sell his bootlaces?" Tellman asked quickly. "Did he say?"

"Yes, yes, he did. Corner of Lincoln's Inn and Great Queen Street."

"Thank you."

It took Tellman the rest of the day, but he found George Mason and Willie Strong, the two men the salesclerk had named, and they were both quite definitely alive.

Then he made enquiries about the peddlers in Lincoln's Inn Fields and learned that there was normally an old soldier named Albert Cole on the northwest corner near Great Queen Street. However, no one recalled seeing him for five or six days. Several barristers from the Inns of Court habitually bought their bootlaces from him and described him passably well. One of them offered to come to the mortuary the next day and identify the body if he could.

"Yes," the barrister said unhappily. "I am afraid that looks very much like Cole."

"Can you say for sure that it's him?" Tellman pressed. "Don't say if you aren't happy about it."

"I'm not exactly happy about it!" the barrister snapped. "But yes, I am quite certain. Poor devil." He fished in his pocket and brought out four guineas. He put them on the table. "Put this towards a decent burial for him. He used to be a soldier. Served his Queen and country. He shouldn't end up in a pauper's grave."

"Thank you," Tellman said with surprise. He had not expected such generosity towards a stranger, and a peddler at that, from a class of man for whom he had an innate contempt.

The barrister gave him a chilly look and turned to leave.

"Do you know anything else about him, sir?" Tellman said as he followed him into the street. "It's extremely important."

The barrister slowed unwillingly, but his training in the law was deeply implanted.

"He was a soldier. Invalided out, I think. I don't know what regiment, I never asked."

"I can probably find that out," Tellman said, keeping step. "Anything else, sir? Don't know where he lived or if he had any other place except Lincoln's Inn Fields?"

"I don't think so. He was usually there, any weather."

"Ever mention where he got his bootlaces?"

47

The barrister looked at him with surprise. "No! I merely purchased the odd pair from him, Sergeant. I did not indulge in long conversations. I am sorry this man is dead, but I cannot be of further assistance." He pulled his gold watch out of his pocket and opened it. "Now, I have spared as much time as I can afford—in fact, rather more. I must take a cab back to my office. I wish you Godspeed in finding his killer. Good day to you."

Tellman watched him disappear into the crowd. At least he now knew the identity of the dead man, and from as good a witness as he was likely to find—certainly one who would stand up in court.

But what had Albert Cole, ex-soldier, present seller of bootlaces, been doing in the middle of the night in Bedford Square? It was less than a mile away, but peddlers rarely moved even a couple of blocks. If they did they were on somebody else's patch, and that was a mortal offense and likely to bring them considerable unpleasantness. Peddlers were very seldom violent people, but even if they were, it would be cause for a severe fight, but not murder, except by accident.

But one did not peddle bootlaces at midnight.

Obviously, something quite different had taken him to General Balantyne's front doorstep. He could not have been courting a maid. That would have taken him to the back. The last thing he would want would be to go to the front door, exposed to the street, the beat constable, any passerby. And certainly no maid keeping an assignation would let him in at the front.

For that matter, why would anyone intending burglary be a moment longer at the front than necessary? Surely he would slip from one back alley to another, through the mews if possible, backyards and tradesmen's entrances where coal and kitchen goods were delivered and rubbish was taken away.

So why was he at the front door, and with Balantyne's snuffbox in his pocket?

Tellman walked along the footpath with his head down, deep in thought. He could not formulate a satisfactory answer, but he felt sure that somehow the Balantyne house had something to do with it. It was not chance. There was a reason.

He needed to know more about General Brandon Balantyne, and also about Lady Augusta.

He did not really suspect her of anything, certainly not alone, and he had very little idea of how to go about investigating her. He was not a cowardly man and held no innate respect for anyone because of their position or wealth, but he still quaked at the thought of addressing Augusta.

The General was different. Tellman understood men far better, and it would be a relatively easy business to check the General's military career. Much of that would be public knowledge through the army. Similarly, he could find and check Albert Cole's record of service.

"Albert Cole?" the military clerk repeated. "Middle name, Sergeant?"

"No idea."

"Where was 'e born?"

"Don't know."

"Don't know much, do you!" He was a middle-aged man who was bored by his job and made as much of it as possible, particularly in this instance of its complication and its inconvenience. Tellman was civil only with difficulty, but he needed the information.

"Only that he's been murdered," he replied.

"I'll see what I can do." The man's face tightened and he went away to search, leaving Tellman sitting on a wooden bench in the outer office.

It was the best part of an hour before he returned, but he had the information.

"Albert Milton Cole," he said with great importance. "This'll be your man. Born May 26, 1838, in Battersea. Served in the 33rd Foot, it says here." He looked up at Tellman. "That's the Duke of Wellington's regiment! Got a bullet wound in 1875. Left leg, 'igh up. Broke the bone. Sent

49

'ome and pensioned off. Nothing after that. Nothing against him though. Never married, according ter this. Any 'elp?"

"Not yet. What can you tell me about General Brandon Balantyne?"

The man's eyebrows shot up. "Generals now, is it? That's a different kettle o' fish altogether. You got some authority for that?"

"Yes. I'm investigating the murder of a soldier who was found with his skull broken . . . on General Balantyne's doorstep!"

The clerk hesitated, then decided he was curious himself. He had no particular love for generals. If he had to do this, and he thought he probably did, then he would look less unimportant if he did it willingly.

He went away again and came back fifteen minutes later with several sheets of paper and presented them to Tellman.

Tellman took them and read.

Brandon Peverell Balantyne had been born on March 21, 1830, the eldest son of Brandon Ellwood Balantyne of Bishop Auckland, County Durham. Educated at Addiscombe, graduated at sixteen. When he was eighteen, his father had purchased him a commission and he had sailed for India as a lieutenant in the Bengal Engineers, and was immediately involved in the Second Sikh War, where he was present at the siege of Multan and served with distinction, although wounded, at the battle of Gujrat. In 1852 he had led a column in the First Black Mountain Hazara Expedition on the Northwest Frontier, and the year after he was with an expedition against the Jowaki Afridis in Peshawar.

During the Indian Mutiny he had been with Outram and Havelock in the first relief of Lucknow, and then in its final capture. There he had served brilliantly, chasing rebel bands in Oudh and Gwalior in '58 and '59. He had gone on to command a division in the China War of 1860, where he had been decorated for valor.

He was in the Bombay army with General Robert Napier when Napier had been ordered to command the expedition to Abyssinia in '67. Balantyne had gone with him.

50

After that Balantyne had been promoted to command himself, and remained in Africa, fighting with continued distinction in Ashantiland in '73 and '74, then in the Zulu Wars of '78 and '79. After that he retired and returned home to England permanently.

It was a career of apparent distinction and honor, and undeserved privilege, paid for in the first place by his father.

That was a deep offense to Tellman, an injustice inherent in a social system he despised. On the surface, he was more angered that apparently Balantyne's path had never crossed that of Albert Cole.

He thanked the clerk for his assistance and left.

The following morning Tellman began the task of learning about Balantyne in earnest. He waited outside the house in Bedford Square, standing across from it on the pavement under the trees, alternatively kicking his heels or pacing back and forth, always swinging around to look at the front door or the main entrance. He had little hope that any of the servants would talk. In that sort of establishment, he knew, they had loyalties, and it was more than a servant's job was worth to gossip about his or her employers. No one could afford to be dismissed without a reference. It was ruin.

General Balantyne emerged from the front door a little after half past ten and walked uprightly along the pavement along Bayley Street and turned left into the Tottenham Court Road down towards Oxford Street, where he turned right and walked westward. He was dressed formally in dark trousers and a beautifully tailored coat. Tellman had vivid opinions about anyone who required a servant to dress him satisfactorily.

The General spoke to no one and appeared not to look either to right or left as he went. *Marched* would have been the appropriate word. He looked stiff, as if he were going into battle. A cold, rigid man, Tellman thought as he walked behind him. Probably proud as Lucifer.

What was he thinking about the crowds he passed through? That they were the civilian equivalent of foot soldiers, people it was not necessary to make way for, even to regard at all?

Certainly he barely seemed to be aware of them, and he spoke to no one, nor raised his hat. He passed two or three soldiers actually in uniform, but ignored them, and they him.

At Argyll Street he turned sharply right, and Tellman almost missed him climbing the steps of a handsome house and going inside.

Tellman went to the door after him and saw the brass plate on which was engraved the words THE JESSOP CLUB FOR GENTLEMEN. He hesitated. There would be a steward of some sort in the vestibule. He would no doubt know all the members. He would therefore be an excellent source of information, but again, one whose livelihood depended upon his discretion.

He must be inventive. He was serving no purpose standing in the street. People would think him a peddler! He jerked his lapels straighter, squared his shoulders and pulled the doorbell.

It was answered by a middle-aged steward in well-cut, slightly faded livery.

"Yes sir?" He regarded Tellman blankly, summing up his social status in a glance.

Tellman felt the blood burn in his face. He would have liked to tell the man his opinion of gentlemen who spent their days with their feet up or playing games of cards or billiards with each other. Parasites on decent people, the lot of them. He could also have added his contempt for those who earned their living by pandering to such leeches.

"Good morning," he said stiffly. "I'm Sergeant Tellman of the Bow Street police station." He held out his card as proof of it.

The steward looked at it without touching it, as if it had been unclean.

"Indeed," he said expressionlessly.

Tellman gritted his teeth. "We are looking for a man who is pretending to be a retired army officer, of distinguished service, in order to defraud people out of considerable sums of money."

The steward's face darkened with disapproval. Tellman

had his attention at least. "I hope you catch him!" he said vehemently.

"Doing everything we can," Tellman replied with feeling. "This man is tall, broad-shouldered, very upright, military looking in his bearing. Dresses well."

The steward frowned. "That describes a few that I can think of. Can you tell me anything else about him? I know all our members, of course, but sometimes gentlemen bring in guests."

"So far as we know, he's clean shaven," Tellman went on. "Although of course that can change. Fairish hair, thinning a bit, gray at the temples. Aquiline features. Blue eyes."

"Can't say as I've seen him."

"I followed a man here just this moment."

The steward's face cleared.

"Oh! That's General Balantyne. Known him for years." His expression suggested something close to amusement.

"Are you certain?" Tellman persisted. "This devil uses other people's names pretty freely. Was General . . . Balantyne? Yes . . . did General Balantyne seem his usual self to you?"

"Well . . . hard to say." The steward hesitated.

Tellman had a stroke of genius. "You see, sir," he said confidentially, leaning forward a little, "I think this bounder may be using General Balantyne's name . . . running up bills, even borrowing money . . ."

The steward's face blanched. "I must warn the General!"

"No! No sir. That would not be a good idea . . . just yet." Tellman swallowed hard. "He would be extremely angry. He might unintentionally warn this man, and we need to catch him before he does the same thing to someone else. If you would be so good as to tell me a little about the real General, then I can make sure that the other places he frequents are not taken in by the impostor."

"Oh." The steward nodded his understanding. "Yes, I see. Well, he belongs to one or two services clubs, I believe. And White's, although I don't think he goes there so often as here." This last was added with pride, a slight straightening of the shoulders.

"Not a very social sort of man?" Tellman suggested.

"Well . . . always very civil, but not . . . not overfriendly, if you get my meaning, sir."

"Yes, I do." Tellman thought of Balantyne's rigid back, his rapid stride along Oxford Street, speaking to no one.

"Does he gamble at all, do you know?"

"I believe not, sir. Nor drink very much either."

"Does he go to the theater, or the music hall?"

"I don't think so, sir." The steward shook his head. "Never heard him refer to it. But I think he has been to the opera quite often, and to the symphony."

Tellman grunted. "And museums, no doubt," he said sarcastically.

"Yes sir, I believe so."

"Rather solitary sort of occupations. Doesn't he have any friends?"

"He's always very agreeable," the steward said thoughtfully. "Never heard anyone speak ill of him. But he doesn't sit around talking a lot, doesn't . . . gossip, if you know what I mean. Doesn't gamble, you see."

"No sports interests?"

"Not that I ever heard of." He sounded surprised as he said it, as if it had not occurred to him before.

"Pretty careful with money?" Tellman concluded.

"Not extravagant," the steward conceded. "But not mean either. Reads a lot, and I overheard him once say he liked to sketch. Of course he's traveled a lot—India, Africa, China too, so I heard."

"Yes. But always to do with war."

"Soldier's life," the steward said a trifle sententiously and with considerable respect. Tellman wondered if he had the same respect for the foot soldiers who actually did the fighting.

He went on talking to the steward for several minutes more, but little was added to the picture he was forming of a stiff, cold man whose career had been purchased by his family and who had made few friends, learned little of comradeship and nothing of the arts of pleasure, except those he

54

considered socially admirable, like the opera . . . which was all foreign anyway, so Tellman had heard.

None of it appeared to have anything whatever to do with Albert Cole. And yet there was a connection. There must be. Otherwise how had Cole got the snuffbox? And why was that the only thing taken?

General Brandon Balantyne was a lonely, unbending man who followed solitary pursuits. He had been privileged all his life, working for none of the advantages he possessed, money, rank, position in society, his beautiful house in Bedford Square, his titled wife. But he was also a troubled man. Tellman was a good enough judge of character to know that. And he intended to find out what that trouble was, most especially if it had cost ordinary, poor, underfed and ill-clothed Albert Cole his life. Honest men reported thieves, they did not murder them.

What could Albert Cole, poor devil, have seen in that house in Bedford Square for which he had been killed?

3

P*ITT WAS CONCERNED* with the murdered man who had been found in Bedford Square, but Cornwallis's problem preyed more urgently upon his mind. For the time being there was not a great deal he could accomplish that could not be done equally as well by Tellman as far as discovering who the man was and, if possible, what had taken him to Bedford Square in the middle of the night. He still thought it most likely to be a burglary which had in some disastrous way gone wrong. He hoped profoundly that Balantyne was not involved, that the man had burgled Balantyne first, taking the snuffbox, and then gone on elsewhere and been caught in the act and killed, perhaps accidentally. The killer had removed his own belongings but had not taken the snuffbox in case the possession of it incriminated him.

It was probably a footman or butler in one of the other houses. When it was discovered which, then great tact would be necessary, but all the discretion in the world would not much alter the final outcome. And he had confidence in Tellman's ability to pursue the trail quite as well as he would have himself. Meanwhile, he would do all he could to help Cornwallis.

He set out from home in the morning as usual, but instead of going either to Bow Street or to Bedford Square, he caught a hansom and requested the driver to take him to the Admiralty.

It took considerable argument and persuasion to obtain the naval records of H.M.S. *Venture* without explaining why he wanted them. With much use of words like *tact*, *reputation*, and *honor*, but mentioning no names, by mid-morning he finally sat alone in a small, sunlit room and read what he had asked for.

The record was simple: Lieutenant John Cornwallis had been on duty when a seaman had been injured attempting to reef the mizzen royal in rising bad weather. According to his own account, Cornwallis had gone up to help the man and had brought him down, half conscious, the last few yards assisted by Able Seaman Samuel Beckwith.

Beckwith was illiterate, but his verbal account, taken down by someone else, was largely the same. Certainly he had not contradicted any part of the official version. The words recorded were bare, just a few sentences on white paper. There was no sense of the people behind it, none of the roaring wind and sea, the pitching deck, the terror of the man trapped up the mast, one minute over the wooden boards which would break his bones if he were to fall on them, the next over the howling, cavernous depths of water which would swallow him beyond any human power to rescue. Any man who fell into that would be gone forever, as completely as if he had never existed, never had life or laughter or hope.

There was no sense of what manner of men they had been, brave or cowardly, wise or foolish, honest or lying. Pitt knew Cornwallis, at least knew him as he was now, an assistant commissioner in the police force, taciturn, painfully honest, out of his depth with politicians, having no conception of their deviousness.

But he did not know how he had been fifteen years before as a lieutenant, faced with physical danger, the chance of admiration and promotion. Had this been an otherwise honorable man's one mistake?

He did not believe that. Such deceit would surely have left a deeper mark. If Cornwallis had profited from stealing another man's reward, praise for someone else's act of courage, would it not have stained everything else he touched? Would he not have spent the rest of his career looking backward over his shoulder, fearing Beckwith's telling of the truth? Would he not have built guards for himself against just this eventuality, knowing there was always a chance? And would that not have shown in all else that he did?

Would he have allowed Pitt to know of it?

Or was he so arrogant he thought he could use Pitt, and Pitt would never realize?

That was such a distortion of the man Pitt perceived that he discarded the notion as close to impossible.

That left the question, did the blackmailer believe it was true or did he simply know that Cornwallis could not prove its untruth?

Beckwith was dead, according to Cornwallis. But had he relatives alive, someone to whom he had told the story, perhaps boasting a little, elaborating on his own part until he appeared the hero, and this person had taken him at his word, as perhaps a son or a nephew might do?

Or for that matter, a daughter. Why not? A woman was as capable as any man of cutting out letters from newspapers and framing a threat.

While he was there, Pitt decided, he should find all he could of the rest of Cornwallis's naval career, and all there was available on Samuel Beckwith as well, particularly if he had a family still alive, and where they might be now.

More argument and more persuasion were necessary before he was given a very abbreviated summary of Cornwallis's career, only those things which were largely a matter of public knowledge anyway, such as any other naval personnel might know from their own observation.

He had been promoted and changed ship within two years. In 1878 and 1879 he had been in the China Seas, involved with distinction in the bombardment of Borneo against the pirates.

Within a year after that he had had his own command. He had sailed in the Caribbean and been involved in several actions of a minor nature, largely skirmishes to do with slavers still operating out of West Africa.

He had retired from the sea in 1889 with distinction and an

unblemished record. There was a list of ships on which he had served and the ranks he had held, nothing more.

Pitt compared it with Samuel Beckwith's career, which had been cut short by death at sea, carried overboard by a spar broken loose in a gale. He had never married, and left behind a sister, living in Bristol at the time of his death. His effects and his back pay had been sent to her. She was listed as a Mrs. Sarah Tregarth. Her address was given.

But Beckwith had been unable to read or write. The letter sent to Cornwallis was quite articulate and contained several complex words. Had Sarah Beckwith learned such an art in spite of her brother's inability?

A discreet letter to the Bristol police would confirm that.

Now Pitt looked at the names of the ships on which Cornwallis had served and copied down a dozen or so names of other men who had served at the same times, including the captain of the *Venture* and the first lieutenant.

Next he showed his list to the man who had so far assisted him and asked for the addresses of all those who were not currently at sea.

The man looked at Pitt narrowly, then read through them.

"Well, he was killed in action about ten years ago," he said, biting his lip. He moved to the next one. "He's retired and gone to live in Portugal or somewhere. He's in Liverpool. He's here in London." He looked up. "What do you want all these men for, Superintendant?"

"Information," Pitt replied with a tight smile. "I need to know the truth about an incident in order to avert a considerable wrong . . . a crime," he added, in case the man should miss the urgency of it or doubt his right to involve himself.

"Oh. Oh, yes sir. It'll take me a little while. If you'd come back in an hour or so?"

Pitt was hungry, and even more he was thirsty. He was delighted to accept the suggestion and go out and buy himself a ham sandwich from a stall, and a cup of strong tea. He stood in the sun on the street corner enjoying them, watching the passersby. Nursemaids in starched aprons wheeled perambulators. Their older charges rolled hoops or pretended to ride

59

sticks with horses' heads. A small boy played with a spinning top and would not come when he was told. Little girls in frilly pinafores mimicked their elders, walking daintily, with heads high. He thought with a wave of tenderness of Jemima and how quickly she had grown up. Already she was beginning to be self-conscious, aware of coming womanhood. It felt like only months ago she had been struggling to walk, and yet it was years.

When he had first met Balantyne she had not even been born. And she had been stumbling with speech, often unintelligible to anyone but Charlotte, when Balantyne had lost his only daughter in the most fearful way possible.

Memory of that turned the sandwich in his mouth to sawdust. How could a man bear such grief and survive? He wanted to rush home and make doubly, triply sure Jemima was all right . . . even hold her in his arms, watch her all the time, make any decisions for her, decide where she should go and who befriend.

Which was ridiculous. It would make her hate him—rightly so.

How did anyone endure having children and watching them grow up, make mistakes, get hurt, perhaps even destroyed, suffer pain worse, more inexplicable, than death? Had Augusta been any help to Balantyne, any comfort at all? Had their common grief brought them closer together at last or merely driven them each into greater isolation, even more alone in their grief?

What was this new tragedy? Perhaps he shouldn't have left it to Tellman to investigate. And yet he could not abandon Cornwallis.

He threw away the rest of his sandwich, drank the last of his tea, and strode back to the Admiralty. There was no time for standing around.

He began with Lieutenant Black, who had served as first officer with Cornwallis in the China Seas. He was home on shore leave and might be called back to sea quite soon. He lived in South Lambeth, and Pitt took a hansom over the river.

He was fortunate to find Lieutenant Black at home and

willing to speak with him, but unfortunate in that what Black had to say was so punctiliously honorable it conveyed very little at all. His professional loyalty to a brother officer was so great as to rob his comments, even his memories, of any individuality or meaning. It conveyed much of Black himself, his perception of events, his fierce patriotism and allegiance to the service in which he had spent all his adult life, but Cornwallis remained only a name, a rank and a series of duties well performed. He never became a man, good or bad.

Pitt thanked him and looked for the next name on his list. He took another hansom and went north over the Victoria Bridge to Chelsea, watching the pleasure boats in the river full of women in pale dresses with bright hats and scarves and men with bare heads in the sun, children in sailor suits, eating toffee apples and striped peppermint sticks. The music of a hurdy-gurdy drifted loudly on the air, along with shouts, laughter and the swish of water.

He found Lieutenant Durand a very different man, lean, sharp featured, roughly the same age as Cornwallis, but still a serving officer.

"Of course I remember him," he said sharply, leading Pitt into a very pleasant room filled with naval memorabilia, probably from several generations, and overlooking a garden full of summer flowers. It was obviously a family home, and judging from the portraits Pitt had glimpsed in the hall, he came from a long and distinguished line of naval officers, going back long before Trafalgar and the days of Nelson.

"Sit down." Durand indicated a well-worn chair and sat in one opposite it himself. "What do you want to know?"

Pitt had already explained his reasons, but this time he must phrase it more skillfully and learn something of the man. "What qualities made him a good commanding officer?"

Durand was obviously surprised. Whatever he had been expecting, it was not this.

"You assume I thought he was a good commander," he said with raised eyebrows, looking at Pitt very directly and with amusement. His face was burned by wind, his eyebrows fair and sparse.

"I assumed you would say so," Pitt replied. "I was wanting something a little less dry. Was I mistaken?"

"Loyalty before honesty. Is that no use to you?" The faint thread of humor was still there. He sat with his back to the window, leaving Pitt to face the garden and the sunlight.

"None at all." Pitt sat back in the chair. It was very comfortable. "Sometimes it is all I can find."

"A naval failing, at times," Durand observed, a flicker of bitterness in his voice. "And the sea has no such sentimentality. She forgives nothing. She'll find the measure of a man faster than anything else. In the end the only honor is the truth."

Pitt watched him carefully, already aware of strong undercurrents of emotion, perhaps of anger or a belief of injustice or tragedy somewhere.

"And was Cornwallis a good commander, Lieutenant?"

"He was a good sailor," Durand answered. "He had a feeling for the sea. In a way I would say he loved it, insofar as he loved anything."

It was an odd remark, said without affection. His face was shadowed, difficult to read.

"Did his men trust him?" Pitt pursued. "Have confidence in his ability?"

"Ability to do what?" Durand was not going to answer anything lightly. He had decided to be frank, and that meant no evasions simply to satisfy.

Pitt was obliged to think harder, more clearly. What did he mean?

"To make the right judgments in bad weather, to know the tides, the wind, the . . ."

Durand smiled. "You are not a seaman, are you." It was a statement, not a question, and made with patience, even condescension, the amusement returned. "I think the questions you want to ask are, for example, was he thorough? Yes, extremely. Was he competent to read a chart, take a ship's position, and judge the weather? Yes, to all of those. Did he think ahead and plan accordingly? As much as any man. Occasionally he made mistakes. When he did, could he think quickly,

62

adapt, get out of the danger? Always, but sometimes more successfully than at other times. He had his share of losses." His voice was dry, the emotion carefully controlled.

"Of ships?" Pitt was horrified. "Men?"

"No, Mr. Pitt, if he had done that he'd have been retired ashore a long time before he was."

"He wasn't retired for loss?" Pitt demanded too quickly.

"Not so far as I know," Durand said, leaning back a little, still staring at Pitt. "I think he simply realized his career was going no further, and he got tired of it. Wanted to come ashore, and somebody offered him a comfortable option, so he took it."

A tart response about the reality of Cornwallis's present job was on Pitt's lips, but he could not afford to alienate Durand if he were to gain any useful information, strong as his impulse was to do so. And Durand obviously had not liked Cornwallis. Perhaps the fact that Cornwallis had reached captaincy while Durand was still serving, and only a lieutenant, had much to do with it.

"What other questions would I ask, if I knew something of the sea?" Pitt said a little stiffly, trying to mask his own feelings.

Durand seemed quite unaware of it. There was a concentration apparent in the angle of his head and shoulders against the light. He was eager to talk.

"Was he a good leader?" he started. "Did he care for his men, know them individually?" He gave a slight shrug. "No, he never gave that impression. If he did, they did not believe it. Did his officers like him? They barely knew him. He was private, withdrawn. He had a captain's dignity, but he had a cold man's isolation, and there is a difference." He was studying Pitt's face as he spoke, watching his reaction. "Did he have the art to communicate to the crew his belief in them, in the mission the ship was bound on?" he continued. "No. He had no humor, no common touch, and no visible humanity. That was what lifted Nelson above all the rest, you know, his mixture of genius and humanity, sublime courage and foresight, with a complete vulnerability to the ordinary

63

aches and losses of other men." His voice hardened. "Corn-wallis had none of that. The men respected his naval ability, but they did not love him." He drew in his breath. "And to be a really good commander, you must be loved . . . that is what inspires a crew of men to go beyond their duty, beyond even what can be expected of them, to dare, to sacrifice, and to achieve what to a lesser crew, with the same ship, would be impossible."

It was a masterly summary, and Pitt was obliged to admit it to himself, whether it was true or not. It was not how he saw Cornwallis, or how he wished to. Honesty and fear both forced him to stay and listen. He was afraid they showed in his face, and he resented the thought that Durand could read them there.

"You mentioned courage," Pitt said, clearing his throat, trying to keep his voice from betraying his dislike of the man and his own loyalties. "Was Cornwallis brave?"

Durand's body stiffened. "Oh yes, undoubtedly," he con-ceded. "I never saw him show fear."

"That's not quite the same thing," Pitt pointed out.

"No—of course it isn't. In fact, I suppose it's almost the opposite," Durand agreed. "I imagine he must have been afraid at times. Only a fool would not be. But he had the sort of icy self-control which hides all emotion. One never saw the humanity in him," he repeated. "But no, he was not a coward."

"Physically? Morally?"

"Certainly not physically." He hesitated. "Morally, I can-not say. There are few great moral decisions at sea. Such judgments of command as he made were not in the time that I knew him. I think he is too orthodox in his thinking, too unimaginative to be a moral adventurer. If you are asking if he ever got drunk and behaved with abandon . . . no! I don't think he ever even behaved with indiscretion." There was a curious contempt in that remark. "Rethinking your question, yes, perhaps he was a moral coward . . . afraid to take life by the horns and . . ." He lost his metaphor and shrugged, a

64

gesture of inner satisfaction. He had painted the picture he wanted, and he knew it.

"Not a man to take risks," Pitt summed it up. Durand's judgment had been cruel, intended to injure, but perhaps in his ignorance of the issues he had said precisely what Pitt wanted to hear—not that Cornwallis was too honest to take credit for another man's act of courage but that he was too much the moral coward to take the chance. The fear of discovery would have crippled him.

Durand sat comfortably with the sunlight at his back.

Pitt stayed for another fifteen minutes, then thanked him and left, glad to escape the claustrophobic feeling of envy that permeated the comfortable house with its family portraits of men who had succeeded and who had expected future generations to follow in their steps and provide even more glittering pictures with their gold braid and proud faces.

The following day Pitt found two able seamen and a naval surgeon. The first was MacMunn, retired after a pirate raid on Borneo, having lost a leg. He lived with his daughter in a small, neat house in Putney where the carpet was patched and the furniture gleamed and smelled of wax. He was more than willing to talk.

"Oh, yeah! I 'member Mr. Cornwallis well. Strict, 'e were, but fair. Always very fair." He nodded several times. " 'Ated a bully, 'e did. Couldn't stand 'em. Punish 'em summink 'orrible. Weren't free wi' the cat, but 'e'd see a man wot bullied them wot was beneath 'im flogged raw, 'e would."

"A hard man?" Pitt asked, afraid of the answer.

MacMunn laughed a rich, happy sound. "Nah! Not 'im. You in't seen nuffink! Mr. Farjeon, now 'e were wot yer'd call 'ard." He pulled a face, turning his mouth down at the corners. "I reckon as 'e'd 'ave keel'auled yer if 'e could. He'd a' liked the days o' floggin' through the fleet!"

"What was that?" Pitt's naval history was shallow.

MacMunn squinted at him. "Put a man in a longboat an' 'ave 'im rowed 'round an' flogged on the deck o' every ship in the fleet. Wot yer think?"

"It would kill him!" Pitt protested.

"Yeah," MacMunn agreed. "Mind yer, a good ship's surgeon'd see a man numbed ter the point 'e'd not know. Die pretty quick, so me grandpa told me. 'E were a gunner at Waterloo, 'e were." Unconsciously, he straightened up as he said it, and Pitt found himself smiling at him without knowing quite why, except a heritage shared, and a knowledge of courage and sacrifice.

"So Cornwallis wasn't hard or unjust?" Pitt said quietly.

"Gawd no!" MacMunn waved the idea away. " 'E were just quiet. I never fancied bein' an officer meself. Lonely kind o' way o' doing things, I reckon." He slurped his tea. "Everybody got their place, an' w'en there's dangers o' yer in one rank, all the same, yer got companions like. But w'en there's only one o' yer, yer can't talk ter them above, an' they can't talk ter you, an' yer can't talk ter them below. Can't make a fool o' yerself if yer an officer, 'cos people expect yer ter be right all the time. An' Mr. Cornwallis took 'isself very serious. Didn't know 'ow ter unbend 'isself, if yer know wot I mean."

"Yes, I think I know." Pitt recalled a dozen times when Cornwallis had hovered on the brink of candor and at the last moment retreated self-consciously. "A very private man."

"Yeah. Well, I suppose if yer want ter be captain, yer gotta be. Make a mistake, show a weakness, an' the sea'll 'ave yer. Makes men 'ard, but makes 'em loyal too. An' yer could always rely on Mr. Cornwallis. Bit stuck kind o' by the book, 'e were, but honest to a fault." He shook his head. "I 'member one time w'en 'e 'ad ter punish a feller wot done summink wrong, don't rightly recall wot now. But it weren't much, but regulations said 'e 'ad ter be lashed wi' the cat . . . answered back the bo'sun or summink. Yer could tell Mr. Cornwallis din't wanna do it. Bo'sun were a right bastard. But yer can't break ship's discipline or ye're all lost."

He twisted up his face, thinking back to the incident. "But Mr. Cornwallis, 'e made 'ard work of it. Paced the quarterdeck all by 'isself fer days, 'e did. Mad as 'ell. Then suffered like 'e were the one wot 'ad bin beat." He took a deep breath.

"Bo'sun got lost overboard an' Mr. Cornwallis bust a gut tryin' ter find if 'e were pushed." He grimaced. "Never did find out, though."

"And was he?" Pitt asked.

MacMunn grinned at Pitt over the top of his mug.

"Yeah, 'course 'e were! But we all reckoned as Mr. Cornwallis din't really wanter know that."

"So you didn't tell him?"

"S'right! Good man, Mr. Cornwallis. Wouldn't wanter make things 'ard fer 'im. An' if 'e'd a' know'd, 'e'd a' 'ad the poor sod 'anged from the yardarm, no matter 'ow much 'e'd a' felt fer 'im, an' like ter 'ave pushed the bo'sun over 'isself." He shook his head. "Got 'is imagination all in the wrong places. Feels for folk summink terrible, but takes everythin' too exact, if you know wot I mean?"

"Yes, I think I do," Pitt answered. "Would he ever take credit for another man's act of bravery, do you think?"

MacMunn looked at him incredulously.

"More likely 'ang for another man's crime, 'e would! 'Oo ever said that's both a liar and a fool. 'Oo is 'e?"

"I don't know, but I intend to find out. Can you help me, Mr. MacMunn?"

" 'Oo, me?"

"If you will. For example, did Captain Cornwallis have any personal enemies, people who were envious or who cherished a grudge?"

MacMunn screwed up his face, his tea forgotten. " 'Ard ter say, if ye're honest like. Nothin' as I knows of, but 'oo can say wot goes on in a man's mind w'en 'e's passed over in the ranks, or w'en 'e 'as ter be told orff fer summink. Honest man knows it's 'is own doin' . . . but . . ." He shrugged expressively.

But no matter how hard Pitt pressed, MacMunn had few practical suggestions to make, and Pitt thanked him again, and left him feeling considerably lighter in spirits, as if he had met with something essentially clean which had washed away the sense of oppression which had weighed him down after speaking with Durand. A fear inside him had eased.

The early afternoon found him in Rotherhithe with Able

Seaman Lockhart, a taciturn man rather the worse for drink who gave him no information of value and seemed to remember Cornwallis as a man to be feared, but respected for his seamanship. He disliked all senior officers, and said so. It was the only subject upon which he would offer more than single-word replies.

By late afternoon, when the air was hot and still and a haze had settled over the City, the river winding below in a glittering ribbon, Pitt walked up the hill from the landing stage towards the Greenwich Naval Hospital to see the onetime ship's surgeon, Mr. Rawlinson.

Rawlinson was busy, and Pitt had to wait in an anteroom for over half an hour, but he was reasonably comfortable and the unaccustomed sights and sounds held his interest.

When Rawlinson came he was dressed in a white shirt with the neck open and the sleeves rolled up, as if he had been hard at work, and there were bloodstains on his arms and several places on his body. He was a big man, well muscled, with a broad, amiable face.

"Bow Street police station?" he said curiously, eyeing Pitt up and down. "Not one of our people in trouble, surely? Not over the river and on your patch, anyway."

"Not at all." Pitt turned from the window, where he had been watching the water and the traffic going up to the Port of London. "I wanted to ask you about an officer who served with you in the past . . . John Cornwallis."

Rawlinson was incredulous. "Cornwallis! You can't mean he's come to your attention. I thought he was in the police himself. Or was it the Home Office?"

"No, police." It seemed explanations were unavoidable. He had promised discretion. How could he honor that and still be of any use? "This is an incident in the past that has been . . . misinterpreted," Pitt replied tentatively. "I am looking into it on Captain Cornwallis's behalf."

Rawlinson pursed his lips. "I was a ship's surgeon, Mr. Pitt. I spent a great deal of my time in the orlop."

"The what?"

68

"The orlop. The lower deck, aft, where the wounded are taken and we do our operating."

Below them on the river a clipper with canvas full set was drifting up tide towards the Surrey Docks, its magnificent sails white in the sun. There was something sad about it, as if its age were already dying.

"Oh. But you did know Cornwallis?" Pitt insisted, dragging his mind back.

"Certainly," Rawlinson agreed. "Sailed under his command. But being the captain of a ship is not a very sociable position. If you haven't been at sea you probably haven't much of an idea of the power a captain has and the necessary isolation that requires." Unthinkingly, he wiped his hands on the sides of his trousers, unaware of smearing them with traces of blood. "You can't be a good commander without keeping a certain distance between yourself and the men, even the other officers." He turned and led the way into a wide gallery through a glass-paned door and down the steps to the grass, the panorama of the river beyond the sloping ground.

Pitt followed, listening.

"The whole structure of the crew is built on a very tight hierarchy." Rawlinson waved his hands as he spoke. "Too much familiarity and men lose that edge of respect for the captain. He has to be more than human to them, close to infallible. If they see his vulnerability, his doubt, ordinary weaknesses or fears, something of the power is lost." He glanced at Pitt. "Every good captain knows that, and Cornwallis did. I think much of it came naturally to him. He was a quiet man, solitary by choice. He took his position very seriously."

"Was he good?"

Rawlinson smiled, leading the way across the grass in the sun. The breeze from the river smelled of salt. The tide was running sharply. Overhead, gulls circled, crying loudly.

"Yes," he answered. "Actually, he was very good."

"Why did he come ashore?" Pitt asked. "He's comparatively young."

Rawlinson stopped, his expression guarded, defensive for

the first time. "Forgive me, Mr. Pitt, but why does that concern you?"

Pitt struggled for the right reply. Surely only some element of the truth would serve Cornwallis now?

"Someone is endeavoring to hurt him," he replied, watching Rawlinson's face. "Damage his reputation. I need to know the truth in order to defend him."

"You want to know the worst they could say, with any honesty?"

"Yes."

Rawlinson grunted. "And why should I not suspect that the enemy you speak of is you yourself?"

"Ask Cornwallis," Pitt responded.

"In that case, why don't you ask him what the worst or the best is of his career?" It was said with wry amusement, no ill will at all. He stood in the sun with his bloodstained arms folded, a smile on his face.

"Because we don't always see ourselves as others do, Mr. Rawlinson," Pitt replied. "Does that need explaining?"

Rawlinson relaxed. "No, it doesn't." He began to walk again, waving his hand in invitation to Pitt to accompany him. "Cornwallis was a brave man," he answered. "Both physically and morally; perhaps a trifle short in imagination. He had a sense of humor, but it didn't show very often. He took his pleasures quietly. He liked to read . . . all manner of things. He was a surprisingly good artist with watercolors. Painted light on water with a sensitivity that astounded me. Showed a completely different side of the man. Made one understand that sometimes genius is not in what you put in but what you leave out. He managed to convey"—he circled his hands in a sweeping motion—"air! Light!" He laughed. "Would never have thought he had such . . . daring . . . in him."

"Was he ambitious?" Pitt tried to phrase it to earn an honest answer, not one motivated primarily by loyalty.

Rawlinson considered for a moment before he replied. "In his own way, yes, I think so. But it wasn't readily observable, not as it was in many men. He did not want to seem excellent so much as actually to be so. The pride in him, the hunger, was not for appearances but for reality." He looked at Pitt quickly, to see if he understood. "It made him . . ." He searched for a way to express what he was looking for. "It made him seem remote at times. Some people even thought him evasive, where I think he was only complex, and different from them. He was his own hardest taskmaster. He was driven, but not in order to please or impress anyone else."

Pitt walked beside him in silence, thinking that if he did not speak, then the other man would continue.

He was right.

"You see," Rawlinson went on, "he lost his father when he was quite young, eleven or twelve, I think. Old enough to know him, from a boy's eye, not old enough to be disillusioned or challenge him in any way."

"Was his father in the navy?"

"Oh, no!" Rawlinson said swiftly. "He was a nonconformist minister, a man of profound and simple belief, and the courage both to practice and to preach it."

"You knew him better than you intimated."

Rawlinson shrugged. "Perhaps. It was only one night, really. We'd had a bad skirmish with a slaver. Boarded them and took the ship all right, but it was teak and burned." He glanced at Pitt. "I see that means nothing to you . . . how could it? Teak splinters are poison, not like oak," he explained. "We had a few men hurt, but our first officer, a good man—Mr. Cornwallis had a great affection for him—was in a bad way. He helped me remove the splinters and do all we could for him. But he went into a fever and we sat up all night, spelled each other the next day and the next night." He reached the gravel path and turned to walk back up the slope, Pitt keeping pace with him.

"Not a captain's job, you'll say, and neither was it. But we were well away from the coast by then and the slaver was dealt with. He took one watch on deck, the other with me." His mouth pulled tight. "God knows when he slept. But we saved Lansfield. Lost a finger, that's all. I suppose we talked a bit then. Men do, in the watches of the night, when they're desperate and there's nothing they can do to help. Didn't see

71

much of him after that, except as duty required. I suppose I always think of him as he was then, the lamplight yellow in his face, gaunt with worry, angry and helpless, and so tired he could hardly keep his head up."

Pitt did not bother to ask if he would have taken credit for another man's act of courage; there was no need. He thanked Rawlinson and left him to go back to his patients. He walked in the bright, late-afternoon light down towards the river and the landing stage where he could catch a ferry back up past Deptford, Limehouse, Wapping, the Tower of London, under London Bridge, Southwark Bridge, and probably get off at last at Blackfriars.

He knew far more of Cornwallis, and if anything he was even more determined to defend him from the blackmailer, but he had little more idea of who that might be, except that it was even harder to think it was anyone who had served with him and genuinely believed the charge to be true.

He remembered the way the letter was written, the grammatical correctness, not to mention the spelling and the choice of words. It was not an ordinary seaman, nor was it likely to be one of their dependents, such as a wife or sister. If it was the son of a seaman, then he had definitely improved his position in the world since childhood.

As he reached the river's edge the smells of salt and weed sharp in his nostrils, the slap of water, the damp air, the cry of gulls, light on their wings, he knew he still had a very long way to go.

That morning Charlotte opened the first delivery of mail and found a letter addressed to her in handwriting which swept away the years like leaves on the wind. Even before she opened it she was certain it was from General Balantyne. What was written inside was very brief:

My dear Mrs. Pitt,
    It was most generous of you to be concerned for my welfare, and to offer your renewed friendship in this present unpleasantness.

72

I thought of taking a brief walk around the British Museum this morning. I shall be in the Egyptian exhibit at about half past eleven. If you should find yourself free, and passing that way, I should be delighted to see you.

I remain your obedient servant,

Brandon Balantyne

It was a stiff and very formal way of saying that he very much needed the friendship she had offered, but the fact that he had written at all made his feelings most plain.

She folded the paper with a quick movement and rose from the kitchen table to lift the lid from the stove and put it in. The flames consumed it with an instant flare, and it was gone.

"I shall be going out this morning," she told Gracie. "I have a desire to look at the Egyptian exhibit in the British Museum. I cannot say when I shall be back."

Gracie shot her a look of fierce curiosity, but she forbore from asking any questions.

"Yes, ma'am," she said with wide eyes. "I'll see ter everythink."

Charlotte went upstairs and took out her second-best summer morning dress, not the pale yellow which was her best—she had worn that the first time—but a pink-and-white muslin she had been given by Emily, whom it had not become as she had hoped.

The British Museum was in comfortable walking distance, which was presumably why he had selected it, and she set out at ten past eleven in order to be at the exhibit by half past. This was a meeting of friendship, not a romantic or society appointment where lateness could be considered fashionable or a suitably modest reluctance.

She was there by twenty-five minutes past, and saw him immediately, standing upright, shoulders straight, hands behind his back, the light on his head, catching the fair hair turning to gray. He looked extraordinarily lonely, as if the other people passing by were all part of some great unity which excluded him. Perhaps it was his stillness that marked

73

him apart. He was very obviously waiting for someone, because his gaze did not appear to move as it would were he actually looking at the mummified figures in front of him or at the intricate carving and gold of the sarcophagus.

She walked over to him, but for a moment he was unaware of her.

"General Balantyne . . ."

He turned quickly and his face filled with delight, and then embarrassment at his betrayal of emotion.

"Mrs. Pitt . . . how kind of you to have come. I hope I do not presume . . . I . . ."

She smiled. "Of course not," she assured him. "The Egyptian exhibit is something I have always wished to see, but no one else I know has the least interest in it, and if I came down and stood around looking at it alone, I might be taken for a most undesirable kind of woman and attract attention I do not wish."

"Oh!" He obviously had not thought of that. Being a man gave him a freedom he had taken for granted. "Yes . . . indeed. Well . . . let us look at it."

He had misunderstood. She could have seen it any time—with Emily, or Great-Aunt Vespasia, or Gracie, for that matter. She was trying to make him feel a little less ill at ease by making a joke of it.

"Have you ever been to Egypt?" she asked, staring at the sarcophagus.

"No. Well . . . only to pass through." He hesitated, then, as if making a great decision, he continued. "I have been to Abyssinia."

She glanced at him. "Have you? Why? I mean, was it to do with interest in the country or were you sent there? I didn't know we had ever fought Abyssinia."

He smiled. "My dear, we have fought just about everywhere. You would be hard put to name a place on the face of the earth where we have not meddled at some time or other."

"Why did we meddle in Abyssinia?" she asked with genuine interest, as well as a desire to make him speak of something in which he was comfortable.

"It is a preposterous story." He was still smiling.

"Good," she encouraged. "I love preposterous stories, the more so the better. Tell me."

He offered her his arm, and she took it as they walked slowly around the exhibits one after another, without seeing any of them.

"It was in January of 1864," he began, "that it really came to a head. But it started long before. The Emperor of Abyssinia, whose name was Theodore—"

"Theodore!" she said with disbelief. "That doesn't sound like an Abyssinian name. It should be . . . I don't know . . . African! At least foreign. I'm sorry—please go on!"

"He was born of very humble family," he resumed. "His first calling was as a scribe, but he earned very little at it, so he took to banditry instead, at which he did so well that by the time he was thirty-seven he was crowned Emperor of Abyssinia, King of Kings, and Chosen of God."

"I have obviously underrated banditry!" She giggled. "Not only its social acceptability but its religious significance."

He was smiling broadly now. "Unfortunately, he was quite mad. He wrote a letter to the Queen—"

"Our Queen, or his own queen?" she interrupted.

"Our Queen! Victoria. He wished to send a delegation to England to see her, in order to let her know that his Muslim neighbors were oppressing him and other good Christians in Abyssinia. He asked her to form an alliance with him to deal with them."

"And she wouldn't?" she asked. They were now in front of a magnificent stone carved with hieroglyphics.

"We will never know," he answered. "Because the letter reached London in 1863 but someone in the Foreign Office mislaid it. Or else they could not think what to say in reply. So Theodore became very angry indeed, and imprisoned the British consul in Abyssinia, one Captain Charles Cameron. They stretched him on a rack and flogged him with a hippopotamus hide whip."

She stared at him, uncertain if he was absolutely serious. She saw from his eyes that he was.

75

"So what happened then? Did they send the army to rescue him?"

"No . . . the Foreign Office looked very hastily for the letter, and found it," he answered. "They wrote a reply requesting Cameron's release and gave it to a Turkish Assyriologist named Rassam and asked him to deliver it. The letter was written in May of 1864, but it did not reach the Emperor in Abyssinia until January nearly two years later, when Theodore welcomed Rassam warmly . . . and then threw the poor man into prison with Cameron."

"Then we sent in the army?" she said.

"No. Theodore wrote to the Queen again, this time asking for workmen, machinery and a munitions manufacturer." The corners of his lips twitched with wry humor.

"And we sent the army?" she concluded.

He glanced sideways at her. "No, we sent a civil engineer and six workmen."

In spite of herself, her voice rose. "I don't believe it!"

He nodded. "They got as far as Massawa, waited there for half a year, and were finally sent home again." Then his expression became serious again. "But in July of that year, 1867, the Secretary of State for India telegraphed the Governor of Bombay asking how long it would take to mount an expedition, and in August the cabinet decided on war. In September they sent Theodore an ultimatum. And we set sail. I came from India and joined General Napier's forces: Bengal Cavalry, Madras sappers and miners, Bombay native infantry and a regiment of Sind horse. We were joined by a British regiment, the 33rd Foot, although actually half of them were Irish and there were almost a hundred Germans, and when we landed near Zula, there were Turks and Arabs and all kinds of Africans. I remember a young war correspondent named Henry Stanley writing about it. He loved Africa, fascinated by it." He stopped. He was looking at the exhibit in front of them now, an alabaster carving of a cat. It was exquisite, but there was no pleasure in Balantyne's face, only embarrassment and pain.

"You fought in Abyssinia?" she asked quietly.

76

"Yes."

"Was it very bad?"

He moved slightly, with just a flinch of the body, a gesture of denial. "No worse than any fighting. There is always fear, mutilation, death. You care about people and see them reduced to the least—and rise to the most—a man can be: terror and courage, selfishness in some, nobility in others, hunger, thirst, pain . . . fearful pain." He kept his face away from her, as if to meet her eyes would make him incapable of saying what he felt. "It strips away all pretense . . . from others and from yourself."

She was not sure whether to interrupt or not. She tightened her fingers on his arm a little.

He stood silently.

She waited. People moved past them, some of them turning to stare for a moment. She wondered fleetingly what they thought, and did not care.

He took a deep breath and let it out silently.

"I did not wish to talk about battle. I'm sorry."

"What did you wish to say?" she asked gently.

"I . . . perhaps . . ." He faltered again.

"I can forget it afterwards if you would rather I did," she promised.

He smiled, a harsh curling of the lips. He remained facing forward, not looking at her. "There was one action in that campaign where we were ambushed. Thirty men were injured, my commanding officer among them. It was something of a fiasco. I was shot in the arm, but not badly."

She waited for him to continue without prompting him.

"I have received a letter." He said it with great difficulty, his words coming as if forced out of him, his face stiff. "It accuses me of being the cause of that rout . . . of—of cowardice in the face of the enemy, of being responsible for the injuries of those men. It says . . . that I panicked and was rescued by a private soldier, but that that fact was covered up to save the honor of the regiment, and for morale. It is not true, but I cannot prove that." He did not tell her that such a charge, if known, would ruin him. He expected her to know.

77

And she did. Anyone would, especially just at the moment, with the Tranby Croft affair all over the newspapers and on everyone's tongue. Even those who would not normally take the slightest interest in such people were now talking about them and awaiting the next development, eager for disaster.

She must answer with intelligence. Sympathy was fine, but it was of no practical use, and he needed help.

"What did they ask for?" she said quietly.

"A snuffbox," he answered. "Just as a token of good faith."

She was surprised. "A snuffbox? Is it valuable?"

He gave a sharp bark of laughter, raw, self-mocking. "No . . . a few guineas. It's pinchbeck, but it is beautiful. Highly individual. Anyone would know it was mine. It is a token of my willingness to pay. Some would say it is a sign of guilt." His hands clenched, and she could feel the muscles of his arm hard under her fingers. "But it's only a mark of my panic . . . exactly what he accused me of." The bitterness in his voice was close to despair. "But I never turned my back on the enemy of the body . . . only of the mind. Odd . . . I had not imagined I lacked moral courage."

"You don't," she said without a moment's hesitation. "It is a delaying tactic . . . until we know the strength of the enemy and a little more of his nature. Blackmail is a cowardly thing . . . perhaps the most cowardly." Her anger was so burning hot, she had not even been aware of using a plural that included herself.

He moved his other hand and very gently, just for a moment, touched her fingers where they lay on his arm, then turned away and began to walk towards the next exhibit, several pieces of ancient glass in a case.

She followed after him swiftly. "You cannot become involved in this," he said. "I told you simply because . . . because I needed to share it with someone, and I knew I could trust you."

"You can trust me!" she said urgently. "But not to stand by and watch you tortured for something you did not do. Not that I would stand by even if you had. We all make mistakes, are weak or frightened or stupid sometimes, and that in itself is usually punishment enough." She stood next to him but did

78

not link her arm in his this time. He was not looking at her.
"We are going to fight!"

Now he did face her. "How? I have no idea who he is."

"Then we must find out," she retorted. "Or else we must contact someone who was there and can disprove what this person is saying. Make a list of everyone who even knows about it."

"The army," he said with the ghost of a smile.

She was determined. "Come, now! It was a skirmish in Abyssinia . . . it was hardly Waterloo! And it was twenty-three years ago. They will not all even be alive."

"Twenty-five," he corrected with a sudden softness in his eyes. "Shall we begin over luncheon? This is not the most convenient place for writing anything."

"Certainly," she agreed. "Thank you." She took his arm again. "That would be an excellent beginning."

They ate together at a most agreeable small restaurant, and were she less preoccupied with the problem, she would have luxuriated in delicious food in whose preparation she had taken no part. But the matter in hand was far too serious, and it had her entire attention.

Balantyne struggled to remember the names of all the men he knew who had been involved in the action in Abyssinia. With a little effort he managed all the officers, but when it came to the private soldiers he could bring to mind only about half.

"There will be military records," he said somewhat glumly. "Although I doubt they will be able to help. It was so long ago."

"Somebody remembers," she pointed out. "Whoever sent that letter is connected one way or another. We'll find these people." She looked down the page from the small notebook he had purchased before coming to dine. There were fifteen names. "The army will know where they live, won't it?"

He looked deeply unhappy. "After this length of time they may well have settled anywhere in the country—or the world, for that matter. Or, as you pointed out, they may no longer be alive."

She felt his misery and understood his fear. She had certainly felt it herself several times, not the sharp, sick terror of physical pain or destruction, but the cold, creeping fear of loss, hurt to the mind and the heart, loneliness, shame, guilt, the desert of being unloved. She was not threatened by this. She must be strong for both of them.

"Well, the person we are looking for is definitely alive, and I imagine living here in London," she said firmly. "Where did you send the snuffbox to?"

His eyes widened. "A messenger called for it, a boy on a bicycle. I spoke to him, but he had no idea where it was going, except that a gentleman had paid him and would meet him in the park at dusk. He couldn't describe this gentleman at all, except that he was wearing a checked coat and a cloth cap, also with checks. It is presumably a disguise. No one would dress like that for any other reason. Whether he was the blackmailer or not, I don't know. He might have been passing it on again." He took a deep breath. "But you are quite right. He is here in London. There is something I did not tell you . . . the man who was found dead on my doorstep had my snuffbox in his pocket."

"Oh . . ." She realized with a drenching coldness how that could be read by any investigating police, even Pitt. "Oh . . . I see." Now Balantyne's fear was better explained.

He was watching her, waiting for the anger, the blame, the changed perception.

"Do you know who he is?" she asked, meeting his eyes.

"No. I expected to, when I went to the mortuary to look at him for Pitt, but so far as I know I have never seen him before."

"Could he have been a soldier?"

"Certainly."

"Could he have been the blackmailer?"

"I don't know. I half wish he were, and then he would be dead." His fingers on the tablecloth were stiff. It took him a deliberate effort of will not to clench them. She could see it in the knotting and then relaxing of his hand. "But I did not kill him . . . and who else would . . . on my doorstep? Except the real blackmailer—to draw police attention to me!" He was shaking now, very slightly. "I watch every delivery of the post for another letter, telling me what he wants. I shall not give it to him. And then he will spread the story—perhaps to the police as well."

"Then we must find someone who was there and can disprove the story," she said with more anger and hope than conviction. "You must have friends, connections, who can tell you where to find these people." She indicated the list. "Let us begin now!"

He did not argue, but the misery in his face and the weariness in the angles of his body betrayed the fact that he did not hope to succeed. He was doing it simply because it was not in his nature to surrender, even when he knew he was beaten.

Tellman was convinced that in some way Albert Cole was connected with General Balantyne, and he was determined that he would discover what it was. Having exhausted the immediate avenues of knowledge regarding Balantyne, he returned to Cole's military career. That was the most obvious possibility.

It was in reviewing the history of Cole's regiment, the 33rd Foot, that he saw that it had served in the Abyssinian Campaign of 1867–68. That was where it crossed Balantyne's Indian service, when he, too, had been briefly sent to Africa. That was it! Suddenly it made sense. They had served together. It was something in that campaign which had brought Cole to Bedford Square, and led to his murder.

He could feel his pulse quicken and a thin thread of excitement stir inside him. He must go to Keppel Street to report this vital piece of news to Pitt.

He took the omnibus and got off at Tottenham Court Road and walked across the few hundred yards to Pitt's house.

He rang the bell and stepped back. Of course it would be Gracie who would answer. Unconsciously, he ran his fingers around inside his collar, as if it were too tight, then ran his

81

hands over his hair, pushing it back quite unnecessarily. His mouth was a little dry.

The door opened. Gracie looked surprised. She smoothed her apron over her hips while looking at him very directly.

"I've come to report to Mr. Pitt," he said rather too abruptly.

"I s'pose yer'd better come in," she said before he had a chance to explain himself more graciously. She moved to allow him past her.

He accepted, hearing his boots clattering over the linoleum all along the corridor to the kitchen. Gracie's feet behind him sounded light, tapping, feminine. But she was as small as a child.

He went into the kitchen expecting to see Pitt sitting at the table, then realized his mistake. He would be in the parlor, naturally. Gracie would fetch him in here to see Tellman, not at the front of the house. It was not a social call.

He stood stiffly in the middle of the room, smelling the warmth, the flour from baking, the clean linen, the steam from the kettle on the stove, the faint grit of coal. The early-evening sun shone through the window onto the blue-and-white-ringed china on the dresser. Two cats lay by the fire, one ginger and white, one black as the coal in the scuttle.

"Don't just stand there like a lamppost," Gracie said sharply. "Sit down." She pointed to one of the wooden chairs. "D'yer want a cup o' tea?"

"I've come to report some very important information to Mr. Pitt," he said stiffly. "Not to sit in your kitchen drinking cups of tea. You'd better go and tell him I'm here." He did not sit.

" 'E in't 'ere," she told him, moving the kettle onto the center of the hob. "If it's that important then yer'd best leave a message wif me. I'll see as 'e gets it as soon as 'e comes in."

He hesitated. It was important. The kettle was steaming nicely. It was a long time since he had sat down, let alone had anything to eat or drink. His feet were hot and aching.

The black cat stretched, yawned, and went back to sleep.

"I made some cake, if yer like?" Gracie offered, moving

82

quickly around the kitchen, fetching the teapot down and then trying hard to reach the tea caddy, which had been pushed to the back of the shelf. She stretched, then tried jumping. She really was very small.

He went over, reaching it effortlessly. He handed it to her.

"I can get it meself!" she said tartly, taking it from him. "Wot d'yer fink I do w'en yer in't 'ere?"

"Drink water," he replied.

She shot him a razor-sharp look, but took the caddy in her hand and went over to the stove. "Yer'd best get some plates down too, then," she instructed. "I want some cake, whether you do or not."

He obeyed. He might as well leave the message with her. It would get to Pitt the fastest way.

They sat on opposite sides of the kitchen table, stiff and very formal, sipping tea that was too hot and eating the cake, which was excellent.

He told her about Albert Cole and the 33rd Foot Regiment, and the Abyssinian Expedition, and that Balantyne had been there too, seconded from India.

She looked very serious indeed, as if the news upset her.

"I'll tell 'im," she promised. "D'yer think as General Balantyne did this feller in, then?"

"Could have." He would not commit himself too far. If he said yes, and was then proved mistaken, she would lose respect for him.

"Wot'll yer do next?" she asked gravely, her eyes steady on his face.

"Learn everything else I can about Cole," he told her. "He must have had a reason for finding Balantyne again after all this time. It's nearly a quarter of a century since then."

She leaned forward. "It must be summink terrible important. If yer find it, yer'll 'ave ter tell Mr. Pitt . . . w'erever 'e is or whatever 'e's doin'. Yer'd best come 'ere an' leave a message wif Mrs. Pitt or me. It can get real serious w'en it's quality, like generals. Don't you go doin' nothin' by yerself." She looked at him with deep anxiety. "In fact . . . yer'd better let Mrs. Pitt know afore yer tell anyone else, 'cos she's quality

83

'erself, so she can 'elp. She'd stop you an' the Master from goin' about it wrong, jus' 'cos yer in't the same kind o' persons." She looked at him with deep concern that he should understand.

She was just a maid, she had only very recently learned to read and write and she came from the back street of . . . he did not know where. Probably the same sort of place as he had himself, somewhere like Wandsworth or Billingsgate, or any of a hundred other downtrodden, overcrowded warrens of the poor. But she was a girl, and therefore not given even the rudiments of an education. Tellman, on the other hand, had definitely bettered himself.

But her suggestion did make a certain amount of sense.

She refilled his cup and cut him another slice of cake.

He accepted both with pleasure. She was a good cook, which surprised him. She looked too small and thin to know anything about food.

"You come an' tell me," she repeated. "An' I'll make sure the Mistress keeps the Master from gettin' inter trouble 'cos o' folks wot 'ave influence an' could 'urt 'im, if it in't done right."

He was getting more and more comfortable in the kitchen. He disagreed with Gracie about all sorts of things. She had a great deal to learn, especially about social issues and fairness, and justice for people, but she was well-meaning, and no one could say she wasn't brave and prepared to fight for her beliefs.

"I suppose that would be quite a good idea," he conceded. He did not want Pitt to get into political trouble if it could be avoided, not necessarily entirely from loyalty to Pitt, about whom he told himself he was still ambivalent. But there was the matter of justice. If General Balantyne thought himself above the law, it would take skill, as well as good detective work, to catch him and prove it.

"Good," Gracie said with satisfaction, taking a large piece of cake. "So yer'll come 'ere an' tell me, or the Mistress, wot yer know, an' she'll tell the Master, an' at the same time 'elp 'im ter not go chargin' in an' mebbe the real truth'll never get told. Back stairs and front stairs is different, yer know." She watched him carefully to make sure he understood.

"Of course I know!" he said. "But they shouldn't be. Rich men don't make any better soldiers than poor men. In fact, worse!"

She squinted at him. "Wot yer talkin' about?"

"General Balantyne is only a general because his father bought his commission for him," he explained patiently. Perhaps he was expecting her to grasp too much. "He probably never did any real fighting, only ordering others around."

Gracie jiggled in her seat as if she were making such a mighty effort at self-control that she could not keep still.

"If 'e's got enough money ter do that, then we gotta be very careful," she said crossly, and without looking at him. Then she raised her head, her eyes blazing. "Are yer sure yer can buy bein' a general? An' if anybody were that rich, why'd 'e buy bein' a soldier? That's daft."

"You wouldn't understand," he said loftily. "People like that are different from us."

"They're not any different if they get shot," she said instantly. "Blood's blood, 'ooever's it is."

"I know that, and you know that," he agreed. "But they think theirs is different, and better."

She sighed very patiently, as she did with Daniel when he was obstructive and deliberately disobedient just to see how far he could push her.

"I daresay yer know more about it than I do, Mr. Tellman. I spec' Mr. Pitt's very lucky ter 'ave someone like you ter 'elp keep 'im straight an' out o' mistakes."

"I do my best," he agreed, accepting a third piece of cake and allowing her to refill his cup yet again. "Thank you, Gracie."

She grunted.

But when he left half an hour later, without having seen either Pitt or Charlotte, he was overtaken by acute anxiety as to exactly what he had promised. It had been a long and very busy day. It was hot. His feet ached. He had walked miles and not had more to eat than a cheese-and-pickle sandwich and

Gracie's cake. She had made him welcome, and without realizing it, he had given his word that he would tell her what he uncovered in the Albert Cole case before he told Pitt. He must be losing his wits! He had never done anything so totally foolish in his life before. It was contrary to everything he had been taught.

Not that that was normally a reason. He was not a man to follow anyone's commands against his own judgment.

He was too tired to think clearly, he just had a terrible feeling of being out of his depth, of following impulse more than his own nature and habit, all the path he was used to.

But he had given his word . . . and to Gracie Phipps, of all people.

86

4

P*ITT HAD HEARD* Tellman's news from Gracie when he finally came home, and he was deeply saddened that the evidence seemed to be connecting Albert Cole more closely with Balantyne. He must instruct Tellman to learn all he could about Cole, most particularly if he had any pattern of burglary or attempts at extortion. Not that he could imagine anything in Balantyne's life that would offer an opportunity for such a thing. The poor man's tragedies had been forced into public knowledge years ago, every shred of misery ripped open.

He was reminded of the circumstances again as he passed a newspaper boy and heard him calling the headlines.

"Dead body on general's doorstep! Police baffled by murder of old soldier in Bedford Square! Read all about it an' see if you can do any better! So, wanna paper, sir? Ta. There y'are!"

Pitt took it from him and opened it up. He read it with mounting anger and dismay. Nothing was said directly enough to be actionable, but all the implications were plain: Balantyne was a general and the dead man must have served with him at some time. There was some bond between them, of love or hate, knowledge, revenge or conspiracy. Even treason was hinted at—so subtly that some might have missed it, but not all. Any of it could conceivably have been true.

And any of it would ruin Balantyne.

He closed the newspaper and, ramming it under his arm,

he strode along the pavement to the steps of the Bow Street Station.

As soon as he was inside a constable came in to tell him that there was a message to say Assistant Commissioner Cornwallis wished to see him immediately. There was no reason given.

Pitt stood up again without even glancing at anything on his desk. The first fear that took him was that Cornwallis had received another letter, this time stating the terms for which the blackmailer would keep silent. All sorts of things entered his mind, from simple money through information on criminal cases, even to actual corruption of evidence.

He did not bother to leave any message for Tellman. The sergeant could proceed perfectly well alone. He did not need Pitt, or anyone else, to instruct him in the pursuit of the recent life and habits of Albert Cole.

Back in the street, Pitt walked around to Drury Lane and almost immediately found a hansom. He was aware of nothing as the cab turned and went south: not the other traffic; the fine, blustery morning; two brewers' draymen shouting at each other; or the traffic stopping for a magnificent hearse with four perfectly matched black horses, their black plumes waving. Nor did he notice, three blocks farther on, an open brougham with six pretty girls giggling and showing off, waving parasols to the imminent peril of all other horse-drawn vehicles within striking distance of them.

He was admitted to Cornwallis's office immediately and found him standing, as so often, by the window overlooking the street. Cornwallis turned as Pitt came in. He looked pale, and there were dark shadows around his eyes and a thin tenseness in his lips.

"Good morning," he said quickly as Pitt closed the door. "Come in." He waved in a very general way towards the chairs in front of the desk, but remained standing, balanced as if he would begin to pace back and forth the moment he had Pitt's total attention. "Do you know of Sigmund Tannifer?"

"No."

Cornwallis was staring at him. His body was rigid, his

hands behind his back. "He's a banker, very prominent in the City, very powerful man in financial circles."

Pitt waited.

As if driven by compulsion, Cornwallis began to pace: five strides one way, turn smartly, five strides the other. The office could have been the quarterdeck sailing before the wind into battle.

"He called me last night," he began, speaking jerkily. "He sounded . . . distressed." He reached the end and turned again, glancing at Pitt. "Wouldn't say what it was, but asked me about the Bedford Square business. Asked me who was in charge of the case." He swiveled around and came back. "When I told him you were, he asked if he could see you . . . privately . . . as soon as possible—in fact, this morning." He started back again, hands still locked behind him. "I asked him if he had any information regarding it. Thought he might have been burgled or know someone who had . . . someone in Bedford Square." He stopped, his eyes puzzled, his face almost bruised looking. "He said he didn't know anything about it. It was another matter, private and very grave." He reached over to the desk and passed Pitt a slip of paper. "This is his address. He is at home, waiting for you."

Pitt took the paper and glanced at it. Tannifer lived in Chelsea.

"Yes sir. I'll go now."

"Good. Thank you." Cornwallis stood still at last. "Let me know what it is. I'll be back by the time you are . . . I daresay."

"Back?" Pitt asked.

"Ah . . . yes." Cornwallis let out his breath slowly. "Have to go to my club . . . the Jessop Club. Don't really want to, can't spare the time." He smiled fleetingly, an effort to hide his reluctance. He was dreading it, as if already his friends and colleagues would somehow know what was in the letter and believe it, or at best wonder. "Have to," he went on explaining. "On a committee for charity. Too important not to go. For children." He looked vaguely embarrassed as he said

89

it, and turned quickly to pick up his hat and follow Pitt out of the door.

Pitt took a hansom and rode, again deep in thought, to Queen Street, just off the Chelsea Embankment. It was a beautiful neighborhood, near the Botanical Gardens, just past the facade of the Chelsea Hospital and the wide space of Burton's Court. The end of the street opened directly onto the river, which was blue and gray, sparkling in the sun.

He knocked on the door of the number he had been given, and when the footman answered he presented his card. He was shown across the stone-flagged hall with scattered Persian rugs. The walls were hung with an array of historical weapons, from a crusader's two-handed sword through a Napoleonic saber to two pairs of dueling pistols and two rapiers. Within moments he was taken into an oak-paneled study, where he was left for no more than five minutes before the door opened and a tall man with receding dark hair came in. He was of striking appearance, although there was too much power in his features for handsomeness, too much flesh.

Pitt guessed him to be in his middle fifties, and extremely prosperous. His clothes were perfectly cut and of fabric which draped as if there could be silk in it. There was a sheen to his cravat as if it, too, were silk.

"Thank you for coming, Superintendent. I am much obliged. Please be comfortable." He indicated the well-worn dark chairs, and as soon as Pitt was seated, he sank into the opposite one, but did not relax. He remained upright, his hands joined together. He was not openly nervous, but he was apparently deeply worried over something.

Several questions came to Pitt's mind, but he did not speak them aloud. He would leave Tannifer to say what he wished without prompting.

"I understand that you are investigating this miserable business in Bedford Square?" Tannifer began tentatively.

"Yes," Pitt agreed. "My sergeant is presently looking into the life of the dead man to see if we can learn what he was doing there. His usual area was Holborn. He sold bootlaces on the corner of Lincoln's Inn Fields."

"Yes." Tannifer nodded. "I read in the newspapers that he was an old soldier. Is that true?"

"It is. Do you know something about him, Mr. Tannifer?"

Tannifer smiled. "No . . . I'm afraid I know nothing at all." The smile vanished. "It was only the suggestion in the press regarding poor Balantyne's possible involvement which made me wish to see you. You are obviously a man of sensitivity and discretion, in whom Cornwallis has the greatest trust, or he would not have assigned you to such a matter." He was regarding Pitt narrowly, weighing him in his own judgment.

Pitt did not feel any response was required. A denial dictated by modesty would be inappropriate now. Obviously, Tannifer had looked into the subject.

Tannifer pursed his lips.

"Mr. Pitt, I have received a most disturbing letter. One might call it blackmail, except that nothing is asked for, as yet."

Pitt felt almost winded with shock. It was the last thing he had expected. This affluent banker in front of him had none of the haunted look that Cornwallis had, but perhaps that was because he had not yet realized the full import of what the letter meant. The strain, the fear, the sleepless nights would come.

"When did you receive it, Mr. Tannifer?" he asked.

"Last post yesterday evening," Tannifer replied quietly. "I informed Cornwallis straightaway. I know him slightly, and I felt I could take the liberty of going to him directly, even to troubling him at his home." He took a very deep breath and let it out, consciously easing his shoulders. "You see, Mr. Pitt, I am in a very delicate position. My entire ability to follow my career, to be of service to anyone, depends upon trust." He watched Pitt's face to see if he understood. A look of doubt flashed across his eyes. Perhaps he was expecting too much.

"May I see the letter?" Pitt asked.

Tannifer bit his lip, moving uncomfortably in his chair, but he did not argue.

91

"Of course. It is there, on the corner of the desk." He indicated it with his hand as if he were reluctant even to touch the thing again himself.

Pitt rose and picked the envelope off the polished surface where it was lying. The name and address were cut out of letters from newspapers, but with such painstaking precision, and glued so carefully, that at a glance it seemed to be printed as if by a machine.

The postmark was "Central London," the previous evening. He opened it up and read the single sheet he found inside.

Mr. Tannifer,

You have grown rich and respected by exercising your financial skills, all with the money of others. It is based upon their trust in you, in your unquestioned honesty. Would they feel the same if they were to know that once you were far less scrupulous, and prospered your own fortune using funds embezzled from your clients?

Warburton and Pryce, I believe. I do not know the sum, perhaps you no longer even know it yourself. Perhaps you never did. Why count what you will never repay? Have you a sense of the absurd?

You must have, or you would not allow other men to trust you with their money. I would not!

Perhaps one day no one will.

And that was all. The meaning was perfectly plain, as it had been in Cornwallis's letter. And like his, nothing was asked for, no precise, explicit threat was made; but the ugliness, the malice and the danger were extremely clear.

Pitt looked across at Tannifer, who was watching him almost unblinkingly.

"You see!" Tannifer's voice was harsh, rising a little as if the veneer were thin. "He doesn't ask for anything, but the threat is there." He leaned forward across the desk, pulling his jacket out of shape. "It is completely untrue! I have never stolen a halfpenny in my life. I daresay with sufficient time and a careful enough audit of the bank's books I could prove it."

He stared at Pitt, searching his eyes, his face, as if desperate to see some hope or understanding.

"But the very fact that I would, or thought I had to, would make people wonder why," he went on. "The suggestion is enough to ruin me . . . and the bank too, if they did not dismiss me. The only course possible would be to resign." He waved his hands wide, jerkily. "And then there would be those who would take that as an admission of some kind of guilt. For God's sake . . . what can I do?"

Pitt longed to be able to give him some answer that would offer the hope he longed for, but there was no such thing that would be remotely honest.

Should he tell him there had been others?

"Is anyone else aware of this?" he asked, indicating the letter.

"Only my wife," Tannifer replied. "She saw my distress, and I had either to tell her the truth or invent some lie. I have always trusted her absolutely. I showed it to her."

Pitt thought that a mistake. He feared her reaction might be to become so afraid that she would unintentionally betray her distress, or even feel the need to confide in someone further, perhaps her mother or a sister.

Tannifer must have read his feelings in his expression. He smiled.

"You have no need to fear, Mr. Pitt. My wife is a woman of remarkable loyalty and courage. I would rather trust her than anyone else I know."

It was an unusual statement to make, and yet when he thought about it, Pitt would have said the same thing of Charlotte, and he blushed now with some guilt that he should have assumed less of Mrs. Tannifer without the slightest evidence.

"I apologize," he said contritely. "I was only—"

"Of course," Tannifer dismissed it, speaking across him, and for the first time allowing himself to smile. "In most circumstances you would be quite right. There is no need to feel the least discomfort." He reached for the embroidered bell cord and pulled it.

Within moments a footman appeared.

93

"Ask Mrs. Tannifer to join us, will you," Tannifer instructed, then as the man went out, he regarded Pitt seriously again. "What can you do to help us, Superintendant? How should I behave regarding this . . . threat?"

"To begin with, tell no one else," Pitt replied, watching him gravely. "Do not even allow them to suspect. If anyone observes your anxiety or distress, think in advance of some other believable cause, and attribute it to that. Better not to say there is nothing wrong, when they may find that difficult to believe. Give no cause for speculation."

"Of course. Of course." Tannifer nodded.

There was a light rap on the door, and a moment later it opened and a woman came in who at first glance appeared quite ordinary. She was of average height, a trifle thin, her shoulders angular, her hips in her very lightly bustled gown too lean to be fashionable, or even very feminine. Her fair hair was naturally wavy and of a soft honey shade. Her features were not beautiful. Her nose lacked elegance, her eyes were wide, blue, and very direct. Her mouth was sensitive and curiously vulnerable. It was her bearing which made her remarkable. There was an extraordinary grace within her which would have marked her out from any crowd, and the longer one looked at her, the more attractive did she seem.

Both men rose to their feet.

"Parthenope, this is Superintendent Pitt, from Bow Street," Tannifer introduced them. "He has come about this wretched letter."

"I'm so glad," she said quickly. Her voice was warm and a little husky. She looked at Pitt earnestly. "It is pure evil! Whoever wrote it does not even imagine it is true; he is simply using the threat of lies to hurt and to—to extort . . . I don't know what. He doesn't even say what he wants! How can we fight him?" She moved to stand closer beside her husband, and almost unconsciously she slid her arm into his. It was a casual gesture and yet intensely protective.

"First, behave as naturally as possible," Pitt repeated, this time to Parthenope Tannifer. "But if anyone realizes you are anxious, give them some other cause to explain it, don't fob them off with a denial they will not believe."

"My wife's brother is in India; Manipur, to be exact. The news from there is sufficient to worry anyone. . . ." He saw Pitt nod, and continued. "As you know, there was a palace coup in September last year. Our people decided that it constituted a rebellion, and in March of this year our man in Assam took four hundred Gurkhas and marched to Imphal, the capital of Manipur, to talk. They were promptly seized and killed."

He furrowed his brow as if he could still hardly believe what he said next. "Apparently, there was no commanding officer of sufficient rank left, so the young widow of the political agent led the surviving British officers and the Gurkhas out of the city, through the jungle and up the mountains towards Assam. They were rescued by a troop of Gurkhas coming the other way." He gave an abrupt little laugh. "I can always say I am worried about him. I should be believed." He glanced at Parthenope, who indicated her agreement, her eyes alight with imagination and pride.

Pitt dragged his attention back from the extraordinary story of Manipur to the present, grim situation in London. A deep chill settled inside him that two prominent men were being threatened with a very particular form of public ruin, but no price was asked.

It also forced itself into his mind to wonder if General Balantyne might be a third victim of the same plan, but had been too afraid, or too ashamed, to speak of it. And of course the threat to him was far greater . . . there was a dead body on his doorstep which made the whole issue public and brought the police to investigate.

Was Albert Cole the blackmailer?

It seemed highly unlikely. The more Pitt considered it, the less did it seem credible. He picked up Tannifer's letter and read it again. It was complex and literate, not the work of a private soldier turned peddler of bootlaces.

And yet he had had in his pocket Balantyne's snuffbox,

95

which, as it transpired, was not valuable, but still extremely beautiful, and possibly unique.

Both Tannifer and Parthenope were staring at him.

"Is there something of importance that you are not telling me, Superintendent?" Tannifer said with concern. "Your expression causes me considerable anxiety."

Parthenope's face was tight, her mouth pulled crooked with fear.

Pitt made an instant decision.

"You are not the only person to suffer from this man's threats, Mr. Tannifer—" He stopped as he saw Tannifer's amazement and something which could have been relief.

"This is monstrous!" Parthenope burst out, stiffening her body and removing her arm from Tannifer's. She clasped her hands tightly in front of her. "Who else is . . . Oh! I'm sorry. What a stupid question. Of course you cannot tell us. At least I know you would not, because if you did it might mean you would tell others of our predicament."

"No, Mrs. Tannifer," Pitt agreed. "I would certainly not mention it without his specific permission. Like your husband, he is a man of dignity and honor whose reputation has never been questioned before. He is accused of the offense which would be most repugnant to him, and yet which, although he is totally innocent, he cannot prove himself innocent of. At least at the present he cannot prove it. With diligent work it may become possible. But his act also lies in the past, and many of those who could have disproved what is charged are no longer alive."

"Poor soul," Parthenope said with profound feeling. Her face was flushed, her eyes direct. "What can we do, Mr. Pitt?"

He was desperate to offer some answer which would comfort her and make her feel she was participating in the battle. But he turned to Tannifer himself as he spoke.

"There are certain things which will define this person," he said thoughtfully. "He must know of the earlier matter you mentioned . . . how public was it?"

"Not at all." Tannifer's face brightened. "I see what you mean. It must be limited by those who either knew for themselves or had heard of it from those who did. That does circumscribe it considerably. But you said two things. What is the other?"

"He must want something from you which will profit him. If you think what you can do—other than merely pay him money, of course—then you may learn something about who it is."

Tannifer frowned. "Do you not think it will be money, when he has felt the exactness of his power well enough?"

"It may be," Pitt replied. "Are you a wealthy man, with funds available?"

Tannifer hesitated. "I—I could not pay a large amount in any haste. Even if I were to sell property, such a thing takes time—"

"Influence!" Parthenope put in quickly, her expression eager. "Of course. That would make the most excellent sense." She looked from Tannifer to Pitt. "Has this other man influence, Superintendent?"

"More than money, yes, Mrs. Tannifer. He has great influence in certain areas."

A bitter smile touched Tannifer's mouth. "I assume you are not referring to Brandon Balantyne but to someone else? Balantyne has no influence now." He shook his head minutely, an oddly hopeless little gesture. "This is a filthy business, Superintendent. I pray most profoundly that you can help us."

Parthenope looked at him earnestly also, but she did not add anything to her husband's words.

"If you would make such a list, Mr. Tannifer?" Pitt prompted.

"Of course. I shall send it around to you at Bow Street the moment it is accomplished," Tannifer promised. He held out his hand. "Thank you for coming, Mr. Pitt. I rest my trust in you. We both do. Please convey my thanks to Cornwallis for sparing you so instantly."

Pitt left oppressed with foreboding and a sense that behind the threatening letters to both Cornwallis and Tannifer was a far greater power than he had at first imagined. There was nothing clumsy or hasty in it, not a greedy man simply taking

97

a chance at extorting money from a mistake he had observed and seen an opportunity on which to capitalize. It was a more carefully laid plan, possibly over a period of time, to obtain power by the deliberate corruption of men of influence.

And in spite of what Tannifer had said about Balantyne's having now retired, Pitt could not help wondering if he, too, was the victim of blackmail. He was certain Balantyne had been deeply afraid of something, and it was connected with the pinchbeck snuffbox found in Albert Cole's pocket. How had Cole come by it? In the answer to that would lie a great deal of the answer to his death.

Pitt returned to Bedford Square, determined to speak to Balantyne again and see if he could learn from him anything further, possibly even ask him outright if he had received a letter. But when he enquired, the footman told him the General had gone out quite early and had not said at what hour he would return. He did not expect it to be before dinner that night.

Pitt thanked him and went to see what he could learn about Sigmund Tannifer in the City, his reputation and standing as a banker, and if possible, what particular or delicate influence he might have upon the finances of others, and if there was any known connection with Cornwallis, or even Balantyne.

Charlotte had no intention whatever of abandoning General Balantyne to hunt for the blackmailer on his own. She joined forces with him the next morning. They met on the steps outside the British Museum. Again she saw him from several yards' distance, even though there were a number of people coming and going and at least half a dozen standing around or speaking with each other. He was probably more conspicuous than he realized due to his ramrod stiffness. She thought he looked as if he were expecting to face a charge any moment, a platoon with fixed bayonets, or perhaps a band of Zulu warriors.

His face lit when he saw her, but in spite of his obvious pleasure, the tension did not slip from him.

"Good morning, Mrs. Pitt," he said, stepping down onto the pavement to meet her. "It is most generous of you to help in this way, giving up your time in a pursuit that may meet with no success."

"It is not much of a battle if there is no chance of failure," she reminded him sharply. "I do not require assured success before I begin."

He flushed faintly. "I did not mean to sound as if I doubted your courage. . . ."

She shot him a dazzling smile. "I know that. I think you are just a little despondent this morning because this is such a cowardly thing for anyone to do, and we cannot strike back at something we cannot see." She moved forward purposefully along Great Russell Street. Although she had no idea where they were going, it was simply better than seeming to stand still. "With whom do we begin?"

"The nearest geographically is James Carew," he answered. "He lives in William Street, near the park." He raised his arm to call a hansom, and a moment later one stopped. He handed her up and followed after, sitting beside her, straight-backed, staring ahead. He had given the driver the address, and they began to move swiftly, weaving through the traffic of carts, wagons, drays, omnibuses and carriages.

She thought of several things to say, but glancing sideways at him she decided that anything at all would be an interruption to his thoughts, and so she remained silent. It was plain that idle talk would not lift his mind from his anxiety, only irritate him beyond bearing. It would indicate she had failed to understand the depth of his concern.

They alighted in William Street and he paid the driver. However, when they rang the doorbell of the address they had been given, the footman who answered informed them that James Carew had undertaken an adventure to the Mountains of the Moon, and no one knew when, or even if, he would return.

"The Mountains of the Moon!" Charlotte said as she strode towards Albany Street, her skirts swirling around her ankles, Balantyne lengthening his stride to keep up with her. "Impertinent oaf!"

He took her arm, restraining her with a gentle pressure.

"They are in Ruwenzori, in the middle of Africa," he explained. "Discovered by the same Henry Stanley I mentioned to you before, if you recall? Two years ago—"

"Two years ago?" She was confused.

"He discovered them two years ago," he elucidated. "In 1889."

"Oh. I see." She slowed her pace, and walked for several yards in silence, feeling a trifle foolish. "Who is next?" she asked as they reached Albany Street.

"Martin Elliott," he answered without looking at her. There was no lift of hope in his voice.

She forgot her own irritation. "Where does he live?"

"York Terrace. We might walk there . . . unless . . ." He hesitated. It was plain in his face that it had suddenly occurred to him she might not wish to walk so far, or be accustomed to it.

"Of course," she agreed firmly. "It is an excellent day. We might usefully discuss what further plans to make after we have seen Mr. Elliott. If he does know who it is, or if it is himself, then he is unlikely to tell us the truth. What manner of person is he?"

Balantyne looked startled. "I can hardly remember him. He was rather older than I, a career officer from an old military family. I seem to think he had fair hair, and grew up in the Border Country, but I cannot remember whether it was the English side or the Scottish." He lapsed into silence again and walked with his eyes down as if studying the pavement.

Charlotte gave her mind over to the evidence such as they possessed. Cole had been found dead on Balantyne's doorstep with the snuffbox in his pocket. He had served on the same Abyssinian campaign twenty-five years before. Somebody had sent the threatening letter to Balantyne but had not yet actually asked for anything, except the snuffbox, as a pledge of intent, and Balantyne had been too aware of the damage they could do him to refuse it.

"What else might they want, apart from money?" she said aloud.

100

He swung around, startled. "What?"

She repeated the question.

A slow color spread up his cheeks, and he looked away.

"Perhaps just the exercise of power," he replied. "For some people that is a purpose in itself."

She spoke from impulse, before she had time to question herself and perhaps lose her courage, or think better and be more tactful.

"Have you some idea who it is?"

He stopped, wide-eyed, staring at her with amazement.

"No. I wish to God I had." He colored faintly. "I'm sorry. But that is one of the very worst aspects of it all . . . I think of everyone I can imagine, every man I know and have considered a friend, or at least someone I could respect, whether I liked him or not, and now I wonder. It is beginning to poison my views of everyone. I catch myself wondering if people know, if they are secretly smiling, watching me and knowing what I fear, and waiting for me to lose my nerve. And all of them but one will be totally innocent." A bitter anger filled his eyes. "That is one of the greatest evils of secret accusation; the poison of it, how it slowly destroys your trust in all those to whom you should be able to turn with honor and regard. And how could the innocent forgive you for not having known they were innocent, for having allowed it to even enter your thoughts that they could do such a thing?" His voice dropped. "How could I ever forgive myself?" A woman walking a small dog passed them, and Balantyne was too distracted even to acknowledge her by raising his hat, a gesture so automatic to him he would normally have done it without thought.

Impulsively, Charlotte reached out her hand and rested it on his arm, holding him lightly. "You must forgive yourself," she said earnestly. "And no one else will need to forgive you, because they will not know. This may be precisely what the blackmailer wants, to make you so demoralized that when he asks for whatever it is, you are willing to give it to him simply to be rid of the fear and the doubts, to know at last who your enemy is so you can also know your friends."

101

She felt the muscles in his arm tighten as he clenched them, but his hand did not move and he stayed close to her.

"I have had a second letter," he said, watching her face. "It was much the same as the first. Cut from the *Times* again and pasted onto paper. It came by first post this morning."

"What did it say?" she asked, trying to keep perfectly steady. He must not see how alarmed she was.

He swallowed. He was very pale. It was obviously difficult for him even to repeat the words. "That my friends would shun me, cross over in the street to avoid me, if they knew I was a coward and ran from battle, and was saved by a private soldier, and then would not even own up to my shame but let him conceal it for me." He swallowed, his throat jerking painfully. His voice was hoarse. "That my wife, who had already suffered so much, would be ruined, and my son would have to disown his name or his career would be finished." He stared at her in helpless misery. "And not a word of it is true, I swear that in the name of God."

"I had not doubted you," she said quite calmly. The depth of his distress had the strange effect of setting a deep resolution in her to fight the issue in his defense to the very last iota of her strength or imagination, and not give in even after that. "You must never allow him to think he has won," she said with utter conviction. "Unless, of course, it should be a tactical ploy, to lead him to betray himself. But I cannot see, at the moment, how that would be an advantage."

He started to walk again. They passed half a dozen people, laughing and talking together: women with tiny waists and sweeping skirts, flowers and feathers on their hats; men in summer coats. And all the time carriages were busy along the street.

They found the house where Elliot had lived, only to be told that he had died of a kidney ailment two months previously.

They ate luncheon in a small, quiet restaurant, trying to keep each other's spirits up, and then took the underground railway right across the city to Woolwich to find Samuel Holt. It was an extraordinary experience, and entirely new to Charlotte, although she had heard about it from Gracie. It was acutely

102

claustrophobic, and the noise was beyond belief. The whole train shot through long, tubelike tunnels, roaring like a hundred tin trays dropped upon a paved yard. But it did achieve the journey in a remarkably short time. They emerged into the blustery, mild wind north of the river and only two streets from Holt's house.

He received them with great pleasure, although unable to rise from his chair and apologizing for it with some embarrassment; old wounds and rheumatism had disabled him. But when asked, he said that yes, most certainly he had been on the Abyssinian Expedition and remembered it quite clearly. How could he assist?

Charlotte and Balantyne accepted the seats offered.

"Do you recall the storming of the baggage train on the Arogee Plains?" Balantyne said eagerly, unable to keep hope out of his voice.

"Arogee? Oh, yes." Holt nodded. "Nasty."

Balantyne leaned forward. "Do you remember a small bunch of men panicking before enemy fire?"

Holt thought for a few moments, his blue eyes misty and far away, as if he were seeing the plains of Abyssinia again, the brilliant skies, the dry earth and the colors of fighting men a quarter of a century before.

"Nasty," he said again. "Got a lot of men killed that way. Never panic. Worst thing you can do."

"Do you remember me?"

Holt squinted at him. "Balantyne," he said with evident pleasure.

"Do you remember me going back for the wounded?" Balantyne said eagerly. "My horse fell. I was thrown, but I got up after a moment or two. Got Manders and helped him back. He was shot in the leg. You turned and went for Smith."

"Oh, yes . . . Smith. Yes, I remember." He looked at Balantyne with a charming, wide-eyed smile. "How can I help you, sir?"

"You remember it?"

"Of course. Dreadful business." He shook his head, the sunlight catching his white hair. "Brave men. Too bad."

103

A shadow crossed Balantyne's face. "The Abyssinians?" he questioned.

Holt frowned. "Our men. Remember the jackals . . . eating the dead. Fearful! What makes you mention it now, sir?" He blinked several times. "Lose a lot of friends, did you?"

Balantyne's face tightened; a bleakness crossed it as if in that instant some hope in him had died.

"Do you remember that attack and my going back for Manders? Do you remember how it happened?"

"Of course I do," Holt insisted. "I said so, didn't I? Why does it matter now?"

"Just recollections," Balantyne replied, leaning back. "Bit of a difference of opinion with someone."

"Ask Manders himself, sir. He'll tell you. You rescued the poor devil. He'd have been dead for certain if you hadn't. What any officer worth his salt would do. Who says otherwise?" Holt was puzzled; it upset him. "Terrible bloodshed. Remember the stench of bodies." His face pinched with distress.

Charlotte looked at Balantyne. He, too, was torn with the pain of memory.

"Good men," Holt murmured sadly. "Manders wasn't one of them, was he?"

"Killed in India a couple of years later," Balantyne said quietly.

"Was he? I'm sorry. Lost count, you know. So many dead." He stopped, searching Balantyne's face.

Balantyne took a deep breath and stood up, extending his hand.

"Thank you, Holt. Good of you to spare me your time."

Holt remained seated in his chair. His face lit with pleasure, and he clasped Balantyne's hand fiercely, clinging to it for several moments before he let go. His eyes shone. "Thank you, General," he said with deep feeling. "It was a great thing that you came to see me."

Outside in the street, Charlotte could hardly wait to turn to Balantyne and see his relief.

"That proves it!" she said exultantly. "Mr. Holt was there. He can make nonsense of the whole charge."

104

"No he can't, my dear," Balantyne answered quietly, controlling his emotions with such difficulty he would not look at her. "We lost no men at Magdala. In fact, there were only two men killed in the entire campaign. Many wounded, of course, but only two dead."

She was astounded, confused. "But the stench," she protested, still trying to force away what he was saying. "He remembered it."

"Abyssinians . . . seven hundred at Arogee with the baggage train. God knows how many at Magdala. They slew their prisoners. Hurled them over the walls. It was one of the worst things I ever knew."

"But Holt . . . s-said . . ." she stammered.

"His mind is gone . . . poor creature." He walked quickly, his body tight. "He is lucid in moments. I think when I left he actually did remember me. Most of the time he was simply lonely . . . and wanted to please." He kept his face straight ahead, and she saw the pain in it, heard the thick huskiness in his voice. She knew it was not for himself. The hollowness of failure would come later.

She did not know what to do, whether touching him would be an intrusion. He was walking very rapidly. She had to pick up her skirts and stride to keep up with him, but he was unaware of it. She moved beside him in silence, every now and again giving a little skip not to be left behind. Loyalty was all she could offer.

Tellman was very fully occupied learning more about the recent life of Albert Cole. He began at Lincoln's Inn Fields with a pair of bootlaces. He found the corner where Cole had stood, and already there was someone else there, a thin man with an unusually long nose but a cheerful expression.

"Laces, sir?" He held out a pair in a fairly clean hand.

Tellman took them and examined them closely.

"Best you'll find," the man assured him.

"You get them the same place as the fellow who was here before you?" Tellman said casually.

The man hesitated, not sure which was the best answer. He looked at Tellman's face and learned nothing.

"Yeah," he said eventually.

"Who was that?"

"You buy 'em from me, guv. I got the best laces in London."

Tellman held out the appropriate money; it was little enough. "I still want to know where you get them. Police business."

"They ain't nicked!" The man's face paled.

"I know that. I want to learn all I can about Albert Cole, who had this patch before you."

" 'Im wot was croaked?"

"Yes. Did you know him?"

"Yeah. That's 'ow I got the patch. Poor sod. 'E were a decent bloke. Soldier, 'e were. Got shot somew'ere out in Africa, or somew'ere like that. Don't know wot the 'ell 'e were doin' in Bedford Square."

"Thieving?" Tellman suggested dourly.

The peddler's body stiffened. "Beggin' yer pardon, sir, but yer din't oughter say that, 'less you can prove it, like. Albert Cole were an 'onest man wot served 'is country. An' I 'ope as yer find the bastard wot topped 'im."

"We will," Tellman promised. "Now, where'd he get the bootlaces?"

"Good man," the bootlace stockist said when Tellman found him. He nodded his head sadly. "London ain't safe no more. When a quiet fellow doin' nobody 'arm can get killed like that, the p'lice ain't doin' their jobs."

"Did he have any money trouble?" Tellman ignored the criticism.

" 'Course 'e did. Anyone wot peddles bootlaces on a street corner's got money troubles," the man said dryly. "You work fer a livin', or wot? You just do this 'cos yer like it, mister?"

Tellman held his temper with difficulty. He thought of his father, who had left their two rooms in Billingsgate at five in the morning and worked carrying bales and boxes in the fish

106

market all day. In the evening he had relieved a friend driving hansom cabs, often until midnight, all seasons of the year: in the swelter of summer when the traffic was jammed head to tail and the smell of manure filled the air; when the rain made the gutters swim and the rubbish and effluent swilled across the road and the cobbles shone black and glistening in the lamplight; in the winter when the wind chapped the skin and the ice made the horse's hooves slide dangerously. Even the pea soup fogs had not stopped him.

"I've got nothing except what I work for," Tellman said, the anger edging his voice till it cut. "And my pa could teach you what that word means, or any man."

The bootlace supplier backed away, frightened not by Tellman's words but by the well of rage he had unwittingly tapped into. Tellman was mollified. The ache of memory was not healed. He could still see in his mind his father's gaunt face, worried, cold, too tired to do anything but eat and sleep. There had been fourteen children, eight of whom lived. His mother cooked and washed, and sewed and swept, scrubbed and carried buckets of water, made soap out of lye and potash, sat up at night with sick children or sick neighbors. She laid out the dead, too many of them her own.

Most of the people he worked with now did not even imagine what exhaustion, hunger and poverty really meant; they only imagined they did. And those like General Brandon Balantyne, with his bought and paid for career, they lived in another world, as if they were more than human and Tellman and his like were less. They had more respect for their horses . . . come to think of it, a great deal more! And their horses had a far better life: a warm stable and good food, a kind word at the end of the day.

But alarmed as he was, the supplier could tell him nothing more about Albert Cole, except that he was absolutely honest in his dealings and worked as regularly as most men, only missing the odd few days through illness. That was until his disappearance, a day and a half before his body was found in Bedford Square. And no, he had no idea what Cole could have been doing there.

107

Tellman took the omnibus and rode back towards Red Lion Square. He started visiting the pawnshops and asking about Albert Cole. No one knew him by name, but the third one he visited seemed to recognize the description Tellman gave of him, particularly the break in his left eyebrow.

" 'Ad a feller like that in 'ere fairly reg'lar," he said with a gesture of resignation. "Always 'ad summink a bit tasty, like. Last time it were a gold ring."

"A gold ring?" Tellman said quickly. "Where'd he get it?"

"Said 'e found it," the pawnbroker replied, looking straight at Tellman without blinking. "Goes down the sewers sometimes. Comes up wi' all sorts." He scratched his ear irritably.

"Down the sewers?" Tellman said.

"Yeah." The pawnbroker nodded. "Find gold, diamonds, all sorts down there."

"I know that," Tellman said. "That's why it costs a fair penny to buy a stretch of sewer to patrol. And any tosher'll knock your head in if you trespass."

The pawnbroker looked uncomfortable. Apparently, he had not expected Tellman to be so familiar with the facts of scavenging.

"Well that's wot 'e told me!" he said abruptly.

"And you believed it?" Tellman gave him a withering look.

"Yeah. Why not? 'Ow was I ter know if 'e were tellin' the truth?"

"Haven't you got a nose on your face?"

"A . . . nose?" But the pawnbroker knew what he meant. The smell of a sewer scavenger was unmistakable, just like the smell of a mudlark, a man who sifted the river silt for lost treasures.

"A thief," Tellman said scathingly. "But of course you wouldn't know that. How often did he come here with stuff?"

The pawnbroker was now extremely uncomfortable. He scratched his ear again.

"Six or seven times, mebbe. I din't know 'e were a thief. 'E always 'ad a good tale. I thought 'e were a . . ."

"Yes, a tosher," Tellman supplied for him. "You said. Always jewelry? Did he ever come with paintings, ornaments, or the like?"

"From down the sewers?" The pawnbroker's voice rose an octave. "I may not be as clever as you are about toshers, but even I know as nobody loses paintings down the bath 'ole!"

Tellman smiled, showing his teeth. "And no pawnbroker buys gold rings from a tosher without knowing that either. No need to fence it if it was fair pickings."

The pawnbroker glared at him. "Well, I dunno w'ere 'e got 'is things, do I? If 'e were a thief it weren't nuthin' ter do wif me. Now, if yer in't got nuffink else ter ask me, will yer get out o' me shop. Yer puttin' orff me proper custom."

Tellman left feeling angry and puzzled. This was a very different picture of Albert Cole from the one he had gained previously.

He went back and had a late luncheon at the Bull and Gate public house in High Holborn. It was only a few yards from the corner where Cole had had his position selling bootlaces. Perhaps on a cold day he had come in here, even if only for a mug of ale and a slice of bread.

He ordered ale for himself and a good, thick sandwich of roast beef and horseradish sauce. He sat where he hoped to fall into conversation easily with some regular of the place. He began to eat. He was hungry. He had been walking all morning and was glad to sit down. He had not cared a great deal about clothes until lately. He had bought one or two things in the last couple of months, a new coat in good dark blue, and two new shirts. A man should have some self-respect. But boots that fitted were his greatest expense, and had not been skimped on since his very first wage.

He bit into the bread, and thought of Gracie's cake. There was something about home cooking, eaten at the kitchen table, which sat better in the stomach than the best meat eaten in some anonymous place, and paid for. Gracie was a funny mixture of a person. At times she sounded so independent, even bossy. And yet she worked for Pitt and lived in his house, without any place that was really her own. She was at his beck and call all hours, not only day but night too.

He pictured her as he sat chewing on the beef sandwich. She was very little, nothing really but skin and bone, not the sort of woman to attract most men. Nothing to put your arms around. He thought of other women he had found pleasing at one time or another. There was Ethel, all fair hair and soft skin, plenty of curves there, and nice-natured too, agreeable. She had married Billy Tomkinson. At the time that had hurt. He was surprised that he could think of it so easily now, even with a smile.

What would Gracie have made of Ethel? His smile widened. He could hear her voice in his mind. "Great useless article!" she'd have said. He could imagine the tolerant scorn on her face with its wide eyes and thin, strong features. She was strong. She had all the courage and determination in the world. She'd never let you down, never run away from anything. Like a little terrier, face anyone. And she knew right from wrong. Conscience like iron. No, maybe more like steel, sharp . . . and bright. Funny how much that sort of thing could matter when you really thought about it.

Not that Gracie wasn't pretty, in her own way. She had a beautiful neck, very smooth, and the daintiest ears he had ever seen. And nice fingernails, oval-shaped and always pink and clean.

This was ridiculous. He should stop daydreaming and get on with his job. He needed to find out a great deal more about Albert Cole. He bought another pint of ale and struck up a conversation with a large man standing at the bar.

He left an hour later, having heard nothing but good of Cole. In the opinion of the barman and other regulars he had spoken to, Cole was a decent, cheerful, hardworking man as honest as the day, careful with his money but always ready to stand a friend a drink when it was his turn.

And occasionally, on a wet evening when the weather was too harsh to expect anyone to buy bootlaces, he would take three or four pints and make them last several hours, and then he would tell tales of his military career. Sometimes there were past war stories of Europe, sometimes heroic deeds of his regiment, which had been the Duke of Wellington's own

and had fought brilliantly against the French in the Napoleonic Wars. And sometimes, if thoroughly pressed—and it
needed that because he was a modest man, even shy when it
came to his own deeds—he would talk of the Abyssinian
Campaign. He reckoned General Napier was the equal of any
soldier on earth, and was immensely proud of having served
under his command.

Tellman left thoroughly angry and confused. The conflicting views of Cole made no sense. He presented two faces:
one honest, ordinary, a man like ten thousand others, who had
served his country and now lived in a boardinghouse and sold
bootlaces on a street corner, patronized by the well-to-do of
Lincoln's Inn Fields, drinking at the Bull and Gate among
friends. The other was a thief who sold his takings to a pawnshop, presumably broke into houses in places like Bedford
Square, and was murdered for his pains.

And he had had the snuffbox in his pocket.

But if he was killed because he was trying to rob someone,
what was he doing outside the house, not inside it?

Could he have been struck somewhere else and left for
dead, and then crawled away? Was he attempting to get help
when he dragged himself up General Balantyne's step?

Tellman walked smartly east along High Holborn and
turned north up Southampton Row towards Theobald's Road.
He would make more enquiries.

But they elicited nothing that clarified the situation. A running patterer, chanting the latest news and gossip for the entertainment of the public, recounted Cole's death in doggerel
verse. Tellman paid him handsomely and learned that Cole
was an ordinary man, a trifle sober but a good enough seller
of bootlaces, and well liked by the people of the area. He was
known for the odd kindness, a hot cup of soup for the flower
seller, bootlaces for nothing as a present to an old man, always a cheerful word.

A constable at the local police station who had seen his
sketched picture in the newspaper said he recognized him as
a petty thief of a particularly quarrelsome nature who lived
around Shoreditch, to the east of there, where he had last

been posted. The man had an odd gap in his left eyebrow where a childhood scar ran across it. He was vicious, given to sudden outbursts of temper, and had running feuds with at least one of the local fencers of stolen goods in Shoreditch and Clerkenwell.

A prostitute said he was funny and extravagant, and she was sorry he was dead.

By the time Tellman left the neighborhood of Lincoln's Inn Fields and High Holborn, it was too late to go to Bow Street, but the contradictions in Albert Cole's character weighed too heavily on him not to report them to Pitt as soon as possible.

He thought about it for several minutes. It was still light, but it was nearly eight o'clock. The sandwich in the Bull and Gate was a long time ago. He was thirsty and tired. His legs ached. A really hot, fresh cup of tea would be marvelous, and time to sit down—for at least half an hour, if not an hour.

But duty must prevail!

He would go and report all this at Keppel Street. That was the proper answer. He could walk it in twenty minutes, easily.

But when he got there, his feet hot, his legs aching, Pitt was not at home; neither was Mrs. Pitt. Gracie answered the door looking cool and fresh in a starched apron.

He was dismayed.

"Oh . . ." he said, his heart racing as he stood on the front step. "That's a shame, because I really should tell him what I've learned today."

"Well, if it's important yer'd better come in," she answered, pulling the door wider and staring at him with a mixture of satisfaction and defiance. She must really want to know about Albert Cole very much.

"Thank you," he said stiffly, following her inside and waiting while she closed the door, then walking behind her along the passage back to the kitchen. It had the same warm comfortable smell it always did: scrubbed boards, clean linen, steam.

"Well, sit down then," she ordered. "I can't be getting' on wif anything wif you standin' in the middle o' the floor. Spec' me ter walk 'round yer?"

112

He sat down obediently. His mouth felt as dry as the pavements he had been walking.

Gracie surveyed him critically from his slicked-back hair to his dusty boots.

"Look like a fourpenny rabbit, you do. I s'pose you in't 'ad nuffink ter eat in hours? I got some good cold mutton an' mashed potatoes an' greens. I can make you bubble an' squeak, if yer like?" She did not wait for him to answer but bent down and pulled the skillet out of the cupboard and set it on the top of the stove. Automatically, she pulled the kettle over as well.

"If you've got it to spare," he said, breathing in deeply.

" 'Course I 'ave," she answered without looking at him. "So wot is it yer come ter say as is so important? Yer found out summink?"

"Of course I have." He mimicked her tone. "I've been looking into Albert Cole's life. Something of a mystery, he is." He leaned back in the chair and folded his arms, making himself more comfortable. He watched as she moved about the kitchen swiftly. She cut an onion off the string hanging by the scullery door and took it to the chopping board. She melted a lump of lard in the skillet and then with swift, light movements began to chop the onion into tiny cubes and drop them into the hissing fat. It smelled and sounded good. It was nice to watch a woman busy.

"So wot's the mystery?" she said. " 'Ceptin' 'oo killed 'im or why, an' why did they leave 'im on the General's doorstep."

"Because he's a decent soldier who served his Queen and country in a crack regiment, then, when he was wounded, came home and sold bootlaces in the street," he replied. "And by night he's a quarrelsome thief who picked the wrong house to burgle in Bedford Square."

She swiveled around to look at him. "So yer got it all solved then?" she said with wide eyes.

"No, of course I haven't," he retorted rather sharply. He wished he could have presented her with some brilliant answer, maybe even before Pitt did. But all he had were pieces, and they did not make sense.

113

She remained staring at him. Her face softened.

He thought in her own way that she really was pretty, but with character; not all peaches and cream, with no taste.

"Some people said 'e was good an' said 'e was a thief too?" she asked.

"No. Different people," he answered. "Seems to have had two quite opposite sides to his life. But I don't know why. It's not as if he had any family, or any job where he had to impress people."

"Oh!" She whisked around as the fat in the pan sputtered loudly. She pushed the onions around with a spoon, then stirred the cabbage in with the mashed potato and spooned the whole lot into the skillet. While it was heating and browning nicely, she carved three generous pieces off the cold mutton joint and set them on one of the blue-and-white kitchen plates. She put out a knife and fork for him, then made the tea and fetched him a mug, and then brought the jug of milk back from the larder as she returned the mutton.

When it was all ready she served it up and put it in front of him, tea steaming gently in the mug. He had not meant to smile, but he found himself almost grinning. He tried to change his expression to something less enthusiastic—and less obvious.

"Thank you," he said, lowering his eyes from hers. "Very civil of you."

"Yer welcome, I'm sure, Mr. Tellman," she answered, pouring herself a mug of tea and sitting opposite him. Then she remembered her apron and shot to her feet to remove it before sitting down again, this time a little more daintily. "So 'oo did yer get all this information from, then? I'd better tell Mr. Pitt proper, not just bits an' pieces."

Trying not to talk with his mouth full, he recounted to her all the contradictory facts and opinions he had learned over the last two days. He considered suggesting she should write it down not to forget it, but he was not totally sure she could write. He knew Mrs. Pitt had taught her to read, but writing was another thing, and he did not want to embarrass her.

"Will you remember all that?" he asked. The bubble and

squeak was the best he had ever had. He had eaten rather too much.

" 'Course I will," she replied with great dignity. "I got a perfick memory. 'Ave ter 'ave. Only just learned to write since I come 'ere."

He felt slightly abashed. He really should leave. He would rather Pitt did not come home and find him here with his feet under the table having eaten a thoroughly good meal. The whole room was extraordinarily comfortable, the clean smell of it, the warmth, the kettle singing faintly on the hob, Gracie with a flush on her face and her eyes bright.

It was not only Albert Cole's life which was confusing, it was sitting here having reported to Gracie as if she were his superior, at the same time being waited upon and spoiled and made welcome.

"I've got to go," he said reluctantly, pushing his chair back. "Tell Mr. Pitt I'm following up on Cole. If he used to quarrel over the spoils of his thieving, that may be what happened to him. I've got to find out who he worked with."

"I'll tell him," she promised. "Mebbe that is wot 'appened. Makes more sense'n anythin' else."

"Thank you for supper."

"S'only bubble an' squeak."

"It was very good."

"Yer welcome."

"Good night, Gracie."

"Good night, Mr. Tellman."

That sounded so formal. Should he tell her his name was Samuel? No. Don't be absurd! She did not care what his name was. She had been in love with that Irish servant in Ashworth Hall. Anyway, they disagreed about everything that mattered—society, politics, justice, a man's rights and obligations in the world. She was perfectly happy being a servant, and he deplored the entire concept as beneath the dignity of any human being.

He marched over to the door.

"Your bootlace is undone," she commented helpfully.

He was obliged to bend down and retie it, or risk tripping over his own feet as he went down the hall.

"Thank you," he mumbled furiously.

"S'all right," she answered. "I'll see yer ter the front door. Only manners. It's what Mrs. Pitt would do."

He stood upright and stared at her.

She smiled at him brightly.

He turned and went down the hall to the door, her light, quick steps after him.

5

CHARLOTTE KNEW that Gracie had had something to report to Pitt from Tellman's visit the previous evening, but it was one of those mornings when nothing seemed to be straightforward, and she was not in the kitchen at the time, at least only dashing in and out. The day before had been mild and sunny, but now the wind had a sharp edge and it was threatening rain. The clothes she had put out for Jemima to go to school in were now not warm enough. Jemima was very serious and did not complain about her pinafore as usual. That meant something else was worrying her, which was more urgent.

It took patient and careful questioning to elicit exactly what the difficulty was, and the answer, most solemnly given, reminded Charlotte how intensely important social questions were even at the age of nine. The precise way of dealing with a matter of accepting favors from the acknowledged leader of the twenty or so little girls in the classroom was a matter of great consequence. Debts were incurred and must be lived up to. Refusals must be explained without offense or one would be placed outside the magic circle of those who were favored.

She treated the problem with appropriate gravity. She had not gone to school herself. Having two sisters, she was taught by a governess in the classroom at home. But the principles were the same as in adult society, and sometimes the pattern of hierarchy lasted as long. Certainly the wounds of exclusion were as deep.

All of which meant that Daniel, two years younger, felt that something of importance was going on and he was not part of it. He knocked and banged around, dropping things and making loud comments, ostensibly to himself but really to take Charlotte's attention.

So when she had finished with Jemima she decided she would walk to school with Daniel, instead of sending Gracie. The result was that by the time she had returned, dealt with the laundry, decided exactly how much longer the socks would last, which shirts needed their collars and cuffs turned (a job she hated), it was late morning when she sat down at the kitchen table for a cup of tea and Gracie told her what Tellman had said about Albert Cole's strange, contradictory character.

"You did very well," she said sincerely.

"I give 'im dinner, jus' cold mutton an' bubble an' squeak. I 'ope that's all right?" Gracie answered, blushing with satisfaction.

"Of course it's all right," Charlotte assured her. "In return for information, he can have the best food in the house. I'd even buy in for him." She thought privately that the food was incidental; it was Gracie's company which brought him. She had seen the slight flush in his face, the way, in spite of all his intentions to the contrary, his eyes softened when he looked at her. Above all, she had felt for his awkwardness and his grief for Gracie when she had had to face the loss of her dreams in Ashworth Hall.

But she did not say so. It would embarrass Gracie and perhaps make her feel as if her most personal affairs were the subject of other people's thoughts and plans.

"That in't necessary," Gracie dismissed it. "Give 'im airs above 'is station. Jus' so's it's all right ter give 'im suffink."

"Most certainly. Use your own judgment." What Tellman had said about Cole weighed heavily on Charlotte's mind. She believed Balantyne, both as to his innocence of the original cowardice in Abyssinia, and certainly of the murder of Cole, but the more she learned the less chance did she see of proving it. So far she had not told Pitt about the blackmail,

118

but it would strain her conscience to withhold it a great deal longer, and he must surely already have considered the possibility, in view of Cornwallis's similar plight.

She needed to be able to discuss it with someone whom she could trust absolutely, not only for her discretion but also for an understanding of the sort of men both Cornwallis and Balantyne were, and of the world in which they moved. Great-Aunt Vespasia was perfect in both respects. She was in her mid-eighties, of an unassailable position in society, and in her day had been the most beautiful woman in London, if not in England. She had excellent judgment of people, and as sharp a tongue to express it as Charlotte had ever known, coupled with the wit to do so with very little unkindness. She also had the courage to follow her own conscience and to fight for the causes she believed in, regardless of other people's tastes. Charlotte had never liked anyone more.

"I shall go and visit Lady Vespasia Cumming-Gould," she announced to Gracie as she stood up from the table. "I think we need her view of this matter."

"She couldn't know about the likes o' Albert Cole, ma'am," Gracie said with surprise. "At 'is best 'e were an ordinary soldier, an' from what Mr. Tellman says, 'e were a thief. Looks like 'e fell out wif 'is mate over wot they took, an' 'e came orff worst. Mr. Pitt said as 'e looked like 'e bin in a fight."

Charlotte felt considerably comforted by that thought. It did seem to make sense. However, it still left the uneasy knowledge that he had had the snuffbox.

"Mebbe more was took," Gracie went on, as if sensing Charlotte's thoughts. She stood by the sink with the dishcloth in her hand. "An' the other feller 'as 'em. 'E just missed the box 'cos 'e were in an 'urry. P'raps the lamplighter were comin', an' 'e scarpered?"

"Yes, perhaps," Charlotte agreed. She could not tell Gracie, or anyone, that Balantyne had given the box to the blackmailer. Did that make Cole the blackmailer, or not? Or his messenger? Or had he stolen it from the blackmailer . . . by an extraordinary chance? "I still think I shall go and see Lady Vespasia," she stated. "I shall probably take luncheon out."

Gracie looked at her keenly, but she made no remark other than to acknowledge that she had heard.

Charlotte went upstairs and took several minutes to select an appropriate gown. On past occasions when she had needed to look more glamorous or impressive than her own very limited wardrobe allowed, she had been given clothes by Aunt Vespasia: dresses and sometimes capes or hats which she no longer used. Vespasia's maid had altered them to fit Charlotte's rather fuller figure, and changed the style a little, usually bringing it both up-to-date and making it a trifle more practical and less formal than it had been when Vespasia had worn it. Vespasia had always loved clothes and had every intention of leading fashion, not following it.

The only problem was that Vespasia was in her eighties, a trifle thin; her hair was silver and her tastes extravagant, to go with her station in life. Charlotte was in her thirties and dark with a rich tint of chestnut in her hair, her skin a warm honey tone. Some adjustments needed to be made.

She chose a pale blue muslin. It had gorgeous sleeves, a very slight bustle gathered from an overskirt of green which took from it the delicacy which on her looked not sophisticated, as it had on Vespasia, but rather insipid. She had a pale blue hat, which complemented the gown. She was reasonably satisfied with the result, and left at a quarter to twelve. The only way to travel dressed like this was by hansom—unless, of course, one had one's own carriage.

She arrived at Vespasia's house shortly after noon, and was admitted by the maid, who by now knew her very well.

Vespasia was sitting in her favorite room, opening onto the garden. She was dressed in her favorite ivory lace gown with ropes of soft, gleaming pearls. The sunlight made a pool around her, and her black-and-white dog was lying on the floor beside her feet. It rose and greeted Charlotte with enthusiasm. Vespasia remained where she was, but her face lit with pleasure.

"How nice to see you, my dear. I was rather hoping you

120

would come. I am bored to weeping with the season this year. There doesn't seem to be anybody with the slightest flair for the unpredictable. Everyone says and does precisely what I expect them to." She moved one shoulder in elegant dismissal. "They even wear what I expect. It is very fashionable, but of no interest whatever. It is frightening. I begin to fear I am growing old. I seem to know everything . . . and I hate it!" She raised her eyebrows. "What is the point in being alive if you are never taken completely by surprise, all your ideas scattered like leaves before a gale, and you have to pick them up and put them together again and find the picture is new and different? If you are not capable of passion or surprise, you really are dead."

She surveyed Charlotte critically, but with affection.

"Well, you are wearing something I had not predicted. Where on earth did you get that gown?"

"It is one of yours, Aunt Vespasia." Charlotte leaned over and kissed her delicately on the cheek.

Vespasia's eyebrows rose even higher.

"Good heavens! Please be good enough not to tell anyone. I should be mortified."

Charlotte did not know whether to be hurt or to laugh. She wanted to do both. "Is it really so awful?"

Vespasia waved her to stand back a little, and regarded the gown critically for several moments.

"The pale blue doesn't suit me," Charlotte explained. It was the addition of the green which seemed to be the focus of Vespasia's displeasure.

"It would if you added cream," Vespasia replied. "That green is far too heavy. You look as if you had fallen into the sea and come out covered in weed!"

"Oh! A sort of drowned look—like the Lady of Shalott?" Charlotte asked.

"Not quite as peaceful," Vespasia said dryly. "Don't tempt me to go further. Let me take that and find you something better." She rose to her feet, leaning a little on her silver-topped cane, and led the way upstairs to her dressing room. Charlotte followed obediently.

121

It was while Vespasia was looking through various swathes and shawls and other accessories that she said quite casually, "I suppose you are concerned about that peculiarly unfortunate matter in Bedford Square? As I recall, you were fond of Brandon Balantyne."

Charlotte found herself blushing quite hotly. That was not at all the way she would have phrased it. She looked at Vespasia's elegant back as she fingered a piece of silvery cream silk and considered its suitability. If Charlotte were to argue over Vespasia's choice of words she would only draw attention to her self-consciousness. She took a deep breath.

"I am upset about it, yes. I went to see him. Please don't tell Thomas; he doesn't know. I . . . I went on impulse, without thinking about it, except that I wanted him to have some . . . sense of friendship . . ." She faltered to a stop.

Vespasia turned around holding the cream silk. It was soft as gauze, faintly shimmering. "This will lighten it," she said with decision. "This piece as a fichu, and this around the bustle and down the front. It will warm the whole effect. Of course you went to see him because you care for him, and you wanted him to know that that was not changed by this new circumstance." Her face become more grave, touched with a gentleness. "How was he?" She looked very carefully at Charlotte, and her own perception of distress became deeper as she read Charlotte's feelings. "Not well . . ."

"He is being blackmailed," Charlotte replied, surprised how sharply it troubled her to say so, as if she were learning it for the first time herself. "Over something he did not do, but he cannot prove it."

Vespasia remained without speaking for several moments, but it was transparent in her face that it was the silence of thought, not of indifference or a failure of understanding.

Charlotte had a sudden, chill feeling that Vespasia knew or guessed something which she herself did not. She waited with a tightening of her throat.

"For money?" Vespasia said, almost as if she did not expect an answer in the affirmative.

"Not for anything," Charlotte replied. "Just . . . just to show that the blackmailer has the power, so far . . ."

"I see." Vespasia draped the silk over Charlotte's gown and tied it expertly. She fiddled with it, pulling it here and there, rearranging it, but her fingers moved absentmindedly. "There," she said when she had finished. "Do you care for that more?"

Charlotte surveyed herself in the glass. It was a great deal better, but that was hardly important.

"Yes, thank you." She turned. "Aunt Vespasia . . ."

But Vespasia was already walking away towards the landing and the stairs down. She held the banister to steady herself, something she would not have done a year or two before. Charlotte had an acute sense of her fragility, and painful knowledge of how much she loved her. She wanted to say so, but it might be overfamiliar; after all, they were not really related. And this was not the time.

At the bottom of the stairs in the hall, Vespasia started back towards the morning room, now full of sunlight.

"I have a friend," she said thoughtfully. "Mr. Justice Dunraithe White."

Charlotte caught up with her and they went into the pale, bright room. There were early white roses in the green bowl on the center table, and the sun through the leaves outside made shifting patterns on the carpet.

"Theloneus tells me he has made some very . . . odd . . . decisions lately, quite out of the character he has hitherto shown. He has delivered opinions which at the very kindest could be described as eccentric." Theloneus Quade was also a judge, and a longtime admirer of Vespasia. Twenty years before he had been deeply in love with her, and would have married her had she accepted him, but she had felt the difference in their ages to be too great. He was still in love, but now it was also a deeper friendship.

She sat down on her favorite seat near the window and let the stick go. The black-and-white dog thumped its tail with pleasure. Vespasia looked steadily at Charlotte.

"You think he is ill . . . or . . ." Charlotte began, then

realized her slowness of perception. "You think he is being blackmailed too!"

"I think he is under very great pressure of some sort," Vespasia said more exactly. "I have known him for many years, and he has always been a most honorable man, scrupulously so. His responsibilities to the law are central to his life, second only to his love for Marguerite, his wife. They have no children, and perhaps have consoled each other for this and grown closer than many others."

Charlotte sat opposite her, rearranging the newly glamorous gown. She was hesitant to ask the next question, but it burned in her mind, and her concern for Balantyne gave her a boldness she would not normally have had.

"Are these decisions in favor of anyone in particular, or any interests?"

A flash of understanding lit Vespasia's eyes, and wry sadness.

"Not yet. According to Theloneus these are merely erratic, ill thought out, quite unlike his usual careful consideration and weighing of all factors." She frowned. "It is as if his mind were only half on what he is doing. I was most concerned about him. I thought perhaps it was illness, which it may be. I saw him two or three days ago, and he looked most unwell, as if he had slept very little. But there was more, a sense of abstraction in him. Only when you told me of Brandon Balantyne did the thought of blackmail occur to me." She moved her hands fractionally. "There are so many things a man may not be able to disprove once the suggestion is made. One only has to look at this ridiculous Tranby Croft affair to see how easily ruin may come simply by a misplaced word, a charge, whether it can be proved or not."

"Is Gordon-Cumming going to be ruined?" Charlotte asked. "And is he innocent?" She knew Vespasia would be at least to some degree acquainted with the principal characters concerned, and very probably know a good deal about their private lives.

Vespasia shook her head slightly. "I have no idea whether he is innocent, but it is perfectly possible. The whole matter should never have arisen. It was handled appallingly badly. When they believed he was cheating they should have called an end to the game, without requiring him to sign a piece of paper promising never to play cards again, which was tantamount to an admission of guilt. Condemning who was present, somebody was bound to speak of it, and then scandal was inevitable. With two wits to rub together they could have foreseen that." She shook her head with impatience.

"But there's got to be something we can do about this threat of blackmail!" Charlotte protested. "It is monstrously unjust. It could happen to anyone."

Vespasia was very tense, unaccustomed lines of anxiety in her face.

"What worries me is what this blackmailer may ask for. You say he has made no demand of Balantyne yet?"

"No . . . except a snuffbox . . . and that was found on the body of the man who was murdered on his doorstep." She found her own fingers clenching. "Thomas knows all about the murder, of course, because it is his case. But that is not all. . . ."

"There is worse," Vespasia said quietly; it was more of a conclusion than a question.

"Yes. Assistant Commissioner Cornwallis is being blackmailed too. Also for something in the past in which he cannot prove his innocence."

"What, precisely?"

"Taking the credit for another man's act of courage."

"And General Balantyne?"

"That he panicked in the face of the enemy and allowed someone else to conceal it for him."

"I see." Vespasia looked deeply troubled. She understood only too bitterly how such rumors, no matter how softly whispered, how passionately denied, would make a man's life nigh to intolerable. Less vicious charges than either of those had at best driven men to retire from all public life and move to some remote spot in the wilder parts of Scotland, or even to leave Britain altogether and become expatriates without a purpose. At worst, they had caused suicide.

"We must fight," Charlotte urged, leaning forward a little. "We can't let it happen."

"You are right," Vespasia agreed. "I have no idea whether we can win. Blackmailers have all the advantages." She rose to her feet, again using the cane. The dog uncurled itself and stood up also. "They use methods we cannot and would not," she continued. "They fight from the shadows. They are the ultimate cowards. We shall have luncheon, then we shall call upon the Whites." She reached for the bell rope and pulled it. When it was answered she informed the butler of her plans, for him in turn to tell the cook and the coachman.

Dunraithe and Marguerite White lived in Upper Brook Street, between Park Lane and Grosvenor Street. Charlotte and Vespasia alighted from the carriage in the bright mid-afternoon sun. Vespasia knew all the proper etiquette for calling on "at home" days, once or twice a month. Any-one with a suitable degree of acquaintance might come. All "morning calls" actually took place in the afternoon, from three o'clock until four for the most formal and ceremonial, from four to five for those less formal, and from five until six for those which were quite intimate or between close friends.

However, there were certain advantages to high birth and the passage of time. When Vespasia chose to break the rules no one complained, except those who would like to have done so themselves but did not dare to, and they made their comments very quietly—and if overheard, denied them.

Fortunately, this was not an "at home" day. Mrs. White was without company, and a somewhat startled maid took Vespasia's card and returned a few moments later to say that Mrs. White would receive them.

Charlotte was too concerned about the issues which had brought them there to take anything but the slightest notice of the house or its furnishings. She had a fleeting impression of heavy, gold-framed pictures, rather a lot of carved oak and curtains with fringes.

In the withdrawing room, Marguerite White stood near a chaise longue covered with cushions, rather as if she had just risen from it. She was slender and pale, with a mass of dark hair. Her eyes were hollow, heavy lidded, her brows delicate. She was a beautiful woman, but Charlotte's most powerful impression was that she was not strong and the slightest exertion would tire her. She was dressed in a dark muslin gown, which was obviously not what she would have chosen had she expected callers.

A greater surprise was that her husband was standing behind her. He was only a little taller than she, a trifle portly now, and broad shouldered. But in spite of his ample frame and genial features, he looked as if he, too, had been ill. There was no color in his skin, and the shadows under his eyes were dark.

"Vespasia! How charming of you to call." He made an effort to be courteous, and a genuine good nature was unmistakable in his voice. Nevertheless, he could not entirely conceal that he was puzzled to see her, and of course he was unacquainted with Charlotte.

Vespasia greeted him with warmth and made the appropriate introductions. All the usual remarks were made about health and weather, and tea was offered, although no one expected it to be accepted at this hour.

"Thank you," Vespasia said with a smile, sitting down on the wide sofa and arranging her skirts with the merest flick of her hand, indicating that she fully intended to stay.

Marguerite looked startled, but there was nothing she could do about it short of extreme rudeness, and it had been apparent from her first response to Vespasia that she was fond of her, and perhaps a little in awe.

Charlotte sat down nervously. What could she possibly say in this absurd but desperately important situation? Something flattering but innocuous. She glanced out of the window.

"What a delightful garden you have, Mrs. White."

Marguerite looked relieved. It must be a subject that gave her pleasure. Her face eased of some of its tension; her eyes brightened.

"Do you like it?" she asked eagerly. "I wish it were larger, but we do what we can to give the illusion of space."

"You succeed admirably." Charlotte was able to say it with sincerity. "I should love to have such a skill, or perhaps I should say an art? I doubt it is something which can be learned."

"Would you like to see it more closely?" Marguerite offered.

It was precisely what Vespasia had most hoped for and intended to bring about were she able. Charlotte had accomplished it within the first few minutes of their visit.

Charlotte turned to her. Enquiring if it were acceptable was a necessary courtesy.

Vespasia smiled, but casually, as if it were of no importance.

"By all means, my dear. I should go while the sun is out and you can enjoy it to its very best advantage. I am sure Mrs. White will be willing to allow you to look at it closely enough to see the delicacy of the details."

"Of course," Marguerite agreed. "It is one virtue most gardeners possess: we all love to show off, but we seldom mind sharing our ideas." She turned to her husband. "You will excuse us, won't you? I seldom have anyone here whose interest is more than an indulgence of my passion. I am so tired of polite nothings."

"Of course, my dear," he said gently, and his regard for Charlotte changed in that moment. It was clear in his expression, the way his shoulders relaxed as he moved to open the French doors for them both, that she had in that one gesture become a friend.

When they were gone—two graceful figures across the small strip of green lawn, outlined by the background of trees, urns of pale flowers reflecting the sunlight, white petunias dramatic against the dark flames of cypress—he closed the doors and came back across the room to Vespasia.

"You look tired, Dunraithe," she said gently.

He remained standing, half turned away from her.

"I was awake a little last night. It is nothing. It happens to all of us now and again."

She must not waste precious time while Marguerite was

128

occupied outside. He would certainly not tell her anything once his wife returned. He had always done everything in his power to protect her from distress of any kind. And yet if Vespasia were precipitate he would regard it as intrusive and be offended. Not only would she not have helped but she would also have damaged a friendship which she valued.

"It does," she agreed with a self-deprecatory little shrug. Then an idea came to her. There was no time to weigh its merits. The garden was small, and Charlotte could keep Marguerite outside only a given length of time. "I have lost some sleep myself recently."

He wished to be courteous, but his attention was only half upon her, and in spite of his efforts, she was aware of it. Theloneus was right, Dunraithe White was deeply worried about something.

"Oh . . . I'm sorry," he said with an absentminded smile. It did not occur to him to enquire as to what the cause might be. She was going to have to be far more blunt than she had wished.

"It is the curse of an imagination," she responded.

That was something to which he could not easily think of a casual reply.

"Of an imagination?" His attention was real at last. "Are you afraid of something, Vespasia?"

"Not for myself," she answered, meeting his eyes. "For my friends, which I suppose in the end is the same thing. We are given pain or happiness through those we care for."

"Of course." He said it with sudden intensity. "It is the core of what we are. Without the ability to love we would be half alive . . . less. And what we have would be of no value . . . no joy."

"And no pain," she added.

His eyes clouded, and there was a fierce tenderness in his face. Suddenly his emotions were raw. She had always known he loved Marguerite, but in that moment she saw something of the depth of it, and the vulnerability. She could not help wondering if Marguerite White was really as fragile as he believed. But it was a judgment only he had the right to make.

129

"Yes, of course," he said in little more than a whisper. "The two are inseparable."

She waited, but he did not go on. Either he was too absorbed in his own feelings or he believed that asking her about herself would be intrusive.

She took a deep breath and let it out silently.

"One cannot see a true friend suffer, perhaps even be ruined, without attempting to help." She watched him as she spoke.

His head jerked up, his body became rigid. It was as if she had struck him. The quiet room, sunlit from the garden beyond, was permeated with fear. Still he said nothing.

She would not let it go, she could not. "Dunraithe, I need your advice. That is really why I have come at this very inappropriate hour. I do know better than to call unannounced at three in the afternoon."

A flash of painful humor crossed his face and vanished.

"You, of all people, do not need to apologize. How can I help you?"

At last!

"Someone I know and care for," she answered, "and for reasons which will be obvious to you, I should prefer not to name him, is being blackmailed." She stopped. The expression on his face did not change in the slightest; indeed, it was unnaturally frozen. But the blood rushed into his cheeks, and then fled, leaving him ashen. If she had ever doubted that he, too, was a victim, she could not possibly do so now.

Had he any idea how his color had betrayed him? Did he feel the heat in his skin, and then the faintness? She looked into his eyes and still was not certain. She continued because the only alternative was to retreat.

"Over something which, in fact, he did not do." She gave a tiny smile. "But he cannot prove it. It was all many years ago, and rests now on the word of people whose memories are dulled or whose testimony may not be sufficient." She gave the minutest shrug. "Anyway, I daresay you are as aware as I that a whisper can be enough to cause irreparable damage, whether it is true or not. Many of the people one would like to

130

admire actually have very little charity when it comes to the chance to cause a stir with a piece of gossip. One has not far to look to know that is true."

He started to say something, then swallowed convulsively.

"Do sit down, Dunraithe," she said softly."You look as if you are quite ill. A stiff brandy might help, but I think a word of friendship might do more. You also are carrying a great burden of some sort. One does not need the eye of a friend to see that. I have shared my concern with you, and feel better for it, even if you are not able to give me any practical advice. And I admit, I cannot think what such advice might be. What can one do against blackmail?"

He avoided her eyes, looking down at the roses in the Aubusson carpet beneath his feet.

"I don't know," he answered, his voice husky. "If you pay, then you only dig yourself in the more deeply. You have created a precedent, and shown the blackguard that you are afraid of him and will yield."

"That is part of the trouble." She watched him intently. "You see, he has not asked for anything."

"Not . . . asked for anything?" His words were stilted, his face drained of color.

"Not yet." She kept her own voice level. "It is most unpleasant, and of course my friend fears that in time he will. The question is what will it be?"

"Money?" There was a lift of hope in him now, as if a demand for money would have been almost a relief.

"I imagine so," she answered. "If not, then it may be something far uglier. He is a man of influence. The worst possibility is that he may be asked to do something corrupt . . . to misuse his power. . . ."

He closed his eyes, and for a moment she was afraid he was actually going to faint.

"Why do you tell me this, Vespasia?" he whispered. "What do you know of it?"

"Only what I have told you," she replied. "And that I fear he may not be the only victim. Dunraithe . . . I am very much afraid there may be a far larger conspiracy involved than

131

merely the misery of one man, or even two. One cannot keep one's reputation, however justly earned, by committing an act of dishonor, possibly even greater than that with which one is falsely accused."

Suddenly he looked at her very directly, anger and desperation in his face. "I cannot tell how much you know, even if that is why you are here, and what of your friend is mythical, what true." His voice was rough, almost angry. "But I confess I also am being blackmailed for something of which I am totally innocent. But I will not risk having it said . . . by anyone! I shall pay him whatever he asks, but I will keep him silent." He was shaking. He looked so ill as to be on the point of collapse.

"My friend is as real as you are." It mattered to her that he did not think she had lied, no matter for what reason. "I did not know you were also a victim, but your distress caused me to wonder. I am profoundly sorry. It is the filthiest of crimes." She spoke more fervently. "But we must fight him. We must do it together, if necessary. We must believe in one another. My friend was accused of cowardice in the face of the enemy . . . a sin which would be anathema to him, a shame he could not live with."

"I'm sorry." The words were wrung from him. She could not doubt he meant them passionately. It was in his face, the angle of his body, the clenched shoulders. "But to allow what I am accused of to be said aloud would be a torment Marguerite could not live with. And that I will not allow . . . whatever he does to me. There is no use arguing with me, Vespasia. I will do anything on earth before I permit her to be hurt. And she would be devastated."

This was no time for tactful evasions. Charlotte and Marguerite would return at any moment. Charlotte had already kept the conversation on gardening alive miraculously long.

"What are you accused of?" Vespasia asked.

He was pale to the lips. Again, the answer seemed forced from him. "Suit for the paternity of the child of one of my closest friends." He struggled for breath. "The husband passed away recently. He cannot even deny that he contemplated such a thing." His voice rose. "Of course he did not! The child was his, and he never could have thought otherwise. But even a whisper of doubt would ruin the mother's reputation, and mine, the more so since we were friends . . . and even call into question the son's inheritance, both of his father's title and his considerable wealth."

His face crumpled and his voice trembled now.

"To have anyone think that I could have behaved in such a way would kill Marguerite. She is . . . very frail. You know that. She has never ever been strong, and of late she has suffered . . . I simply will not allow it!"

"But you have done nothing wrong," she pointed out. "There is nothing for you or Marguerite to be shamed by."

His lip curled. The bright sunlight streaming through the windows showed the contempt in his face. "And do you imagine people will believe that . . . all people? There will be whispers, glances." He laughed derisively. "Some well-meaning busybody will be sure to tell Marguerite what is being said, probably in the guise of forewarning her, perhaps in simple malice."

"And so you will do what he asks of you," Vespasia said. "The first time, and the second . . . and maybe the third? By which time you will truly have done something to be ashamed of, and his hold upon you will be real!" She leaned forward a little. "How far will you go? You are a judge, Dunraithe. Justice must be your first loyalty."

"Marguerite is my first loyalty!" His voice was raw, his fists clenched. "I have loved her nearly all my life, and I will do anything to protect her."

Vespasia said nothing. He did not need her to repeat that for him to betray his trust, sell his honor, would also devastate Marguerite. He must see it all in her eyes. He could not bear to look beyond the first danger and deal with them one at a time, pay the cost and think about tomorrow's evil afterwards, hope then for some escape. Perhaps someone else would defeat the blackmailer before that?

The French doors opened, and Charlotte and Marguerite came in in a gust of bright wind and billowing skirts. There was color in Marguerite's cheeks, and she looked excited and happy.

Dunraithe made a mighty effort to master the pain and the fear that had been so naked in him a few moments before. His whole expression changed. He straightened his body. He smiled at both the women, extending his warmth towards Charlotte as well.

"Your garden is quite lovely," Charlotte said with very real admiration. "What marvelous things can be achieved when you have both the art to see what should be done and the skill to do it. In the nicest way, I am perfectly envious."

"I am so glad you enjoyed it," he said. "She is very clever, isn't she?" The pride in him was enormous, a thing of unalloyed pleasure.

Marguerite beamed with happiness.

The tea was brought, and it was now almost four o'clock anyway. They sat making another half hour's trivial conversation, then said their farewells and the carriage was called.

Vespasia told Charlotte what she had learned as they traveled back to Keppel Street.

"I am very afraid that this is far bigger than we had at first supposed," she said grimly. "I am sorry, my dear, but you can no longer keep your knowledge of Brandon Balantyne's involvement from Thomas. I realize it will not be easy for you to tell him how you have become aware of it, but you have no alternative now."

Charlotte looked at her steadily. "Do you really think this is some kind of conspiracy, Aunt Vespasia?"

"Do you not think it looks like it?" Vespasia replied. "Cornwallis, Balantyne, and now Dunraithe White."

"Yes . . . I suppose so. If only he had asked for money!"

"He would still have to be stopped," Vespasia pointed out. "Money is only the beginning."

"I suppose so."

It was not an easy conversation, as Vespasia had predicted, but Charlotte broached the subject as soon as Pitt returned home. For once he was quite early, coming into the kitchen

134

in his stocking feet and finding her busy putting away clean crockery. She did it immediately because once she had determined to do it, she could not settle to any kind of peace of mind until it was accomplished. She had rehearsed it several times, never entirely satisfactorily.

"Thomas, I have something I must tell you about the Bedford Square case. I don't know whether it is relevant or not . . . I hope not, but I feel you should know."

It was not her usual pattern of speech, and he caught the difference, turning from the sink, where he was washing his hands, and looking at her with surprise.

She stood in the middle of the kitchen floor, half a dozen plates in her hand. She took a deep breath and then spoke, without waiting for him to ask or allowing him to interrupt.

"I spent the afternoon with Aunt Vespasia. One of her friends, Judge Dunraithe White, is also a victim of this blackmailer who is threatening Mr. Cornwallis."

He stiffened. "How do you know? Did he tell Vespasia?" His voice was high and sharp with incredulity.

"Not easily, of course," she answered, putting the plates back on the table and passing him a clean towel. "But they are old friends. I occupied his wife, who is a most excellent gardener. I must tell you more about that—I know! Later," she interrupted herself quickly.

"Vespasia spoke alone with Mr. White, and he confessed to her his situation. He is absolutely distracted with worry and fear, but the accusation is that he fathered the eldest son and heir of one of their closest friends. And now that the friend is dead and cannot deny it, the blackmailer is saying that he was actually going to sue Mr. White. . . ."

Pitt winced, his expression conveying plainly how he appreciated the hurt. He dropped the towel over the back of the chair nearest to him.

"And Mr. White said such a thing would devastate his wife. She is very frail and so they have no children of their own. He adores her, and will pay any price asked of him rather than allow that."

Pitt hunched his shoulders and pushed his hands hard down

135

into his pockets. "That's Cornwallis, White, and, I heard today, also a man named Tannifer, a merchant banker in the City. He's accused of fraud with his clients' funds."

"Another one!" She was startled. It was looking increasingly as if Vespasia was right and the problem was far larger and more serious than any individual blackmail for greed.

He looked at her gravely. "Have you considered that perhaps General Balantyne is also being blackmailed? I know you would rather not think so, in view of the murdered man on his doorstep, but I can't dismiss it just because I would prefer to."

Now was the time. "He is." She watched his face to see how angry he might be. He stood absolutely still, all kinds of emotions conflicting in his eyes, anger and amazement, pity, understanding, and something which for an instant she thought was a sense of betrayal. She went on talking, quickly, trying to cover the moment. "I went to convey my sympathy for his new tragedy . . . really that the wretched newspapers had raised the Christina business all over again, as if living it once were not enough." Now what was in his face was unmistakably pity, memory of indescribable pain, not for himself but for Balantyne, and understanding of what she had done. "I knew something else was extremely wrong," she went on, smiling at him now. "And I offered my friendship, for whatever comfort that was. He told me, with great embarrassment, that he is being blackmailed over an incident in the Abyssinian Campaign twenty-five years ago which never happened, but he cannot prove it. Most of the other people concerned are either dead or abroad, or senile."

She took a breath and hurried on again. "No one has asked him for money either, or anything else, but he has had a second letter, and it is very threatening. Such a charge would ruin him and Lady Augusta, whom I don't care about, but Brandy too. He is trying to find anyone from the campaign who can help, but he hasn't succeeded so far. What can we do, Thomas? This is dreadful!"

He remained silent for several moments.

"Thomas . . ."

"What?"

"I'm sorry I didn't tell you about General Balantyne earlier. I wanted to see if I could find something and prove his innocence of the accusation."

"You also didn't want me to know because it would make me suspect him of killing Albert Cole, because the snuffbox was his," he said levelly. "Did he give it to Cole?"

"No . . . he gave it to the blackmailer. He was asked for it, as a pledge, and it was collected by a boy on a bicycle." She waited for what he would say next. How angry would he be about that? She really should have told him.

He regarded her steadily.

She felt the color hot in her face. But if she were in the same position over again, she would do the same thing. She had no doubt whatever that Balantyne was innocent. He needed defending. And Augusta would certainly not do it.

Pitt smiled with a curious little twist. He knew her rather too well for comfort at times.

"Your apology is accepted, even if it is not entirely believed," he said gently. "I suggest for your leisure-time reading you try *Don Quixote*."

She winced now, and lowered her eyes. "Are you ready for supper?"

"Yes." He sat down at the table and waited for her to lay plates for them, put away the rest of the plates, finish preparing the meal and then serve it.

Vespasia did not know about Sigmund Tannifer, but what she did know was enough to cause her such grave concern that she used the telephone, an instrument which she found quite marvelous, to ask her friend Theloneus Quade if she might call upon him that evening.

He responded by offering to call upon her instead. She was tired enough to accept with gratitude. Had the offer come from anyone else she might have declined, even with asperity. She refused to concede any more to age than was forced upon her, and most certainly not in front of others. But Theloneus was different. She had come to realize that his love for her had transcended his initial fascination with the beauty she had possessed even into her sixties, and the core of which was still with her. Now it was a love for the person she was and the experiences they had shared over a lifetime through a tumultuous century. It had begun, for her at least, when the Emperor Napoleon had threatened the very existence of Britain. She remembered Waterloo. Queen Victoria had been a child then, and relatively unknown.

Now she, too, was an old woman, who wore black and was empress of a quarter of the world. Steamships sailed the seas, and the Thames Embankment was illuminated by electric lights.

Theloneus arrived a little before eight. He kissed her on the cheek, and for a moment she smelled the faint perfume of clean skin, laundered cotton, and felt the warmth of him.

Then he stood back. "What is it?" he asked with a frown. "You look extremely worried."

They were in her sitting room. There was still bright sunlight outside. It would not be dark for nearly two hours, but there was a coolness already in the air, in spite of its golden brilliance.

He sat down, because he knew how it irritated her to have to stare upwards.

"I spent much of the day with Charlotte," she began. "We called upon Dunraithe White. I am afraid you were correct in your fears for him. He confided in me the source of his anxiety. It is worse than you thought."

He leaned forward, his thin, gentle face creased with worry.

"You feared premature senility, or even madness, didn't you?" she asked.

He nodded. "At worst, yes, I did. What could he have told you that you find even more serious?"

"That he is being blackmailed. . . ."

"Dunraithe White!" He was aghast. "I find that almost impossible to believe. I never knew a more predictably righteous man in my life. Or a more transparently honest one. What on earth can he have done for which anyone could

138

blackmail him, let alone which he would pay to keep secret?" His face was creased in lines of pity and concern, but underlying it all was still incredulity.

Vespasia understood. Only his love for Marguerite made Dunraithe White vulnerable, and that was what was so frightening. The blackmailer must be close enough to him to have known that, otherwise he would not have wasted his time with the attempt.

Theloneus was waiting for her to explain, watching her.

"He is not guilty of anything," she said softly, "except the desire to protect Marguerite from the whisper of unkindness, true or untrue." Then she told him of the accusation and Dunraithe's response.

Theloneus sat for some time without answering.

The black-and-white dog lay asleep in the sun, snoring gently and occasionally giving a little whimper as she dreamed.

"I see," Theloneus said at last. "You are right; it is far worse than I thought."

"He will not refuse the man, whatever he demands," she said gravely. "I tried the arguments of reason. I told him that he has nothing whatever of which to be ashamed now, and Marguerite will understand that. But if he does something because this man forces him to, something he would not do of his own will, then he will have, and she will know that too."

"Did he not perceive it for himself?" He leaned forward a little.

"I think he is too frightened for her to look beyond tomorrow," she answered. "Sometimes fear can be like that . . . paralyzing the will or the ability to see what is too horrible."

"Is she really so delicate, Vespasia?" He looked uncomfortable, unwilling to appear harsh, and yet he needed to ask.

She considered hard before she answered him, thinking of all she knew of Marguerite White over the years, piecing together memories, wondering how she had interpreted them then, and how with hindsight they might be different now.

"Perhaps not," she said at length, speaking slowly. "Certainly she does not have good health, that has always been true. How ill she is would be difficult to say. She is in her mid-forties at least, perhaps a trifle more, so the delicacy that was feared in her youth must have been overestimated. She was told that she could not bear children, that to do so would certainly jeopardize her life."

He was watching her closely, listening.

She wished to be fair, but memory crowded in, and doubt. She was glad she was speaking to Theloneus, whom she loved, and would not have him think ill of her, but also whom she trusted well enough that she dared allow him to see in her what was vulnerable, and perhaps frightened, or weak, or less than beautiful. He would judge with the eyes of a friend.

"Yes?" he prompted.

"She is also used to thinking of herself as the one to be protected," she went on. "The one who must never be distressed or asked too much of. Dunraithe has spoiled her . . . with the very best intention. Perhaps he was sometimes too careful to be wise. She might have become stronger, at least in spirit, had she faced reality more often. Most of us will run away if there is someone who will protect us, face all the unpleasantness for us, and count it a privilege to do so."

"Could she face this?" he asked, his eyes wide and intent, unwavering from hers.

"I don't know," she replied. "I have been asking myself that, considering all the avenues one might take, even to precipitating some crisis to draw out this blackguard. I can hardly bear to think what will happen if he asks Dunraithe to do something which would be an abuse of his office. . . ."

Theloneus put his hand over hers, very gently, touching rather than holding. She noticed with surprise how thin it was, how visible the veins. His face had changed so much less; the curve of the nose was the same, the steady eyes, the sensitive mouth. It was so natural to protect someone you loved, someone you saw as vulnerable and to whom you felt a burning loyalty, someone without whom you would have no happiness, no laughter, no sharing, perhaps above all someone who loved you.

"The answer is that whether Marguerite would survive it or not, my dear," she said with absolute conviction, "Dunraithe will never be sure enough of it to take that risk. We must assume that if some demand comes, he will accede to it."

He sat back. "Then I shall have to watch all his decisions with the greatest care, a thing I do not wish at all. I do not ask what this person accuses him of, but I think perhaps I need to know whether it is an offense in law which may affect his position."

"No, it is purely a moral one," she replied with a twisted smile. "If this were to be an offense in law our prisons would be full and the Houses of Parliament empty."

"Oh!" His answering smile was instant. "I see . . . of that nature. I should find it difficult to believe of Dunraithe, but I can see how difficult that might be for Marguerite, even if the better part of her knew it was untrue. Sometimes laughter is the cruelest judgment."

She must tell him the rest. "That is not all . . . it is not even the worst of it, Theloneus."

Something in her voice, an edge of fear, caught him with a sudden sharpness, it was so unlike Vespasia to be afraid of anything. She was far more likely to respond to evil with anger.

"What is it?"

"Dunraithe White is not the only one. John Cornwallis and Brandon Balantyne are being blackmailed also, almost certainly by the same person . . . or people."

"Brandon Balantyne?" His eyes widened in amazement. "John Cornwallis? I find that . . . almost impossible to credit. And you said 'people'? Do you imagine more than one?"

She sighed. Suddenly she was weary with the effort of the ugliness she could imagine. "Perhaps. Nothing has been asked for yet. Dunraithe is not a wealthy man, but he has great power, great influence. He is a judge. To corrupt a judge is very wicked. It strikes at the root of the only barrier between the people and injustice, the loss of trust in society to protect its members, in the end against chaos and the rule of the jungle."

She saw his agreement in his face. He did not interrupt.

"And John Cornwallis similarly," she went on. "He is not

141

wealthy, but as assistant commissioner of police he, too, has great power. If the police are corrupted then what protection has anyone against violence or stealth? Order begins to fail, and men take the law into their own hands because they trust no other. The one I do not yet understand is Brandon Balantyne." She saw the lack of comprehension in his face.

"Did he tell you that he is being blackmailed?" he asked quickly.

"No. Charlotte did. She is most concerned about it. She is very fond of him. And that is an entirely different problem."

He did not understand that either; she saw it plainly in his eyes.

"No," she said with the ghost of a smile. "That is not what I mean at all," she answered the question he was only thinking. "But she has little perception that he may be fonder of her than either of them realizes." She moved her other hand slightly, dismissing the idea for the moment. "But I am deeply afraid, Theloneus. What does this blackmailer want? If he exercises his power with sufficient skill, the damage he may do is incalculable. Who else may be affected?"

He was very pale. "I don't know, my dear. But I think we must face the possibility that there are more, and that we may not be able to find them, or even to guess who they are. Vespasia, this may be very serious indeed. Far more than the reputation of any one person may rest on it, important as that is. Is it possible that Brandon Balantyne may be persuaded to stand out against the pressure?"

"Perhaps." She thought of all she knew of Balantyne, the fleeting memories, his face as a young man, the grief that had come to him since. "The accusation against him is cowardice in the face of the enemy. . . ."

Theloneus winced. He was not a military man, but he knew enough of war and honor to grasp at least something of what such a thing meant.

"He has already been hurt so much . . ." she said quietly. "But perhaps with having endured that, he can face public ignominy again with more courage than others. I pray that it will not be necessary."

142

"And Cornwallis?" he asked.

"Taking credit for another man's act of courage at sea," she replied. "In each case the charge is the most painful that particular man could face. We are dealing with someone who knows his victims well and can hurt with a unique skill."

"Indeed," he said grimly. "We shall need as much skill if we are to beat him, and I think a great deal of luck as well."

"A great deal," she agreed. "Perhaps we should not go into battle on an empty stomach. Would you care for a little late supper? I believe Cook has asparagus, brown bread and butter, and I expect there is champagne."

"Knowing you, my dear, I am quite sure there is," he accepted.

Cornwallis paced along the pavement outside the Royal Academy of Art. He was suffering a kind of pain he had never experienced before. He was long familiar with loneliness, the physical discomfort of coldness, exhaustion, miserable food, stale sea biscuit and salt bacon, brackish water. He had been seasick, feverish, injured. He had certainly been frightened, ashamed, torn with pity he did not know how to bear.

Only since he had met Isadora Underhill, the wife of Bishop Underhill, had he understood what it was to think of a woman with a pleasure and a pain which were inextricably bound together, to long to be in her company, and to be so terrified of hurting or disappointing her that the thought of it made him sick.

Nothing in the world was as sweet as the thought that she also cared for him. In what way he had not dared to contemplate. It was sufficient that she thought well of him, that she believed him to be a man of honor and compassion, of courage and that inner integrity which no outside circumstance can tarnish or bend.

The last time they had met, she had mentioned that she would attend the exhibition of paintings by Tissot at the Royal Academy. If he did not go, she would believe he did not wish to see her. Their relationship was far too delicate for him to offer any explanation, as if she had expected him. And yet

143

if he did go, and they were to meet, and they would, and fall into conversation, as they must, would she see the fear in him caused by the letter? She was so perceptive; in some ways she understood emotions in him no one else had even guessed at. If he could agonize as he was doing, and she were to walk and talk with him, and be unaware of it, then what was their affection worth?

And yet if she did see it, how could he explain it?

Even as he was saying this to himself, he was mounting the steps and going in. The room of the exhibition was posted. He walked past the grave, delicate beauty of a Fra Angelico Madonna, which normally would have stirred a unique joy in him. Today he barely noticed it. He would not go to the room with the Turners. Their passion would overwhelm him.

Without realizing it he was already at the exhibition of Tissot. There was Isadora. He could always see her at a glance, her dark head held at just such an angle. Her hat had a sweeping brim, very plain. She was alone, regarding the paintings as if she took great pleasure in them. They were not really her taste, he knew that, too stylized. She preferred landscape, vision and dream.

He walked across to her as if drawn by a power beyond him to resist.

"Good afternoon, Mrs. Underhill," he said quietly.

She smiled at him. "Good afternoon, Mr. Cornwallis. How are you?"

"Very well, thank you. And you, Mrs. Underhill?" He wanted to say how lovely she looked, but that would have been far too familiar. There was a perfect grace in her bearing, a beauty in her far deeper and more pleasing to the mind than simple perfection of line or coloring. It was in the expression of her eyes and her lips. He wished he could tell her that. "A fine exhibition," he said instead.

"Indeed," she answered without enthusiasm, a very slight smile touching her lips. "But I prefer the watercolors in the next room."

"I too," he agreed immediately. "Shall we look at them instead?"

144

"I should like that," she accepted, taking his arm and walking beside him past a small group of gentlemen admiring a portrait of a young woman in a striped gown.

In the room beyond they were almost alone. As one, they stopped in front of a small seascape. "He has caught the effect of light on water very well, don't you think?" he said with fierce admiration.

"I do," she agreed, turning to glance at him momentarily. "The touch of green is exactly right. It makes it look so cold and translucent. It is difficult to make water look liquid." There was concern in her eyes, as if she saw in his face the marks of sleeplessness, fear, the mistrust which was beginning to creep into every waking thought, and last night, even into his dreams.

What would she think if she knew? Would she believe that he was innocent? Would she understand why he was afraid? Might she even be afraid herself, in case others believed it and she would want to distance herself from the shame of it, the embarrassment of having to say she did not believe it, explain why, see the looks of polite amusement and wonder . . . and then afterwards be abashed?

"Mr. Cornwallis?" There was a lift of concern in her voice.

"Yes!" he said too quickly. He felt a slight warmth in his cheeks. "I'm sorry, my thoughts were wandering. Shall we move to the next picture? I always find pastoral scenes most agreeable." How stilted he sounded, as if they were strangers forcing a meaningless conversation, and how cold. *Agreeable.* What a lukewarm word to use for beauty of such deep and abiding peace. He looked at the black-and-white cows grazing in dappled sunlight and the rolling countryside glimpsed through summer trees. It was land he loved with a passion. Why could he not say so to her?

What is love without trust, forgiveness, patience, and gentleness? Mere hunger and need, joy in another's company, shared pleasures, even laughter and perceptions, are merely the things of good acquaintance. To be more than that must be giving as well as taking, cost as well as gain.

"You look a little concerned, Mr. Cornwallis," she said gently. "Have you a troublesome case?"

He made a decision. "Yes, but I intend to leave it behind for half an hour." He forced himself to smile and linked his arm through hers, something he had never done before. "I shall look at this perfect loveliness which nothing shall fade or destroy, and it will be doubled from now because I shall share it with you. The rest of the world can wait. I shall return to it soon enough."

She smiled back at him, as if she had understood far more than he had said. "How very wise of you. I shall do exactly the same." And she walked close to his side, keeping her arm through his.

6

TELLMAN NEEDED to know more about Albert Cole, most particularly his comings and goings in the last few days of his life. So far every additional fact had only added to the confusion. He must go back to the beginning and start again. The best place for that was Cole's lodgings in Theobald's Road.

The house was shabby, more so in the clear morning sunlight than it had seemed the first time he had been there. But it was clean, and there were neat rag rugs on the board floors and the landlady was busy with pail and scrubbing brush. Her faded blond hair was tied up in a cloth cap to keep it off her face, and her red-knuckled hands were covered in suds.

"Good morning, Mrs. Hampson," he said pleasantly. "Sorry to bother you again when you're busy." He glanced at the half-scrubbed floor of the passage. The smell of lye and vinegar reminded him of the rooms where he had grown up, of his mother kneeling just like this with a brush in her hand, her sleeves rolled high. He could have been a small boy again with bare knees and holes in his boots.

Mrs. Hampson stood up stiffly, smoothing her apron. "S'you again, is it? I dunno any more 'bout your Mr. Cole now than I did w'en yer first come. 'E were a quiet, decent sort o' man. Always got a civil word. I dunno w'y anybody'd wanter go an' kill 'im for."

"Can you think back to the last few days of his life, Mrs. Hampson?" he asked patiently. "What time of the morning did he get up? Did he have breakfast? When did he go out?

147

When did he come back? Did he have anybody call on him here?"

"Nob'dy I ever seen," she answered, shaking her head. "Don't encourage callers. In't room, an' yer never knows wot they'll get up ter. Anyway, decent man, 'e were. If 'e ever did anythink like . . . natural . . . 'e din't do it 'ere."

Tellman did not think Cole's death had had anything to do with women. He did not bother to pursue that path.

"When did he come and go during the last few days of his life, Mrs. Hampson?"

She thought for a moment. "Well, the last day I saw 'im, which were the Tuesday, like, 'e went out abaht seven in the mornin'. Catch them as would buy laces on their way ter work. Can't afford ter miss 'em." She pursed her lips. "Next lot'd be later, more nine or ten, so 'e said ter me. The lawyers start later, bein' gents, like. An' o' course there's casuals all the time."

"And the day before? Can you remember?"

"Some." She ignored the brush in her hand, still dripping water onto the floor. "Can't remember partic'lar, but I'd a' remembered if it a' bin different. Same every day. Gruel fer breakfast, an' a piece o' bread. Look, mister, I got work ter do. If yer wants more'n this, yer'll 'ave ter come inside an' let me get on." She knelt and wiped up the drips and then the last few inches of soap and water and he picked up the pail to carry it for her, their palms meeting on the wooden spool of the handle.

She was so startled she nearly dropped it, but she said nothing.

In the kitchen she left the pail in the corner and began to mix white brick dust into a paste with linseed oil to scour the tabletops. She mixed some more with water to polish the knife blades and the large brass-handled poker by the stove.

Tellman sat in the corner out of her way. He watched her work. He asked her everything he could think of about Albert Cole. An hour later she had finished cleaning the kitchen, and he followed her as she took the besom brush made of coarse twigs to sweep the landing floor and give the mats a hefty

148

beating and return them. By the time Tellman left he had a fairly good idea of Cole's domestic life, ordinary, decent, and comfortably monotonous. As far as she knew, he spent every night alone in his bed, presumably asleep.

Tellman's next stop was the corner of Lincoln's Inn Fields, to ask passersby and local tradesmen if they remembered seeing Cole in his usual spot. It was hard to disentangle memory of one day from that of another.

The flower seller diagonally across leading to New Square was a little more help.

" 'E weren't there Sunday, 'cos folks don't buy on Sunday any'ow. Most of 'em in't 'ere," she said, scratching her head and pushing her bonnet a trifle crooked. " 'E were 'ere Monday, 'cos I seen 'im. 'Ad a word wif 'im. 'E said summink abaht gettin' a bit o' money soon. I laughed at 'im, 'cos I thought as 'e were 'avin' me on, like. But 'e said as 'e were serious. 'E wouldn't say as 'ow 'e were gonner get it. An' I never see'd 'im again."

"That would be Tuesday," he corrected.

"No, Monday," she assured him. "I always know me days, 'cos o' wot's 'appenin' in the *Fields*. Beanpole, 'e's the patterer, 'e tells us everythink. It were Monday. Tuesday 'e weren't 'ere. An' then on Thursday mornin' the police found 'is corpse in Bedford Square. Poor soul. 'E were or'right, 'e were."

"So where was he on Tuesday?" Tellman asked, puzzled.

"Dunno. I took it as 'e were sick or summink."

Tellman learned nothing more in Lincoln's Inn Fields, nor with close questioning at the Bull and Gate either.

In the afternoon he returned again to the mortuary. He loathed the place. On a warm day like this the smells seemed to be heavier, more claustrophobic, sticking in the back of his throat. It was a strange mixture of sharp and sour. But on a cold day the damp seemed to run from the walls and the chill of it ate into his bones, as if the whole place were like some scrubbed and artificial sort of public grave, only waiting to be closed over. He always half expected to find himself locked in.

"Nobody new for you," the attendant said with surprise.

"I want to see Albert Cole again." Tellman forced himself to say the words. It was the last thing on earth he really wanted, but where Cole had been on the day before he was killed could be the only clue as to what had happened to him. "Please."

" 'Course," the attendant agreed. "We got 'im in the ice 'ouse, all tucked up safe. Be with you in a trice."

Tellman's footsteps echoed as he followed obediently to the small, bitterly cold room where corpses were kept when the police still needed to be able to examine them in connection with crime.

Tellman felt his stomach clench, but he lifted back the sheet with an almost steady hand. The body was naked, and he felt intrusive. He knew so much and so little about this man when he had been alive. His skin was very pale over his torso and upper legs, but there was an ingrained grayness of dirt as well, and the stale odor was not entirely due to carbolic and dead flesh.

"What are you looking for?" the attendant asked helpfully.

Tellman was not sure. "Wounds, for a start," he answered. "He was a soldier in the 33rd. He saw a lot of action. He was invalided out. Shot in the leg."

"No, 'e weren't," the attendant said with certainty. "Might a' broke a bone or two. Couldn't tell that without cutting 'im open. But shot goes through the skin, leaves a scar. There's a knife scar on 'is arm, an' another on 'is chest, down the side of 'is ribs. In't nuthink on 'is legs, but look for yerself."

"It was on his military record," Tellman argued. "I saw it. He was wounded very badly."

"Look for yerself!" the attendant repeated.

Tellman did so. The legs of the corpse were cold, the flesh slack when he touched it. But there were no scars, no marks where a bullet or musket ball had smashed in. This man had certainly not been shot, in the legs or anywhere else.

The attendant was watching him curiously.

"Wrong records?" he asked, twisting up his face. "Or wrong corpse?"

"I don't know," Tellman replied. He bit his lip. "I suppose

150

any records could be wrong, but it doesn't seem likely. But if this isn't Albert Cole, who is it? And why did he have Albert Cole's socks receipt on him? Why would anybody steal a receipt for three pairs of socks?"

"Beats me." The attendant shrugged. " 'Ow are yer gonner find out 'oo this poor devil is, then? Could be anyone."

Tellman thought furiously. "Well, it's someone who spends a lot of time out on the streets, in boots that don't fit very well. Look at the calluses on his feet. And he's dirty, but he's not a manual worker. His hands are too soft, but his nails are broken, and they were before he fought off his attacker because the dirt is in them. He's thin . . . and he looks a lot like Albert Cole . . . enough that the lawyer who passed Cole regularly and bought bootlaces from him thought it was him."

"Lawyer?" The attendant shrugged. "Don' suppose 'e looked at 'is face much. More like looked at the laces an' jus' passed a word or two."

Tellman thought that was very probably true.

"So where yer gonner start lookin', then?" The attendant was eager, almost proprietorial about the matter.

"With people who said Albert Cole was a thief," Tellman replied with sudden decision. "Beginning with the pawnbroker. Maybe it was this man who took the stolen things to him."

"Good thinking," the attendant said respectfully. "Drop in when yer passin' by. 'Ave a cup o' tea and tell me wot 'appens."

"Thank you," Tellman answered with no intention whatever of coming back if he were not driven by inescapable duty. He would write a letter!

The pawnbroker was anything but pleased to see him. His face registered his disgust when Tellman was barely through the door.

"I told yer! I get nothin' 'ere as is stolen, far as I know. Get orff me back and leave me alone!"

Tellman stood exactly where he was. He stared at the man, seeing his anger and discomfort with pleasure.

151

"You said Albert Cole came in here and sold you gold rings and other bits and pieces he found in the sewers."

"That's right. An' so 'e did." The pawnbroker squared his chin.

"No, you said it was the man whose picture I showed you," Tellman corrected. "Thinnish sort of man, fair hair going bald a bit at the front, hatchet face, break in one eyebrow . . ."

"An' you said it were a geezer called Albert Cole wot was a soldier and got 'isself killed in Bedford Square," the pawnbroker agreed. "So wot of it? I din't kill 'im an' dunno 'oo did."

"Right! I told you it was Albert Cole." Tellman hated having to admit it. "Well, it seems it wasn't. Army records. So now I'd like to know who it was. And I'm sure you would like to be of assistance in identifying the poor devil, since you can earn the favor of the police without dropping anyone else in it. Think again . . . anything you can tell me about this man who claimed he was a tosher. Perhaps he really was, and not a bootlace peddler at all?"

The pawnbroker's face twisted with contempt. "Well if 'e were a tosher 'e didn't find much as I ever saw. Some o' them toshers down west does real well. I'd a' never believed rich folks was so careless with their gold an' stuff."

"So tell me everything you know about him," Tellman insisted, letting his eyes wander around the shelves speculatively. "That's a nice clock. Handsome for the kind of person who needs to pawn their things."

The pawnbroker bristled. "We get some very classy people in 'ere. And bad times can 'it anyone. 'It you one day, mebbe, then yer'll not look down on folks so easy."

"Well, if they do, I won't have a clock like that to hock," Tellman replied. "I'd better go to the police station and make sure the owner isn't suddenly in a position to redeem it. Like perhaps it's on a list of missing property. Now, this man who came and sold you jewelry, what do you remember about him—everything!"

The pawnbroker leaned forward over his counter. "Look, I'll tell yer everything I know, then will you get aht an' leave me alone? 'E came in 'ere once an' some woman came in. Lottie Menken; she lives up the corner about fifty yards. She come ter 'ock 'er teapot, does it reg'lar, poor cow. She knows 'im. Called 'im Joe, or summink like that. Go an' find 'er. She'll tell yer 'oo 'e is."

"Thank you," Tellman said gratefully. "If you're lucky, you won't see me again."

The pawnbroker breathed out a prayer, or it might have been a blasphemy.

It took Tellman nearly an hour to find Lottie Menken. She was a short woman, so immensely stout that she moved with a kind of rolling gait. Her black, ringletted hair sat on her head in uncombed profusion, rather like a hat.

"Yeah?" she said when Tellman addressed her. She was busy in her scullery making soap, which she did for a living. There were tubs of animal fats and oils to mix with soda for hard soap, but far more in quantity to mix with potash to make soft soap, which was more economical to use. He saw on shelves above her, which she presumably used the kitchen stools to reach, jars of powder blue and stone blue for the final rinse which would help remove the coarse yellowish color given by starch or natural in linen of a lower quality.

He knew better than to interrupt her work. He leant against one of the benches, casually, as if he belonged in this neighborhood, as indeed he had once in one just like it.

"I believe you know a thinnish sort of fair-haired bloke called Joe who sells things to Abbott's pawnshop now and again. That right?"

"What if I do?" she asked without looking up. Measurements must be right or the resultant soap would be no good. "Dunno 'im much, just ter see, or pass a word."

"What's his full name?"

"Josiah Slingsby. Why?" Still without looking up, she asked him, " 'Oo are yer, an' w'y d'yer care? I in't gettin' mixed up in any o' Slingsby's business, so yer can take yerself orff outa 'ere. Go on—get aht!" Her face closed in anger, and perhaps it was also fear.

"I think he may be dead," he said without moving.

153

For the first time she stopped working, her hands still, the liquid almost up to her rolled sleeves. "Joe Slingsby dead? Wot makes yer say that?"

"I think he was the body found in Bedford Square, not Albert Cole."

This time she actually turned to look at him. There was an expression in her face which Tellman thought was hope.

"Perhaps you would come and take a look at him?" he asked. "See if it is. You'd know." He understood the cost of wasting time for her. "It would be a service to the police which naturally you would be paid for . . . say, a shilling?"

She looked interested, but not yet certain.

"Cold work, identifying corpses," he added. "We'd need a good hot dinner afterwards, and a glass of porter."

"Yeah, I suppose we would at that." She nodded, setting her ringlets turning. "Well then, we'd best be about it. W'ere is this corpse that's mebbe Joe Slingsby?"

The following day Tellman went straight to see Pitt at Bow Street, to catch him before he should go out and to inform him that the body was definitely not that of Albert Cole but of Josiah Slingsby, petty thief and brawler.

Pitt looked nonplussed.

"Slingsby? How do you know?"

Tellman stood in front of the desk as Pitt stared up at him over the scattered papers on its surface.

"Identified by someone who knew him," he replied. "I don't think she was mistaken or lying. She described the gap in his eyebrow and she knew about the knife wound in his chest. Remembered when it happened a couple of years ago. It certainly isn't Albert Cole; military records make that plain, because of the shot. Cole was invalided out of the army with his leg wound. The corpse had none. Sorry, sir." He did not elaborate. Pitt deserved an apology, but not a long story, and certainly not an excuse.

Pitt leaned back in his chair and pushed his hands into his pockets. "I suppose the barrister who identified him did his best. I daresay he wasn't used to corpses. Most people aren't. And we rather assumed it was Cole because of the socks. Which brings us to the interesting question of why he had Albert Cole's receipt in his pocket. Or was it his own?"

"Don't think so. He didn't live anywhere near Red Lion Square; lived miles away, in Shoreditch. I checked yesterday afternoon. Nobody around Holborn had ever seen or heard of him—not on the streets, not in the pub. Far as I can see, he never met Albert Cole or had anything to do with him. The more I think of it, the less sense it makes. Slingsby was a thief, but why would anybody steal a receipt for socks? They're only worth a few pence. Nobody keeps that sort of thing more than a day or two, if that."

Pitt chewed his lip. "So what was Slingsby doing in Bedford Square? Thieving?"

Tellman pulled the other chair over and sat down. "Probably. But the funny thing is, nobody's seen Cole either. He's disappeared as well. His things were left in his room and his rent is paid up, but nobody's seen him on his patch or in the Bull and Gate. But he was there on Monday, when Slingsby was in his usual haunts as well. We are definitely dealing with two different men who only happen to look alike."

"And Slingsby was found dead with Cole's receipt in his pocket," Pitt added. "Did he take it from Cole for some reason we haven't thought of? Or did someone else, some third party we don't know about, take it from Cole and give it to Slingsby? And if so, why?"

"Maybe there's some stupid little reason we haven't thought of," Tellman said without meaning it. He was just casting around hopefully. "Maybe it doesn't have anything to do with why Slingsby was killed."

"And why he had General Balantyne's snuffbox in his pocket," Pitt added. "General Balantyne was being blackmailed. . . ."

Tellman was startled. His opinion of Balantyne was poor, as it was of all privileged men like him, but it was a contempt for those who took from society more than they put in and

155

who assumed an authority they had not earned. It was something most people accepted, and it was certainly not a crime.

"What did he do?" he asked, tilting his chair back a little.

A quick flare of anger crossed Pitt's face, and suddenly a gulf opened up between them. All the old hostilities and barriers were there again, just as when Pitt had first been given command of Bow Street. They were both of humble origin. Pitt was no more than a gamekeeper's son, but he had aspirations to something more. He spoke like a gentleman and tried to behave as if he were one. Tellman was faithful to his roots and his class. He would fight the enemy, not join them.

"He did nothing," Pitt said icily, and perhaps rashly. "But he cannot easily prove it, and the accusation would ruin him. It refers to an incident in the Abyssinian Campaign, in which, as you proved, Albert Cole was also involved. Whether Josiah Slingsby had anything to do with the blackmail is what we have yet to learn."

"The snuffbox!" Tellman said with satisfaction. "Payment?" And the moment the words were out he regretted them. Automatically, he straightened up in his chair.

Pitt's face was a picture of scorn. "For a pinchbeck snuffbox? Hardly worth the effort, is it? Josiah Slingsby might murder for a few guineas, but Balantyne wouldn't."

Tellman felt himself clench with anger, for his own stupidity. He knew it showed in his face, much as he tried to conceal it.

"The snuffbox might not be all of it," he said sharply. "Might only be one payment. We don't know what else he may have given him. Maybe that was the last of many, and the General just lost his temper? Perhaps he realized he was never going to be rid of him and would just be bled dry and then maybe ruined anyway?"

"And Cole's socks?" Pitt asked.

"Makes sense." Tellman leaned forward, eagerly now, putting one hand on the desk. "Cole and Slingsby were in it together. Cole was the one who told him, maybe he knew how he would use the information, maybe not. Maybe Slingsby killed Cole over the proceeds?"

156

"Except that it's Slingsby who's dead," Pitt pointed out.

"All right, then Cole killed him," Tellman argued.

"Which leaves Balantyne innocent," Pitt said with a tight smile.

Tellman refrained from swearing only with difficulty. "That's one thing that would be possible," he conceded. "Don't know enough to say yet."

"No, we don't," Pitt agreed. "So you'd better find out all you can about it. See if you can discover any connection between Slingsby and Balantyne, and if Balantyne had paid out anything apart from the snuffbox, or done anything that could have been forced on him by Slingsby."

"Yes sir." Tellman stood up, but casually, not to attention.

"And Tellman . . ."

"Yes?"

"This time you'd better report direct to me, here, not at home. . . ."

Tellman felt the heat burn up his face, but there was nothing he could say that would not only make it worse. He refused to stoop to giving explanations that might be taken for excuses. He stood stiff and unanswering.

"I don't want anyone else to know you are enquiring into his life," Pitt emphasized. "Or following him. Is that clear? And 'anyone' includes Gracie and Mrs. Pitt."

"Yes sir. Is that all?"

"It's enough," Pitt replied. "At least for the present."

The following morning's newspapers were filled with two scandals. One was the continuing saga of the Tranby Croft affair, growing increasingly ugly with every new revelation. It now appeared that, after the initial accusation of cheating at baccarat, Gordon-Cumming had been persuaded to sign a letter promising never to refer to the matter with another soul.

Then two days after Christmas, Gordon-Cumming had received an anonymous letter from Paris mentioning the Tranby Croft affair and advising him never to touch cards if he should come to France, because there was much talk about the subject.

157

Naturally, he was horrified. The pledge of secrecy had very obviously been broken.

Nor had that been the end of it. Shortly after that, news had come of the story from another source, the Prince of Wales's latest mistress, Lady Frances Brooke, an inveterate gossip nicknamed "Babbling Brooke."

Gordon-Cumming wrote to his commanding officer, Colonel Stracey, sending in his papers and asking leave to retire from the army on half pay.

A week later General Williams and Lord Coventry, the two friends and advisers of the Prince, visited Sir Redvers Butler at the War Office and formally told him all about the events at Tranby Croft that weekend, then requested a full enquiry by the military authorities at the earliest possible moment.

Gordon-Cumming appealed to Butler to delay such an enquiry in order not to prejudice his own pending civil action for slander.

The Prince of Wales wound himself into a state of all but nervous exhaustion over the prospect of having to testify, but to no effect. The other witnesses, the Wilsons, the Lycett Greens and Levett, all refused to withdraw their charges of cheating.

Now the case was being heard before the Lord Chief Justice, Lord Coleridge, and a special jury. In the glorious sunshine of a hot, early July, the courtroom was packed, and the public hung on every word.

Pitt was interested in the case only for its reflection on the fragility of reputation, and how easily a man, any man, could be ruined by a suggestion, let alone a fact.

Lower down the page, another scandal caught his eye. It was a story printed beneath a photograph of Sir Guy Stanley, M.P., speaking with a very strikingly dressed woman named in the caption as Mrs. Robert Shaughnessy. They had been caught in a moment's close conversation. Mr. Shaughnessy was a young man with radical political ambitions, contrary to government policy. He had lately succeeded in a brilliant move towards his aims, greatly assisted by what looked like inside information. In the picture, he had his back turned to his wife and Sir Guy and was looking away.

The story below suggested that Sir Guy, a favored candidate for a ministerial position, had been far more intimate with Mrs. Shaughnessy than was consistent with morality or honor, and threaded through the ambiguous phrases was the implication that he had let slip government business in return for her favors. There was also a difference of some thirty years in their ages, which made it uglier and lent it a sordid and pathetic air.

If Sir Guy Stanley had been hoping for preferment, he would not now receive it. A blow like this to a man's reputation, whether the suggestion was founded or not, would make him an impossible choice for the post in the government for which his name had been put forward.

Pitt sat at the breakfast table holding the newspaper in his hand, his toast and marmalade forgotten, his tea growing cold.

"What is it?" Charlotte asked anxiously.

"I'm not sure," he said slowly. He read out the article about Guy Stanley, then lowered the paper and met her eyes. "Is it coincidence, or is this the first threat carried out as a warning to the others?" He wondered what could have precipitated it.

"Even if it isn't," she pointed out, "it will serve the same purpose." She was pale faced as she put her cup down in its saucer. "As if the Tranby Croft business were not enough without this. It will reinforce the blackmailer's message, whether this was his doing or not. Do you know anything about Guy Stanley?"

"No more than I've read here."

"And this Mrs. Shaughnessy?"

"Nothing at all." He took a deep breath and pushed away his plate. "I think I must go and see Sir Guy. I need to know if he had a letter. More than that, I need to know what he was asked to do . . . and had the courage to refuse."

Charlotte remained silent. She sat with her body tense, her shoulders pulling at the rose-colored cotton of her dress, but there was nothing more to say.

159

He touched her lightly on the cheek as he passed, and went out to collect his boots and his hat.

The newspaper had given Guy Stanley's address, and Pitt alighted from the hansom half a block away and walked briskly in the warm morning air up to the house and rang the doorbell.

It was answered by a footman who informed him that Sir Guy was not in and would not be receiving callers. He was about to close the door again, leaving Pitt on the step. Pitt produced his card and held it out.

"I am afraid it is police business about which I need to see your master and it cannot wait," he said firmly.

The footman looked highly dubious, but it was not within the bounds of his authority to refuse the police, in spite of the orders he had been given to admit no one.

He left Pitt on the step while he went to enquire, carrying the card on his silver tray.

The slight wind was already welcome in the rising heat of this unusual July. By midday it would be sweltering. It was an uncomfortable wait, reminding Pitt sharply of his social status. A gentleman would have been asked in, even if left in the morning room.

The footman returned with a look of slight surprise and conducted Pitt into a large study, where he had only a moment to wait before the door opened and Sir Guy Stanley came in. He was a tall, thin man only barely recognizable from the newspaper photograph, which must have been taken at least two or three years previously. His white hair was markedly thinner now, and his side-whiskers shorter and neater. He walked carefully, as if uncertain of his balance, and he banged his elbow against the oak-paneled door as he closed it. His face was almost bloodless.

Pitt's heart sank. Stanley did not look like a man who had faced the enemy down, at whatever the cost, but like someone who had received a fearful and unexpected blow. He was still reeling with the shock and barely in command of himself.

"Good morning, Mr. . . ." He glanced at the card in his hand. "Mr. Pitt. I am afraid this is not a fortunate morning for me, but if you tell me in what way I may be of assistance, I shall do what I can." He indicated the overstuffed chairs, leather buttoned into complex patterns. "Please sit down." He almost fell into the closest of them himself, as if not certain he could remain on his feet any longer.

Pitt sat opposite him. "There is no pleasant or diplomatic way of putting this, sir, so I shall avoid wasting your time and simply tell you the situation. However, I shall omit the names of the people concerned in consideration of their reputations, as I will yours, should you be able to assist me."

There was no understanding in Stanley's face, only polite resignation. He was listening only because he had promised to.

"Four prominent men of my acquaintance are being blackmailed—" Pitt began. He stopped abruptly, seeing the sudden blaze of interest in Stanley's face, the rush of blood up his thin cheeks and the clenching of his hands on the wood-and-leather arms of the chair.

Pitt smiled bleakly. "I believe each to be innocent of the charge leveled against him by the writer of the letters, but unfortunately, in every case it is almost impossible to prove it. They are also, in every case, the offenses of which each would be most profoundly ashamed, and therefore peculiarly vulnerable to pressure."

"I see. . . ." Stanley curled and uncurled his fingers on the arm of the chair.

"No money was asked for," Pitt continued. "In fact, so far nothing at all has been named, or given, except one small token of faith . . . or if you like, submission."

Stanley's hands knotted more tightly.

"I see. And what is it you think I may be able to help you with, Mr. Pitt? I have no idea who it is or how to battle against such a thing." He smiled with bitter self-mockery. "Surely today I am the last man in England to offer advice on the safeguarding of one's honor or reputation."

Pitt had already decided to be honest.

"Before I came here, Sir Guy, I had wondered if perhaps you were also a victim of this man, and when he had named his price for silence, you had told him to go to the devil."

"You thought better of me than I had warranted," Stanley said very quietly, the color bright on his thin cheeks. "I am afraid I did not tell him to go to the devil, in spite of profoundly wishing him there." He looked at Pitt very steadily. "He only asked one very small thing of me, a silver-plated brandy flask, as a token of good faith. Or perhaps 'surrender' would be more accurate."

"You gave it to him?" Pitt asked, dreading the answer.

"Yes," Stanley replied. "His threat was couched in roundabout terms, but it was perfectly plain. As you no doubt observed in this morning's newspapers, he has carried it out." He shook his head a little, a gesture of confusion, not of denial. "He gave me no warning, no further threat, and he did not ask for anything." He smiled very faintly. "I like to think I would not have given it him, but now I shall never know. I am not sure whether I really wish I had tested myself . . . or not. I have my illusions still . . . but no certainty. Is that better, do you think?"

He stood up and walked towards the window facing the garden, not the street. "In my better moments I shall believe I would have damned him, and gone down with my own honor intact, no matter what the world thought. In my worse ones, when I am tired or alone, I shall be convinced my nerve would have failed, and I should have surrendered."

Pitt was disappointed. He was startled by how much he had been trusting that Stanley had actually been asked for something specific, even use of his influence, and had precipitated this act by his refusal. It would have been an indication of what to expect regarding the others. It might even have narrowed the field to who the blackmailer might be.

Stanley saw his face and read the emotion correctly, but misjudged the reason for it. The hurt was in his eyes, and the shame.

Pitt shrugged very slightly. "A pity. I'm sorry to have intruded at such a time. I came because I hoped he had tipped

162

his hand far enough to ask you for some abuse of influence or power, and then we would know what he wanted. You see, the other victims are men in many different fields of achievement, and I can see no common link between them."

"I'm sorry," Stanley said sincerely. "I wish I could be of help. Naturally, I have racked my mind as to who it could be. I have gone over every personal enemy or rival, anyone I might have slighted or insulted, anyone whose career I have affected adversely, whether intentionally or not, but I can think of no one who would stoop to such a thing."

"Not Shaughnessy himself?" Pitt asked with little hope.

Stanley smiled. "I disagree profoundly with everything Shaughnessy believes in and is trying to bring about, with a great deal more chance of success lately, but he is open about it, a man to meet you face-to-face and fight his cause, not resort to blackmail or secrecy."

He gave a very slight shrug, a weary little lift of one shoulder. "Apart from which, if you consider recent political history, such an effort on his part would hardly be necessary. He already has all I could have given. Ruining me will taint his own cause, not help it. And he is not a fool." His lips tightened. "And although this picture"—he gestured to the newspaper lying on the desk—"paints me as gullible and treacherous, it also paints his wife as a whore, not a thing any man wants in the eyes of the public, whatever the truth in private may be. And although I do not know Mrs. Shaughnessy nearly as well as the comments imply, I have observed her on many occasions, and I have seen no cause to doubt her virtue."

"Yes . . . of course," Pitt was forced to agree. Shaughnessy had no motive, whether he had the means and the opportunity or not. "Do you still have the letter?"

Distaste curled Stanley's thin lips. "No. I burnt it, in case anyone should chance to see it. But I can describe it to you. It was cut from the *Times*, in some cases individual letters, sometimes whole words, and pasted onto a sheet of plain white paper. It was posted in central London."

"Can you recall what it said?"

163

"I see by your face that that is what you expected," Stanley observed. "I assume the others were the same?"

"Yes."

Stanley let out his breath in a sigh. "I see. Yes, I think I can, not perhaps word for word, but the intent. It stated that I had given Mrs. Shaughnessy government information helpful to her husband in return for her physical favors, and should such a thing become known I would be ruined, and most certainly fail to receive the ministerial appointment I had hoped for. It asked that as a pledge of my understanding I should give to the writer a token gift; a small silver-plated flask would serve very well. Instructions were included as to how I should parcel it up and give it to a messenger on a bicycle who would call for it."

Pitt sat forward a little. "How did he know that you possessed such a thing?"

"I have no idea. I admit, his knowledge unnerved me considerably." Stanley shivered very slightly. "I felt . . . as if he were observing me all the time . . . unseen . . . but always there. I suspected everyone. . . ." His voice tailed off, defeated, full of pain.

"And did you give him the flask?" Pitt asked in the silence that followed.

"Exactly as instructed," Stanley replied. "In order to give myself time to think. It was asked for immediately, to be collected that day."

"I see," Pitt replied. "It fits the pattern of the others. Thank you for your candor, Sir Guy. I wish I could offer any way of mitigating this circumstance, but I know of none. However, I shall do everything within my power to find this man and bring some kind of justice on him." He meant it with a vehemence that startled him. There was a rage inside him that was almost choking, as real as for any murder or violence of the flesh.

"Some kind of justice?" Stanley questioned.

"The extortion of a silver-plated flask is not a very great crime," Pitt pointed out bitterly. "And if you can prove that he has libeled you, then you may sue for damages, but that is your decision rather than mine. It is a course most men hesitate to pursue, simply because to take the issue to court brings it far more publicity than to say nothing. Poor Gordon-Cumming and the Tranby Croft affair is surely the most eloquent proof of that that one could ask." He stood up, instinctively holding out his hand.

"I am well aware of it, Mr. Pitt," Stanley said ruefully, taking Pitt's hand and grasping it. "And all the proof in the world would not undo the damage in the public's eyes. That is the nature of scandal. Its tarnish hardly ever wears off. I suppose it will be some satisfaction if you catch the devil. But I daresay he is a man whose own reputation would be little hurt by the exposure of his acts."

"There I disagree with you," Pitt said with sudden satisfaction. "I think he is a man whose intimate knowledge of his victims indicates he may well be of a similar social standing. I travel in hope."

Stanley looked at him very directly. "If I can be of any assistance whatever, Mr. Pitt, please call on me at any time. I am now a far more dangerous enemy than I was yesterday, because I have nothing left to lose."

Pitt took his leave and went out into the hot sun. The air was completely still, and the pungent odor of horse droppings came sharply to his nose. A carriage passed by, loud on the stones, the brass on the harness winking in the light, ladies with parasols up to shade their faces, footmen in livery sweating.

Pitt was not more than fifty yards along the street when he saw Lyndon Remus coming towards him, his expression alight with recognition.

Pitt felt himself tense with dislike, which was unjust, and he knew it. Remus had not written the article exposing Sir Guy Stanley. But he was there ready to make capital of it.

"Good morning, Superintendent!" he said eagerly. "Been visiting Stanley, I see. Are you investigating the allegations against him?"

165

"Whether Sir Guy's relationship with Mrs. Shaughnessy was proper or improper is none of my business, Mr. Remus," Pitt said coldly. "And I don't see that it is any of yours."

"Oh, come now, Mr. Pitt!" Remus's fair eyebrows shot up. "If a Member of Parliament is selling government information in exchange for a lady's favors, that is the business of every man in the kingdom."

"I have no evidence that he has done so." Pitt stood still on the hot pavement, facing him. "I have merely read the implication, made by innuendo in a newspaper. But if it should be, it is still not my concern. There are appropriate people to enquire into it, and I am not one of them, nor are you."

"I ask in the public interest, Mr. Pitt," Remus persisted, standing directly in front of him. "Surely you don't say that the ordinary citizen has no right to be concerned in the honesty and morality of the men whom he elects to govern him?"

Pitt knew he had to be careful. Remus would remember what he said, and perhaps even quote it.

"Of course not," he answered, measuring his words. "But there are proper ways of enquiring, and libel is a moral offense, even where it is occasionally not a civil one. I went to see Sir Guy Stanley on a completely different issue where I thought he might be able to give me some assistance from his experience. He did, but I am not able to discuss it with you because it would jeopardize a current investigation."

"The murder in Bedford Square?" Remus concluded swiftly. "Is Sir Guy involved in that?"

"Do you not understand me, Mr. Remus?" Pitt snapped. "I told you that it is a matter I cannot discuss, and I gave you the reasons. Surely you don't wish to hinder me, do you?"

"Well . . . no, of course not. But we have a right to know—"

"You have a right to ask," Pitt corrected him. "You have asked, and I have answered you. Now, would you please step out of my way. I must return to Bow Street."

Reluctantly, Remus did so.

In his room in the police station, Pitt considered Remus again. Was it worth having anyone enquire a little more closely about him? He was almost certainly simply doing his job with rather more relish than Pitt found pleasant. But investigation of corruption and abuse of office or privilege was a legitimate part of his duties, just as it was of Pitt's own. Society required such men, even if on occasion they trespassed into people's private lives in a way which was intrusive, painful and unjustified. The alternative was the beginning of tyranny and the loss of the right of society to understand itself and have any curb upon those who ruled it.

Still, the privilege of the press could also be abused. Membership in its ranks did not confer immunity from police enquiry. He could have someone see if Lyndon Remus had any connection with Albert Cole, Josiah Slingsby, or any of the men who were being blackmailed.

But before he could attend to that he was met with a message that Parthenope Tannifer wished to see him the very first moment it was possible, and would he please call upon her at her home.

He had expected it, not from Parthenope Tannifer, but from her husband, and possibly from Dunraithe White also, although since White had told Vespasia he had no intention of fighting the blackmailer, no matter what he should demand, perhaps he would not wish to draw police attention to himself.

Pitt also thought of how Balantyne would feel when he saw the morning newspapers. He must be ill with anxiety, and helpless even to know which way to turn to defend himself. He could not prove the original charge was untrue. He could not prove he had not killed the man on his doorstep, Cole or Slingsby. The fact that it was Slingsby did not clear Balantyne of suspicion; Slingsby could have been a messenger of the blackmailer.

Most of all as Pitt went down the stairs again and out into the hot, dusty street, he thought of Cornwallis, and the misery which he must feel this morning as he realized that the threats were fully intended and the blackmailer had no hesitation in carrying them out. He had the will and the means. He had demonstrated it now beyond doubt or hope.

Pitt was received in the Tannifer house immediately and was shown to Parthenope's boudoir, that peculiarly feminine sitting room where ladies read, embroidered, or gossiped pleasantly together with very rare intrusion from men.

This particular room was unlike others he had been in. The colors were very simple and cool, with none of the usual oriental affectations that had become so fashionable over the last decade. It was most individual, catering entirely to the taste of its owner, making no concessions to what was expected. The curtains were plain, cool green, no flowers. Similarly, the green glazed vase on the small table had no blooms; its own shape was sufficient ornament. The furniture was simple, old, very English.

"Thank you for coming so rapidly, Mr. Pitt," Parthenope said as soon as the maid had closed the door. She was dressed in dusky blue-gray with a white fichu at the throat, and it became her well enough, in spite of being rather severe. Something softer would have disguised her angular proportions. She looked extremely distressed and made no attempt to hide it. The morning newspaper was lying on the table beside her chair. Her embroidery was in a heap next to it, the needle stuck into the linen. Silks in shades of brown and taupe and cream spilled all around it where she had presumably left it last. Scissors and a silver thimble were on the carpet, as if dropped in haste.

"Have you seen it?" she demanded, pointing her finger at the newspaper. She stood in the center of the room, too angry to sit.

"Good morning, Mrs. Tannifer. If you are referring to the article about Sir Guy Stanley, yes, I have read it, and I have spoken to Sir Guy himself—"

"Have you?" she cut across him. "How is he?" Her eyes were bright, her face full of concern and pity, for a moment the fear overridden.

"Do you know him?" He was interested.

"No." She shook her head quickly. "But I can imagine what pain he is enduring at the moment."

168

"You assume he is innocent of the implications in the article," Pitt said with some surprise. It was a kinder judgment than many people would be making.

She smiled briefly, like a flash of sunlight, there and gone. "I suppose that is because I know my husband is innocent. Am I mistaken?" That was a demand, almost a challenge.

"Not so far as I know," he replied. "Sir Guy is a victim of the same letter writer as Mr. Tannifer, and therefore I believe him when he says the charge is unfounded."

Her voice dropped a little. "But he had the courage to defy him . . . as the Duke of Wellington said, 'Publish and be damned!' How I admire him!" Her voice rang with sincerity, and there was a faint flush in her cheeks. "What a terrible price to pay. I cannot imagine he will now obtain the post in the government that he desired. His only comfort will be his own courage, and perhaps the respect of those friends who know him well enough to dismiss the accusation." She took a deep breath and straightened her slender shoulders. There was a warmth in her tone that lent an extraordinary beauty to her voice. "I hope we shall face the future as well. I shall write to him this morning and tell him of my regard for him. It may be of some small comfort. It is all I can do."

He did not know how to answer her. He did not want to lie, and perhaps he could not afford to if he were to learn anything from her; but neither was he prepared to lay open Stanley's confidences, and his own personal doubts.

"You hesitate, Mr. Pitt," she observed, watching him closely. "There is something you do not wish to tell me. It is worse than I feared?"

"No, Mrs. Tannifer, I was merely considering how to phrase what I say so I do not betray confidences. Even though Sir Guy Stanley and Mr. Tannifer are in the same situation, I would not discuss one with the other to their embarrassment."

"Of course!" she agreed quickly. "That is admirable. But have you learned anything more about who this devil may be? Surely all information must be helpful? I . . . I called you today not just because I am at my wit's end to know what to do, how even to begin to fight this battle, but because I have information to give you myself. Please sit down." She indicated the soft, plain chair opposite her own.

Pitt did as he was bid as soon as she had seated herself. Suddenly there was a lift of hope.

"Yes, Mrs. Tannifer? What have you learned?"

She leaned forward a little, leaving her skirts disarranged as they had crumpled in the chair. "We have received a second letter, in much the same terms as the first, but rather more direct, using words like *cheat* and *embezzler*. . . ." Her cheeks colored with embarrassment and anger. "It is so unjust! Sigmund has never profited a ha'penny except by his own skill and judgment. He is the most honorable man I have ever known. My own father was a soldier, the colonel of a regiment. I know much of honor and loyalty, and the complete trust one must have in everything, and how it must be earned." She lowered her gaze. "I'm sorry. That is not what you want to know. We are already assuming all the accusations are unjust. This one was cut from the *Times* as well, and glued onto a sheet of ordinary paper. It came by the first post. It was put in a box in the City, just like before. Only the wording was different." She looked up at him.

"But did he ask for anything, Mrs. Tannifer?"

"No." She shook her head. Her thin hands were clenched in her lap, her eyes grave and troubled. "He seems to be some kind of monster who merely wishes to inflict pain and terror upon people for no gain to himself beyond the pleasure it affords him." She looked at him with desperate earnestness. "But I believe I know who may be another victim, Mr. Pitt. I have hesitated whether to tell you or not, and the fact that I do so may not please my husband. But I am distracted to know how to face this matter and avoid just the kind of ruin he has cost poor Sir Guy Stanley."

Pitt leaned forward. "Tell me what you know, Mrs. Tannifer. It may help, and I doubt very strongly that it can hurt any more than will be inevitable, regardless of what we do."

She took a deep breath and let it out slowly. She was obvi-

170

ously embarrassed by what she had done, and yet the determination in her to fight, to defend her husband, did not waver in the slightest.

"I had been in the study with my husband, discussing the matter. He is far more troubled by it than I believe he allowed you to see. It is much more than financial ruin or the loss of career; it is the knowledge that ordinary people, friends, those whom one admires and whose opinions mean so much, will believe you to be dishonorable . . . that is what hurts beyond any reparation. Perhaps when all is said and done, a quiet conscience is the greatest possession, but a good name in the eyes of others is second."

He did not argue. He knew how dear to himself he held the belief in others that he was honest, and perhaps even more, that he was generous, that he never deliberately caused pain.

"What did you hear, Mrs. Tannifer?"

"I had just left, but I did not quite close the door. I was in the hallway when I heard my husband pick up the telephone. We have one; it is an excellent instrument. He placed a call to Mr. Leo Cadell, of the Foreign Office. At first I was about to continue on my way to the kitchen—I was intending to speak to the cook— but I heard his voice change. Suddenly he became very grave, and there was both sympathy and fear in his tone."

She regarded Pitt intently. "I know my husband very well. We have always been extremely close, and keep nothing from each other. I knew straightaway that Mr. Cadell had told him something grave and confidential. I concluded from what I could hear of my husband's part of the conversation that Mr. Cadell had asked about raising money, a large amount, at very short notice. He is a man of considerable means, but it does not necessarily follow that a large sum can be realized with ease. Good financial advice is imperative if one is not to lose a great deal." She took a breath. "Sigmund tried to be of every assistance to him, but I know from what he said that he guessed it was to pay some suddenly incurred debt, the size of which was not yet known, but it could not be avoided or delayed in any way."

171

"It does sound as if it could be blackmail," Pitt agreed. "But if that is the case, he is the first one to be asked for anything specific. No one else has been asked for money at all."

"I am not certain that is what it was," she conceded. "But I heard the tone of Sigmund's voice, and I saw his face afterwards." She shook her head quickly. "He would not discuss it with me, of course, because whatever Mr. Cadell told him was in confidence, but it was not an ordinary matter of luxuries. Sigmund was deeply troubled, and when we spoke, he referred to the blackmail letter again and asked me how deeply I would mind if we were to find ourselves in greatly reduced circumstances. Would I be prepared to leave London and live somewhere quite different, even in another country, if it should come to that." Her voice was strong, full of confidence. "I said that of course I would. As long as we kept our honor and went together, I should live anywhere and do anything that necessity drove us to." She lifted her chin and looked very directly into Pitt's eyes. "I should rather be ruined by libel like poor Sir Guy Stanley than pay a halfpenny to this monster and feed his evil."

"Thank you for your frankness, Mrs. Tannifer." Pitt meant intensely what he said. She was a remarkable woman possessed of a courage and loyalty he admired, and at the same time in her there was passion, and a fierce knowledge and ability to feel pain. Her compassion for Stanley was not born purely of imagination.

He rose to his feet to take his leave.

"Will it help?" she demanded, standing also. "Will you be able to learn anything further?"

"I don't know," he admitted. "But I shall certainly go to see Mr. Cadell. He may be able to tell me more about what he has been asked for, and possibly what he is threatened regarding. All information should narrow the possibilities as to who could have known enough to write the letter. In each case the victim is accused of the sort of offense likely to hurt him the most deeply. That speaks of a certain knowledge, Mrs. Tannifer. If you should learn anything more, please call me immediately."

"Of course. Godspeed, Mr. Pitt." She stood in the center of her uniquely peaceful room, a slender, rather angular figure of burning emotion. "Find the devil who does this . . . for us all!"

7

As soon as Pitt had left to go and see Sir Guy Stanley, Charlotte picked up the newspaper and read the article again. She did not know if Stanley had been threatened by the blackmailer or not, or what he might have been asked for, and really it was irrelevant. Whatever the truth of the matter was, the other victims would feel the same horror and pity for him, and fear for themselves. Whether it was a fortuitous accident or a deliberate warning to them, the result would be exactly the same, a tightening of the pressure, perhaps this time almost beyond bearing.

She explained her intentions very briefly to Gracie, then went upstairs and changed into the same yellow morning dress she had worn on the first occasion, because it was the one in which she felt most confident, and then set out to walk to Bedford Square.

Her sense of outrage and anxiety carried her all the way to the doorstep of Balantyne's house, and when the door was opened she explained with the greatest simplicity that she had come to call upon the General, if he was in and would receive her.

However, she was crossing the hall when she encountered Lady Augusta, dressed magnificently in browns and golds. Augusta came down the stairs just as Charlotte reached the foot with its elaborately carved newel.

"Good morning, Mrs. Pitt," she said icily, her eyes wide, her brows arched. "Over what hitherto unknown disaster

174

have you come to commiserate with us today? Has some catastrophe occurred of which my husband has not yet informed me?"

Charlotte was too angry to be awed by Augusta, or anyone else, and she had been lately in Vespasia's presence. Something of the older woman's supreme confidence had rubbed off. She stopped and regarded Augusta with equal chill.

"Good morning, Lady Augusta. So kind of you to be interested. But then as I recall, you were always a person of warmth and most generous judgment of others." She ignored the flush of anger on Augusta's face. "The answer to your question rather depends upon whether you are just descending for the first time today, or if you have already been down, perhaps for breakfast?" Again she overrode Augusta's sharply indrawn breath and obvious irritation. "I am afraid the news is most distressing. There is a highly scurrilous article about Sir Guy Stanley. And of course the usual miserable disclosures about the Tranby Croft affair, although I did not read that."

"Then how do you know they are miserable?" Augusta snapped.

Charlotte widened her eyes very slightly, as if a mere flicker of surprise had touched her.

"I regard it as miserable that an unfortunate matter of gentlemen's behavior while playing cards should have passed into public dispute and comment," she replied. "Was I mistaken in imagining that you would also?"

Augusta's face was tight. "No, of course you weren't!" she said through her teeth.

"I'm so glad," Charlotte murmured, wishing profoundly that Balantyne would appear and rescue the situation.

Augusta was not easily bested. She resumed the attack. "Then since it is not the Tranby Croft affair which brings you here, I must assume it is because you have supposed that Sir Guy Stanley's misfortune is somehow of concern to us. I do not believe I am acquainted with him."

"Indeed . . ." Charlotte said vaguely, as if the remark was completely irrelevant, as indeed it was.

175

Augusta was now visibly irritated. "No! So why should you imagine that I am sufficiently distressed by his misfortune, deserved or not, that I should require your sympathy, Mrs. Pitt? Particularly at"—she glanced at the long case clock in the hall—"half past nine in the morning!" Her tone of voice conveyed how outlandish it was that anyone at all should call at such an unheard-of hour.

"I am sure," Charlotte agreed with surprising calm, wishing even more fervently the General would appear. "Had I thought for a moment you were . . . concerned . . . I should have sent you my card, and called by at three."

"Then not only is your journey unnecessary," Augusta retorted, glancing again at the clock, "but you are somewhat early."

Charlotte smiled at her dazzlingly, wondering frantically what she could say. Apart from her desire to see Balantyne, she hated to be beaten by a woman she realized she loathed— not for anything she might have said or done to Charlotte, but for her coldness towards her own husband.

"I cannot assume you could be aware of General Balantyne's regard for Sir Guy and remain so unconcerned," she said with glittering and spurious charm. "That would be too uncharitable. Indeed, it would be heartless . . . which no one would think of you. . . ."

Augusta drew in her breath and let it out again.

There were footsteps along the passageway, and General Balantyne appeared in the hall. He saw Charlotte and started forward.

"Mrs. Pitt! How are you this morning?" His face was haggard with anxiety, fear and distress. The skin around his eyes was shadowy and paper-thin, the lines at his mouth deeper.

She turned to him with immense relief, effectively dismissing Augusta.

"I am quite well," she answered, meeting his look frankly. "But I found the news appalling. I had not foreseen such a thing, and I don't yet really know what to make of it. Thomas has gone there, of course, but I will not know what he has learned until this evening, if he will discuss it at all."

176

Balantyne looked beyond her to Augusta and saw the expression in his wife's face. Charlotte did not turn.

Augusta made a slight sound, as if she thought of saying something, and then reconsidered. There was a sharp swish of skirts and a rustle and tap of feet as she walked away.

Charlotte still did not turn.

"It was kind of you to come," Balantyne said quietly. "I admit I am extraordinarily glad to see you." He led the way to his study and opened the door for her. Inside was warm and bright, and comfortable with long use. There was no fire lit— the unusually hot summer did not require one—and there was a large, green-glazed vase full of white lilies on the drum table. The flowers perfumed the whole room and seemed to catch the sunlight from the long windows.

He closed the door.

"You read the newspaper?" she said immediately.

"I did. I don't know Guy Stanley well, but the poor devil must be feeling . . . beyond description." He ran his hands over his brow, pushing his hair hard back. "Of course, we don't even know yet if he is one of us, but I dare not believe he isn't. It almost seems irrelevant; this has shown just what ruin can come upon us with a whisper, an innuendo. As if we didn't know . . . with the Tranby Croft affair. Although I think Gordon-Cumming might well have been guilty."

Suddenly his face paled, tightening with pain. "God! What am I saying? I know no more of the man than rumor, the gossip that passes in the club, snatches overheard. That's exactly what is going to happen to all of us." He walked unsteadily over to one of the large leather chairs and sat down heavily. "What hope have we?"

She sat down opposite him. "It is not quite the same as Mr. Gordon-Cumming," she said quietly but very firmly. "There is no question that they were playing baccarat. No one denies that. And Mr. Gordon-Cumming's reputation prior to this is such that there are many who do not find it difficult to believe that he would cheat. Seemingly there have been doubts before. Has anyone ever made so much as a whisper that you could have panicked on the battlefield?"

"No. . . ." He lifted his head a little. He smiled very slightly. "That is some comfort, but there will still be many only too happy to assume the worst. I never heard any question of Stanley's honor or integrity before, and yet look at the newspapers. I doubt he will be able to sue for libel, it is so subtly worded, and what could he prove? Even if he did, what could he win back that would be a quarter the value of the reputation he has lost? Money answers so very little where love or honor are concerned."

It was true, and to argue with him would be not only pointless but offensive.

"No value, except punitive," she agreed. "And I suppose a court case would only give people the opportunity to throw more accusations. And all the charges are so cleverly chosen that one cannot prove they are untrue. He has obviously thought of that." She leaned forward, the sun catching the corner of her sleeve in vivid gold. "But we must not give up trying. There must be someone still left alive from the ambush in Abyssinia who can remember what happened and whose testimony would be believed. We must just keep searching for them."

There was no hope in his face. He tried to compose himself to some kind of resolution, but it was automatic, without heart.

"Of course. I have been thinking who else I might approach." He gave a half smile. "One of the ugliest aspects of all this is that one begins to suspect everyone of being involved. I try hard not to wonder who it is, but when I am awake at night thoughts come into my mind unbidden." His mouth tightened. "I determine not to entertain them, but the hours go by and I find I have done. I can no longer think of anyone without suspicion. People whose decency and whose friendship I had never questioned before suddenly become strangers whose every motive I look at again. My whole life has changed, because I see it differently. I question everything good . . . might it really conceal deceit and secret betrayal?" He looked at her with undisguised anguish. "And in thoughts like that I am betraying all that I am myself, all that I want to

178

be, and thought I was." His voice dropped. "Perhaps that is the worst thing that he is doing to me . . . showing me something in myself I had not known was there."

She understood what he meant; she could see it in him too clearly, isolated, frightened, and alone, so vulnerable, all the certainties he had built over the years dissolving in a space of days.

"It is not you," she said gently, putting out her hand and laying it not on his hand, but on his arm, on the fabric of his coat. "It is just being human. Any of us might be there; the only difference is that most of us don't know that, and we cannot imagine it when it is outside our experience. Some things no imagining can reach."

He sat silently for a few moments. He looked up at her once, and there was warmth in his eyes, a tenderness she was not certain how to interpret. Then the instant passed, and he drew in his breath.

"I have other people in mind whom I could ask about the Abyssinian Campaign," he said in a studiously casual voice. "And I must go to my club for luncheon." He could not hide the sudden tension about his eyes and lips. "I should greatly prefer not to, but I have obligations I cannot avoid . . . I won't. I will not allow this to make me break my promises."

"Of course," she agreed, withdrawing her hand and standing up slowly. She would have liked to protect him from it, but there is no defense against failure except to keep trying, to face the enemy, open or secret. She smiled at him a trifle wanly. "Please always count on me to help in any way I am able."

"I do," he said softly. "Thank you." He colored painfully and turned away, walking to the door into the hall and opening it for her.

She went past him and nodded to the waiting footman.

Pitt stood in Vespasia's pale, calm sitting room staring at the sunlit garden beyond the windows, waiting for her to come downstairs. It was too early in the afternoon for a social call, especially on someone of her age, but his business was

179

urgent, and he had not wished to arrive and find she had gone out to pay calls herself, which could have easily happened if he had left his own visit until a more appropriate hour.

The white lilacs still perfumed the air, and the silence, away from the road, was almost palpable. It was a windless day; there was no rustle of leaves. Once a thrush sang for a moment, and then the sound disappeared again, lost in the heat.

He turned as he heard the door open.

"Good afternoon, Thomas." Vespasia came in, leaning a little on her cane. She was dressed in ecru and ivory lace with a long rope of pearls catching the light almost to her waist. He found himself smiling in spite of the reason for his visit.

"Good afternoon, Aunt Vespasia," he replied, savoring the fact that she permitted him to use that title. "I'm sorry to disturb you at this hour, but it is too important to me to risk missing you."

She brushed the air delicately with one hand, dismissing the idea. "My calls can wait for another day. It was nothing of importance, merely a way to spend the afternoon and fulfill a certain duty. Tomorrow will do as well, or next week, for that matter." She walked across the carpet and sat down in her favorite chair, facing the garden.

"You are very generous," he replied.

She looked at him candidly. "Rubbish! I am bored to tears with idle conversation, and you know it, Thomas. If I hear one more silly woman make some remark about Annabelle Watson-Smith's betrothal, I shall cause my own scandal with my reply. I was going to call upon Mrs. Purves. And how she has an unbroken lamp mantle in her house I cannot imagine. Her laugh would shatter crystal. You know me well enough not to try humoring me."

"I'm sorry," he apologized.

"Good. And for heaven's sake, sit down! I am getting a crick in my neck looking up at you."

He sat obediently in the chair opposite her.

She regarded him steadily. "I assume you have come about this appalling business of Guy Stanley. Have you ascertained if he is another victim?" She shrugged very slightly, just the

180

lifting of one shoulder. "Even if he is not, and this is simply a coincidental tragedy, the effect upon everyone else will be the same. I can imagine what Dunraithe White will feel. Thomas, this is really very serious."

"I know it is." It seemed strange to be speaking of such evil and deliberate pain in this beautiful room with its simplicity and its scent of flowers. "And you do not yet know the full extent of it. I went to see Sir Guy this morning, and it is uglier than I had supposed. He was indeed threatened in exactly the same manner as the others . . ."

"And he refused," she finished for him, her face grim. "And this is the terrible revenge, and the warning to everyone else."

"No . . . I wish it were."

Her eyes widened. "I do not understand. Please be frank, Thomas. Whatever the truth is, I am not too fragile to hear it. I have lived a long time and seen more than I think you imagine."

"I am not being evasive," he said honestly. "I do wish the answer were as simple as Sir Guy's having been asked for something and refusing it. He was not asked for anything at all, except a silver-plated flask, as a token, much as I assume Balantyne was asked for the snuffbox. Just something individual and marking the blackmailer's power. Sir Guy gave him the flask, by messenger. This exposure comes without warning and for no reason other than to make a display of power. It chanced to be Sir Guy who was the victim; it could as easily have been anyone else."

She looked at him steadily, absorbing what he had said.

"Unless Sir Guy has nothing the blackmailer wants," he went on, thinking aloud. "And he was chosen in order to expose him and frighten the others."

"So the poor man never had a chance." She was pale, and she spoke sitting very upright, her back stiff and her chin high, her hands folded in her lap. She would never betray panic or despair—she had been schooled to greater self-mastery than that—but in the early-afternoon sun there was a rigidity in her that spoke of inner pain. "Nothing he could have said or done

181

would have affected the outcome. I doubt the offense with which he is accused has much to do with him either."

"He says not," Pitt agreed. "And I believe him. But it is actually about something else that I have come to you. I know of no way in which you could help me regarding Sir Guy Stanley; in this other matter you may."

Her silver eyebrows rose. "Other matter?"

"Mrs. Tannifer sent for me this morning. She is deeply concerned, having heard the news—"

"Tannifer?" she interrupted. "Who is she?"

"The wife of the banker, Sigmund Tannifer." He had temporarily forgotten that she did not know about him.

"Another victim?"

"Yes. She is a woman of courage and individuality, and Tannifer himself did not keep the truth from her."

The ghost of a smile touched Vespasia's lips. "I assume Mr. Tannifer's supposed offense was not of a marital nature?"

"No, financial." The momentary humor flickered through him also. "The betrayal of trust regarding his clients' funds. Ugly and certainly ruinous if it were even considered possible it were true, but not personal in the same way. Mrs. Tannifer is wholly behind him."

"And she is alarmed, very naturally."

"Yes." He nodded. "But not simply that. She is determined to fight in every way open to her. She called me because she overheard a conversation on the telephone between her husband and Mr. Leo Cadell, who apparently holds a position of importance in the Foreign Office." He stopped, seeing a new pain in Vespasia's face, a very slight tightening of her fingers in her lap. "I came to ask you if you knew Mr. Cadell. I see that you do."

"I have known him for years," she answered, so quietly he had to strain to hear her. She saw him lean forward, and cleared her throat. "I have known his wife since she was born. Indeed, I am her godmother. I was at her wedding . . . twenty-five years ago. I have always liked Leo. Tell me what I can do."

"I'm sorry. I hoped you might know them, but I wish it were not so well." He meant it. The ugliness of this seemed to

182

be touching so many places, the pain and the fear spreading, and he still had so little idea even where to look, never mind where to strike back. "Have you any idea as to a connection between Balantyne, Cornwallis, Dunraithe White, Tannifer and Cadell? Anything at all they have in common?"

"No," she said without waiting to give the matter a thought. "I have already spent too many hours trying to imagine any sphere of influence or power they have in common, or the remotest family connection, and I should be surprised if they were even more than passingly acquainted with one another. I have wondered if there was anyone they could have injured, even unknowingly. But Cornwallis was in the navy; Balantyne, the army. Dunraithe has never been abroad so far as I know, and has always served the law. You say Tannifer is a banker; and Leo is in the Foreign Office. They are not of a generation, so even if they went to the same school, it could not have been at the same time. Brandon Balantyne must be at least fifteen years older than Leo Cadell." She looked confused and at a loss.

"I have tried everything else," he conceded. "I have tried financial and business interests, investments, even gambling or sporting pursuits. There doesn't seem to be anything that ties them all together. If there is, it must be far in the past. I've asked Cornwallis. He is the one man I can press for any detail he can recall. He swears he never even heard of any of them, except Balantyne, until a couple of years ago."

"Then I had better go and call upon Theodosia." Vespasia rose, accepting Pitt's hand reluctantly as he stood more rapidly than she and offered it. "I am not yet decrepit, Thomas," she said a trifle stiffly. "I simply do not shoot to my feet as you do."

He knew she was not angry with him but with her own limitations, most especially now, when she felt helpless to protect her friends and was growing daily more bitterly aware of how serious was the threat to them.

"Thank you for listening to me," he said, walking beside her. "Please do not give any undertaking to keep confidences unless you have no other possible way of learning the truth. I need to know all you hear."

She turned to look at him, her hooded eyes dark silver-gray. "I am as aware as you are of the depth of danger in this case, Thomas, and not only of how deeply it could scar the individual men and women involved but also of the corruption to our society altogether if even one of these men succumbs to whatever it is that is asked of them. Even if it is trivial, and not illegal, the very fact that they can be persuaded to do it at another's command is the first symptom of a disease which kills. I know these men, my dear. I have known men like them all my life. I understand what they are suffering and what they fear. I understand their sense of shame because they do not know how to fight back. I know what the esteem of their fellows means to them."

He nodded. No more words were necessary.

Vespasia alighted from her carriage on the pavement outside the house of Leo and Theodosia Cadell. It was a trifle early to call, except for the most formal of visits, which was the last thing she intended, but she had no inclination to wait. Theodosia could leave a message with the footman that she was not at home should anyone else come. She could select any reason she chose. An elderly relative was unwell. That was hardly true—Vespasia was in excellent health—but it would satisfy. She was certainly distressed.

She told her driver to take the carriage around to the mews, out of sight. She would send for him when she was ready to leave. She permitted him to pull the doorbell for her before moving to obey.

She was admitted by the parlormaid and was shown to the large, old withdrawing room with its burgundy curtains and Chinese vases she had always disliked. They were a wedding gift from an aunt whose feelings they had never wished to offend. Theodosia joined her within moments.

"Good afternoon, my dear." Vespasia surveyed the younger woman carefully. There were thirty-five years between them, but just at the moment that was less than usually apparent. Theodosia also had been remarkably beautiful, perhaps not in the unique way Vespasia had, but sufficient to turn a great many heads—and not a few hearts. Her blue-black hair was touched with silver now, not only at the temples but across the front of the brow. Her dark eyes were magnificent, her high cheekbones just as clear, but there were shadows in her skin and a lack of color that spoke of poor sleep. There was a tightness in her movements and a loss of her usual grace.

"Aunt Vespasia!" No weariness or fear could mar the real pleasure in her greeting. "What a delightful surprise! If I had known you were coming I should have instructed the staff that I am not at home to anyone else. How are you? You look wonderful."

"I am very well, thank you," Vespasia answered. "A good dressmaker can achieve a great deal. However, even the best cannot work miracles. A corset can hold together your body and provide the best posture on earth, but there is nothing that can do the same for the face."

"There is nothing wrong with your face." Theodosia looked surprised and half amused.

"I hope not, except a certain passage of time," Vespasia agreed wryly. "But I cannot be so kind to you, my dear, and do so with the remotest honesty. You look worried sick."

What little color there was blanched from Theodosia's cheeks. She sat down suddenly in the chair opposite Vespasia, who naturally had not risen.

"Oh, dear. Is it so apparent? I thought I had disguised it rather better than that."

Vespasia relented. "From most people, I daresay. But I have known you since you were born. Also," she added, "I have fashioned a few repairs to the appearance myself, well enough to know how they are done."

"I am afraid I have not been sleeping very well," Theodosia said, looking at Vespasia, then away again. "Silly, but perhaps I am coming to the time of life when late nights are not as easy to accommodate as they used to be. I hate to admit that."

"My dear," Vespasia said very gently, "late nights are usually followed by late mornings, and you are in an excellent position to sleep until noon, if you so wish. If you do not

185

sleep well, it is because you are ill, or something is worrying you too profoundly to allow you to forget it, even in your bed. I rather think it is the latter."

It was clear in Theodosia's face that she meant to deny it; it was so plain she might almost have spoken. Then she met Vespasia's unwavering gaze. Her resistance crumpled, but nevertheless she did not explain.

"May I tell you something about a friend of mine?" Vespasia enquired.

"Of course." Theodosia relaxed a little. The immediate pressure had been removed from her. She sat back in the chair, preparing to listen, her skirts in an elegant swirl around her, her eyes on Vespasia's face.

"I shall not tell you a great deal about his history or circumstances," Vespasia began. "Because for reasons which will become apparent, I prefer to keep you from guessing his name. He might not mind in the slightest your knowing his predicament, but that is not my decision to make."

Theodosia nodded. "I understand. Tell me only what you wish."

"He is a military man of distinguished service," Vespasia began, never taking her eyes from Theodosia's face. "He has now retired, but his career was long and honorable. He had great courage and qualities of leadership. He was held in high esteem, both by friends and by those who liked him less, for whatever reason."

Theodosia was attending closely, but with no more than polite interest. It was a great deal easier than being questioned as to her own anxieties. The hands in her lap were loosely folded, the pearl-and-emerald ring catching the light.

"He has had his share of personal grief," Vespasia continued. "As most of us do. However, lately something quite new has happened, without the slightest warning."

"I'm sorry," Theodosia sympathized. It was clear in her wide eyes that she expected some domestic discord, or possibly financial reverse, the sort of misfortune which can afflict most people.

Vespasia's voice did not alter. "He received a letter, anony-

186

mous of course, cut from words in the *Times* newspaper. . . ." She saw Theodosia stiffen and her hands lock, but she affected not to have noticed. "It was very plainly and articulately phrased, accusing him of cowardice in the face of the enemy, a great many years previously, during one of our lesser foreign campaigns."

Theodosia swallowed, her breath rapid, as if she were struggling to gain sufficient air and this warm and pleasant room were actually suffocating her. She started to say something and then changed her mind.

Vespasia hated going on, but if she stopped now she would have served no purpose and helped no one.

"The threat to disclose the details of this incident, entirely false, was quite plain," she said. "As was the ruin it would bring, not only to my friend but of course to his family. He is quite innocent of the charge, but it is all so long ago, and happened in a foreign land with which we now have little connection, so it will be well-nigh impossible to verify it. It is always harder to prove that something did not happen than that it did."

Theodosia was very white, her body so stiff beneath her smoky-blue dress that the fabric seemed strained.

"The curious thing," Vespasia went on in the silence, "is that the writer of the letter did not ask for anything, no money, no favor, nothing at all. He has now written at least twice that I am aware of."

"That is . . . terrible," Theodosia whispered. "What is your friend going to do?"

"There is very little he can do." Vespasia watched her closely. "I am not sure if he is aware that he is not the only person so victimized."

Theodosia was startled. "What? I mean . . . you think there are others?"

"There are four others that I know of. I think there may be five. Don't you, my dear?"

Theodosia licked her lips. She hesitated for several long, silent minutes. The clock in the hall struck the quarter hour.

In the garden, outside the long windows, a bird sang. Some-where, beyond the wall, children were calling out in a game.

"I promised Leo I would tell no one," Theodosia said at last, but the anguish in her face made it desperately clear how she longed to share the burden.

Vespasia waited.

Outside the bird was still singing, the same liquid call over and over—a blackbird, high in a tree in the sun.

"I suppose you already know," Theodosia said at last. "I don't know why I hesitate, except that the nature of the accu-sation is . . . oh, it's all so stupid, and yet so real . . . so . . . almost . . . not true . . . but . . ." She sighed. "What am I mak-ing excuses for? It doesn't matter. It doesn't alter anything." She looked steadily at Vespasia. "Leo has received two of these letters as well, making the charges but not yet asking for anything, just pointing out how if it became public it would ruin him . . . ruin us both . . . and Sir Richard Aston as well."

Vespasia was puzzled. She could imagine no charge that could possibly include Leo and Theodosia and Aston. Aston was Leo's superior in the Foreign Office, a man of highly dis-tinguished career and very great influence. His wife was connected to several of the great aristocratic families in the land. He was a charming man, possessed of both wit and intelligence.

Theodosia laughed, but it was a hollow sound, amusement without pleasure.

"I see you had not even thought of it," she observed. "It was Sir Richard who was responsible for Leo's promotion."

"It was entirely merited," Vespasia replied. "He has amply proved that. But even had it not been, it is a mistake to pro-mote someone beyond their ability, but it is not an offense, and certainly not Leo's offense, or yours."

"Your trust in me is making you naive," Theodosia said with an edge of bitterness. "The suggestion was that Leo paid for his promotion."

"That's balderdash," Vespasia dismissed it, but without conviction or relief. It was so foolish it could be only part of

188

the story. "Aston has all the money he could need, and Leo hasn't sufficient to pay an amount that would make any difference. And you mentioned that you were involved, or at least you implied you had some part in it greater than simply that his ruin would accomplish yours as well." Then even as she spoke a glimmering of another idea came to her; it was repellently ugly, because she cared for Theodosia, but not unbelievable of someone for whom she had no regard. Others would believe it.

"I can see it in your face," Theodosia said gently. "You understand at last. You are right; the letter said that Sir Richard had admired me far more than as a friend, and Leo had sold me to him, as a lover, in return for his promotion, and Sir Richard had accepted." She winced as she gave it words, and her hands were twisting in her lap. "The only part of it that bears any relation to fact is that I was aware that Sir Richard did . . . desire me. But he never made any improper suggestion, let alone advance. I was simply . . . a trifle uncomfortable because of his position regarding my husband." Her jaw set. "Why should I have to apologize for that? I was beautiful. I could name a score of other women, two score, who were the same."

"You do not have to explain," Vespasia pointed out with a flash of humor. "I do understand."

Theodosia blushed. "I'm sorry. Of course you do, better than I. You must have faced envy and discomfort on that account all your life, the little remarks and suggestions."

Vespasia lifted her chin a trifle. "It is not quite in the past, my dear. The body may become a little stiff, and tire more easily, the appetites of the flesh become controlled, the hair may fade and the face betray the years and all that one has made of them, but the passion and the need to be loved do not die. Nor, I am afraid, do the jealousies or the fears."

"Good," Theodosia said after only a moment. "For all its pain, I think I like the way we are. But what can I do to help Leo?"

"Keep silent," Vespasia responded immediately. "If you make the slightest attempt to deny it, you will raise thoughts

189

in people's minds which had never entered them before. Sir Richard will hardly thank you for that, nor will Lady Aston. She is not an easy creature, rather overbearing, and the kindest thing that can be said of her appearance would be to liken her to a well-bred dog, one of those ones that has difficulty breathing. Most unfortunate."

Theodosia tried to laugh, and failed. "She is actually quite pleasant, you know, and even if it was a dynastic marriage to begin with, I believe he is very fond of her. She has humor and imagination, both of which last longer than beauty."

"Of course they do," Vespasia agreed. "And they are a great deal easier and more rewarding to live with. But too few people realize it. And beauty has such an immediate impact. Ask any girl of twenty whether she would rather be beautiful or amusing, and I will be surprised if you find one in a score who will choose humor. And Lucy Aston is undoubtedly one of the nineteen."

"I know. Is that all I can do, Aunt Vespasia, nothing?"

"It is all I can think of, for the moment," Vespasia insisted. "But if Leo should receive a letter which asks him to do something under duress, if you have any love for him, or for yourself, do all you can to dissuade him from it. Whatever the cost of scandal precipitated by his making this charge public, it will be small compared with the ruin agreeing to it will bring. It is no guarantee the blackmailer will keep silent—Guy Stanley is witness of that—and you will add the real dishonor of whatever he would have you do. He may damage your reputation, but only you can damage your honor. Don't let it happen." She leaned forward a little, looking intently at the younger woman. "Assure him you can withstand anything that is said of you wrongly, and all that may come because of it, but not that he should allow this man to turn him into the kind of creature he is, or to become a tool in his evil."

"I will," Theodosia promised. In a quick gesture she reached forward and took Vespasia's hands in her own, gripping them warmly. "Thank you for coming. I should not have had the courage to come to you, but I feel stronger, and quite certain of what I must do now. I shall be able to help Leo."

Vespasia nodded. "We shall stand together," she promised. "There are several of us, and we shall not stop fighting."

Tellman was meanwhile busy tracking the last few days in the life of Josiah Slingsby. Someone had murdered him, either with deliberate intent or accidentally in a fight which had gone too far. That was one of the few things in this whole affair of which he was certain. Whether it had any connection with the blackmail attempt or not, it must be solved. It was the original case, and must not be lost sight of in whatever else was occupying most of Pitt's time. Tellman fully expected the trail he was following to cross General Balantyne's path, and it might be easier to come at it from this angle than from pursuing Balantyne directly, although that, too, would have to be done.

He began by discovering where Slingsby had lived. It was tedious and time-consuming, but not difficult for someone who was used to the mixture of threat, trickery and small bribes necessary to deal with fencers of stolen goods, prostitutes and keepers of "netherskens," as cheap rooming houses were called, where those who wished to keep well out of the way of the police could rent a space to sleep in for a few pence a night. The owners asked nothing about their patrons and simply took the money. None were friends of the law, and whatever business they were involved in was best not discussed.

Lapsing into the attitude of the beggars and pickpockets lounging around the area, Tellman fell into conversation with a bull-chested man whose "terrier-crop" haircut indicated he had not long been out of prison. In spite of his impressive physique he had a hacking cough and dark circles of exhaustion under his eyes.

From him Tellman learned that Slingsby frequently worked in partnership with a man named Ernest Wallace, infamous for his ability to climb up drainpipes and balance along roof ledges and windowsills, and for his filthy temper.

He spent the rest of the day in Shoreditch, learning all he could about Wallace. Little of it was to his credit. He seemed

191

to inspire both dislike and considerable fear. He was very good at his chosen skill of thieving, and his profits were both high and regular. So far he had escaped the attention of the law, who might well have been aware of him but had not yet proved any charge against him. However, he had quarreled with almost everyone with whom he had had dealings, and two or three of them that Tellman found carried the scars.

In this area it was understood that no one cooperated with the police to the extent of betraying one of their own, even at the cost of life. Tellman was the enemy, and he knew it. But revenge might be sought in more than one direction. He needed to find someone whom Wallace had hurt badly enough that he would be willing to savor Wallace's downfall and pay the price. A little fear and a little profit might sway the argument.

It took him another day of slipping in and out of gin mills, crowded markets, being bumped and jostled, carrying nothing in his pockets, and even then the linings were ripped by cutpurses so skilled he did not feel their hands or their knives. He ate from a sandwich stall, walked dripping alleys, stepping over refuse, hearing rats' feet scurrying away, and mixed threats and wheedling, but finally he found the person he sought, not a man but a woman. Wallace had beaten her, and as a result she had miscarried her child. She hated him enough not to care how she took her revenge.

Tellman had to be very careful how he questioned her. He must not prompt her into saying anything intentionally to ruin Wallace, and thereby end up being useless in any trial.

"It's Slingsby I want," he insisted.

She stood leaning against the dark brick wall of the street, her face half shaded in the gloom. The sky was hazed over with chimney smoke, and the smell of effluent was heavy in the air.

"Well, find Ernie Wallace an' yer'll find Joe," she answered. "Joe Slingsby's the only one as'll work wif 'im. Least 'e were. Dunno if 'e still does." She sniffed. " 'Ad a fight summink terrible 'baht a week ago—it were, 'cos o' the big row down at the Goat an' Compasses. Were the same night.

Ernie damn near killed Joe, the bleedin' swine. In't seen Joe around 'ere since then. I 'spec 'e went orff." She sniffed again and passed the back of her hand across her mouth. "I'd a' come back an' stuck a shiv in 'is ribs, if I'd a' bin 'im. Bleedin' bastard. Would now, if I could get near enough the swine. But 'e'd see me comin', an' 'e's too fly by 'alfter 'ang around any dark alleys by 'isself."

"But you're sure Joe Slingsby was with him that night a week ago?" Tellman tried to keep the excitement out of his voice. He could hear his words falling over each other with eagerness. She could hear it too.

"Din' I just tell yer?" She stared at him. "Yer deaf, or summink? I dunno w'ere Joe is. I in't seen 'ide ner 'air of 'im since then, but I know w'ere Ernie Wallace is. 'E's bin throwin' money around summink wild, like 'e 'ad it all."

Tellman swallowed. "You reckon he and Joe Slingsby did a burglary that day and fought over the takings, and Wallace won?"

" 'Course I do!" she said with contempt. "Wot else? Yer in't very bright, are yer?"

"May be true." He must be very careful. He affected doubt, turning away from her. "An' maybe not."

She spat on the narrow pavement. " 'Oo cares!" She took a step back, her voice hard.

"I do!" He reached out and snatched her arm. "I gotter find Ernie Wallace. It's worth something to me to know for sure what happened."

"Well, Joe won't tell yer!" she said derisively. " 'E got the worse of it, I know fer sure."

"How do you know?" he insisted.

" 'Cos I saw it, o' course! 'Ow d'yer think?"

"Did Slingsby say he'd get back at Wallace? Where'd he go after?"

"I dunno. 'E never went anyw'ere." She pulled her arm away roughly. " 'E could a' bin dead, fer all I know." Suddenly her face changed. "Jeez! Mebbe 'e were dead! Nobody in't seen 'im since then."

"In that case," Tellman said very slowly, looking straight at

193

her, "if it can be proved, then Ernie Wallace murdered him, and he'll swing for it."

"Oh, it can be proved. . . ." She stared back at him, wide-eyed. "I'll see ter it. I swear ter that, I do. I'll get it fer yer!"

She was as good as her word. The evidence was all he needed. He took two constables and together they found and arrested Ernest Wallace and charged him with the murder of Josiah Slingsby. But regardless of the subtlety or persistence of questioning, or the threats or promises made to him, Wallace was adamant that he had left the body of Slingsby in the alley where he had fallen, and himself left the scene with all the speed he could muster.

"W'y the bleedin' 'ell should I a' took 'im ter bleedin' Bedford Square?" he demanded with amazement. "Wo' for? D'yer fink I'm gonna carry a corpse wot I done in 'alfway 'roun' Lunnon in the middle o' the night, jus' so as I can leave 'im on someone else's bleedin' doorstep? Wo' fer?"

The notion of placing Albert Cole's bill for socks in the pocket of the corpse had him seriously questioning Tellman's sanity.

"Yer bleedin' mad, you are!" He snorted, his eyes wide. "Wot the 'ell are yer on abaht—socks?" He guffawed with laughter.

Tellman left the Shoreditch police station deep in thought. Unconsciously, he pushed his hands farther into his pockets, not realizing how he was mimicking Pitt. He believed Wallace, simply because what he said made sense. He had killed Slingsby in a fight which was violent, stupid, born of an ungoverned temper and a quarrel over money. There was no forethought in it, no planning either before or after.

So who put the socks receipt in Slingsby's pocket and where had he got it from? Where was Albert Cole now . . . alive or dead? And above all, why?

There was only one answer that came to his mind: in order to blackmail General Brandon Balantyne.

The street was shimmering with heat. It rose in waves from

the stones, and the sheer brick walls on either side seemed to hem him in. The horses trotting briskly between the shafts of hansoms and drays alike were dark with sweat. The smell of manure was sharp in the air. He preferred it to the stale, clinging odor of drains.

A running patterer stood on the corner with a small group of listeners gathered around him. He was spinning a doggerel poem about the Tranby Croft affair and the Prince of Wales's affection for Lady Frances Brooke. His version of the tale reflected rather better on Gordon-Cumming than on the heir to the throne or his friends.

Tellman stopped and listened for a minute or two, and gave the man a threepenny bit, then crossed the street and went on his way.

What did the blackmailer want? Money, or some corrupt action? And there had to be more to it than merely Slingsby's body, even if it were believed to be that of Albert Cole, or Balantyne would never submit. The answer to those questions must lie with Balantyne. He would do as Pitt had told him and investigate the General more thoroughly, but he would be highly discreet about it. And he would tell Gracie nothing. His face burned at the thought, and he was surprised and angry at how guilty it made him feel that he would be keeping it from her, after he had given her his word, at least implicitly, to help.

He pushed his hands deeper into his pockets and strode along the pavement with his shoulders hunched and his lips in a thin line, the smells of rotten wood, soot and effluent catching in the back of his throat.

He began early the following morning by looking again at what he knew of Balantyne's military record. He needed to know something of the man in order to understand his weaknesses, why he might have created enemies and who they would be. According to what little Tellman had learned by following him since the discovery of the corpse in Bedford Square, he was a cold, precise man whose few pleasures were solitary.

195

Tellman squared his shoulders and increased his pace along the footpath. He was absolutely certain there was a great deal more to learn, more that was actually relevant to the blackmail and whoever had moved the body of Josiah Slingsby and left it on the General's doorstep. Perhaps as far as the law was concerned it did not matter a great deal. Tellman had arrested and charged Wallace with the murder. But blackmail was also a crime, whoever the victim was.

He did not want to speak to officers, men of Balantyne's own background and situation in life, who also had purchased their commissions and would close ranks against enquiry as naturally as against any other enemy attacking the quality of their comfortable, privileged lives. He wanted to speak to ordinary soldiers, who would not be too arrogant to answer him man to man and to praise or criticize with honesty. He could speak to them as equals and press them for detail, opinion, and names.

It took him three hours to find Billy Treadwell, who had until five years before been a private in the Indian army. Now he kept a public house down by the river. He was a thin man with a large beak of a nose and a ready smile with crooked, very white teeth, the middle two of which were chipped.

"General Balantyne?" he said cheerfully, leaning on a barrel in the yard of the Red Bull. "Well, Major Balantyne as 'e were then. 'Course, it's goin' back a fair bit, but yeah, I remember 'im. 'Course I do. Wot about it?" It was not said aggressively but with curiosity. Years in India had burned his skin a deep brown, and he seemed not to find this extraordinary heat wave in the least uncomfortable. He narrowed his eyes against the reflection of the sun on the water, but he did not look for shade.

Tellman sat down on the low edge of the brick wall that divided the yard from the small vegetable garden. The sound of the river was a pleasant background just out of sight. But the heat burned his skin, and his feet were on fire.

"You served with him, didn't you? In India?" he asked.

Treadwell looked at him with his head a little on one side.

196

"You know that, or you wouldn't be 'ere askin' me. Wot about it? Why fer d'yer wanna know?"

Tellman had weighed in his mind how to answer this question all the way there on the steamer he had taken up the river. He was still uncertain. He did not want to prejudice the man's answer.

"That's hard to say without breaking confidences," he said slowly. "I think there's a crime going on, and I think the General might be one of the intended victims. I want to stop it happening."

"So why don't you just warn 'im?" Treadwell said reasonably, glancing over his shoulder at a steamer as it passed close to shore, wondering if it might be likely custom.

"It isn't that simple." Tellman had prepared himself for that. "We want to catch the criminal as well. Believe me, if the General could help, he would."

Treadwell turned back to him. "Oh, I believe that!" he said with feeling. "Straight as a die, 'e were. Always knew where you stood with 'im . . . not like some as I could name."

"Strict for law and order, was he?" Tellman asked.

"Not special." He gave his full attention now, business forgotten. " 'E'd bend the rules if 'e could see the reason. 'E understood that men 'ave got ter believe in a cause if yer asking 'em ter die for it. Just like they gotter believe in a commanding officer if they're gonna obey 'im w'en they don't see the reason why 'e gives an order."

"You don't question an order?" Tellman said with disbelief.

"No, 'course not," Treadwell answered disdainfully. "But some yer obeys slow, like, an' some yer trusts."

"Which was Balantyne?"

"Trust 'im." The reply was unhesitating. " 'E knew 'is job. Never sent men ter do summink as 'e couldn't do 'isself. Some men leads from the back . . . not 'im." He moved over and sat on the barrel top, settling to reminisce, squinting a little in the sun but ignoring its heat. "I 'member once when we was up on the Northwest Frontier . . ." There was a faraway look in his eyes. "Yer'd 'ave ter see them mountains ter believe 'em, yer would. Great shining white peaks 'anging

197

over us in the sky, they was. Reckon as they was scrapin' 'oles in the floor of 'eaven."

He took a deep breath. "Anyway, Major Balantyne was told by the Colonel ter take a couple o' score of us an' go up the pass an' come down be'ind the Pathans. 'E were kind o' new at the Northwest. Didn't reckon much ter the Pathans . . . Major Balantyne tried ter put 'im right. Told 'im they was some o' the best soldiers in the world. Clever, tough, an' din't run away from nuffink on God's earth." He shook his head and sighed wearily. "But the Colonel, 'e wouldn't listen. One o' them daft bleeders wot won't be told nuffink." He looked at Tellman for a moment to make sure that he was following the story.

"And . . ." Tellman prompted, shifting his feet uncomfortably. He could feel the sweat trickling down his body.

"So the Major stood ter attention," Treadwell resumed. " 'Yes sir,' 'No sir,' an' took 'is orders. Then as soon as we was well out o' sight o' the post, 'e said in a loud voice as 'is compass was broke, an' gave orders to go about-face, an' followed 'is plan ter come at the Pathans from two sides at once, an' instead o' standin' our ground, ter keep movin' . . . just a couple o' rounds o' shot, an' then, while they was still workin' out which way we was comin', we was gone again." He looked at Tellman narrowly.

"Did you win?" Tellman was caught up in spite of himself.

" 'Course we did," Treadwell said with a grin. "An' the Colonel took the credit for it. Was as mad as all 'ell, but couldn't do nuffink abaht it. Stood an' listened ter them say wot an 'ell of a clever feller 'e was, an' thanked them fer it. 'Ad ter, didn't 'e?"

"But it was the Major's idea!" Tellman protested. "Didn't he tell them, whoever was in charge?"

Treadwell shook his head. "Yer never bin army, 'ave yer?" There was pity in his tone, and a certain kind of protectiveness, as of the world's innocents. "Yer don' show up one o' yer own, even if 'e looks for it. Loyalty. The Major'd never a' done that. One o' the old sort, 'e were. Take wot comes ter 'im an' never complain. I seen 'im so wore out 'e were near droppin' ter the ground, but 'e jus' kep' goin'. Wouldn't let the men down, yer see? That's wot bein' an officer is abaht, them wot's any good. Yer always gotta be that bit better'n others, or 'ow could they foller yer?'"

There was a bellow of laughter from the open door of the public tearoom.

Tellman frowned. "Did you like him?" he asked.

To Treadwell it was an incomprehensible question.

"Wot d'yer mean . . . 'like 'im'? 'E were the Major. Yer don' 'like' officers. Yer either love 'em or 'ate 'em. Yer 'like' friends, fellers wot yer marches beside, not them as yer follers."

Tellman knew the answer before he asked; still, he needed to hear it in words.

"Did you love or hate the Major?"

Treadwell shook his head. "If I din't see yer face, I'd reckon you was simple! In't I just bin tellin' yer, 'e were one o' the best?"

Tellman was confused. He could not disbelieve Treadwell; the light in his eyes was too clear, and the amusement at an outsider's failure to grasp what was so plain to him.

Tellman thanked him and took his leave. What had happened to Balantyne in the intervening years which had made him the stiff and solitary man he was now? Why was Treadwell's view of him so . . . unrecognizable?

The next soldier he found was one William Sturton, another ordinary man, who had risen through long service to the rank of sergeant and was immensely proud of it. He was stiff with rheumatism now, and his white hair and whiskers shone in the dappled shade as he sat on the park bench, eager to talk, remembering the glories of the past with this young man who knew nothing and was so happy to listen.

" 'Course I remember Colonel Balantyne," he said with a lift of his chin, after Tellman had introduced himself. "It were 'im as led us w'en we rode inter Lucknow after the Mutiny. Never seen anyfink like it." His face was set hard as he strove to control the anguish of memory that tore him even now. Tellman could not imagine what lay in his inward vision. He knew poverty, crime and disease; he knew the ravages of cholera in the slums, and freezing corpses of the beggars and the old and the children who lived in the streets. He knew all the agony inflicted by helplessness and indifference. But he had never seen war. Individual murders were one thing; the carnage of mass destruction was beyond his knowledge. He could only guess, and watch the sergeant's face.

"You went in . . ." he prompted.

"Yeah." Sturton was looking beyond him, his eyes misted over. "It was seein' the women and children that got me. I'm used ter seein' men cut ter pieces."

"Colonel Balantyne," Tellman said, forcing him back to the issue. He did not want to hear the other details. He had read about it, been told in school, enough to know he dreaded it.

A thread of breeze stirred the leaves, making a sound like waves on a shore. Away in the distance a woman laughed.

"Never forget the Colonel's face." Sturton was lost in the past. He was in India, not the milder heat of an English summer afternoon. "Looked like death 'isself, 'e did. Thought 'e were gonna fall orff 'is horse. Stumbled w'en 'e got orff. Knees fair wobbled w'en 'e walked over ter the first pile o' corpses. 'E'd seen plenty o' death on the battlefield, but this were different."

In spite of himself, Tellman tried to imagine it, and felt sick. He wondered what Balantyne's emotions had been, how deep? He looked like such a stiff, cold man now.

"What did he do?" he asked.

Sturton did not look at him. His mind was still in Lucknow thirty-four years before.

"We was all took bad at it," he said quietly. "The Colonel took charge. 'E was white as death an' 'is voice were shakin', but 'e told us all wot ter do, 'ow ter search the buildings ter make sure there weren't no ambushes. Ter see if there were anyone 'iding, like." There was fierce pride in his voice, far-away things remembered, and the fact that he had done his duty and survived into these softer times. "Secure the bounds, put a watch in case they returned," he went on, not looking at Tellman beside him. " 'E sent the youngest fer

200

that . . . keep 'em out o' the way o' the dead. Some of us was took pretty 'ard by it. Like I said, it were the women, some of 'em wi' babes even. 'E went 'round 'isself to see if any of 'em was still alive, like. Gawd knows 'ow 'e did it. I couldn't a'. But then that's w'y 'e's a colonel an' I in't."

"He was a colonel because his father bought his commission," Tellman said, then instantly and without knowing why, wished he hadn't.

Sturton looked at him with patient contempt. His face was eloquent that he considered Tellman beneath explaining to.

"You dunno nuffink about duty or loyalty or nuffink else, or yer wouldn't say such a damn stupid thing," he retorted. "Colonel Balantyne were the sort o' man we'd a' followed any place 'e'd a' gorn, an' proud ter do it. 'E 'elped us bury the dead, and stood over the graves and said the prayers for 'em. Even on 'ot nights if I shut me eyes I can still 'ear 'is voice sayin' them words. Never wept, 'course 'e wouldn't, but it were all there in his face, all that 'orror." He sighed deeply and remained silent for several moments.

This time Tellman did not venture to interrupt. He was full of strange and troubling emotions. He tried to imagine the General as a younger man, a man with an inner life of emotions, anger, pain, pity, all masked with a mighty effort because it was his duty, and he must lead the men, never let them doubt him or see weakness, for their sakes. It was not the Balantyne he had believed he knew.

"So wot d'yer want ter know about the Colonel for, then?" Sturton burst across his thoughts. "I in't gonna tell yer nuffink agin 'im. In't nothing ter tell. If yer think as 'e done suffink wrong, yer daft . . . even dafter an' more iggerant than I took yer for, an that's saying a lot."

Tellman took the reproach without argument, because he was too confused to justify himself.

"No . . ." he said slowly, "No, I don't think so. I'm looking for someone who is trying to hurt him . . . an enemy." He saw the look of anger on Sturton's face. "Possibly from the Abyssinian Campaign, perhaps not."

201

"Yer got any idea wot yer doin'?" Sturton said disgustedly. "Wot kind o' enemy?"

"Someone vicious enough to try to attempt blackmail with a false story," Tellman answered, then was afraid perhaps he had betrayed too much. He felt as if any step he took he was on uncertain ground. Suddenly everything was shifting beneath his feet.

"Then yer'd better find 'im!" Sturton said furiously. "An' soon! I'll 'elp yer!" He stiffened as if to move and begin straightaway.

Tellman hesitated. Why not? He could use any expert help he could obtain. "All right," he accepted. "I need to know anything you find out about the attack on the supply train at Arogee. That's the event that's being lied about."

"Right!" Sturton agreed. "Bow Street, yer said. I'll be there."

Tellman spent the next two days discreetly following Balantyne himself. It was not difficult, since Balantyne went out very little and was so deep in thought as never to look to either side of himself, far less behind. Tellman could have been striding step by step with him and probably not have been noticed.

The first time the General went out in a carriage with his wife, a dark, handsome woman Tellman found intimidating. He was very careful not to catch her eye, even by accident. He wondered what had made Balantyne choose her . . . and then realized that perhaps he had not. Maybe it was an arranged marriage, family links, or money. She was certainly elegant enough as she walked across the pavement past the General, barely looking at him, and accepted the coachman's hand up into the open carriage.

She arranged her skirts with a single, expert movement and stared straight ahead. She did not turn as Balantyne got in beside her. He spoke to her. She replied, again without looking at him. She told the coachman to proceed before he moved to do so.

Tellman felt vaguely embarrassed for the General, as if he

had been somehow rebuffed. It was a curious sensation, and one that took him entirely by surprise.

He followed them to an art exhibition where he was not permitted inside. He waited until they emerged a little over an hour later. Lady Augusta looked bright and hard—and impatient. Balantyne was speaking with a white-haired man, and they seemed deep in conversation. They regarded each other with respect which bordered on affection. Tellman remembered that the General painted in watercolors himself.

Lady Augusta tapped her foot.

Balantyne was some minutes more before he joined her. All the way home she ignored him, and back in Bedford Square she alighted from the carriage and went to the front door without waiting for him or looking back.

On the second occasion he went out alone, pale-faced and very tired. He walked quickly. He gave a threepenny piece to the urchin who swept the crossing over Great Russell Street, and a shilling to the beggar on the corner of Oxford Street.

He walked to the Jessop Club and disappeared inside, but he came out less than an hour later. Tellman followed him back to Bedford Square.

Then Tellman returned to Bow Street and went to Pitt's old files to read the case of the murders in the Devil's Acre and the startling tragedy of Christina Balantyne. It left him with a feeling of horror so intense the helplessness to affect it knotted inside his stomach, the anger at the pain he could not reach, the willful destruction and the loss.

He ate a brief supper without any pleasure in it, his imagination in the dark alleys of the Devil's Acre, the blood on the cobbles, but every now and then worse scenes intruded into his imagination: frightened little girls, children no older than Pitt's Jemima, screaming . . . unheard, except by other little girls, cowering and just as helpless.

He wondered about Christina Balantyne and the General. Perhaps in his place he might have chosen solitary pursuits as well. Please God he would never be in such a place to know!

* * *

It was with a very different feeling that he followed Balantyne the next morning, when to Tellman's amazement he met Charlotte Pitt on the steps of the British Museum.

Tellman felt like an intruder, a voyeur, as he saw the joy in Balantyne's face when he caught sight of her. There was an acute vulnerability in him, as if he cared intensely and dared not acknowledge it even to himself, far less to her.

And watching her quick concern, the direct way she met his gaze, her complete candor, Tellman was suddenly aware that she had no idea of the nature or the depth of the General's feelings. She was frightened for him. It was clear in her face. Even had Tellman not known that from Gracie, he could have guessed it watching her now.

They turned to go inside, and without even considering any other possibility, he followed them in. Then, as Charlotte glanced at a woman almost on her heels, he realized with a sudden chill, a feeling of almost nakedness, that if she saw him she would recognize him instantly.

He dropped to one knee and bent his head as if to tie his bootlace, causing the man behind him to trip and only regain his balance with difficulty, and some ill temper. The whole incident drew far more attention to him than if he had simply followed at a more discreet distance. He was furious with himself.

From now on he must remain at the far side of any room and observe them by reflection in any of the glass cases that housed certain of the exhibits. Balantyne disregarded him, he was interested only in Charlotte, but she would recognize Tellman in profile, perhaps even entirely from the back.

For some time he contrived to stay always behind a garrulous woman in black bombazine and watch as Charlotte and Balantyne moved from room to room, speaking together, pretending to look at the exhibits but seeing nothing. She knew of the blackmail, of the murder, and was determined to fight to help him. Tellman had seen her like this before, perhaps never caring quite so passionately, but he knew her capacity to become involved.

Every now and then as they moved to stand in front of another case, he was obliged to pretend to be absorbed in whatever was closest to him. In this place a man alone would be conspicuous if he were not seen to be looking at something.

He found himself next to what was listed on the little plate as a carving from a palace in Assyria, seven centuries before Christ. There was an artist's impression of how the whole building would have appeared. He was amazed at the size of it. It must have been magnificent. He could not pronounce the name of the king who had ruled it. It was surprisingly interesting. One day he would come back here and look at it again, when he had time to read more. He could even bring Gracie.

Now he must follow after Charlotte and Balantyne. He had nearly missed them.

He was beginning to understand why this case mattered to Charlotte. Balantyne was none of the things Tellman had thought of him. Which meant he had been mistaken, full of misjudgments. If he could be so wrong in his assumptions about Balantyne, what about all the other arrogant, overprivileged people he had disliked and dismissed?

What about all his preconceptions?

What kind of an ignorant and prejudiced man did that make him? One Gracie would not want. One who was angry with himself, and confused.

He turned and walked away from the exhibition, out of the museum and down the steps into the sun. He had a great deal of thinking to do, and his mind was in chaos; his emotions even more so.

8

A *FTER WHAT* Parthenope Tannifer had told him, Pitt felt compelled to go and see Cadell. Perhaps he had no idea more than any of the others who the blackmailer was, but even the slightest chance could not be overlooked. It was always possible he would be the first victim to be asked for something specific. And he was certainly in a position of power. From the Foreign Office he could affect the outcome of delicate negotiations in a number of areas. It had occurred to Pitt that perhaps one of the victims was more important to the blackmailer than the others, that one was central to whatever purpose he had in mind, and it could be to influence the government in some policy abroad or within the Empire.

Fortunes could be made and lost on such decisions. Events in Africa alone were highly volatile. Where land and gold were concerned there were many to whom life was cheap, let alone honor. In the rush to explore, to press even farther into that vast continent, such men as Cecil Rhodes and others in his footsteps were used to thinking in terms of armies and nations. A single man's well-being here or there might hardly be noticed.

Pitt had never left England, but he knew enough of those who had to understand that for both men and women on such fringes of ever-expanding civilization, death was around them, frequent and sudden, from violence or the many endemic diseases of tropical climates. It was too easy, in all the other extreme, necessary changes to life and values, to forget the notions of honor which were still powerful in England. The stakes were so high they could dwarf individual considerations.

He had had to make an appointment to see Cadell, and it was two days after speaking with Parthenope Tannifer when he was admitted to his rooms in the Foreign Office. Then he was kept waiting nearly a quarter of an hour.

When finally he was shown in, Cadell rose from his desk with a puzzled look on his lean face. He was not a handsome man, but his features were regular enough, and the lines of habitual expression were good-natured, even gentle. However, today he looked tired and harassed, and obviously was unwilling to see Pitt. He was doing it only because Pitt had insisted it was most urgent police business which could not wait, nor could anyone else help him.

"Good morning ... er ... Superintendent," Cadell said with a slight smile, offering his hand, and then almost immediately withdrawing it, as if he had forgotten what the gesture had been for. "I'm sorry to rush you, but I am due to see the German ambassador in twenty-five minutes. I do apologize, but it is a matter which cannot be delayed." He indicated a very beautiful Queen Anne chair with crimson upholstery. "Please sit down and tell me what I can do for you."

Pitt accepted and began straightaway. Twenty-five minutes was very little indeed to explore such a delicate and painful matter, but he knew Cadell meant what he said.

"Then I will waste none of your time in civilities, if you will excuse me," he said, meeting Cadell's eyes. "This is too grave a subject to leave partway through because other business calls."

Cadell nodded.

Pitt hated being so blunt, but there was no alternative. "What I tell you is in confidence, and I shall keep in confidence anything you say to me, so far as I am able."

Cadell nodded, his gaze straight and unblinking. If he had the slightest idea what Pitt was going to say, he was a superb actor. But then as a diplomat, perhaps he was.

"Several prominent men, of position rather than of wealth, are being blackmailed," Pitt said candidly.

207

Cadell's face tightened so slightly it could have been no more than a change in the bright light from the window. He said nothing.

"No one has been asked yet for money," Pitt continued. "The implication is that it may be influence or power that is demanded instead. A sword is hanging over each of them, and no one knows when it may drop, or in precisely what manner. To the best of my belief, each man is innocent of the accusation, but it is so subtle and so far in the past that not one of them can disprove it."

Cadell let out his breath very slowly. "I see." His eyes did not waver from Pitt's face; they were so intent it was unnatural. "May I ask if Guy Stanley was one of them?"

"You may, and yes, he was," Pitt said levelly. He saw Cadell's eyes widen and heard the very slight sound as he drew in his breath.

"I see. . . ."

"No, I don't think you do," Pitt corrected. "He was not asked for anything, except a relatively worthless silver-plated flask, as a token of submission more than anything else. It was of no value of itself, only symbolic of victory."

"Then why . . . why was he exposed?"

"I don't know," Pitt admitted. "I would guess it is as a warning to the other victims, a demonstration of power . . . and of the will to use it."

Cadell was sitting very still, only his chest rising and falling as he breathed unnaturally slowly. His fingers did not clench on the desk, but they were stiff. He was holding himself in control with a massive effort.

Footsteps passed along the corridor and disappeared.

"You are quite right," he said at length. "I have no idea how you knew I was a victim as well . . . perhaps I should not ask. The suggestion made about me is . . . disgusting, and totally untrue. But there are those who, for their own reasons, would be only too willing to believe it and repeat it. It would ruin not only me but others as well. Even to deny it would suggest the idea to those to whom such a thought would never have occurred. I am helpless."

208

"But you have been asked for nothing so far?" Pitt insisted.

"Nothing whatsoever, not even a token of submission, as you put it."

"Thank you for being so frank, Mr. Cadell. Would you describe the letter for me? Better still, if you have it, may I see it?"

Cadell shook his head.

"I don't have it. It was cut from newspaper, I believe the *Times*, and glued on plain paper. It was posted in the City."

"Exactly like the others." Pitt nodded. "Will you keep me apprised of anything further you may receive, or anything you consider could throw any light on this at all . . ."

"Of course." Cadell stood up and ushered Pitt to the door.

Pitt left uncertain of whether Cadell would tell him or not. Cadell was obviously a man of great self-control, deeply shaken by events. Unlike others, he had not told Pitt what the threat to him had been. It must cut too sharply, cause too deep a fear.

But then Dunraithe White had told only Vespasia. He would not have told Pitt.

He caught a hansom in Whitehall and went straight to see Cornwallis.

He found him at his desk amid a sea of papers, apparently searching for something. He looked up as soon as Pitt came in. He seemed glad to abandon his task. His face showed the marks of tiredness and strain. His eyes were red-rimmed, his skin papery, shadowed on his cheeks and around his lips.

Pitt felt a tug of pity for him, and anger welled up, driven by his own helplessness. He knew that what he had to tell Cornwallis now would make it worse.

"Morning, Pitt. Have you news?" Cornwallis asked before the door was closed. He looked closely at Pitt's face, and understanding of failure came slowly into his eyes. Something in his body relaxed, but it was not ease so much as despair, a knowledge of being beaten again.

Pitt sat down without being asked. "I've spoken with Leo Cadell at the Foreign Office. Mrs. Tannifer was right. He is another victim, just the same."

209

Cornwallis looked at him sharply. "The Foreign Office?"

"Yes. But he hasn't been asked for anything, not even a token."

Cornwallis leaned forward over the desk and rubbed his hands over his brow up onto his smooth head.

"That's a police commissioner, a judge, a junior minister in the Home Office, a diplomat in the Foreign Office, a City banker and a retired general. What have we in common, Pitt?" He stared at him, a flicker of desperation in his eyes. "I've racked my brains! What could anybody want of us? I went to see Stanley, poor devil. . . ."

"So did I," Pitt said, sinking back in the chair and crossing his legs. "He couldn't add anything."

"He didn't defy the blackmailer." Cornwallis leaned forward. "The poor devil didn't have the chance! I think we have to assume that his exposure was a demonstration of power, to frighten the rest of us." He waited to see if Pitt would disagree. When he did not Cornwallis went on, his voice lower, catching a little. "I had another letter this morning. Essentially the same as the others. A little shorter. Just told me I'd be blackballed from all my clubs . . . that's only three, but I value my memberships."

He was looking down at the disordered papers on the desk as if he could not bear the intrusion of meeting anyone's eyes. "I . . . I enjoy going there and being able to feel comfortable . . . at least I did. Now, God knows, I loathe it. I wouldn't go at all if I were not involved in certain duties I would not betray." His lips tightened. "The sort of place where you would wander in if you felt like it, or not visit for a year, and it would be just the same as when you were last there. Big, comfortable chairs. Always a fire in bad weather, warm, crackling. I like the sound of a fire. Sort of a live thing, like the sea around you. Like a ship's crew, stewards know you. Don't have to be told each time what you like. Can sit there for hours and read the papers if you feel like it, or find some decent sort of chap to talk to if you fancy a spot of company. I . . ." He looked away. "I care what they think of me."

Pitt did not know what to say. Cornwallis was a lonely

210

man, without the love or the warmth, the belonging or the responsibilities, of a wife and children such as Pitt had. Only servants waited for him in his rooms. He could come and go as he pleased. He was not needed or missed. His freedom had a high price. Now there was no one to talk to him, demand his attention or offer him comfort, take his mind from his own fears and loneliness, distract him from nightmares or give him companionship and the kind of love that does not depend upon circumstance.

Cornwallis started pushing around the papers on his desk as if he were looking for something, making what had been merely untidy into complete chaos.

"White has resigned," he said, gazing at the shambles in front of him.

Pitt was startled. He had had no idea.

"From the judiciary? When?"

Cornwallis jerked his head up. "No! From the Jessop Club. Although . . ." His voice was strained. "I suppose he might resign from the bench as well. It would at least remove him from the power or the temptation to comply with this man's wishes if that is what they are." He pushed his hand over his head again, as if he had hair to thrust back. "Although judging by his treatment of Stanley, he could be perfectly capable of then exposing White even more violently to warn the rest of us, and surely White will have thought of that?"

"I don't know," Pitt said honestly.

Cornwallis sighed. "No, neither do I. When I saw him at the club, just before he resigned, he looked appalling, like a man who has read his own death warrant. I sat in my chair like a fool, pretending to read some damned newspaper . . . you know I can't look at the *Times* these days?" His fingers were fiddling with the letters, notes and lists in front of him, but idly, not as if he had the faintest interest in what they were.

"I looked at White and I knew what he was feeling. I could practically read his thoughts, they were so like my own. He was ill with anxiety, trying to suppress the fear in case anyone else guessed, attempting to appear natural, and all the time half looking over his shoulder, wondering who else knew, who thought he was behaving oddly, who suspected. That's one of the worst things of all, Pitt." He looked up, his face tense, the skin shining across his cheekbones. "The mind racing away with thoughts you hate and can't stop. People speak to you, and you misinterpret every remark, wondering if they mean something more by it. You don't dare meet a friend's eyes in case you see knowledge there, loathing, or worse, that he should see the suspicion in yours."

Suddenly he stood up and strode over to the window, his back half turned to Pitt. "I hate what I have allowed this to make me into, and even as it happens I don't know how to stop it. Yesterday I met an old friend from the navy, quite by chance. I was crossing Piccadilly, and there he was. He looked delighted and dodged in front of a brougham, nearly being clipped by the wheels, in order to see me. My first thought was to wonder if he could be the blackmailer. Then I was so ashamed I couldn't look in his face. . . ."

Pitt scrambled for anything to say that would be of comfort. Everything would be lies. He could not say the man would have understood or would have forgiven. Does one forgive for being considered a blackmailer, even for an instant? If Cornwallis had suspected Pitt, Pitt could never have liked him the same way afterwards. Something irreparable would have been broken. He should know Pitt better than that. Blackmail was an abysmal sin, cruel, treacherous, and above all the act of a coward.

Cornwallis laughed abruptly. "Thank you at least for not replying with some platitude that it doesn't matter, or that he would never know or do no better himself." He was still staring at the street below, his back to the room. "It does matter, and I wouldn't expect anyone to forgive. I couldn't forgive any man who thought me capable of such a thing. And worst of all, whether anyone else knows, I know it of myself. I'm not what I thought I was . . . I haven't the judgment or the courage. That's what I hate the most." He turned to face Pitt, his back against the light. "He's shown me part of myself I would rather not have known, and I don't like it."

"It has to be someone who knows you," Pitt answered quietly. "Or how would he have learned of that event sufficiently to twist it as he has?"

Cornwallis stood with his feet slightly apart, braced as if against the pitch of a quarterdeck.

"I've thought of that. Believe me, Pitt, in the small hours I've walked the bedroom floor or lain on my back staring at the ceiling and thought of every man I've ever known from schooldays to the present. I racked my brains to think of anyone to whom I might have been unjust, intentionally or not, anyone whose death or injury I could even have been perceived to have caused or contributed to." He spread his hands jerkily. "I can't even think of anything I have in common with the others. I barely know Balantyne to speak to. We are both members of the Jessop Club, and of a Services Club in the Strand, but I know a hundred other people at least as well. I don't suppose I've spoken to him directly above a dozen times."

"But you know Dunraithe White?" Pitt was searching his mind also.

"Yes, but not well." Cornwallis looked mystified. "We've dined a few times. He's traveled a little, and we fell into conversation about something or other. I can't even remember what now. I liked him. He was agreeable. Fond of his garden. I think we spoke of roses. His wife is clever with space and color. He was obviously devoted to her. I liked it in him." Cornwallis's face softened for a moment as he recalled the incident. "I dined with him again another time. He was held in town late, some legal matter. He would have preferred to go home, but he couldn't."

"His decisions have been erratic lately," Pitt said, remembering what Vespasia had told him.

"Are you sure?" Cornwallis was quick to question. "Have you looked into it? Who says so?"

With anyone else Pitt would have hesitated to answer, thinking discretion better, but with Cornwallis he had no secrets in this.

"Theloncus Quade."

"Quade!" Cornwallis was startled. "Surely he is not another victim? God in heaven, what are we coming to? Quade is as honorable a man as any I know of—"

"No, he's not a victim!" Pitt said hastily. "It was he who noticed White's opinions lately and became concerned. Lady Vespasia Cumming-Gould approached White because of it."

"Oh . . . I see." Cornwallis bit his lip. He frowned, walking back towards the desk and staring moodily at the tossed piles of paper. He turned to Pitt. "Do you think his erratic judgments are born of his anxiety over the blackmail, for fear of what will happen next, what he will be asked for? Or could it be the price he is paying to the blackmailer, and somewhere among the eccentric decisions is the one that matters, the one this is all about?"

Pitt considered it seriously. The thought had occurred to him before, briefly. He had given less weight to it only because he was so overwhelmingly concerned about Cornwallis.

"It could be the latter," he replied. "Are you sure that is not the connection between you . . . a case in which you both have some part?"

"But if it is, then where are the others involved?" Cornwallis asked. "Is it political? Stanley is already ruined. His part hardly matters now . . . or does it? Was it always part of this plan to destroy his power, to prevent him from obtaining the position he sought?" He jerked his hands wide. "And Cadell? Is there a foreign power involved? Tannifer's bank certainly deals with many European banks. Enormous amounts of money could be concerned. Balantyne fought in Africa. Could that be it?" His voice rose a tone, suddenly an edge of eagerness in it. "Could it be to do with the financing of diamonds or gold in South Africa? Or simply land, perhaps expeditions inland to claim whole new tracts, like Mashonaland or Matabeleland? Or some discovery we know nothing of."

"Balantyne served most of his time in India," Pitt said thoughtfully, turning it over in his mind. "His only African experience that I know of was Abyssinia, and that's the other end of the continent."

Cornwallis pulled his chair around and sat on it, staring at

Pitt, leaning forward. "A Cape-to-Cairo railroad. Think of the money involved. It would be the biggest thing of the coming century. The African continent is an entire new world."

Pitt caught a glimpse of the vision, but it stayed on the edge of his mind, just beyond clarity. But certainly it was a fortune, a power for which many men would kill, let alone blackmail.

Cornwallis was staring at him, his face dark with the enormity of what he perceived. His voice was urgent when he spoke.

"Pitt, we have to solve this . . . not just for me or for any of the individual men it may ruin. This could be far more widely reaching than a few lives made or lost; it could be a corruption which could alter the course of history for . . . God knows how many." He leaned farther forward, his eyes intense. "Once any of us yields to the threat and does something that really is wrong, perhaps criminal, perhaps even treasonous, then his hold is complete and he could ask anything and we would have no escape . . . except death."

"Yes, I know," Pitt agreed, seeing an abyss of corruption open up in front of him, every man suffering alone, driven by fear, exhaustion, suspicion on every hand, until he could bear the pressure no longer. Simple murder would have been less cruel.

But rage was a waste of energy, possibly exactly what the blackmailer wanted; useless, time-consuming, clouding the mind.

Pitt composed himself with an effort. "I'll look into all Dunraithe White's cases over the last year or so, and all those scheduled to come before him as far in the future as is known."

"Tell me!" Cornwallis demanded sharply. "You had better report every day, so we can compare what we know. At the moment we are in the dark. We don't even know in which direction to begin. It could be fraud or embezzlement, or a simple murder that appears domestic. There must be money, or it wouldn't involve Tannifer, and some foreign interest for Cadell, and possibly Balantyne . . ." His voice sharpened, and he raised his hand, banging his forefinger on the desk. "Mercenaries? A private army? Perhaps Balantyne knows the man who would recruit for it . . . or lead it? He might have knowledge he does not even realize . . . and some criminal case that White and I are both concerned with. Or that I may become concerned with. Perhaps we are beginning to understand something, Pitt?" There was hope in his eyes. "I could have asked White myself, but he's resigned from the Jessop, and I don't have the opportunity to speak to him casually anymore. And Balantyne only comes for the committee meetings. I think he hates it as much as I do. The man looks as if he hasn't had a decent night's sleep in weeks."

Pitt forbore from saying that Cornwallis looked the same.

"Cadell less so," Cornwallis added, rising to his feet again. "But then I suppose it is a week or so since I saw him . . . before poor Stanley was ruined."

"You know Cadell?" Pitt said quickly. He had not been aware of that, although it should not surprise him. Society was small. Hundreds of men belonged to a mere handful of clubs and associations.

Cornwallis shrugged. "Slightly. He was on the committee at the club. It's a group who meet every so often, to do with a charity for orphans. It's the only reason I go now. Can't let them down."

Pitt rose also. "I'll start to look into Dunraithe White's cases. I think that is where we'll find the link. It must be something in the recent past or on the calendar for the future. I think the future is more likely."

"Good. Let me know the moment you find anything, however tentative," Cornwallis urged. "I might be able to see the connection before you do."

Pitt agreed again, and left to begin, collecting a list of all the current investigations over which Cornwallis had a general authority. Then, armed with a brief note of introduction and explanation, he took a hansom to the Old Bailey Courthouse.

* * *

The afternoon had gained him a list of cases, but it was bare information and there were several pending with which both Cornwallis and White had some connection, even if tenuous. What he needed was an informed opinion, preferably that of someone who was aware of the situation. Theloneus Quade was the obvious choice. Pitt had no idea where he lived, and to approach him in court where he was presiding would be difficult, and possibly unwise.

Six o'clock in the evening found him on Vespasia's doorstep.

"Have you news?" she asked him when he was shown into the withdrawing room where she was sitting in the late-afternoon sun reading the newspaper. She put the paper down immediately, not merely from good manners but from a very real concern. The small black-and-white dog at her feet opened one eye to make sure he was who she thought he was, then, satisfied, closed it again and went back to sleep.

"Not really," he replied, glancing at the *Times* where she had let it fall. She had been following the Tranby Croft affair. Black letters proclaimed that the verdict had been brought in: guilty. Pitt found it strangely chilling. He had no idea whether Sir William Gordon-Cumming had been guilty of cheating or not, but that a simple matter of dishonor at cards should have escalated into a formal court case involving so many people in conflicting testimony which had now laid bare hatred and national scandal was a tragedy. And it was one which need not have happened. There was too much that was beyond human ability to avoid; it was absurd that this should have reached such a stage.

"I suppose the Prince of Wales at least will be relieved it is over," he said aloud.

Vespasia glanced at the paper, half on the floor. Her face was bleak with disgust.

"One presumes so," she said coldly. "This is the first day of the Ascot races. He did not stay in court to hear the verdict. Lady Drury called by on her way home. She told me he drove to the royal box accompanied by Lady Brooke, which was

217

tactless to say the least, and was met by boos and hisses from the crowd."

Pitt remembered Vespasia's dislike of craning her neck to look up at him, and accordingly sat down. "What will happen to Gordon-Cumming?" he asked.

She replied unhesitatingly. "He will be dismissed from the army, expelled from all his clubs and boycotted from society in general. He will be fortunate if anyone continues an acquaintance with him." Her face was difficult to read. There was a sharp pity in it, but she could have considered him guilty and still felt that. Pitt knew her well enough to realize how complex were her emotions. She belonged to a generation to which honor was paramount, and the Prince of Wales's own gambling and self-indulgent manner of life were not excused by his royal status. In fact, it made them the more reprehensible. She was of the same generation as Victoria herself, but from all he had heard, as unlike her in nature as possible, although they had lived through the same epoch of history.

"Do you think he was guilty?" he asked.

She opened her amazing silver-gray eyes wide, her perfectly arched brows barely moving.

"I have considered it carefully, for reasons relating to the problem facing us. It serves as something of a measure of public opinion, at least that part of it which would be of concern to men like Dunraithe White and Brandon Balantyne." She frowned slightly, looking directly at Pitt. "It seems undeniable his method of placing his wager was ill advised, most particularly in the company in which he found himself." The expression in her eyes was impossible to read. "No one comes out of this well, neither man nor woman. There has been a suggestion, not entirely absurd, that the whole matter was deliberately brought about in order to discredit Gordon-Cumming and thus disqualify him as a rival of the Prince's for the affections of Frances Brooke."

"The Lady Brooke with whom the Prince arrived at Ascot today?" Pitt asked, surprised. It seemed either extremely stupid or unnecessarily arrogant, and possibly both.

218

"The same," she agreed dryly. "I have no idea whether it is true, but the fact that it can be suggested is indicative of opinion."

"Innocent?" he said quietly.

"I don't know," she replied. "The jury apparently took only fifteen minutes to reach their decision. It was greeted by jeers and hisses also. But after the summation given by the judge little else was possible."

"To save the Prince?" he asked.

She gave a very slight gesture of despair.

"That seems unarguable."

"Then it has no bearing upon our situation. . . ."

She smiled very slightly. "Other things will have, my dear Thomas. Public opinion is a very fickle animal, and I fear our blackmailer has great skill. He has chosen his subjects far too well for us to delude ourselves that he is likely to make mistakes. To answer your question, yes, I think poor Gordon-Cumming may well have been innocent."

"I have looked through all the possible cases where there might be a connection between Cornwallis and Dunraithe White," he said thoughtfully, reverting back to the reason for which he had come. "A very ugly fear is in the back of my mind that the conspiracy may be a great deal more ambitious than I imagined to begin with. Nothing to do with simple payment of money, but the corruption of power . . ." He watched her face as he spoke, seeking to read whether she found his thought absurd. He saw only the greatest gravity. "To do with expansion in Africa, perhaps. That is the area involving all the people we know about which comes most easily to mind."

"Indeed." She nodded. "Of course, we do not know who else may be concerned. That is one of the most frightening aspects of this case. There may be other members of government or the judiciary, or any other area of power or influence. But I agree, Africa does seem likely. The amounts of money to be gained there at present are beyond the dreams of most of us. I think Mr. Rhodes may end up building little short of his own empire. And throughout history people have been dazzled by the prospects of gold. It seems to breed a kind of madness."

He brought out the piece of paper on which he had written the names of the cases in which Cornwallis and Dunraithe White were both involved. There were only five. He showed it to her.

She picked up her lorgnette to read his handwriting.

"What do you need?" she asked when she had finished. "To know more about them?"

"Yes. White would not tell me, because he intends to yield to the blackmailer; you told me that yourself. I should prefer not to ask Cornwallis, because I believe he is politically naive, and I would also rather not compromise him, should we not be able to prevent the matter from becoming public." He felt a weight inside himself, a heaviness of foreboding it was not easy to dispel, even here in this calm, sunlit room with which he had become so pleasantly familiar. "I must be able to help him . . . if it should come to that."

"You do not need to explain it to me, Thomas," she said quietly. "I understand the nature of suspicion, and of honor." She met his gaze steadily. "I think perhaps that you should speak to Theloneus. What he does not know already, he will be able to learn. He is as deeply worried by this as we are. He also fears it may be a political plan of far-reaching nature, with high and irrevocable stakes involved. We shall call upon him . . . unless, of course, you feel it wiser to go alone?" There was no shadow of personal hurt or affront in her silver eyes.

He answered honestly. "I should value your judgment. You may think to ask him questions I would have missed."

She nodded her assent. She was grateful; she loved to be involved. Her intellect and her curiosity were as sharp as ever, and the foibles of society had bored her for years. She knew them all so well she could predict them. Only the rarest, most genuine eccentric still awoke her interest or amusement. But of course she would not say so. She merely smiled, and asked Pitt if he would care for dinner first, which he accepted, asking permission to use the telephone to let Charlotte know that he would not be home.

"Of course, there are many possibilities," Theloneus Quade said as they sat in the late-evening sun in his quiet library, the small summer garden beyond the window filled with the sounds of birdsong and of falling water from a stone fountain. The long light was apricot-gold on the full-blown roses, and a white clematis shone in a flash of silver.

"Tannifer may be pressured to grant a loan which he is aware cannot be satisfactorily guaranteed," he continued earnestly. "Or indeed repaid. Or to overlook dealings which are fraudulent, not to investigate accounts when there has been embezzlement."

"I know." Pitt sat back in the comfortable chair. The room was quiet, charming, and full of individual touches. He had noticed books on a wide variety of subjects as he came in: the fall of Byzantium, Chinese porcelain, a history of the Tsars of Russia, the poetry of Dante and of William Blake and a dozen other unrelated subjects, and on the wall a watercolor of ships by Bonington which he thought was probably quite valuable. Certainly it was very lovely.

"It could also be someone who has already committed some act for which he will shortly be tried," Theloneus went on. "And he hopes to subvert the cause of justice. Possibly, without being aware of it, the other victims may be in some way witnesses to it, and he believes they may be suborned by the threat of disclosure, or their testimony invalidated by their own ruin." He looked at Pitt steadily, the question in his eyes. His features were mild, sensitive, but there was an acute intelligence in him which burned through, and only a foolish man would mistake his quiet voice, his outward gentleness, for any weakness of courage or intent.

"I've not found any connection between all the victims we know of," Pitt explained. "They do not seem to have any common interest or background. They have only the slightest acquaintance, as all London of a certain social level has. There are a limited number of gentlemen's clubs, the museum,

221

the National Geographic Society, the theater, the opera, the races, the same round of social events. Even so, they do not have any interest in common I can find, or any specific acquaintance that does not equally include a thousand others."

"And no one has yet been asked for money?" Theloneus said.

"I am not certain." Pitt thought of Cadell. "It is possible Cadell of the Foreign Office may have." He told him of Parthenope Tannifer's information, and his own visit to Cadell, and his denial.

Theloneus remained silent for several moments, turning it over in his mind.

Outside the light was fading. The lawn was already in shadow, and there was a flush of gold across the sky.

"I cannot help feeling that it is more than money," Vespasia interrupted the silence. "Money could more easily be extracted by slow and reasonable threats, and a means of payment made more obvious. The pattern does not seem to be right."

Pitt turned in his chair to look at her. Her face was very grave in the slanting light, which was gentler than the white clarity of morning. It lent a glow to the beauty of her bones, still exquisite, untouched by the years. Her hair could almost have been gold rather than silver.

"I am inclined to agree with you," Theloneus said at last. "The exercise of power is so deliberate I feel there will be something asked for which will be repugnant to each man we know of, but by the time the demand is made, he will be so weakened by the tension, the fear and the exhaustion that he will not be able to summon the strength to resist. He will be prepared to do almost whatever he is asked, even something he would normally refuse without consideration."

"What concerns me," Vespasia said with a frown, "is why Brandon Balantyne was the one chosen for the dramatic and rather extreme measure of having a corpse placed upon his doorstep." She looked from Pitt to Theloneus, and back again. "That was bound to bring the police into this affair.

Why did our blackmailer wish that? One would have thought it would be the last thing he desired."

"That puzzles me also," Pitt confessed. "Except it would seem that possibly some extreme pressure was desired upon Balantyne, but why, I have no idea."

"I suppose it is not coincidental?" Theloneus asked. "Could it be merely fortuitous that poor Albert Cole died where he did?"

"No." Pitt realized he had not told them about Tellman's discovery. He saw their surprise at his certainty. "No, it's not coincidence," he said. "Tellman has been working on it. We assumed it was Albert Cole because of the bill for socks, which certainly seemed to be his. The lawyer from Lincoln's Inn Fields identified him as Cole." He had their total attention. They both leaned forward, eyes fixed upon his face. "But it turns out it was a petty thief by the name of Josiah Slingsby," he continued, "who quarreled with his accomplice, Ernest Wallace, a man with a violent temper, and Wallace killed him. . . ."

"And left him in Bedford Square?" Vespasia said in amazement.

"They were burgling Bedford Square," Theloneus concluded. "They stole the snuffbox from Balantyne? No . . . you said he admitted giving it to the blackmailer. Thomas, my dear friend, this makes no sense whatever. You had better explain yourself again. We have missed something. To begin with, where is the real Albert Cole?"

"No, Wallace did not kill Slingsby in Bedford Square," Pitt answered. "Or anywhere near it. They quarreled in an alley in Shoreditch, and he left Slingsby exactly where he fell and ran away. He swears he never went anywhere near Bedford Square, and Tellman believed him. So do I."

"And the receipt for socks?" Theloneus asked. "Did he know Albert Cole?"

"He says not, and there seems no reason to suppose he did."

"And what does Cole say?"

"We haven't found Cole. I have Tellman looking for him."

"Then someone else took Slingsby's body, placed Albert Cole's receipt on it, and left it on Balantyne's doorstep," Vespasia said with a shiver she could not control. "Surely there can be no other conclusion than an intention to embarrass Brandon Balantyne, possibly even to have him arrested for murder?"

"You did not add, my dear, that it must be the blackmailer," Theloneus reminded her. "Since he placed the pinchbeck snuffbox in the dead man's pocket as well."

She looked from Theloneus to Pitt. "Why? Under arrest Balantyne could neither pay money nor exert influence, corrupt or otherwise."

"Then that brings to one's mind the only other alternative," Theloneus reasoned. "He may wish Balantyne removed so he cannot have an effect upon whatever it is he is planning to do. Perhaps he tried to corrupt him and failed, and this is his way of neutralizing his ability to affect the issue."

"Which brings us back to the most urgent need to learn what the issue is," Pitt said helplessly. "We don't know! We have found nothing in common between them all, Mr. Quade." He produced the list of cases and handed it to Theloneus. "Can you tell me anything about these? They are all the charges in which Cornwallis was concerned and are due to be heard before Dunraithe White. Is there anything in any of these which could involve the others, however indirectly?"

Theloneus studied the list very carefully, and Pitt and Vespasia remained silent while he did so. Outside the light was dying more swiftly. The roses were a pale blur. Only the tops of the trees were golden. A poplar looked like a shimmering spire as the sunset breeze caught and turned its leaves. A cloud of starlings whirled up into the air, black against the deep, soft blue of the sky. The hustle and squalor of the city was only a matter of yards away, the other side of a high stone wall, but it could have been another land.

The clock in the hall chimed the half hour.

"Some of these cases are merely sad," Theloneus said at last. "People who have allowed shortsighted greed to sweep away their better judgment, individual crimes which will

224

bring down the families of the men concerned, but no more. There is a sense in which it is already inevitable, and nothing Cornwallis or White will do can change that. An able barrister may mitigate the sentence by pleading the circumstances, showing the accused in a more human light, but the verdict will be the same."

"And the others?" Pitt pressed.

"That is a domestic murder. It is unlikely to implicate anyone else, but not impossible. The woman was beautiful, and very liberal with her favors. Other men may be implicated, but I find it difficult to believe blackmail will help the accused husband. And since he is in prison awaiting trial, it would have to be accomplished for him by someone else. He does have two loyal and ambitious brothers. It is not impossible."

"Could it involve all our blackmail victims?" Pitt said dubiously.

"If you are referring to Laetitia Charles, then most certainly not!" Vespasia said tartly. "Certainly she was, at the very kindest, a woman of overgenerous affections. She was also earthy in her tastes, very frank to the point of vulgarity, and had an uproarious sense of the absurd, frequently at the cost of her admirers—and of her husband." She shrugged her thin shoulders very slightly. In the shadows her face was unreadable. "She would have terrified the life from a man like Captain Cornwallis, and he would have bored her to weeping. Leo Cadell would have had more of a sense of self-preservation than to have had anything to do with her, even socially, and Dunraithe White has never looked at another woman in his life. Even if he had wanted to, and I concede that he may, his sense of honor would crucify him if he had, and I, at least, would know of it."

Theloneus smiled bleakly. "You are probably right, my dear. That leaves two cases of fraud and embezzlement, both for very large sums of money. One involves international banking in Europe—Germany, to be precise—and the transfer of funds to a very questionable enterprise in South Africa. The other is an attempt to pass forged bonds and deeds to mines, again in Africa."

"Could they be connected to each other?" Pitt asked quickly.

"Not on the surface, but it is possible." Theloneus regarded the paper again. "One would have to know who purchased the bonds. It is conceivable that it may concern all our victims."

"Where in Africa?" Pitt pressed.

"As I recall, several places." Theloneus frowned. "I think it may bear further investigation. The case is not complete yet. The trial lies some time in the future."

"Is it still under investigation?" Pitt asked with a sinking in his stomach. "By whom?"

"Superintendent Springer," Theloneus replied. "Reporting to Cornwallis." He regarded Pitt steadily, a sadness in his eyes and in the lines of his face, but he would not look away nor temper the perception that was all too plainly in his mind.

"I see," Pitt said slowly, hating himself for the thoughts he could not dismiss. Vespasia was watching him also, less easy to see clearly in the half darkness as no one had wished to light the gaslamps. The last of the day was slipping away rapidly. The rustle of the poplar leaves sounded through the open windows like breaking waves on a shore, far away.

Theloneus said it for him. "Of course, it is a possibility Cornwallis may be pressed to abandon the case, to order Springer to withdraw from it, discontinue investigation, somehow contaminate the evidence. And Dunraithe White may similarly be pressed to render an eccentric or perverse decision."

"Would that not cause a mistrial?" Pitt asked.

"Only if there was a verdict of guilty," Theloneus replied. "The Crown does not have the right to appeal against an acquittal. If it did, cases might never end."

"Of course." Pitt had not been thinking clearly. The idea of Cornwallis in such a situation—that, in fact, he might already be compromised—was even more painful than he had expected. He had said nothing, but he was a uniquely lonely man, used to the isolation of command at sea, where he could never confide in anyone or his power to lead would be damaged beyond repair. The captain was as alone on the quarterdeck as if he were the only man on the face of the ocean. The slightest weakness, indecision, possibility of ignorance or error, and his position was forfeit. Everything in the structure of rank, obligation and privilege conspired to make it so. It was the only way someone could survive in an element which obeyed only its own rules and knew neither thought nor mercy.

Cornwallis could not change in a few short years, perhaps not ever. When he faced danger he would revert to the skills he knew, the ones that had carried him through countless perils before. It was an instinct he probably could not have helped, even had he wanted to.

"Is Tannifer involved?" Pitt asked, thinking of Parthenope and her fierce loyalty.

"It is embezzlement. It is possible," Theloneus answered.

"Cadell?" Pitt went on.

"African funds. The Foreign Office may be concerned."

"Balantyne?"

"I can't see how, but there is much yet to be uncovered."

"I see." Pitt stood up slowly. "Thank you very much for your time . . . and your thoughts."

Vespasia leaned forward to rise, and Theloneus offered her his arm. She took it, but lightly; as a gesture, not an assistance.

"I am afraid we have not helped, have we?" she said to Pitt. "I am sorry, Thomas. The roads of friendship are sometimes strewn with many pitfalls, and some of them can hurt a great deal. I wish I could say Cornwallis will not fail, but it would be a lie, and you would know it. Nor can I say that, even with the utmost courage and honor, he will not be hurt. But we shall not cease to fight with the very few and inadequate weapons we have to hand."

"I know that." He smiled at her. "We are not beaten yet."

She gave a very slight smile back, but was too tense to argue.

They parted from Theloneus, leaving him standing in the lighted doorway, and drove home in her carriage through

227

the lamplit streets, neither feeling it necessary to speak any further.

The following morning Pitt went to see Cornwallis. He was torn between the personal loyalties of friendship and the necessities of his duty to pursue knowledge to its end. Whether Cornwallis understood that or not, he could not deliberately fail in it and remain of use to either of them.

Cornwallis was pacing the floor again. He swung around and stopped as Pitt came in, almost as if he had been caught in some nefarious act. He looked as if he had not eaten properly or slept well in days. His eyes were sunken into his head, and for the first time since Pitt had known him, his jacket did not sit smoothly on his shoulders.

"I have had another letter," he said baldly. "This morning." He waited for Pitt to ask what was in it.

Pitt felt his stomach lurch and his body go cold. This was the demand at last. He could see it in Cornwallis's eyes.

"What does he want?" He tried not to betray his knowledge.

Cornwallis's voice was rough, as if his throat were sore, and he spoke with difficulty.

"That I should drop a case," he replied. "If I don't, then the H.M.S. *Venture* matter will be exposed in every newspaper in London. I could deny it all I wished, but there would always be those who believed, those who doubted my version of events. I . . . I should be blackballed from my clubs, perhaps even lose my naval rank and standing. Look what happened to Gordon-Cumming, and for far less!" His face was ashen, and he controlled his hands from trembling only by supreme effort of will.

"Which case?" Pitt asked, waiting for him to say the embezzlement that Springer commanded.

"This case!" Cornwallis frowned. "The blackmail investigation. The truth about Slingsby and the Bedford Square murder . . . who put the body on Balantyne's steps. What in God's name does the man want from us?" His voice was rising in spite of himself, a note of panic creeping in.

The room seemed to swim with the sunlight blazing in

through the open window, the noise of traffic in the street below rose like thunder.

"But you won't . . ." Pitt said, forcing the words through stiff lips.

A faint patch of color blushed up Cornwallis's haggard cheeks. Something in his mouth softened.

"No! Of course not," he said with intense, choking emotion. It seemed to take him by surprise, as if he had not thought he could feel so passionately about anything. "No, Pitt, of course I won't." He seemed about to add something more, a word of thanks for having assumed so much, but at the last moment the words were too open, too intimate an acknowledgment of friendship, of vulnerability. It was all better understood, where it could be glossed over later. Men did not say such things to each other.

"Naturally." Pitt shoved his hands down inside his pockets. "At least it gives us something further to look into, a better place to begin." He must say something trivial and matter-of-fact. It did not really matter what. "I think I'll go and see Cadell again."

"Yes," Cornwallis agreed. "Yes, of course. Let me know what you learn."

Pitt went to the door. "I might see Balantyne too," he added as he went out. "I'll tell you if there's anything."

9

Pitt *HAD BEEN* late home the previous evening, but even so he had wanted to tell Charlotte what he had learned and the troubling thoughts he could not still in his mind. She had been more than willing to listen, not only in concern for his feelings but because she wished intensely to know for herself. They had sat talking long after midnight, unable to let go of the anxiety and the need to share it with each other.

This morning she was more than ever concerned for General Balantyne. It seemed he was targeted by the blackmailer in a more personal and specific way than any of the other victims. Pitt had very carefully refrained from saying that had the murder of Josiah Slingsby been blamed upon him, he would have been effectively removed from complying with the blackmailer's demands, either for money or for the exercise of influence. Nevertheless, she had understood it perfectly clearly. Therefore it followed that what he wanted might not be anything Balantyne could give but rather his destruction, not an act but the inability to act. And either ruin or death would serve the same end. Pitt had skirted around it, being so careful, trying not to hurt her, but the thought was inevitable once the train of ideas was begun.

It was a brilliantly sunny day, but fortunately a little cooler. At last there was a breath of breeze to break the suffocation of the heat wave. It was too pleasant to be inside if one did not have to. She had agreed to meet Balantyne in the British Museum as before, but was delighted when a boy on a bicycle brought a note to the door asking if she would find it acceptable to meet at the gate of the Royal Botanical Gardens in Regents Park instead.

She wrote a hasty answer that she would be happy to.

Accordingly, at eleven o'clock, dressed in deep pink and wearing one of Vespasia's most extravagant hats, she was standing in the sun just inside the gates, watching the passersby. It was an occupation which in small amounts she found most interesting. She imagined who they were and what sort of homes and lives they had left this morning, why they might have come here, whom to meet.

There were the obvious lovers, strolling arm in arm, whispering to each other and laughing, seeing no one else. There were those less open, pretending they were merely friends and had met by chance, being elaborately inconsequential. Several young girls in pastel dresses passed by, giggling, huddled close together, swinging their petticoats, eyeing the young men and trying to look as if they weren't. Their muslin skirts drifted in the slightest breeze, their hair gleamed, the blood warm in their cheeks.

Two young soldiers paraded by in uniform, dashing and elegant. Charlotte could not help thinking that probably in ordinary browns and grays they would have looked like any other clerks or apprentices. The bravado made all the difference. She smiled as she watched them. They had a kind of brash innocence. Had Balantyne once been like that, thirty years ago?

It was impossible to imagine him so young, so callow and unaware.

An elderly lady came past dressed in lavender. Perhaps she was in half-mourning, or maybe she merely liked the color. She walked slowly, her entire attention upon the flowers, profuse and dazzling in their beauty.

Although Charlotte was waiting for Balantyne, she did not see him until he was at her elbow.

"Good morning," he said, startling her. "They are beautiful, aren't they?"

She realized he was speaking about the roses.

231

"Oh, yes. Marvelous." She was suddenly completely uninterested in them. In the bright sunlight the weariness showed in his face, the network of fine lines about his eyes and mouth, the shadows from too little sleep.

"How are you?" he continued, looking at her as if the answer mattered to him greatly.

"Let us walk," she suggested, reaching to take his arm.

He offered it unhesitatingly.

"I am very well," she answered as they passed between the flower beds, just another two people among the many. "But the situation is hardly better; in fact, I am afraid it is worse." She felt his arm tighten under her hand. "There have been very curious developments which have not been in the newspapers. It is proved beyond doubt that the body was not that of Albert Cole at all, but a petty thief from Shoreditch called Josiah Slingsby."

He stopped and swung around to stare at her. "But that makes no sense!" he protested. "Did he steal the snuffbox? From whom? He cannot have been the blackmailer . . . I received another letter this morning!"

She had known more would come, and yet she still felt a shock as if someone had struck her. He had touched them again, closely, personally, had reminded them of his reality, his power to act, to hurt them.

"What did he say?" She found the words awkward, her lips dry.

"The same," he answered, beginning to walk again. In the shelter they had lost the breeze, and the perfume of the roses was heavy, dizzying in the sun.

"Did he still not ask for anything?" she pressed. She wished he would. Waiting for the blow to fall was almost worse than facing it when it did. But then, that was presumably a large part of the plan, the weakening, the fear, the wearing down before the attack.

"No." He faced straight ahead, avoiding looking at her. "There is still no request for money or anything else. I have lost count of the hours I have lain awake trying to imagine what he could wish of me. I have thought of every area in which I could act, or have influence, of every person I know whose behavior I could affect, for good or ill, and I can think of nothing."

She hated the thought, but it must be faced if it were to be fought against.

"Is there anyone in whose path of promotion or gain you are standing?"

"Militarily?" He laughed with a sharp, desperate sound. "Hardly. I am retired. I have no title or wealth that should pass to anyone but Brandy, and he could not be behind this. You know that as well as I."

"Any other position, social or financial?" she pressed. "Any elected office?"

He smiled. "I am president of an explorers' club which meets once a quarter and tells each other stories, greatly embellished by imagination and wishful thinking, entirely for entertainment. We are all of us over fifty, and many over sixty. We live in the glory and the color of our past exploits. We remember Africa when it truly was a dark continent, full of mystery and adventure. We traveled for love of the unknown, long before anyone thought of it in connection with investment and the extension of empire."

"But you have knowledge of it, real knowledge, from having been there?" she pressed.

"Of course, but I cannot think it is of any use to present-day explorers and financiers." He frowned. "Do you think this has anything to do with Africa?"

"Thomas does ... at least he holds it as a possibility. Great-Aunt Vespasia believes it is a very powerful conspiracy, and great profit for someone lies at the root of it."

They were passing other flower beds now which were brilliant with color and perfume. The drone of bees was audible above the swish of skirts and a faint murmur of conversation.

"That seems likely," he answered.

"Any other offices?" she asked.

"I was president of a society promoting young artists, but my term finished last year." His voice emphasized the triviality of it. "Other than that, newly being a member of a group within the Jessop Club that raises finances for an orphanage. I cannot imagine anyone desiring to take my place in that. It is hardly exclusive anyway. I believe anyone who wished to join it would be welcomed."

"It doesn't sound like the sort of thing one would commit blackmail to achieve," she agreed.

They walked in silence for a hundred yards or so, across the pathway which circled the gardens and out into the main part of Regents Park. The sun was growing hotter and the breeze had dropped. Somewhere in the distance a band was playing.

"I don't think the fact that the body is that of Slingsby, and not Cole, has made any difference to the police's believing I could have been responsible for his death," he said at length. "I suppose he could have been running errands for the blackmailer as easily as anyone else. You say he was a thief?"

"Yes . . . from Shoreditch, nowhere near Bedford Square," she said quickly. "He was killed in Shoreditch, by his accomplice. Thomas knows it had nothing to do with you at all."

"Then why is his sergeant still making enquiries about me?"

"To learn what the blackmailer wants," she said with conviction. "It must be some influence you have, some power or information. What have you in common with the other victims?"

He smiled bleakly, a flash of hard humor. "Since I don't know who they are, I cannot even guess."

"Oh . . ." She was taken aback. "Yes . . . of course. They are a banker, a diplomat, Sir Guy Stanley of course you know . . ." She saw the wince of pity in his face but went on. "A judge . . ." Should she mention Cornwallis or not? Pitt might prefer she did not, but the situation was too serious for secrets that were largely a matter of saving embarrassment. "And an assistant commissioner of police."

He looked at her. "Cornwallis," he said softly. "I don't expect you to answer that . . . of course. I'm sorry. He's a very decent man."

"You know him well?"

"No, very slightly. Simply members of the same club . . .

two clubs, actually. Always thought him a good fellow, very straightforward." Again he lapsed into silence for several yards. "I knew Guy Stanley too. Not well, but I liked him."

"You are speaking of him in the past. . . ."

His face tightened. "So I am. I'm sorry. That is inexcusable. I've been thinking about him a lot since that news broke. Poor devil." He shivered a little and hunched his shoulders, knotting the muscles as if he were cold in spite of the sun. "I called on him. Wanted to tell him . . . I don't know . . . perhaps only what you came to me to say, that I still regarded him as my friend. I don't think him guilty of that charge, but I have no idea if he believed me."

A dog scampered across their path carrying a stick in its mouth.

He stared straight ahead. "Perhaps I should have had the courage to tell him I was a victim of the same blackmail, but I couldn't bring myself to tell even him what it accused me of. I do not admire myself for that. I wish now that I had. Then he might have known I believed him. But I suppose if I were honest, I was afraid he would not believe me." He swung around to face her again. "That is the thing; I am not sure of anybody anymore. I mistrust where I would never have thought of it even a month ago. People offer me decency, friendship, kindness, and I look at them and doubt. I try to see motives behind which are ugliness and duplicity, double meanings to remarks that are made in innocence. I am tainting even the good that I have."

She squeezed his arm more tightly, standing close to him in the bright light. The feathers of her hat fluttered in the breeze, almost close enough to him to touch his cheek.

"You must keep not only your head but also your heart," she said gently. "You know it is not true. You must think better of us than to imagine we are so easily misled or so quick to be cruel." She made herself smile. "You have only one enemy that we know of, and even he does not actually believe it is true. He knows better."

The wind caught a loose strand of her hair and blew it across her brow.

"Thank you," he said very quietly; it was little more than a breath. Then he put out his hand and pushed the hair back where it had come from, under the brim of Vespasia's hat. In that one gesture he had committed himself, and he knew it. In this isolated moment in the sun it did not matter. Tomorrow perhaps it would, but today could not be taken from the memory.

She felt a moment of sweetness, and pain, and a realization that she was guilty of a wild kind of carelessness that she had never intended, and could similarly never be undone.

A little way off a woman with a blue parasol laughed. Two little boys chased each other, tumbling in the grass and getting happily dirty.

She must start to walk again, say something natural.

"As I mentioned, Aunt Vespasia thinks it may have something to do with Africa," she remarked. "The situation there is so volatile, with fortunes to be made and lost."

"She is right," he agreed, also beginning to move forward, his mind returned to the matter in hand. "That would explain the various men he has apparently chosen."

"The Cape-to-Cairo railway?" she suggested.

They discussed African politics for some time: Cecil Rhodes and the expansion northwards, the possibilities of vast quantities of gold to be discovered, land, diamonds, the conflicting interests of other European countries, most particularly Germany.

But by noon when they parted they were no closer to knowing what any such political adventurers could demand of Balantyne, or anything he knew which could stand in any man's way to the fortunes to be exploited in Africa or anywhere else.

While Charlotte was in the Royal Botanical Gardens talking to Balantyne, Pitt returned to see Sigmund Tannifer, at his request. He found him in a grave mood, and this time Parthenope was not present.

"I have discussed this with my wife," Tannifer said as soon as the formalities had been met and he and Pitt were sitting

236

facing each other in his handsome, rather ornate study. "We have given a great deal of thought to who may be involved, and even more as to what they may demand of me, when they finally reach that stage." He also appeared haggard and as if his nerves were stretched almost to the breaking point. His left hand constantly fidgeted, and Pitt noticed that the crystal decanter on the chiffonier behind him was less than a quarter full of brandy. He would not have blamed any man in these circumstances for seeking a little extra comfort.

"And you have some conclusion?" he asked aloud.

Tannifer bit his lip. "Not really conclusions, Superintendent, more speculation I would like to put before you." He gave a half smile. "Perhaps I am looking for excuses to speak with you, obtain some reassurance. I fear it is rather like pulling the dressing off a wound to see if it is healing . . . or not." He shrugged his heavy shoulders. It was an oddly defeated gesture. "It doesn't help in the slightest, neither the wound itself nor one's ease of mind, and yet the compulsion is irresistible."

Pitt understood perfectly. "And what are your thoughts, Mr. Tannifer?"

Tannifer looked slightly self-conscious. "I am not trying to usurp your office, Superintendent. I am sure you know far more about it than I do, but I was considering all the areas in which I might have some ability to act and which could be misused to someone else's advantage." His fingers drummed silently on the arm of his chair. "It always comes back to finance of some sort." He stopped, regarding Pitt gravely.

Pitt nodded, indicating that he understood, but he did not interrupt.

Tannifer could not hide his nervousness.

"The first thing that came to my mind was to wonder what we may have in common. Of course, I do not know the identities of the other victims, beyond what I may deduce with a little common sense. Poor Guy Stanley is obvious, although since in his case the threat has been carried out . . ." His fingers increased in their rhythm of drumming on the chair arm. "And I can assume Brandon Balantyne . . ." He waited to see

237

if Pitt would confirm it or if he could read it from his expression. His lips tightened. Apparently, he could. "And as I believe my wife mentioned—she told me she had spoken with you—I am certain in my own mind that Leo Cadell is also threatened in the same way. He believes he will be asked for money. At least that is the impression he has given me. But I have never thought that was at the root of the blackmailer's aim."

Pitt nodded.

"You agree?" Tannifer said quickly, his voice gaining strength. "I am sure we are right. I have been making certain very discreet enquiries into their affairs, and thinking back upon my own responsibilities. It is within my powers to grant very large loans for investment in certain areas, most particularly land and the development of mining for precious metals such as gold."

Pitt found himself sitting a trifle more upright in spite of his intention to not betray any of his own feelings.

If Tannifer noticed he did not show it. He sat slumped in his own chair, his face heavy with concentration.

"It would be corrupt of me to agree to such loans without proper security," he said thoughtfully. "But not beyond my actual power. In seeking to learn which areas might be involved, so as to decide who might be concerned, I looked into Leo Cadell's recent travels, and what I could discover, with discreet enquiry, of his interests." He was watching Pitt with intense concentration. "In all cases, Superintendent, they centered in Africa. The possibility is barely realized of the enormous treasure lying in the areas Cecil Rhodes is developing. A man who could involve himself now could, in the next twenty years, amass a king's ransom and perhaps build himself an empire."

It was what Vespasia and Theloneus Quade had feared. Now Tannifer was saying virtually the same thing.

Tannifer was watching Pitt acutely, his eyes unblinking, his shoulders hunched.

"I see you follow me perfectly." He took a deep breath. "I was speaking with Cadell, and he let slip a remark which leads me to believe that Mr. Justice Dunraithe White might be another victim. . . ."

Pitt was startled. How could Cadell have known that? Was it observation of White's erratic behavior, or the emotional strain under which he labored, almost to the verge of illness? Perhaps it was not so difficult to detect a fellow victim, being acutely aware of one's own suffering?

"I cannot comment," Pitt said quietly. "But you may assume that at least one judge is involved. Does that make your deductions any plainer?"

"I am not sure. I see it very murkily, I admit." Tannifer smiled grimly. "Perhaps I am wasting your time, but I find it almost impossible to sit and wait until the blow falls, and do nothing to try to ward against it." He seemed embarrassed, uncertain how to continue, and yet obviously there was something further he wanted to say.

"Be frank, Mr. Tannifer," Pitt urged. "If you are correct, then this conspiracy is wide and deep, and the effects, if it succeeds, will be far greater than the ruin of a few good men and their families."

Tannifer looked down. "I know. It is only some feelings for the privacy of others which hold me, and perhaps at this stage such delicacy is misplaced." He looked up quickly. "Cadell indicated to me that there was some incident in the naval career of Assistant Commissioner Cornwallis which could be open to misinterpretation, and therefore to the same kind of pressure as is being exerted upon me." He was watching Pitt with acute concern. "I am deeply afraid that the blackmailer may attempt to have this whole enquiry dropped in order to protect himself. Perhaps Cornwallis could not further his African ambitions, but he might be persuaded to manacle you. . . ." He let out his breath in a heavy sigh. "This is hideous! Everywhere we turn we are faced with blind alleys and new threats."

Pitt made some sign of assent, but his mind was racing on the remark Tannifer had made about Cadell without realizing its importance. The incident in Cornwallis's naval career was not questionable; only the blackmailer had seen it as such.

Tannifer would not know that, but Pitt did. He must not betray his understanding.

"It is a profound danger," Pitt said, and he had no need to invest his expression of face and voice with any false anxiety. The fear was very real. His regard for Cornwallis made it the more painful, because he could foresee it happening. It was the next, obvious step for the blackmailer, and he now knew Cornwallis would suffer, perhaps already was suffering. If it happened, would he even tell Pitt?

He hated himself for allowing the thought to enter his mind, but it was there like a knife, pricking him at every turn, and surprising in its painfulness.

"But you will not permit it to . . . prevent you?" Tannifer said huskily. "You will . . ." He let the rest of the sentence fall away.

Pitt did not answer. What would he do if Cornwallis were threatened in such a way, and if he asked Pitt to protect him? He had not doubted Cornwallis's innocence. Would he allow him to be ruined, shamed, publicly driven from all he valued? He could not honestly make such promises.

Tannifer looked away. "It is not so easy, is it?" he said softly. "We like to think we would have the courage to tell him to go to the devil . . . but embarrassment, loneliness and humiliation are real." He looked back at Pitt levelly. "To speak of ruin is one thing, to face it is another. I thank you at least for your honesty."

"We had considered the possibility of the extortion of agreement to large funds for expedition into Africa, north from the Cape into Mashonaland and Matabeleland," Pitt said thoughtfully. "Or an investment in a Cape-to-Cairo railroad . . ."

Tannifer sat up sharply. "Brilliant!" He clenched his fists on the arms of his chair. "I commend you, Superintendent. Your perception is more finely attuned than I had given you credit for, I admit. I am most encouraged . . . perhaps foolishly so, but I shall cling onto it." He rose to his feet and held out his hand.

Pitt took it, and was startled by the strength of Tannifer's grip. He left feeling as if at last he had taken a step forward, even if it was towards an unknown and certainly harsh conclusion.

He had no alternative but to go again to see Leo Cadell. He was unable to do this at the Foreign Office, where Cadell was fully engaged for the afternoon, but he called at his home and was waiting for him when he arrived. It was not an interview he was looking forward to, and Cadell's weary face made it more difficult.

He rose to his feet from the sofa where he had been sitting.

"Good evening, Mr. Cadell. I am sorry to trouble you at the end of the day, but I am afraid there are matters I need to discuss with you, and you were not available earlier."

Cadell sat down. He did it as if his body ached, and it was apparent he was using all his reserves of inner strength to maintain an air of courtesy.

"What is it you wish to discuss, Mr. Pitt?"

"I have been giving a great deal of thought to what unjust pressures might be brought to bear upon you, particularly with regard to your position in the Foreign Office," Pitt began. It was difficult to maintain the anger he had felt when he was in Tannifer's house. He had to remind himself of the pain the man opposite him might be inflicting on others, of the ruin that the blackmailer had unquestionably already unleashed on Guy Stanley without giving him any chance to fend it off, even dishonorably. It was not impossible that the blackmailer might disguise himself as one of the victims. What better way to ensure that he knew the direction of the investigation or its success? Who knew what lay behind Cadell's anxious face and the polite, patient smile? He was a diplomat. He had made his career successfully masking his emotions.

He was watching Pitt now, waiting for him to make his point.

"You have considerable interest and responsibility in African affairs," Pitt continued. "Particularly in the exploration of such areas as Mashonaland and Matabeleland."

"I am concerned with relations with other European powers

241

who have interests in the area," Cadell corrected slightly. "Germany, in particular, is also concerned in East Africa. The situation is far more sensitive than perhaps you are aware. The potential for making vast amounts of money is immense. Most of the population of South Africa is not British but Boer, and their feeling towards Britain is not kindly—nor, I fear, in any way to be relied upon." He watched Pitt's face as he spoke, trying to gauge his understanding. "Mr. Rhodes is a law unto himself. Dearly as we would wish it, we have little control over him."

Pitt was unwilling to allow Cadell to know too much of his thoughts. Perhaps the knowledge Tannifer had given him was his only advantage. However smooth a face a blackmailer wore, he was a ruthless man without scruples as to whom he hurt, or how deeply. It would seem he enjoyed the taste of his own power. The ruin of Guy Stanley would suggest as much.

He looked steadily at Cadell. "If you were to be asked by the blackmailer, Mr. Cadell, what would be within your ability to do to serve his ends, were he interested in African expansion, a private fortune in that country, or perhaps domination of a Cape-to-Cairo railroad?"

Cadell was startled. "Good God! Is that what you think he wants?"

Was it the idea which shocked him or Pitt's perception of it?

"Would it be possible?" Pitt insisted.

"I . . . I don't know." Cadell looked acutely uncomfortable. "I suppose there is . . . information I might pass to certain people . . . information as to Her Majesty's government's intentions which would benefit—could benefit—such a person."

"How about a military adventurer?" Pitt went on. "Someone intending to raise a private army, for example."

Cadell was white-faced. He sat forward in his chair. "This is far more serious than I had imagined. I . . . I supposed it would be a matter of money. Perhaps I was naive. Believe me, if anyone should approach me with any such suggestion I should report it immediately to Sir Richard Aston, whether I knew who it was or not. The consequences would have to follow as they may. I would not betray my country, Mr. Pitt."

Pitt wanted to believe him, but what else would he say, whatever he would actually do? Pitt could not rid his mind of the knowledge that this man sitting so innocently opposite him had told Tannifer of Cornwallis's vulnerability, a thing he could not know other than from the blackmailer. In truth, it did not exist. That was the only thing all the men unarguably had in common; the blackmailer knew them well enough to be familiar with what could be manufactured from their pasts to destroy all their usual courage and resolve, reduce them to nerve-racked, self-doubting men living in a waking night-mare, suspicious of even those closest to them.

"Do you know Assistant Commissioner Cornwallis?" Pitt asked abruptly.

"What?" Cadell was taken by surprise. "No . . . well . . . slightly. Belong to the same clubs. See him occasionally. Why? Or should I not ask?"

Did he say that because he knew? Or was it the intelligent guess any man might make in the circumstances? He must think of a noncommittal answer. And he should not betray Tannifer's confidence. If Cadell was the blackmailer he was cruel enough to exact a vicious revenge.

"He is in charge of the case . . . ultimately," he said aloud. "He mentioned the possibility of a political motive."

"I cannot help you," Cadell replied wearily. "Believe me, Mr. Pitt, if I knew anything at all which could be of use, and I were free to discuss it with you, I would. I presume I do not have to explain to you that a great deal of the information I have about Africa concerns the government's plans regarding Mr. Rhodes and the British South Africa Company, and is confidential. So also are all matters to do with the settlement of Mashonaland and Matabeleland, or our relations with other European powers who have interests in the continent of Africa. It would be an act of treason for me to speak of them to you except in the broadest way, which would be of no use to you."

Pitt realized that there was no purpose in pressing him further, and after thanking Cadell, he took his leave.

Vespasia was walking slowly across her lawn, thinking that it was time it was mown again, when she saw Pitt standing in the open French windows of her sitting room. She was startled to find her breath catching in her throat and her heart racing, fearing what news he might have brought. She walked rapidly towards him, barely leaning on her stick.

"Good evening, Thomas," she said as soon as he joined her on the grass. She refused to betray her anxiety. "I am afraid the best of the tulips are over. They are beginning to look dreadfully blowsy."

He smiled in the evening sun, glancing at the heavy roses in full bloom, and the cascade of wisteria, and a few huge, gaudy tulips past their best.

"It looks perfect to me."

She regarded him up and down. She remembered that he liked gardening, when he had the opportunity. "I agree, but perhaps the purist would not."

He offered her his arm and she took it as they walked slowly back across the grass to the terrace and up the steps.

"I am afraid I have very unpleasant news, Aunt Vespasia," he said when they were inside and she was seated.

"I can see it in your face, my dear," she replied. "You had better tell me what it is."

"Tannifer sent for me today. He also seems to be of the opinion that the blackmailer's ultimate goal may be to influence African affairs to his own advantage."

"That is not news, Thomas," she said a trifle sharply. She had not realized how tense she was. She heard the edge in her own voice. "We had assumed as much," she continued. "Did he offer any evidence?"

He must have caught her emotion. He came directly to the point. "He mentioned Cadell's name in two regards, one intentionally, concerning his professional interest in African affairs."

His face was filled with distress, and it touched her with increasing fear. She found herself swallowing with an effort, but she did not interrupt.

"The other was accidental, at least as to meaning," he continued quietly. "He was concerned that Cornwallis might also be a victim, and that thought was prompted by Cadell's having referred to an incident in Cornwallis's career which was open to misinterpretation and therefore made him vulnerable."

For a moment she did not understand. Her concern was for Pitt.

"But Cornwallis said that he saved the man," she argued. "Does that now make you reconsider his innocence?"

"No." He shook his head minutely. "It makes me wonder how Cadell knew of it and why he should even consider Cornwallis as a victim."

Then she understood. A great weight of coldness settled inside her. She dared not think of the tragedy that might lie ahead. She had known Theodosia and cared for her since her birth; she had watched her grow up as she had her own children.

"Leo Cadell is a victim also," she said, and knew the remark was pointless even as she made it. The blackmailer could easily pose as a victim. It would serve his purpose in many ways.

Pitt did not argue with her. He knew it was unnecessary.

"I realize that does not exclude him," she said very deliberately. "But I have known Leo for a great many years. I have watched his pattern of behavior. And don't tell me people can change with pressure or temptation. I know that, Thomas." She was talking too quickly, too vehemently, and she could hear it in her voice, and yet it seemed to be beyond her control. Her thoughts were far ahead, and already inescapable. "He has his weaknesses, of course. He is an ambitious man and a good judge of other men's characters, but he is fiercely patriotic, in a conventional way." She felt a thin shudder of horror. "He is not a greedy man, nor an adventurous one."

Pitt was listening to her, his face grave. The sunlight through the French windows lengthened across the carpet, apricot gold. The black-and-white dog had gone back to sleep as it lay in the warmth.

"I do not believe Leo has the cruelty, or the ingenuity, to have conceived a scheme like this," she said with conviction. "But that he should use Theodosia's beauty to win advancement is not impossible. He would deny doing it, even to himself." She hated what she was saying; it was repugnant in every way. It felt like a betrayal to admit such a thing, even to Pitt, but it was true. It had crossed even her mind to wonder if the accusation could hold some truth. That in itself was the most powerful illustration of the blackmailer's brilliance. Even she had entertained the idea . . . how much more easily would others believe it? She was ashamed of herself for her disloyalty, not only to Leo, but even more to Theodosia. And yet the thought had come, and the doubt.

Pitt was still talking.

"I called on him," he said gravely, watching her face. "He seems to consider he may be asked for money. Mrs. Tannifer overheard a conversation about raising a large, unspecified amount."

"But the blackmailer has not asked for money," she responded. "That makes no sense." But even as she said it the thought darkened in her mind. She refused to accept it. It was disloyal . . . untrue. She was doing exactly what the blackmailer wanted . . . she had yielded her independence, her belief. "It's rubbish!" she said too loudly.

He did not argue. They discussed it a little longer and then he took his leave. But even when he had gone, she could not rid her mind of the thought and the unhappiness which oppressed her, and she spent a long and surprisingly lonely evening.

While Pitt was talking to Vespasia, Charlotte was sitting in her kitchen pouring tea for Tellman, who had called expecting to find Pitt at home. To judge from the expression on his face, he was both disconcerted and pleased to find that Pitt was unexpectedly late and the only people home to hear his report were Charlotte and Gracie.

He sipped the tea appreciatively and rested his feet. He

would probably have liked to take his boots off, as Pitt himself would have done, but that was far too much of a liberty.

"Well?" Gracie said, watching him from where she stood at the sink. "Yer must 'ave come fer summink, 'ceptin' ter sit down."

"I came to see Mr. Pitt," he replied, avoiding meeting her eyes.

Gracie kept her patience with difficulty. Charlotte could see the temper in her face and watched her thin chest rise and fall as she took a deep breath.

Archie, the marmalade-and-white cat, stalked across the floor, found just the right place in front of the stove and sat down.

"That means yer don't trust us ter pass it on ter 'im?" Gracie said quietly.

Tellman seemed almost to have forgotten Charlotte. The idea that Gracie thought he did not trust her was obviously acutely uncomfortable to him. His struggle within himself was palpable.

Gracie did not help him at all. She waited, her arms folded, regarding him, her small face full of impatience.

"It's nothing to do with trust," he said at last. "It's police business, that's all."

Gracie thought about that for a moment or two.

"I s'pose you're 'ungry too?" she said.

That took him by surprise. He looked up quickly. He had been expecting an argument or a flash of temper.

"Well, are yer?" she demanded. "Cat got yer tongue?" Her tone became sarcastic. "That in't a p'lice secret, is it?"

"Of course I'm hungry!" he said, coloring dull pink. "I've been walking around the streets all day."

"Follerin' poor General Balantyne, 'ave yer?" she said, also ignoring Charlotte. "Well, that must a' bin 'ard work. W'ere'd 'e go, then?"

"I didn't follow him today," he replied. "Nothing to follow him for."

"So 'e din't do nuffin', then?" she concluded. "Never thought as 'e did." She sniffed.

Tellman was silent. If anything, his discomfort seemed to have increased. Watching him, Charlotte was aware that his mind was going through a kind of turmoil quite unfamiliar to him. His ideas had been challenged and found severely wanting. He had been forced to change his opinions about someone, presumably General Balantyne, and so perhaps a great many other people he had previously grouped together as a class and now had been obliged to see as individuals. To have one's prejudices overthrown is always painful, at least at first, even if one can eventually accommodate them, and it becomes liberating in some distant future.

She felt sorry for him, but that would be the last thing he would want. She still remembered now and then how when she had first met Pitt he had shown her another world, full of individual people with loves and dreams, fears, loneliness and pain, perhaps different in cause but essentially the same as her own. Before that she had barely noticed some of the ordinary men and women in the streets; they had been a class to her rather than people just as unique as she was, with lives as full of incident and feeling as her own. The realization of how blind she had been was painful. She had despised her own narrowness, and it was not easy to acknowledge it even now.

She could see the confusion in Tellman's face, his bent head, his bony hands lying on the table beside the mug of tea Gracie had given him.

Angus, the black cat, came in through the back door and sauntered across to sit so close to Archie that he was obliged to move. Angus began to wash himself.

Gracie cleared her throat. "Well, if yer like I can get yer a kipper an' some bread an' butter?" she offered, barely glancing at Charlotte to gain her permission. She was about detecting business, and that did not really require any additional sanction.

Tellman hesitated, but his desire to accept was far plainer than he could possibly have realized.

Gracie gave up, shrugging her shoulders. She treated him as she would seven-year-old Daniel; she took the decision out of his hands. She snatched the skillet from the rack and put it

248

on the hob, poured water from the kettle into it, then went for the kipper.

"Yer 'avin' it poached," she said over her shoulder. "I in't messin' around wif fryin'. Anyway, tenderer poached." And she disappeared into the larder to fetch it.

Tellman glanced up to Charlotte anxiously.

"You are very welcome, Mr. Tellman," she said warmly. "I'm glad you have discovered General Balantyne is not involved in the death of Josiah Slingsby, and I am grateful to hear it."

He bit his lip. He was still confused inside himself.

"He seems to be a good man, Mrs. Pitt, a good soldier. I spoke to quite a few men who served with him. They have a lot of . . . respect for him . . . more than that . . . a kind of . . . loyalty . . . affection." The surprise and reluctance was still in his voice.

Charlotte found herself smiling, partly with sheer relief. She had not thought differently, but it was important to have Tellman say so. She was also amused to see his expression.

Gracie came back with a large kipper and, ignoring both of them, placed it in the simmering pan with satisfaction. Both cats immediately sat up, noses quivering, startled, and went eagerly towards the stove. Then Gracie went to the wooden breadbox and took out a loaf. Cutting them first from the end, she buttered several thin slices and laid them on a plate. She refilled the kettle and set it on the hob, working busily, as if she were alone in the room.

Still smiling to herself, Charlotte decided to leave them. Tellman could work through his awkwardness the best he was able. He gave her a quick, rather desperate look as she went to the door, but she pretended to have no idea of the emotion in the room, and excused herself to have a game of charades with Jemima and Daniel, leaving Gracie to finish the kipper.

Pitt was later than usual in to Bow Street the following morning; in fact, he had only just arrived when there was a sharp bang on his office door. Before he could answer, it opened to admit a breathless sergeant, his face filled with consternation.

"Sir . . . Mr. Cadell has been found shot!" He swallowed hard, catching his breath. "Looks like suicide. He left a note."

Pitt was stunned. Even as he sat motionless with the sense of shock sinking into him like ice, his brain told him that he should have expected it. The signs had been there; he had simply refused to recognize them because of the pain it would cause Vespasia. He thought of her now, and of Theodosia Cadell. For her this would be almost unbearable, except that one had to bear it because there was no alternative.

Was he to blame? Had his visit to Cadell yesterday evening precipitated this? Would Vespasia hold him responsible for it?

No, of course not. It would be unjust. If Cadell were guilty, then it was his own doing.

"Sir!" The sergeant shifted from one foot to the other, his eyes wide and anxious.

"Yes." Pitt stood up. "Yes. I'm coming. Is Tellman in?"

"Yes sir. Shall I get 'im?"

"Send him to the door. I'll get a hansom." He went straight past the sergeant, not even thinking to pick up his hat from the stand, only snatching his jacket off its hook.

Downstairs he met Tellman, coming from the back of the station, his face grave and pale. He did not say anything, and together they went out onto the pavement and walked in the sun smartly along to Drury Lane. Pitt stepped into the road waving his arms, startling a shire horse pulling a wagon full of furniture. He shouted at a hansom coming around the corner from Great Queen Street and started running towards it, holding up all the traffic and being very thoroughly sworn at.

He scrambled in, calling out instructions to the driver, and slid across the seat to make room for Tellman. Of course, it was pointless—a few minutes here or there in reaching Cadell's house could make no difference now—but the urgency of action released some of the anger and misery inside him.

Two or three times as they rode, Tellman made as if to speak, then, seeing Pitt's face, changed his mind.

When they arrived Pitt paid the driver and strode across the pavement to the front door. There was a constable posted outside, his face stiff, his body at attention.

"Mornin', sir," he said quietly. "Sergeant Barstone's inside. He's expecting you."

"Thank you." Pitt brushed past him, opened the door and went in. It was absurdly like yesterday evening. The elaborate long case clock in the hall still ticked loudly, the hand moving from second to second with a little jerk each time. The brass edge of the umbrella stand still gleamed, but now from the sunlight streaming under the closed withdrawing room door. The bowl of roses had not shed any petals, or the maid had picked them up already.

All the doors were closed. He had not thought to ask where Cadell's body was, and he had let himself in. There was no one else in the hall. He went back to the door again and rang the bell, then returned to wait.

"Do you want me to speak with the servants?" Tellman asked. "Don't know what we could find. This looks like the end of it. Not really what I expected."

"I suppose you might as well," Pitt agreed. "Somebody might tell us some small thing which will explain how it all happened. Yes . . . yes, of course." He straightened up. He was being careless. "We don't know it was suicide yet. We are assuming."

"Yes sir." Tellman went willingly. Pitt knew why. He hated having to face the families of the dead. Corpses did not trouble him the same way—they were beyond their pain—but the living, the shocked, bewildered, grieving, were different. He felt helpless and intrusive, even though he could have justified his role to anyone. Pitt understood exactly; he felt the same.

The butler appeared from the green baize door into the servants' quarters. He looked startled and angry to see Pitt already in the hall. In the distress of the morning he had apparently forgotten who Pitt was.

"Good morning, Woods," Pitt said gravely. "I'm sorry for Mr. Cadell's death. Is Mr. Barstone in the withdrawing room?"

251

Woods recollected himself. "Yes sir." He swallowed, moving his neck as if his collar were too tight. "The . . . the study is locked, sir. I assume you will be needing to go in?"

"Is that where Mr. Cadell is?"

"Yes sir . . . I . . ."

Pitt waited.

Woods searched for words. He was obviously troubled by profound emotions.

"I don't believe it, sir!" he said gruffly. "I've been with Mr. Cadell for nearly twenty years, and I don't believe he'd take his own life. It has to be something else, some other answer."

Pitt did not argue. Denial was the natural response to something so ugly, and from this man's point of view, so utterly inexplicable. How could it make any sense to him?

"Of course we'll investigate every possibility," he said quietly. "Would you let me into the study; Sergeant Tellman has gone to speak with the rest of the staff. Who found Mr. Cadell this morning?"

"Polly, sir. She's the downstairs maid. Went in to dust and make sure the room was clean and tidy. I'm afraid you can't speak to her yet, sir. She's taken it terribly hard. Awful thing for a young girl to find." He blinked several times. "She's usually very sensible, good worker, no trouble, but she just fainted clear away. She's in the housekeeper's sitting room, and you'll just have to give her time. Can't help that, sir."

"Of course. Perhaps you can tell me most of what I need to know to begin with."

"If I can, sir," Woods conceded, perhaps helped in the immediate moment by the fact that he was able to be engaged in doing something. He fished in his pocket and produced a small brass key. He stood with it in his hand, waiting.

"What time was that?" Pitt asked him.

"Just after nine, sir."

"Was that the usual time for Polly to go into the study?"

"Yes sir. Things sort of fall into a routine. Best way. Then nothing gets forgotten."

"So everyone would know that Polly would go into the study at that time?"

252

"Yes sir." Woods looked deeply troubled. It was easy to understand, and his thoughts were plain in his face. Cadell himself would have to have been aware of the almost certainty that a young maid would be the one to find him.

"And the door was unlocked. . . ." Pitt stated the obvious, but with surprise. People who intended killing themselves very often ascertained that they would have privacy.

"Yes sir."

"Did anyone hear the shot? It must have made a considerable noise."

"No sir, not that we realized, if you know what I mean?" Woods looked embarrassed, as if he had been at fault; if they had heard it they might have prevented the tragedy. It was irrational, but grief and incomprehension had numbed his faculties. "You must understand, sir, most of the staff were busy about their duties that hour of the day. The kitchen was full of comings and goings. There were tradesmen's boys in the yard with deliveries and the like, wagons and carts and things clattering up and down the road, and with the windows open to air the house, there was a certain amount of noise anyway. I expect we heard it but never realized what it was."

"Did Mr. Cadell have breakfast this morning?"

"No sir, just a cup of tea."

"Wasn't that unusual?"

"No sir, not lately. I'm afraid Mr. Cadell was not himself as far as his health was concerned." He blinked again, stirring to govern his emotions. "He seemed very preoccupied, if you understand me. I daresay there is some foreign business that gives cause for concern. It is an extremely responsible . . ." He tailed off, suddenly remembering again that his master was dead. His eyes filled with tears and he turned away, embarrassed to lose such control of himself in front of a stranger.

Pitt was used to distress. He had been in situations like this countless times. He affected not to have noticed.

"Where did Mr. Cadell take his tea?"

It was a moment before Woods replied. "I believe Didcott the valet took it up to his dressing room, sir," he said at last.

"And then he went down to the study?"

"I believe so. Didcott would know."

"We'll ask him. Thank you. Now I'll go to the study, if you will let me in."

"Yes sir, of course." And with slightly shaky steps, Woods led the way across the hall and down a fairly long passage to an oak door which he opened with the key. He remained outside while Pitt went in.

Leo Cadell was slumped forward over the desk, his hands on top of it a trifle awkwardly, his head on one side. Blood from a wound to his right temple spilled out over the wooden surface of the writing top. A dueling pistol lay touching his right hand, two inches from a quill pen, the ink dried. There was also a cushion on the floor near the chair. Pitt bent and picked it up, putting it to his nose and sniffing. The smells of gunpowder and charring were plain. That explained why nobody had heard the sharp report of the shot.

It did not explain why Cadell had not locked the door from the inside, so people would know there was something wrong, and it would not be a young maid, or even his wife, who would be the first to find him.

But then a man capable of the kind of blackmail which had been practiced was hardly likely at this point to consider the feelings of a maid or of anyone else. How easy it is to be totally and disastrously mistaken in one's judgment of people. Pitt still found it hard to accept, and Vespasia possibly never would. Apparently, even as wise and shrewd as she was, she could be utterly wrong.

He looked at the papers on the top of the desk. Half a dozen in a neat pile were letters and minutes from the Foreign Office; one, alone, to the left of the pile, was composed of pieces clipped from newspapers . . . probably the *Times* again, and pasted onto plain white paper. He read it.

I know the police are close behind me now. I cannot succeed, and I will not wait for them to arrest me. I could not face that.

This is a quick, clean end, and I shall not be aware of

what happens after I am gone, except that the case is
ended. It is all over.

Leo Cadell

It was terse; no regrets, no apologies. Perhaps there was
another letter somewhere to Theodosia. Pitt could not believe
she had known his guilt

He looked closely at it again. It appeared exactly the same as
the others he had seen. The spacing was a trifle different, less
precise, but then in the circumstances that was unsurprising.

There were scissors along with a paper knife, a stick of
sealing wax, a small ball of string and two pencils in a holder
on the desk. He could not see any glue or paste. Perhaps it had
been used up and the container thrown away.

Where was the newspaper from which the words and letters had been cut? It was not on the desk or on the floor. He
looked in the wastepaper basket. It was there, folded neatly.
He took it out. Yesterday's copy of the *Times*. It was easy to
see where the pieces had been cut.

He let it fall again. There seemed little more to say. Cadell
was right; as far as the police were concerned, the case was
complete. For the victims, most of all for Theodosia, it never
would be.

The sharp morning sunlight fell through the clear glass of
the French doors into the garden. The maid had been too dis-
traught to think of closing the curtains. There was no one in
sight. He moved across and did it now, closing the latch on
the door and then drawing the heavy velvet across.

He went out and locked the hall door behind him. He must
speak with Theodosia. Speaking to the family of the victim,
and the ultimate arrest of someone, the shock and anguish of
their family, were the two worst times in any investigation. In
this one they were bound together in one occasion, and the
grief in one person.

She was sitting in the withdrawing room, gray-faced, her
body stiff, her hands clenched together in her lap so hard her
knuckles shone where the skin was stretched tight. She stared

at him wordlessly out of eyes almost black. She was alone, no maid or footman with her.

He came in quietly and sat down opposite her. Not only had she lost her husband, a man Vespasia said she truly loved, and her future was gone, but—immeasurably more painful—her past was destroyed as well. The whole precious image of her world and all it had meant was shattered. The foundation upon which she had built her beliefs was gone. Everything about her husband that truly mattered, that formed the structure of her relationships, even of her understanding of herself and her own judgments, was proved a lie. She had been misled, deceived in everything. What was left?

How often do we perceive the world and those we love not as they are but only as we want them to be?

He wished he could offer her any comfort at all, but there was none.

"Would you like me to call Vespasia for you?" he asked her.

"What? Oh." She remained silent for a few moments, struggling within herself. Then she seemed to reach some inner conviction. "No . . . thank you. Not yet. She will find this very difficult. She was—" Her voice cracked. "She was fond of Leo. She thought well of him. Please wait until I am more composed. Until I have a better idea of what happened so that I can tell her."

"Would you like me to tell her?" he offered. "I can go to her home. Otherwise she will read it in the newspapers."

The very last vestige of blood drained from her face, and for a moment he was afraid she was going to collapse. She struggled for breath.

Instinctively, ignoring conventions, he moved forward to kneel on the floor beside her, holding her hands where they were knotted iron hard on her lap. He put his other arm around her. "Slowly!" he commanded. "Breathe slowly. Don't gasp."

She obeyed, but even so it was several minutes before she regained physical control of herself.

"I am sorry," she apologized. "I beg your pardon. I had barely thought of the newspapers."

"I'll call on Vespasia as I leave here," he said decisively. "I am sure she will wish to be with you. It will be easier for her to face this if she is not alone."

She looked at him, and there was a warmth of gratitude momentarily in her eyes. She did not question his decision. Perhaps she was glad to have any step taken for her, anything that relieved a bit of the weight she must bear alone from now on.

"Thank you," she accepted.

There was nothing else to ask her. He rose to his feet. She could summon the maid if she wished. She might prefer just at the moment to be alone, perhaps to weep, although that would probably come later.

He was at the door when she spoke.

"Mr. Pitt . . . my husband did not kill himself . . . he was murdered. I don't know how, or by whom, except that I have to presume it was the blackmailer. If you stop now, he will get away with it." The last sentence was said with sudden, choking anger, and her eyes blazed a challenge to him, on the brink of blame.

He did not know what to say. There were no grounds for her charge except loyalty, pain and despair.

"I won't take anything for granted, Mrs. Cadell," he promised. "I shall look for proof of every detail before I accept it."

He and Tellman questioned all the household staff, but there had been no break-in; no strangers had been seen. The delivery boys at the back door had not gone through the wooden gate in the wall to the garden; indeed, they had been too busy flirting with the scullery maid and the lady's maid, respectively, to leave the step at all. They had barely succeeded in doing the duty they were employed for.

No one had come through the house, and the only person to go through the garden door was the gardener's boy delivering ties and doing a little work on the old white climbing rose which was in bloom and in need of holding up.

No one knew anything about the gun. Cadell must have had it for some time. There were a pair of pistols in a case locked into the corner cupboard in the study, but this was not one of them. Theodosia said she had never seen it before, but admitted that she hated guns and would not recognize one from another.

The staff were not permitted to touch them or have anything to do with them, so they could offer no information at all. It seemed that where Cadell had obtained it or how long he had owned it would remain a mystery, like much else to do with his whole blackmail scheme.

Pitt called at Vespasia's house before returning to Bow Street. She, too, was shocked by the news of Leo Cadell's death, and found it almost impossible to believe that he was responsible for the blackmail, but she did not deny it as Theodosia had done. She thanked Pitt for coming to tell her personally rather than allowing her to read of it in the newspapers, then she called for her carriage and her lady's maid, and prepared to go and offer whatever comfort she could to her goddaughter.

Pitt decided then to tell Cornwallis. He also should not learn it from the evening editions of the newspapers.

"Cadell?" he said in amazement. He was standing in the middle of his office as if he had been pacing the floor. His face was haggard. He had neither eaten nor slept well in weeks. There was a very slight nervous tic in his left temple. "I . . . I presume you must be sure?"

"Can you think of another explanation?" Pitt asked unhappily.

Cornwallis hesitated. He looked profoundly miserable, but even as they spoke, some of the agonized tension had eased out of his body, and his shoulders were lowering into a more natural position. Whatever the surprise or the understanding of grief, his own ordeal was over, and even if he despised himself for it, he could not help but be aware of that.

"No . . ." he said at last. "No. From what you say, that must be the answer. What a damned tragedy. I'm sorry. I could have wished it were . . . someone I didn't know. I suppose that's idiotic. It had to be someone I knew. . . . It had to be someone we all knew. Well done, Pitt . . . and . . ." He wanted to thank Pitt for his loyalty, it was there in his eyes, but he did not know how to word it.

"I'll go back to Bow Street," Pitt said briefly, "and tidy up the details."

"Yes." Cornwallis nodded. "Yes. Of course."

10

$V_{ESPASIA}$ *WENT* immediately to Theodosia, taking her lady's maid with her, and such necessities as she would require to remain overnight, or longer. She had no intention of allowing Theodosia to remain alone in the grief, confusion and despair which must follow upon such an appalling loss. In her long life she had encountered suicide before. It was in many ways the hardest of all to endure, and the loneliness and the guilt which invariably followed all but doubled the pain.

There was nothing to do that first afternoon and evening but to survive them, to be there and allow Theodosia to begin to realize that Leo was truly dead. Of course, tomorrow morning would be worse. Sleep, however little of it, would bring respite, then with waking there would be a few moments before memory returned. That would be like hearing it all over again, only without the numbing mercy of shock.

They sat up and talked in Theodosia's boudoir. She seemed to need to speak of Leo, most particularly of the kind of man he had been when they first met. With a rising tone of desperation she recalled dozens of good things he had done, brave or kind or wise, acts of honesty where less would have passed uncriticized, even unnoticed, but he had silently done his best.

Vespasia listened, and indeed she could remember a great many of them herself. It was only too easy to recall all that was likable in him, all she had admired over the years.

A little before midnight Theodosia suddenly found she

was able to weep, and the release of tears exhausted her. After that Vespasia's maid brewed her a sleeping draft and she went to bed. Vespasia took a draft herself and retired fifteen minutes later.

The morning was even worse than she had expected, then she was angry with herself for not having foreseen it. She met Woods in the hallway as she was crossing to the breakfast room. He looked pale and red-eyed.

"Good morning, your ladyship," he said hoarsely, and cleared his throat. "How is Mrs. Cadell?"

"Asleep," Vespasia answered. "I shall not disturb her. Will you be good enough to bring me the newspapers."

"The newspapers, your ladyship?" His eyebrows rose.

"Yes, please."

He stood unmoving. "Did you mean the whole newspaper, your ladyship?"

"Of course, the whole newspaper, Woods. Am I not making myself plain?" It would have been pleasanter to have them burnt. It was her first instinct, but she needed to know what they said. There were truths that could not be avoided. "I shall be in the breakfast room. I shall have tea and toast. No more will be necessary."

"Yes, your ladyship," Woods said hastily. "I'll . . . I'll have them ironed. . . ."

"Don't bother." She realized that with the master dead the usual duties in this respect had been abandoned. "I'll look at them as they are." And without waiting for argument, she passed him and went to the breakfast room.

He brought them on a tray, smoothed but unironed, and she took them from him. They were uniformly dreadful. One of them summed up everything that was worst in all three and added a great deal of speculation that was both cruel and destructive. It was written by Lyndon Remus. He had done his own investigation into the corpse found in Bedford Square and its possible connection with General Balantyne. He must have followed Pitt because he also was aware of his visits to Dunraithe White, Tannifer and Sir Guy Stanley.

In his article on Cadell's suicide he suggested a conspiracy that Pitt had discovered and that he had been on the brink of arresting Cadell.

Superintendent Thomas Pitt refused to comment, but Bow Street police station did not deny that Mr. Cadell was being investigated in connection with a very serious matter involving extortion and murder, and figures in the establishment, both financial and military, as well as in the government.

Since Mr. Cadell, who shot himself to death in his study yesterday morning, held a high position in the Foreign Office, one cannot but wonder if the conspiracy concerned the interests of Great Britain abroad, and even treason may have been narrowly averted by swift action from the police.

It is to be hoped that if there are other guilty parties they will not now be protected from answering for their crimes, whether carried out or simply intended. Lesser men have been exposed for lesser offences, and paid the cost.

He continued for several paragraphs in a similar vein, and by the time Vespasia came to the end of it she was so angry she could hardly hold the paper still enough to read it. She set it down on the table. Lyndon Remus might have begun as a sincere journalist intending to expose corruption, but he had allowed ambition to warp his judgment. The chance of his own fame and the power that the pen afforded had prompted him to make unfounded assumptions. All of them had a marked lack of compassion for the results of his speculation upon the bereaved, who might have been innocent but for whom proof of that would come too late to undo the pain or the ostracism that went hand in hand with suspicion.

"I have read them," she said to Woods when he returned to see if she was ready to have the table cleared. "You may burn them now. There is no need for Mrs. Cadell to see them."

"Yes, your ladyship," he said quickly. His opinion was clear in his face, and his hands, when he took the papers, shook a little.

"How are the staff?" Vespasia asked him.

"We are managing, your ladyship," he replied. "I regret to say there are persons outside in the street attempting to ask questions . . . for the newspapers. They are . . . most . . . ill mannered. They are intrusive and have no respect for . . . death."

"Have you locked the areaway doors?" she asked. "We can do without deliveries today."

"I . . . I hadn't," he admitted. "With your permission I shall do so."

"You have it. And no one is to answer the front door unless they have first ascertained who is outside and sought either my permission or Mrs. Cadell's. Is that clear?"

"Yes, indeed. Cook asked me to enquire what you would like for luncheon, Lady Vespasia. I assume you will be remaining?" He looked a little desperate.

"Most certainly," she answered him. "I think whatever Cook cares to prepare will be excellent. May I suggest something very light. An egg custard would be a suitable pudding, or a fruit fool."

"Yes, thank you, your ladyship."

Vespasia went to the withdrawing room; somehow the formality of it seemed appropriate to the mood.

Theodosia came down a little after ten. She looked exhausted and wretched, dressed entirely in black, but her head was high and she wore an expression of resolution.

"There is a great deal I need to do," she said even before Vespasia had the opportunity to ask her how she was, although it would have been a pointless question. She would probably never in her life suffer more than she was doing this morning. "And you are the only one I can ask to help me," she finished.

"Leo must have had a man of affairs," Vespasia replied, regarding Theodosia gravely. "There is very little you're required to do yourself. Even that, I can do for you, if you wish."

Theodosia's eyebrows rose. "I am not referring to that sort of thing, Aunt Vespasia. I am quite sure Mr. Astell can do all

263

of that. Although I should welcome your advice as to what you think would be suitable." She frowned very slightly, concentrating. "I am quite certain Leo did not take his own life. No one could drive him to that, no matter what he thought or feared. I am even more certain he was not behind the blackmail."

She stood with her back to the room, her face towards the garden but blind to its flowers and dappled light. "I do not delude myself I know everything about him," she said slowly. "One never does . . . nor should one. It would be intrusive, and more dangerous than that, it would be boring. But I really do believe I knew Leo too well for him to have deceived me either to his elation when the plan seemed to have been succeeding or his despair when he would have felt such imminent failure as to have driven him to this."

Vespasia was uncertain what to say. She had often imagined she knew people better than events had proved. But Theodosia had spoken of emotions, not morality, and that was a matter of observation. It was less easy to dismiss.

"There is no need to humor me," Theodosia said quietly, still facing the window. "I realize how I sound. What woman could admit to such a thing of her husband without struggling against it? But I intend to do a great deal more than wring my hands in protest."

"It will not be easy," Vespasia pointed out tentatively. "I am afraid you must be prepared for a great deal of opposition. . . ."

"Of course." Theodosia did not move. "If Leo did not do this, then someone else did. They are hardly going to welcome my disturbing what they wish to appear a very tidy end to the affair." She turned at last. "Will you help me, Aunt Vespasia?"

She looked at Theodosia's haggard face, her stiff shoulders and the desperation in her eyes. It might be hopeless. It might bring more grief upon them than there was already. But how could she refuse? It would not prevent Theodosia; it would only leave her more isolated to do it.

"Are you sure you wish to?" she asked gently. "What we

discover may not all be what you would like, my dear. Sometimes one is better knowing less of the truth, rather than more. And you will assuredly make enemies."

"Of course." Theodosia remained standing. "Do you imagine it will be much worse for me than it will be anyway when this becomes known? Mr. Gordon-Cumming will not be the only person who will find it unbearable to remain in London or the Home Counties. The blackmailer has taken so much from me he has left me very little still to lose now. I do not need you to promise me fairy-tale endings, Aunt Vespasia. I know there are none. I only wish you to lend me your intelligence and your support. As I daresay you know, I shall persist whether you give it me or not, but I shall have much less chance of success."

Vespasia smiled dryly; a small, sad gesture. "Put like that, you leave me little choice, unless I wish you to believe I preferred you to fail. Nothing would please me better than to discover Leo was innocent, both of the blackmail and of taking his life. We must consider carefully how to proceed, and of course where to begin."

Theodosia moved back across the room and sat down heavily, looking suddenly a trifle lost.

"I'm sorry," she said. "But who else could I turn to? And who better?" For all her determination, she actually had very little idea what she could do.

"Are you sure you are willing to face whatever we may discover?" Vespasia asked for a last time. "It may not be what you wish."

"No." The word was flat and certain. There was no happiness in it, but there was conviction. "But it will not be what they are saying at the moment. Where do we begin?"

"With logic ... and a hot cup of tea," Vespasia said decisively.

Theodosia gave a ghost of a smile and walked over to the embroidered bell rope. When the maid came she ordered hot tea.

"Now for the logic," she requested when they were alone again.

Vespasia settled herself to begin. "Whoever the black-mailer is, he is personally acquainted with all of his victims, because he is aware of their past experiences sufficiently well to know to what charge they would be most vulnerable and where in their careers he can make it most reasonably believable."

"Quite," Theodosia agreed. "You say he. Does it have to be a man? Could it not be a woman? It is naive to suppose a woman incapable of such intelligence or such cruelty."

"Of course it is," Vespasia answered. "But I think that might be to suppose that the placing of the corpse on Brandon Balantyne's doorstep was unconnected, which seems to me unlikely. I find it difficult to imagine circumstances where a woman who had the acquaintance of the victims would also be aware of the death of Slingsby and have the means to move his body. Although I suppose it is not impossible."

"I had forgotten about that," Theodosia admitted. "We shall consider men first. I know something about most of Leo's life, where he was born, grew up, went to school and to university and then into the diplomatic service. I have already racked my mind to think of any enemies who could be responsible for this." She frowned. "Anyone who succeeds is bound to arouse envy, if nothing else. And it is regrettable, but many of those who succeed far less will explain it to themselves by blaming others."

The maid arrived with fresh tea on a tray, and set it down on the low table between Vespasia and Theodosia. She offered to pour, but Theodosia declined, preferring to do it herself.

When they were alone again, Vespasia replied, "I do not believe this is a matter of personal vengeance, unless we can find some affair in which all the victims were involved. Did Leo even know them all?"

Theodosia looked at her with a thin shred of humor. "I don't know. You have been far too discreet to tell me who they are."

"Oh!" Vespasia had forgotten that. There seemed little point in worrying about indiscretion; clearing Leo's name

266

and finding the true blackmailer, if it was not he, were more important. "General Balantyne, John Cornwallis, Sigmund Tannifer, Guy Stanley and Dunraithe White."

Theodosia looked startled. "I did not know that," she said quietly. "They are different generations and quite different kinds of men. I know Parthenope Tannifer. She has called several times. A most interesting woman. And is not Dunraithe White a judge?"

"Yes. And John Cornwallis is assistant commissioner of police," Vespasia added. "One wonders if some subversion of the law is intended. Except how could that involve Brandon Balantyne?"

"There must be some connection," Theodosia said fiercely. "It is up to us to find it. It cannot be professional. It cannot be from school or university."

"Then it must be social," Vespasia deduced, sipping her tea. The hot liquid was peculiarly refreshing, even though the room was warm and bright in the summer morning sun. The whole house was unusually silent, the servants on tiptoe. Someone had thought to put straw in the street outside to muffle the hooves of passing horses. Vespasia had a sudden thought. "Or financial! Could Leo have invested in some scheme or other, and those other people also?"

"And there is something wrong in it?" Theodosia seized the idea eagerly. "Yes! Why not? That would make some sense of it." She rose to her feet. "There will be notes of it in his study. We shall look."

Vespasia went with her, the tea abandoned.

They spent the rest of the morning and early afternoon there, stopping for a brief luncheon only because Vespasia insisted for Theodosia's sake, and Theodosia obeyed for hers. They searched for records of all Leo Cadell's investments of any nature whatever, and discovered that he had been, on the whole, extremely prudent. There had been one rather rash backing of an adventure in the Caribbean which had lost him a modest amount, but all the rest were either adequate or extremely good. There was startlingly little invested overseas in anything speculative, and he had been scrupulous to avoid anything with even the semblance of profiting from his knowledge gained as a member of the diplomatic service.

Vespasia became increasingly saddened reading the dry facts of investment and return over the years. They demonstrated the financial life of a man who made good provision for his family but was extraordinarily careful, erring on the side of loss, never to make a penny from his professional advantage. It reflected the man she knew, nothing like the person Lyndon Remus wrote of in the newspapers, or the police presumed from the manner of his death. Funny that a series of figures should convey so much.

"There's nothing here," Theodosia said desperately a little after half past three. She was sitting at the desk with papers strewn all around her. She looked wretched and exhausted. "He gave to certain charities, but that's about all I can think of that he could have had in common with the other people you mention, and then it wasn't much. I mean, not the sort of money anyone would blackmail over."

"What charities?"

Vespasia asked simply for something to say, to not allow the silence to make it seem she had given up.

Theodosia was surprised. "Specifically? An orphanage that was governed by several members of the Jessop Club. I knew he still went on attending that committee most of the time even when he was exceptionally busy. He mentioned that General Balantyne was on it also." And without saying anything further she took a bundle of letters out of the desk drawer and began to read through them.

Vespasia went to one of the other drawers and found some more.

For half an hour she saw nothing that seemed of any relevance at all. It was unpleasant reading through another person's letters which had been intended as private. There was nothing Leo would have had cause to be embarrassed or ashamed of, not even anything especially personal; it was simply intrusive for a third person to read them. She had a terribly oppressive sense of his death. Going through his belongings made its reality almost tangible.

She read one letter through, although it was more of a memorandum, and then she nearly missed the relevance. It was on the letterhead, printed below that of the Jessop Club. The handwritten part was addressed to Leo Cadell and concerned the patronage of a fund-raising art exhibition. A notable society lady was to attend. It had been held over six months before, and was of no importance. Leo had presumably kept it only because he had written an address on it, some collector of Chinese ginger jars living in Paris. It was the names of the committee that caught Vespasia's eye: Brandon Balantyne; Guy Stanley, M.P.; Lawrence Bairstow; Dunraithe White; John Cornwallis; James Cameron, Sigmund Tannifer and Leo Cadell.

She looked up. Theodosia was still reading, a growing pile of discarded papers strewn around her.

"Do you know Lawrence Bairstow?" Vespasia asked. "Or James Cameron?"

"I knew Mary Ann Bairstow," Theodosia replied, looking up. "Why? What have you found?"

"Could Lawrence Bairstow be another victim?"

There was sudden disappointment in Theodosia's face.

"No. The poor man is senile. He is a great deal older than she is. I am afraid he would be incapable of exerting any influence at all, for good or ill. And I believe his personal affairs are looked after by the family solicitors." She could not keep the weariness of pain out of her voice.

"And James Cameron?" Vespasia pressed, not sure why, or if there was any purpose in it; it was simply unbearable to give up.

"The only James Cameron I knew of went to live abroad several months ago," Theodosia answered. "He has poor health, and he moved to a drier, warmer climate. India, I think, but I'm not sure. Why? Why are you asking? What is that?"

"I think, just possibly, we may have discovered what they have in common," Vespasia said slowly. "Although I cannot see, for the life of me, what conceivable profit there could be in it."

269

Theodosia shot to her feet and snatched the paper from her. She read it, then looked up, puzzled. "They are all on this committee within the Jessop Club. But it's for an orphanage. That is what the money is for. Could that be it . . . misappropriation of funds?" The expression in her eyes hovered between hope and despair. "It hardly seems worth it. How much could it be?"

"A great deal of disgrace, if it were discovered," Vespasia answered gravely, trying to keep the emotion calm in her voice. "To steal from an orphanage is particularly despicable."

"I hadn't thought of that." Theodosia's hands were trembling. She gripped them together to control the movements. She so fervently wanted this new information to mean something she dared not hope too much, and yet she was so close to surrendering to grief she could not let go either. "That . . . that could be it . . . couldn't it?"

Vespasia did not have the heart to deny it, even though she felt it could not be true. Perhaps to give Theodosia some shred of light now was more important than a probable truth. She must survive.

"It could," she agreed. "Let us see if there is any other reference to it here, then I shall take it to Thomas and see what he makes of it."

"You mean Superintendent Pitt?" The hope fled from Theodosia's face. "He is sure Leo was guilty."

"He will listen if I tell him about this." Vespasia filled her voice with an absolute conviction she did not feel.

"Will he?" Theodosia clutched at it.

"Most certainly. Now, let us see what else we can find."

In another two hours of meticulous reading of every piece of paper in the desk and in the drawers of the cabinet they found only one other thing which seemed to have any bearing. It was a letter dated some two weeks earlier.

My dear Cadell,

Perhaps I am being over zealous, but I am concerned about the amount of money going to the orphanage at Kew. I have re-read the accounts and it seems to me to require

270

some more detailed evaluation. I have raised the matter in committee once, but was overruled.

Of course it is possible I am out of touch with the cost of things, but I would value your opinion. I hope we may discuss the subject at a time suitable to you.

I remain,

your most obedient servant,

Brandon Balantyne

Theodosia was so encouraged by it that Vespasia could not bring herself to point out how trivial the matter almost certainly was.

"You'll take it to Superintendent Pitt?" Theodosia urged.

"Of course."

"Immediately?"

"I shall call on him before I return home," Vespasia promised. "Now, my dear, I am far more concerned about you. Will you be all right alone tonight? I can return if you wish me to. It is not an inconvenience in the slightest. I can send for a change of linen without any trouble at all."

Theodosia hesitated. "No . . . I shall have to learn . . . to become used to it . . . I think . . ." She tailed off.

Vespasia made the decision for her. "I shall return when I have seen Thomas. I do not know how long it shall be, as I may not find him immediately. Please do not wait supper for me. I shall be perfectly happy with whatever Cook can make for me then."

"Of course," Theodosia agreed, her face filled with gratitude. "I . . . thank you!"

In the event, Vespasia did find Pitt in his office in Bow Street. As far as anyone could tell, the case was closed, and he was now obliged to deal with a great many other matters that had arisen while he was wholly occupied with the Bedford Square murder and the blackmail. He was delighted to see her and welcomed her with enthusiasm.

She regarded his piled desk critically.

"I can see that I am interrupting you," she said with very

271

gentle sarcasm. "Perhaps I should wait, and call upon you at home?"

"Please!" He readjusted the chair he was holding for her. "There could be nothing more urgent than seeing you."

"It looks extremely urgent," she observed with a dry smile, sitting carefully in the chair. "But perhaps also rather arduous. I shall not keep you for very long."

"Never mind." He smiled back at her, his eyes alight for the first time in weeks. He returned to his own seat. "I shall have to make do with what time you can spare. What is it?"

She sighed, her humor vanishing. "Almost certainly nothing. But in going through Leo Cadell's papers I have discovered one thing which all the blackmail victims had in common and which was a cause of concern to at least one among them . . . the one who was most viciously accused, by implication."

"Balantyne?" He looked surprised. "What is it?"

She took the letter and the memorandum on the Jessop Club paper from her reticule and passed them both over to him.

He read them carefully and then looked up. "An orphanage? What about those other two people, Bairstow and Cameron? Are they victims as well?"

"I have no reason to suppose so; in fact, every reason to believe they are not, and could not be," she replied. "Bairstow is senile, according to Theodosia, and Cameron has left England to live abroad. That leaves of the committee members only those we know." She watched his face closely. She saw the lift of interest and the slight change in his expression. "Will you do me the favor of investigating it, Thomas, for Theodosia's sake? I appreciate that it is extremely unlikely to be anything other than what it seems, a worthy cause assisted by a group of gentlemen who happen to belong to the same club. But I am extremely fond of Theodosia, and I, too, find it difficult and painful to believe that Leo was guilty of blackmail and of suicide. I am compelled to explore any possibility that it is not so, however remote."

She hated asking favors, and she saw the understanding of that in his face.

"Of course," he agreed. "I shall go out to Kew tomorrow and require to see their books, and send men to check on Bairstow and Cameron. Cornwallis will give me all the excuse I need."

"Thank you, Thomas. I am most grateful." She rose to leave. It had been an exhausting two days, and now suddenly the grief overtook her and she found it difficult to muster the strength to face returning to Theodosia and staying awake long into the night to offer her what comfort and companionship she could. She could not lessen Theodosia's pain, only share it. But she could hardly love her and do less.

The next day was beautiful. The heat wave continued, bright and hot, but there was a clarity to the air and every now and then a breeze. People were out in the streets and parks, and on the river were scores of little boats, pleasure steamers, ferries, barges and every other kind of vessel that could take to the water. The sounds of singing, barrel organs and pennywhistles drifted on the air. Children shouted to one another, and every so often there was a burst of laughter.

Pitt took the boat up the river to Kew. It seemed not only the pleasantest way to travel but also probably the fastest.

As he stood on the deck between a fat woman in a striped blouse and a man with a red face, he wondered if he should really be doing this at all. It was an escape from the paperwork that had piled up while he was occupied with the blackmail case, and he did not want to refuse Vespasia. She had looked unusually tired. Grief had taken none of her spirit or her determination, but there was an acceptance of defeat in her which was the profoundest change he could have imagined. It troubled him enough to justify this trip up the river with the sun and the breeze on his face as the steamer made its way up past Battersea and turned south towards Wandsworth. There was another complete S bend before Kew. He would enjoy it.

He found himself smiling as he watched the rowing boats plying back and forth, narrowly avoiding getting in everyone's way. Little boys in sailor suits stood up precariously and

273

anxious women held them by the britches. Little girls with ribboned straw hats waved excitedly. Fathers bent their backs to the oars with proprietorial satisfaction.

On the shore people picnicked on stretches of grass. He thought idly that a few of them were going to be burned by this evening. At the water's edge they did not realize how strong the sun was.

He was wasting his time going to an orphanage. Even if there had been petty pilfering, and Balantyne had suspected it, it was not the same degree of crime as the sort of blackmail they had been dealing with. It could only be a few hundred pounds at the very most, and that would have to have been over years or it would have been noticed long before now.

Why had Balantyne questioned it instead of requiring an audit of the books? He had written to Cadell about his concerns. Cadell would hardly be blackmailing him with something as extreme as a murdered man on the doorstep in order to stop him from pursuing such a request.

But that did raise a genuine question to which Pitt had seen no satisfactory answer . . . who had moved the body of Josiah Slingsby from Shoreditch to Bedford Square? Who had put Albert Cole's receipt for socks in Slingsby's pocket? How had he had it in the first place?

For that matter, where was Albert Cole now? If he was alive, where had he gone and why? And if he was dead, why had Slingsby's body been left on Balantyne's step and not Cole's body? Had he coincidentally died of natural causes?

That seemed to be stretching unlikelihood too far.

And it did not answer the questions about Slingsby's body and how Cadell had even heard of it, let alone how he'd moved it to Bedford Square.

Did any of it matter now, except that it was a puzzle?

A pleasure steamer went by, its passengers shouting and waving, its wake setting the ferry rocking. The sun was dazzlingly bright on the water.

Was he being self-indulgent, expecting every case to have a complete solution, wanting to understand exactly what had happened? Or was he being diligent, making sure of the truth?

What he was really doing was taking a trip up the river instead of sitting in Bow Street doing his paperwork, and trying to help Vespasia a little . . . although she would have to accept in the end that Leo Cadell was the blackmailer. He had confessed it . . . in a letter exactly like all the others. Possibly he had gained his knowledge of the lives of the other victims through knowing them in the Jessop Club. One could learn a great deal about people from casual conversation, expanded by a little questioning as if from interest or admiration. The rest he could have gleaned from public records; army and navy details he could easily have asked for on the pretext of having some need to know in his position at the Foreign Office.

But the question remained, how did he know Slingsby at all, let alone remark his resemblance to Cole?

Pitt put it out of his mind for a while and enjoyed the river and the brilliance of the day. All around him people were having fun.

The orphanage at Kew Green was a large, rambling old house with a garden walled around and overhung with trees. It looked spacious enough to house fifty or sixty children, at the very least, and the appropriate number of staff to look after them.

He walked up to the front door, noticing the clean scrubbed step, and pulled the bell. It was answered within minutes by a girl of about seventeen. She was wearing a dark blue cotton dress, starched apron and cap.

"Yes sir?" she said helpfully.

Pitt explained who he was and asked if he might speak to whoever was in charge. He conveyed in his manner that refusal was not to be tolerated.

She conducted him to a very pleasant room facing the front entrance and invited him to sit in one of the threadbare but surprisingly comfortable seats while she went for Mr. Horsfall.

When he arrived, closing the door behind him with a snap,

he was taller even than Pitt, very rotund around the middle, and with a genial face, as if he smiled often and easily.

"Yes sir," he said agreeably. "What can we do for you? Dolly said something about the police. I hope none of our charges have been creating a nuisance? We do the best we can to see they are well behaved, and if I say so myself, I think we more than succeed, most times. But children will be children."

"I have no reason to doubt it," Pitt replied honestly. "I am from Bow Street, not Kew." He ignored the surprise in Horsfall's face. "And it is regarding financial matters I have come. The recent suicide of one of the committee of beneficiaries who donate a large amount to your establishment had raised some questions as to possible irregularities."

Horsfall looked suitably saddened. "Oh, dear. How painful. Well, sir, of course you may examine our books, with pleasure. But I do assure you, if there has been anything amiss, it has not been after any funds have reached us. We are very careful." He nodded. "We have to be. We mustn't lose sight of the fact that we are dealing with other people's money. If they cannot trust us, then there will be no more." He looked at Pitt with wide eyes.

What he said was transparently true, and Pitt felt foolish for wasting both Horsfall's time and his own. But he could hardly say so now.

"Thank you," he replied. "It is merely to complete the matter. I would be negligent to overlook it."

"Of course. Of course." Horsfall nodded again, hooking his thumbs in his waistcoat. "Shall I bring them to you here, or would you prefer to come through to my office, where you can sit at a desk?"

"That would be very courteous of you," Pitt accepted. He was aware that there was always the possibility of two sets of books, but he acknowledged to himself that he had never really expected anything from his visit beyond being able to tell Vespasia he had tried.

He spent the rest of the morning and most of the afternoon, apart from a brief respite for luncheon at the local public house, going over endless receipts both for money and for goods, food, fuel, clothes, wages, and found everything in the most meticulous order. Had Horsfall not explained his need for exactness, he might have found the perfection suspicious. But there was not a farthing unaccounted for, and he did not doubt for a moment that if he went equally carefully through the Jessop Club's donations, he would find a faultless match.

He was barely aware of the children who must fill the building. As Horsfall had said, they were remarkably well behaved. He did see two little girls, walking hand in hand, aged about five and six, respectively, and suddenly one of them began to run, pulling the other along. They were followed a moment later by a girl of ten or so, carrying a boy not more than two. Other movements caught the corner of his vision, and he heard voices.

He closed the books, thanked Horsfall and apologized for troubling him, then took his leave of the orphanage, feeling a trifle foolish. There seemed no reason whatever why Balantyne—or Cadell, for that matter—should have been concerned. Perhaps it was a matter of raising funds, rather than their use, which had worried him.

He could ask Balantyne, but it hardly seemed worth it.

The question of how Cadell had known of Slingsby's death, and how he had moved the body, seemed far more important. And where was Albert Cole? If he was dead, they should know if it had been a result of natural causes, and if not, then what had happened to him? He would put Tellman onto that as soon as he returned to Bow Street . . . tomorrow. Tonight he would write to Vespasia and tell her that the orphanage books were immaculate.

Charlotte was grieved by the news of Leo Cadell's death, largely for Aunt Vespasia, but her imagination extended to how his widow must feel. However, she was relieved of an immense weight of anxiety, even of fear, regarding both General Balantyne and Cornwallis. She liked Cornwallis profoundly, and she knew also how deep was Pitt's affection for him.

She knew Balantyne must have read of Cadell's death in the newspapers. He could hardly have missed it. It was sprawled across the front page, along with Lyndon Remus's speculations as to what sort of long and tragic story might be behind Cadell's fall from brilliant diplomat to blackmailer, extortionist and, ultimately, suicide.

Half of her mind could understand the necessity for freedom to question and investigate the lives of all public figures. Without such liberty, secrecy begot oppression and ended in tyranny. But with freedom came responsibility, and the immense power of the written word could so easily be abused. There was a sense in which Lyndon Remus was doing exactly the same thing as Cadell had attempted. The fact that Cadell and his family were now the victims did not leave her with any sense of satisfaction or poetic justice, just an awareness of the vulnerability of reputation and the thought of how Theodosia Cadell must feel.

An errand boy delivered a note from General Balantyne, and she gave him the answer that she would be happy to meet him, again in the Royal Botanical Gardens, at three o'clock in the afternoon.

The day was less oppressively hot, and a considerable crowd was taking the air for one sort of pleasure or another. She marveled at how many people seemed to have no other call upon their time and were free from the necessity of any form of work. Before she had met Pitt such a thought would never have crossed her mind. Young ladies of her social class then had far too much time and too little to fill it that gave anything but the most momentary satisfaction. Then she seemed always to have been looking forward to tomorrow for something that might happen.

She saw Balantyne as soon as she was through the gates. He was standing alone, facing the parade of soldiers in uniform, couples arm in arm, girls with parasols accompanied by their mothers, parasols swinging dangerously as they glanced at the young men and pretended they weren't. He appeared to be watching them, but the stillness of his head betrayed that his thoughts were elsewhere.

Charlotte walked over to him and was almost beside him before he noticed her.

"Mrs. Pitt!" He looked at her gravely, searching her eyes. "How are you?" He paid not the slightest regard to her appearance; he was concerned entirely with her feelings.

"I am quite well," she answered, equally concerned for him. Looking at his face, she could see little of the relief she would have expected, considering that the threat of ruin that had dogged him for weeks was now lifted. "And you?"

He smiled very slightly. "I had expected to feel better," he admitted. "Perhaps I am still bemused. I liked Cadell." He offered her his arm. "Isn't that ridiculous? But I cannot rid myself of the emotion in a single day, in spite of knowing now what he was really planning. I suppose I am not the judge of men's characters that I thought I was." He gave a very slight, rueful shrug.

"I'm sorry," she said simply. "I don't think Great-Aunt Vespasia has ever been so fearfully mistaken either. Mrs. Cadell is her goddaughter, you know."

"I didn't." He walked in silence a few yards. "Poor woman. I can imagine the devastation she must be feeling now, the confusion and loss."

Charlotte thought of Christina. Perhaps he was remembering her when he spoke. Time might have blunted the edge of his own pain, but nothing could remove it. Looking sideways at him now, she would not intrude, it would be inexcusable, but she imagined him thinking of Theodosia Cadell with a pity that could only spring from his own knowledge. His mouth was tugged tight at the corners, the muscles in his neck tense.

"We are all relieved of our fears," he said after a little while, moving between the banks of roses heavy with perfume in the sun. "We need no longer dread the delivery of mail. We can encounter our friends in the street and meet their eyes without wondering what they are thinking, what double meaning may lie behind the simplest remark. I feel guilty for the people I doubted. I hope to heaven they will never know it. Oddly, in all my suspicions, I never thought of Cadell."

She wanted to answer with something intelligent, but she could think of nothing.

He did not seem to be waiting for her to say anything, merely glad of her companionship and grateful for the presence of someone to whom he could speak his thoughts as they came to him.

"It is terrible that our relief, the end of our ordeal, has to be the beginning of someone else's," he went on. "How will Mrs. Cadell endure this? The knowledge will destroy everything of the past as well as the future. Does she have children, do you know?"

"No . . . I don't. I think Aunt Vespasia said something about daughters; I'm not sure. I wasn't really listening. How shatteringly life can change from one day to another." She looked at the people passing by them, all seeming so carefree, as if there were nothing on their minds more serious than whether their gowns were fashionable or not, whether a young man had smiled at them, or the girl behind them. And yet underneath, their hearts could be breaking too. Every one of them must succeed in some way, or fail, and the price of that was heavy, perhaps poverty, perhaps loneliness. She had been as young, and as desperate in her own way, once.

"What I don't understand," Balantyne went on, frowning, "is why Cadell put the body of Slingsby on my doorstep with Albert Cole's receipt on him and the snuffbox in his pocket. What was he trying to do? Have me arrested for his murder?" He turned and looked at her, his eyes full of confusion. "Did he hate me so much? Why? I liked him. . . ."

"I don't know," she confessed. "What is more difficult to understand for me is how he got the body. Slingsby was killed in Shoreditch."

He sighed. "I suppose we shall never know. The man must have had a life quite separate from anything we guessed. I have never found myself so mistaken in anyone." He gave a very slight laugh. "When I was worried about the orphanage in Kew, he was the one I wrote to."

"What worried you?" she asked, not that it mattered; it was simply something to continue the conversation.

"The money," he replied, smiling at her ruefully. "It all seems terribly trivial now. It wasn't even a large amount."

"Missing?" she asked.

"No . . . quite the contrary I thought we were not giving enough . . . enough to meet the demands, that is. Perhaps I am a trifle naive as to how one may manage if one is skilled in housekeeping. I daresay they have a good kitchen garden. I have forgotten what children eat. I seem to recall rice pudding, plum duff and bread and jam. I suppose there must have been a great deal else."

They walked a little farther in silence. Five minutes later they had completed the circle and were back at the gates again. He stopped.

"I . . ." He cleared his throat. "I . . . I am deeply grateful for your friendship." He coughed, removing his arm from hers. "I value it a great deal more than you know—or than it is remotely suitable that I should tell you." He stopped abruptly, knowing he had already said too much.

She saw the passion of gentleness in his eyes, and understood all that he could never say and she should not have allowed to happen.

She closed her eyes, not to meet his.

"I acted on impulse," she said almost under her breath. "Sometimes . . . in fact, quite often . . . I have more feeling than sense. I apologize for it. But I never believed you were guilty and I cared so much to prove it." She made herself smile, still with her eyes lowered. "I am very glad that that at least has been proved. I wish we could have solved all the other things too, but they will have to remain as they are." For an instant she looked at him, then after a moment turned and walked away back towards the gates and outside, knowing that he watched her until was she out of sight, but she could not look back. She must not

11

P*ITT ARRIVED HOME* late after seeing Vespasia on the way back from Kew. He felt deeply sorry for her. Nothing he had been able to tell her was anything but crushing to the last shred of hope.

Now he sat in front of the empty fireplace in his parlor. The doors to the garden were closed after having been open nearly all day. It was still light, but there was a coolness in the air that could be felt if one were sitting still. The sweet smell of the neighbor's new-cut grass lingered in the room, reminding him it was time he attended to his own lawn, not to mention the weeding.

Charlotte was sitting opposite him, her sewing discarded. He could see from the rough shape of it that it was a dress for Jemima. There seemed so much material he recalled with a jolt how rapidly she had grown. She was not a little girl anymore, and she most decidedly had opinions of her own. That had come forcibly to his attention a few times lately. It made him think with sharp pity of Christina Balantyne, and brought an awareness of how time can change people and one can be too preoccupied to notice it. Girls grow up and become women.

"Was there nothing at the orphanage?" Charlotte asked, interrupting his thoughts.

He was pleased to be able to share his findings with her. It did not make it any better; it simply hurt less.

"No. Everything was in exceptionally good order. I went

through the books in detail. Every penny was accounted for. Not only that, but it was all clean and obviously well cared for, and the half dozen or so children I actually saw seemed happy and in good health, well clothed and clean also."

"But General Balantyne was worried about it." She frowned slightly. "He told me that himself." She looked at him very steadily, and he knew she was waiting to be asked when she had seen him again.

He found himself smiling in spite of the gloom that he felt. She was very transparent.

"Well, it looks as if he need not have been," he answered. "I wish all institutions were as well run."

"He didn't think they were misappropriating funds," she explained. "He thought they weren't using enough." She took a deep breath. "But he did admit that perhaps he didn't know very much about budgeting. I daresay he hasn't much idea what you can do with things like potatoes and oatmeal and rice pudding, and of course bread."

"I assume he doesn't know much about army catering, then?" he observed.

"I didn't ask," she admitted. "I think honestly he was more troubled by his misjudgment of Leo Cadell. He truly liked him . . . and trusted him."

"I know," Pitt said quietly. "It has wounded Aunt Vespasia profoundly as well. I think . . ."

"Yes?" She was quick to respond, her face earnest.

"You might visit her a little more often . . . for a while. At least offer to . . . somehow make it tactful."

She smiled a little ruefully. "It is not easy to be tactful with Aunt Vespasia. She can read my thoughts almost before I have them."

"Then perhaps you had better not try. Simply offer."

"Thomas . . ." she said tentatively.

"Yes?"

"What did he want? I mean, what was Cadell going to ask them all for? Was it just money, or something to do with Africa, as you thought?"

"I don't know. His note said very little. What puzzles me

far more is how he knew about Slingsby at all, that he resembled Cole, let alone that he was dead."

"You don't know?" She was startled.

"No. I can see why he wanted Slingsby's body to be taken for Albert Cole's . . . to increase the pressure on Balantyne . . . but why not use the real Albert Cole? He would be far more likely to have met him. He worked in Lincoln's Inn Fields, where Cadell could easily have been. Any of the victims could have, and Dunraithe White assuredly has."

"Well, what happened to Albert Cole?" she asked, her face puckered. "Where is he?"

"I have no idea."

"Why didn't he come forward when his death was reported in the newspapers?" she pressed.

"I don't suppose he reads the newspapers," he answered with a smile. "He may not read at all."

"Oh. I never thought of that." She showed a moment's consternation at her own blindness, then hurried on. "Even so, other people do. And he isn't anywhere in his usual places, is he? He's gone from his lodgings and from the corner where he sold bootlaces, and from the public house where he drank. You told me that."

His brief moment of humor vanished. "I am afraid he may also be dead. Perhaps he died of some cause that didn't suit their purpose."

"Such as what?" she demanded.

"Illness of some sort or, for example, drowning. We could hardly blame General Balantyne for a drowned body that turned up on his doorstep."

In spite of herself she laughed. It was absurd, grotesque. But the moment was soon gone.

"Poor man," she said, more to herself than to him. "But that doesn't answer how Cadell knew about Slingsby and just happened to be in Shoreditch at the time. What on earth would he be doing in Shoreditch at all?"

He shrugged. "I don't know. I'm not sure whether I need to know. I want to, but does it matter now?"

"Yes." There was no hesitation in her at all. "This doesn't

make any sense. You need to know at the very least what happened to Albert Cole. Just because nobody misses him doesn't mean he doesn't matter."

He did not argue. Perhaps it was the excuse he had been wanting.

Pitt went to see Cornwallis in the morning. He looked a different man. The shadows of tiredness were still in his face, but the haunted air had gone from his eyes and he stood upright, his shoulders square again, and he met Pitt's gaze almost eagerly.

In the first moment after coming into the room, Pitt realized just how heavy had been the weight upon Cornwallis, how very sharp the fear. Now that it was gone, every aspect of his life had changed again. Courage and belief in himself had returned.

Pitt almost let it rest. Whatever had happened to Albert Cole, it could not be undone. Did they really need to know? Cadell was guilty, by his own admission. It filled all the facts. He was in a position to have gained all the information about the other victims. He knew them all from the Jessop Club.

"Good morning, Pitt," Cornwallis said cheerfully. "Excellent job. I'm most extremely grateful." His expression darkened. "Although I'm damned sorry it turned out to be Cadell. I liked him. At least . . . I liked what I believed him to be. It is hard to discover that someone is not remotely what you supposed. It shakes your confidence in your own judgment. I used to think I knew a man's character." He frowned. "It was part of my job."

"Everyone was mistaken in him," Pitt replied, standing a little rigidly.

Cornwallis relaxed. "I am afraid so. Still, it's over now." He raised his eyebrows. "Have you something else on your mind?"

This was the moment to make his decision. There were too many questions. He thought of Vespasia.

"No . . . I'm afraid it is still the same case. I'm not satisfied yet. . . ."

Cornwallis looked startled, and dismay flashed in his eyes. "What? You can't have any doubt that Cadell was guilty. For heaven's sake, he confessed and shot himself. You can't imagine he was doing it to protect someone else." He spread his hands jerkily. "Who? If he wasn't guilty, then he was as much a victim as the rest of us. Are you suggesting there was a conspiracy?"

"No!" Pitt was beginning to feel foolish. "Nothing like that. I just want to understand how he did it—"

"I've been thinking about it," Cornwallis interrupted, jamming his hands into his pockets and walking back towards his desk. "It seems fairly clear now we know who it was. He knew us all reasonably well—at least at the Jessop, if nowhere else." He sat down and leaned back in his chair, crossing his legs. He looked up at Pitt earnestly. "I can remember dining with him. I don't know now what we talked about, but different places we'd been. I could easily have mentioned which ships I'd served on. From there he could have looked up my naval record. As a member of the Foreign Office he wouldn't need much of an excuse." He smiled bleakly.

Pitt sat down as well, ready to argue when the time came.

"Similarly, he could have looked up Balantyne's career," Cornwallis went on. "It's amazing how comfortable one can get over a good dinner at the club." He smiled a little. "You reminisce, and with a fellow you like, who is a good listener, maybe tells a bit about himself as well, you find yourself talking into the small hours. No one disturbs you or tells you it's time to leave. He could have learned all manner of things about any of us." He looked at Pitt with a sudden bleakness. "If you think it's worth going to the Jessop and asking the stewards if they remember Cadell sitting up late with anyone, do so. But it would prove nothing either way. They could have forgotten, or it could have been somewhere else. Most of us belong to more than one club."

"I hadn't doubted where he got the information," Pitt replied. "A little conversation, some enquiries and then some imaginative guesses would be quite sufficient."

286

"The snuffbox?" Cornwallis said quickly. "He may have visited Balantyne's home, but even if he hadn't, I can remember Balantyne having it at the club, because I've seen it myself, when I think back. Not closely. I wasn't paying attention. It's the sort of thing you see but don't see. I daresay Guy Stanley used his flask the same way. Some people prefer their own particular whiskey or brandy. I have half a memory that he liked a single malt."

"Yes, that's all simple enough," Pitt agreed again. "It wasn't that I was thinking about." How much should he say? Were Vespasia's doubts anything more than the loyalty of a friend? "How did he know about Slingsby's death in Shoreditch, and how did he get the body back to Bedford Square? More than that, how did he know Slingsby resembled Cole, and so would be any use to him? How did he get Cole's receipt, and where is the real Cole?"

"I've no idea why he was in Shoreditch," Cornwallis replied with a frown. "The man seems to have had a life we knew nothing about. Perhaps he gambled?" His face creased with distaste, and there was an edge of exasperation in his voice. "He could have had a liking for bare-knuckle fighting or any of a dozen other things. Some men do. A darker side to the character. You must know that even better than I do. Perhaps he was there when Slingsby was killed, and saw his chance."

"To pass him off as Cole and leave him on Balantyne's doorstep?" Pitt asked. "Why? Why take the risk of carrying him halfway through London in the middle of the night? And what happened to the real Albert Cole? Where is he?"

"Obviously, Cadell was a man who liked taking risks," Cornwallis said a little sharply. "It would seem his respectable life as a diplomat, married to one woman all his adulthood and always behaving with the utmost correctness, oppressed some part of his nature. I've known it to happen before." Unconsciously, his hand on the desk clenched and there was an increased edge to his voice. "For heaven's sake, Pitt, plenty of men behave like fools. Women too, for all I know." He leaned forward. "Why do we gamble, drive

287

carriages too fast, ride dangerous horses, fall in love with all the wrong women? Why do we even try to do something pointless and dangerous, climb mountains or pit ourselves against nature to test our strength? Nine times out of ten there's nothing at the end of it except the knowledge that we succeeded. That's all we want."

"And you think Cadell was that sort of person?" Pitt could not keep the doubt from his face.

"I hadn't thought so, no," Cornwallis answered. "But I was obviously mistaken. I hadn't thought he was a man to blackmail his friends for the sheer pleasure of exercising power over them and watching them suffer," he added bitterly. "I can't begin to understand why anyone should take delight in such a thing. I can only suppose he was in desperate need of money he'd lost gambling, and he intended to ask us all for everything we could afford when he was ready, when he was sure we would pay."

Pitt chewed his lip. "And where is Albert Cole?"

Cornwallis stood up abruptly and walked over to the window. He stared out of it with his back to Pitt.

"I've no idea. It's probably a coincidence; he went away or died. It had nothing to do with Cadell."

"And the receipt?" Pitt could not give up, not only for Vespasia but because reason demanded better answers than he had.

Cornwallis remained staring at the street. "I don't know," he admitted. "Perhaps it was a mistake. The man in the shop was in error. Does it matter now?"

Pitt looked at Cornwallis's broad, straight shoulders. "Balantyne went to Cadell about the orphanage funds. He was worried they were insufficient."

Cornwallis turned around, puzzled. "Why do you mention that? What has it to do with . . . anything?"

"It probably hasn't," Pitt confessed. "I went out to the orphanage. The books are perfect."

"Why?"

"Lady Vespasia Cumming-Gould still finds it very difficult to believe Cadell was guilty—"

"Of course she does!" Cornwallis came back across the

room, frowning with annoyance. "His widow is her god-daughter. It is difficult for anyone to believe someone they cared for could have been guilty of a wretched, vicious crime. I don't find it easy myself. I liked the man." He took a deep breath. "But the longer she resists it, the harder it will be to accept, and the more painful."

Pitt spoke more from emotion than reason.

"If you think Aunt Vespasia is simply being an old lady who is refusing to accept an unpalatable truth, you know very little of her and underestimate her profoundly. She knew Leo Cadell since before his marriage, and she is a woman of considerable wisdom and experience. She has seen more of the world than either you or I, particularly of men like the ones we are concerned with." He had spoken more sharply than he intended, but it was too late to moderate it.

Cornwallis blushed. For a moment Pitt thought it was from anger, then he realized it was from shame.

Cornwallis turned away. "I'm sorry. I have the greatest regard for Lady Vespasia. My own relief has . . . has blinded me for a moment to the reality of other people's grief." His voice thickened with tightly suppressed emotion. "I want this to be the end of it so fiercely I cannot bear to believe otherwise. It has obliged me to think about a great many things, events and people which I had taken for granted most of my life . . . other men's opinions of me I assumed I knew. Even my career has . . . still, that is hardly important now." He let out his breath in a soundless sigh and turned back to face Pitt. "You had better find Cole . . . or at least have Tellman look for him. There is nothing else pressing . . . is there?"

Before Pitt could answer that there was not, there was a sharp rap on the door.

"Come in," Cornwallis replied, looking towards it.

The man who came in looked startled.

"Mr. Justice Quade is here to see you, sir," he said to Cornwallis. "He is extremely perturbed and says the matter is urgent."

"Send him in," Cornwallis directed. "Pitt, you'd better stay."

Theloneus Quade appeared the moment after, and indeed, the clerk had not exaggerated. Quade's thin, gentle face wore an expression of deep concern.

"I apologize for intruding upon you, Mr. Cornwallis." He glanced at Pitt. "Fortunate to find you also here, Thomas. I am afraid there has been a development I find disturbing—most disturbing—and I felt I should inform you of it in case it has meaning." He looked abashed, and yet perfectly determined.

"What is it?" Pitt asked with sinking misgiving, though with less surprise than he should have felt.

Theloneus looked from one to the other of them. "Dunraithe White has just excused himself from a case he was scheduled to hear. It was rather an important one, involving a major fraud in one of the large investment trusts. His withdrawal will severely inconvenience everyone and delay the hearing until someone can be found to replace him."

Cornwallis stood motionless. "Is he ill?" he said without hope.

"He has said so," Theloneus replied, "but I saw him at the opera yesterday evening, and he was in excellent health then." His lips tightened. "I happen to be acquainted with his doctor. I took the liberty of calling him when I heard. I am afraid I practiced an untruth. I asked if Dunraithe had been taken to a hospital, that I might send him a letter or attend to anything he might wish. His doctor quite obviously had no idea what I was talking about, and assumed I must be mistaken. He may, of course, be ill at home and not have found it necessary to send for any medical help, but that would be an unusual way to behave, and Dunraithe is a conventional man. Mrs. White would have sent for someone, even if he had not."

Cornwallis opened his mouth to argue with some reasonable answer and then changed his mind. Without being aware of it, his body was tense again, the ease gone from his face.

"It occurs to me," Theloneus said sadly, "that a letter has been overdue in the mail, and perhaps he received it only this morning. He may imagine that Cadell was not alone in his crime and that a threat still exists." He looked from one to the other of them. "I don't know if you know the answer to that,

290

but if you do, then you might persuade him of it. If not, then we had better continue our work. It would seem it is not entirely finished."

Cornwallis glanced at Pitt, then back to Theloneus.

"We don't know the answer," he said frankly. "We were discussing it before you arrived. We don't know exactly what Cadell wanted. We have assumed it was money, but it is only an assumption. We also assumed he was alone, and perhaps we should not have." His voice was rough-edged. The weight of fear he had only just cast aside had descended upon him again. It seemed the heavier for the short respite. Quite suddenly he was once more haggard, the color gone from his skin. The one night's untroubled sleep need never have been given him, or the few meals eaten with pleasure.

"I'll go and see Mr. White," Pitt said quietly. He looked at Theloneus. "Will you come with me? He may simply refuse to admit me. He could send his butler with a message that he is too ill. I can scarcely argue that I know he has not yet sent for a doctor."

"Of course," Theloneus agreed. "I had thought of it myself. I can persuade him, on judicial business, if nothing else. He cannot refuse to speak to me on that, whatever his state of health." He gave a sad little grimace. "I do not know whether to wish he is telling the truth or not."

It proved a wise decision. When the butler opened the door there was a cool refusal in his face prepared for whoever should consider disturbing his master's peace. However, when Theloneus introduced himself and declared the nature of his business, the butler recognized that it was not within his jurisdiction to refuse, and he dutifully carried Theloneus's card upstairs on his silver tray.

He returned several minutes later, his face grim.

"Mr. White is not well this morning, sir, as I explained. If the matter truly cannot wait, then of course he will see you. Perhaps you would not mind doing him the favor of allowing him a few minutes to compose himself and come downstairs." It was not really a question.

"Of course," Theloneus said sympathetically. He sat down in one of the large chairs in the study where they had been shown. Pitt could not help thinking that it was one of the few rooms in the house where Marguerite White would almost certainly not interrupt them. Dunraithe would not have to explain their presence to her.

Pitt and Theloneus sat in silence. Several times Pitt nearly spoke, then changed his mind. They had already said all there was until they knew whether White had indeed received a letter, or if perhaps he had some genuine illness. Perhaps he had, and the anxiety and distress of the past few weeks had so worn down his courage that he no longer had the strength to fight back.

The door opened and Dunraithe White came in, closing it behind him. He was dressed in trousers and a soft smoking jacket. He looked gray-faced, as if he had not slept for nights on end, and there was a dry, stiff texture to his skin. He had shaved, but poorly, as if his attention had not been upon the task. As well as a small missed patch on his chin, there were two tiny spots of blood where the blade had caught him. The butler had simply reported Pitt as "another gentleman," and White was profoundly shaken to recognize him.

"Superintendent! Has something further happened?" He cleared his throat. "Stokes did not tell me you were here. Only you . . ." He turned to Theloneus. "I . . . I thought it was a judicial matter."

"It is," Theloneus replied, staring at him levelly and without the slightest evasion. "I am deeply concerned over your withdrawal from the Leadbetter case. As you must know, it will cause the deepest inconvenience to the court calendar, and a considerable cost due to the delay, which must necessarily follow, until someone else can be found to hear it. Is there any way whatsoever, with your physician's assistance, that in a day or two you may be recovered sufficiently to resume your role?" He regarded White with innocent concern.

"No." White answered without hesitating to give the matter thought. "It would be quite misleading of me to allow you to think I will be well . . . I really cannot say that." He swallowed. "In . . . in fairness to all concerned, the prosecution and the defense . . . you must replace me." He looked at Theloneus with something like despair in his eyes.

Seeing the compassion in Theloneus's face, Pitt expected him to relent, but he did not. Without a moment's change in the gentleness in his eyes or his voice, he continued as if White had not spoken.

"I am sorry, my dear fellow. I must know the truth of this. You do indeed look as if you are suffering greatly, but you do not seem unwell, which is a different thing."

White made as if to protest, but he could not find the words.

"If you have some ailment," Theloneus went on, "then allow me to send for your physician. I know him well, and I have no doubt he will come to you within the hour."

"Really!" White protested. "I am perfectly able to . . . to send for him myself, should I require his assistance. You take too much . . ." He half turned away, moving his arm ineffectually. "Please accept my word, Quade, and my apologies, and let the matter be. I have said all I have to."

Theloneus remained where he was.

"I think not," he said very quietly. "Perhaps I wrong you, and if so I am in your debt, but I think you are not ill in any medical sense, and even the Lord Chancellor would understand if—"

White wheeled around. "Are you threatening me?" he accused, his eyes hot and angry.

Theloneus did not even look surprised.

"Is somebody threatening you even though Cadell is dead?" he asked mildly.

What shred of color there was left White's face. For several moments he did not speak, and neither Theloneus nor Pitt broke the silence.

"Are you sure Cadell was the blackmailer?" White said at last, his voice strained to cracking.

"He confessed," Pitt said, speaking for the first time. "His note was exactly the same as the blackmail letters, and on the same white notepaper."

"I want to believe that," White said desperately. "Dear God, you don't know how much I do. . . ."

Theloneus frowned. "Why do you find it so hard? Have you received another letter? Were you told to drop the Leadbetter case?"

White shook his head; there was a bitter laughter in him close to hysteria. "No . . . nothing to do with the Leadbetter case." His voice cracked. "I simply can't face it. I think I shall resign from the bench altogether. I cannot go on like this." He held his hands out in front of him, palms down. They trembled very slightly. "But you are correct; I did receive another letter in the post this morning."

"May I see it?" Pitt requested.

White gestured towards the fireplace. "I burnt it . . . in case Marguerite found it. But it was just the same as the others . . . threats . . . talks of ruin and pain, but nothing asked for." Unconsciously, his hands clenched. "I cannot continue like this . . . I will not!" He looked from one to the other of them. "My wife is terrified. She has no idea what is wrong, but she cannot help but be aware that I am beside myself with worry. I have told her it is a case I am concerned with, but she will not believe that forever. She knows little of the ways of the world, but she is not a foolish woman, nor unobservant." In spite of himself his voice softened. "And she cares for my welfare with the tenderest concern. The whole matter is beginning to affect her health also, and I cannot keep it from her indefinitely. She will begin to know I am lying, and that will make her even more afraid. She has always trusted me. It will destroy every shred of peace of mind she has." He lifted his chin, and his shoulders stiffened. "You may enquire all you wish, Quade. I shall do whatever this blackguard asks of me. I will not subject Marguerite to scandal and ruin. I have told you this before, and I fail to see why you did not believe me then. I thought you knew me better." He turned away, his back rigid, his jaw set.

A dozen arguments rose to Pitt's lips, but he knew Dunraithe White was not listening. Fear, exhaustion and the passionate desire to protect his wife had closed his mind to argument of any sort.

Theloneus tried a last time.

"My dear fellow, Cadell is dead. He cannot hurt you or your family. Please reconsider before you commit yourself to a course of action which will bring to an end a long and memorable career. I shall deem that I did not hear your last words . . ."

White turned around, glaring at him.

". . . because if I had," Theloneus continued, "I should have to inform the Lord Chancellor of their import. He might then find it most difficult to keep you in a position of high trust, knowing that you would place the love of your family before the duty of your calling."

White stared at him, ashen-faced, swaying a little on his feet.

"You are very brutal, Quade. I had not seen it like that." He swallowed with difficulty. "I suppose it may look like that to you."

"It would look like it to you, my dear fellow, were our places reversed," Theloneus assured him. "And if you think of it for a moment, you know that. Would you prefer I told you only after you had made your decision?"

White took several moments to answer.

"No . . ." he said at last. "No, I should not. I have enjoyed my career. I shall be at a loss without it. But I can see that my present ill health must become a permanent thing. I shall write my resignation to the Lord Chancellor this morning." There was a finality of despair in his voice. "It will be in the afternoon post. You have my word. Then I shall disregard this damnable letter, whoever it is from. I think that perhaps my wife and I should take a short holiday in the country, for recuperation. Perhaps a month or so."

Theloneus did not make any further attempt to dissuade White. He took his leave quietly, and he and Pitt went out into the sun and the noise and ordinariness of the street. Neither spoke of it, except on parting when Pitt thanked Theloneus for having come with him. There really was nothing that needed more words.

Pitt's mind was still troubled over the details of Cadell's knowledge. How he had learned, and invented, sufficient detail with which to blackmail his fellow members of the Jessop Club was not difficult to imagine. But Pitt could still think of no answer to the question of how Cadell knew of Slingsby and Cole, not to mention Ernest Wallace and the murder in Shoreditch. Had it been simply money he was after, eventually? And if so, why? What was he spending it on that he needed more than his very ample salary and his inherited wealth?

Or was it the sadistic power to hurt, to torment and to ruin? Such a thing was entirely outside anything Aunt Vespasia had observed in the man in over quarter of a century's acquaintance.

Or was it, as they had considered before, some mad African venture into speculation and empire building?

Whatever it was, a more careful scrutiny of all his papers and a more thorough and directed questioning of his wife and his household staff should reveal a thread, a shadow, some indication of an answer.

Accordingly, Pitt hailed the next cab which passed him and gave the driver directions to Cadell's house.

There was still straw muffling the street outside, and of course all the curtains were drawn, giving the windows a blind look, almost as if the house itself were dead.

But when he pulled the bell he was let in immediately, and Theodosia herself came into the withdrawing room within minutes. She was dressed in black with no relief except a jet mourning brooch at the throat. Her eyes were hollow and her skin had no color at all. Anything artificial would have stood out like a clown's makeup. Even so, she was a beautiful woman; her high cheekbones and long slender throat could not be affected by any grief, nor the thick, carefully dressed dark hair with its silver streaks. She reminded him of Vespasia.

"Is there something further I can do for you, Superintendent?" she asked. "Or have you discovered . . . ?" She tried with painful intensity to keep hope out of her voice, and almost succeeded.

How could he answer without the cruelty of suggesting something only to snatch it away again?

"Nothing new," he said immediately, and saw the light fade from her eyes. "Just questions to which I can't find any answers, and I must at least look."

She was too well-bred to be impolite, and perhaps she remembered he was a friend of Vespasia's.

"I assume that you wish to look here?"

"Please. I would like to go through Mr. Cadell's letters and papers once more, everything he kept at home, and speak to the staff again, in particular his valet and the coachman."

"Why?" she asked, then immediately comprehension flooded her face, and a darkness of misery. "You don't believe he killed that wretched man who was found in Bedford Square, do you? You can't! How would he even know him?"

"No, I don't believe he killed him," he said quickly. "We know who did that. It was witnessed. We have the man arrested and charged. But he swears that he did not move the body from Shoreditch to Bedford Square. He simply fled. That was witnessed as well. I want to know how the body got to General Balantyne's step and who put his snuffbox in the pocket and tried to have the body identified as Albert Cole."

"What snuffbox?" She was completely bemused.

"General Balantyne had a highly unusual snuffbox," he explained. "Like a reliquary, only made of pinchbeck. He gave it to the blackmailer"—he saw her wince at the word, but there was no other he could use—"as a token of surrender. It was found in the corpse's pocket, along with a receipt for socks, from which we identified him—wrongly, as it turns out—as Albert Cole, a man who had served with Balantyne on the campaign where the incident occurred over which he was threatened."

"And you believe my husband found the body, wherever it was, and moved it, and put those things on it?" she asked with disbelief, but no strength to deny. She was dizzy with

297

confusion and pain. "Do the details matter now, Mr. Pitt? Do you need to dot every *i* and cross every *t*?"

"I need to understand more than I do now, Mrs. Cadell," he replied. "There is still too much of it which seems inexplicable. I feel as if I have left something undone. And I want to know what happened to the real Albert Cole. If he is alive, where is he? And if he is dead, did he die naturally or was he also murdered?"

She stood very still. "I suppose you must. I . . . I want to hope that you will find some other explanation, something that does not involve my husband. Every fact you have found so far makes that impossible, and yet I cannot believe it of the man I knew . . . and loved." Her lip trembled a little, and she gestured impatiently. "You must think me a fool. I imagine every woman whose husband has done something criminal says the same thing. You must expect it by now."

"If people were so easy to read, Mrs. Cadell, anyone could do my job, and far better than I do it," he said softly. "It can take me weeks to solve a case, and too often I don't succeed at all. Even when I do, I am frequently just as surprised as anyone else. Most of the time we see what we expect to see, and what we want to."

The ghost of a smile touched her face. "Where would you like to begin?"

"With the valet, if you please."

But Didcott, the valet, proved of little use. He was obviously suffering from shock and bewilderment, and the very natural anxiety as to what his own future would be. He would have no employment once Cadell's belongings were disposed of. He answered every question to the best of his ability, but he could shed no light on the subject of Cadell's life outside what was generally known of his work at the Foreign Office and the social and diplomatic functions that one might have expected him to attend. If he owned any clothes suitable for venturing to the East End, or attending the rougher gambling houses, let alone such sports as bare-knuckle fighting or dog fights, he did not keep them in the house.

Pitt went through all the cupboards and drawers himself.

Cadell had been a fastidious man, well dressed, as Pitt would have expected, but considering his position and his income, certainly not extravagant. Almost all his suits were formal; there was little of a more casual nature.

Didcott kept a diary of events Cadell attended in order that he might make sure every garment was ready, clean and pressed, when it should be required and that there were always sufficient clean shirts to hand. Pitt read it carefully, going back over the previous three months. If Cadell had kept every appointment, and Didcott assured Pitt that he had, then his schedule allowed very little time indeed for self-indulgence of any sort. It was difficult to see when he could have had time to go to Shoreditch, or anywhere else, to overspend money on private vices.

It also appeared, incidentally, that he had very seldom been to the Jessop Club lately, not above three times in the previous eight weeks, at least according to Didcott's diary. Perhaps Pitt should go to the club and ask there? Maybe it was irrelevant, but it was a silly little fact that did not fit the picture.

He went downstairs and outside to the mews, where he found the coachman, but even with the most detailed questioning, he also could offer nothing of use. He had driven Cadell regularly over the previous eight years and had never taken him to Shoreditch, or anywhere like it. He looked at Pitt with wide, sad eyes, and seemed confused by almost everything Pitt said.

It seemed that if Cadell had gone on any private journeys, he had done so by hansom or some other form of public transport, or less likely, with an associate.

Was that the answer, a conspiracy?

With whom?

He should go through all the papers again. Reread everything to see if there was any indication of another person, another mind involved.

He was offered luncheon, and accepted it, eating it in the servants' hall. They treated him civilly enough, but their grief was very obvious, and they spoke little.

He returned to his task, and it took him the rest of the afternoon, going through every drawer and cupboard. He even leafed through books from the shelves in the study, the only room in the house which was private to Cadell and not touched by any of the servants except in his presence. It was where he had kept certain of his work when he had brought it home.

Pitt questioned all the servants about the posting of a letter on the day before Cadell's death, or that morning, but no one knew of a letter, to Dunraithe White or anyone else.

There was no glue in the study desk drawer. There was notepaper, but it was of a different texture and a slightly different size from that of the letters. It would seem Cadell had not written them at home. Could he really have done it at the Foreign Office? Or was there a third place, one they knew nothing of?

The only other thing that caught Pitt's attention was a note on the side of Cadell's appointment diary: "Balantyne still worried about Kew. He is not a fool. I should take it seriously."

He thanked Theodosia and left to go to Bedford Square. He had been to Kew himself. Charlotte had spoken to Balantyne also, but perhaps there was something Pitt could ask that would elicit an explanation as to why the General was concerned that made some kind of sense.

He did not believe it, but he could not leave it undone.

As he was shown in by the footman he was greeted with icy disdain by Augusta. She was dressed in a gray striped gown and looked magnificent. Pitt was jolted by memory of the past, her courage and resolution, her grief, and the loneliness that must haunt her solitary hours. There was no happiness in her, only cold strength. There was something admirable about her, something frightening, and not a little that evoked a sense of pity.

"What tragedy is it this time, Mr. Pitt?" she enquired, coming towards him with a remarkably graceful step for a woman of her age. There was nothing whatever fragile in her, nothing that spoke of vulnerability. "And what makes you imagine that we can assist you in your confusion?"

"The same tragedy, Lady Augusta," he answered gravely, standing in the middle of the wide hall. "And I am not at all sure that General Balantyne can help, but I have to ask."

"Do you?" she said with faint sarcasm. "I find that difficult to understand, but I suppose you have to justify yourself somehow."

Pitt did not argue. He probably was wasting not only his own time but Balantyne's. Nevertheless, he would still ask him about Kew.

"The orphanage?" Balantyne said with surprise. He stood with his back to the oak fireplace in the morning room, staring at Pitt. "Yes, I did speak to Cadell about it. Twice, I think . . . possibly three times." He was frowning slightly. "I don't understand why you are concerned now. If they are incompetent, or short of funds, it is hardly a police matter."

"Incompetence? Is that what you were concerned about when you contacted Cadell two or three times?" Pitt asked with surprise. "Why Cadell? Did you speak to the committee in general?"

"Yes, of course I did. No one else seemed to consider the matter of any substance."

"You thought the funds were insufficient," Pitt said again. "You did not suspect that anyone was misusing them or diverting them to private profit?"

"No," Balantyne said. "I don't know what I thought was happening, just that sufficient care was not being taken."

"So you spoke to Cadell? Why him?"

"I believed he would listen and take the matter up with the man in charge . . . Horsfall."

"I went there myself," Pitt confessed. "I looked through the financial books. They were faultless."

"I don't doubt it," Balantyne said a little sharply. "I was not suspecting dishonesty . . . only a reluctance to demand more money, sufficient to care properly for the children there. I was concerned that they might be cold . . . or hungry."

301

"I saw the children," Pitt replied. "They were clean and well clothed and looked in excellent health."

Balantyne was puzzled. "Then it would seem I was mistaken." But there was disbelief in his voice. He was reluctant to let go of the conviction he had held.

"What made you think there was something wrong?" Pitt was puzzled also, because he respected Balantyne and could not dismiss his ideas lightly, even if they appeared to have no foundation.

Balantyne frowned. "I go to Kew every so often. I am familiar with the size of it, and how many children it could accommodate. I do not understand how they can manage adequately on the funds they have. It seems to me . . . far too little. . . ." He lifted one shoulder very slightly. "I don't know why they didn't press for more."

"Were you alone in this?" Pitt thought of the other members of the committee in the Jessop Club. Surely no stretch of the imagination could connect the orphanage with blackmail or death?

"I don't believe so," Balantyne answered a trifle ruefully. "I raised the subject when we all met. Cornwallis seemed to think I was mistaken. But then he is used to naval catering, which is hardly the same." His lips tightened. "Nor is it ideal . . . especially for children. I thought Cadell at least considered the possibility of examining the situation."

"I see," Pitt replied with a sudden and profound sense of disappointment. What had he hoped for? It was never going to be a motive for blackmail, far less murder. "Thank you for giving me your time, General. I really should let this subject go."

"The orphanage at Kew?" Balantyne asked.

"No . . . no, I meant the possibility of it being connected with Cadell's blackmail attempts or his death. Even if you are right, it is hardly a motive."

Balantyne's surprise showed in his face. "Had you thought it was?"

"I don't know. It seemed to be the one thing you all had in

302

common, but I realize now it was membership of the committee, not its purpose, that counted."

"What happened to the real Albert Cole?" Balantyne asked.

"I don't know. But we shall go on looking for him." Pitt held out his hand. "Thank you. I hope I shall not need to disturb you again."

Balantyne clasped Pitt's hand warmly, but he said nothing further.

Pitt walked home in the warm twilight, still filled with unease, trivial questions unanswered, pricking his mind, leaving him no sense of completion.

12

F_{IND} *ALBERT COLE,* Pitt had said to Tellman. Alive or dead. If he is alive, find out why he disappeared from his lodgings and from Lincoln's Inn Fields; and if he is dead, find out how he died, naturally or otherwise. If he was killed, who killed him and why, and also when. And where.

Tellman had made a sarcastic reply, wondering why Pitt had bothered to trail all the way out to Kew and what on earth an orphanage, very satisfactorily run, could have to do with any of it.

Pitt had had no answer for that, and left Tellman to go about his search. He himself had begun with more about Cadell's movements. Could he have transported Slingsby's body from Shoreditch himself, and if not, which was probably the case, then who had? He had told Tellman of his intention to visit Cadell's widow and enquire from the valet and coachman, and see if he could trace Cadell to Shoreditch from that end.

Tellman acknowledged the instruction tersely, but if he were honest, he was not unwilling to obey. He thought that suicide was a frustrating way to conclude a case. Too much was unexplained. They would probably never learn what had made a man like Leo Cadell jeopardize everything he had, which was a vast amount, wealth and happiness beyond Tellman's dreams . . . although his dreams had included some happiness lately, and he blushed hot at the thought.

But he did not expect to understand the man, only the facts of the case, the logical, material details. And finding Albert Cole was part of that. He set out with a profound determination.

Pitt addressed himself to the task of learning how Slingsby's body had been moved from Shoreditch to Bedford Square, and more importantly, by whom. Naturally, he began with Cadell. Since he was dead, the Foreign Office would not protect him in the way it had previously.

Pitt had little trouble in tracing Cadell's movements on the day before the body had been found. He had worked either in his office or at various meetings with officials from the German embassy. At the time Slingsby and Wallace were fighting in Shoreditch, Cadell had actually been in negotiation with the German ambassador himself.

Like almost anyone else, he could have gone to Shoreditch in the small hours of the morning, presuming someone had moved Slingsby's body from the street where it had fallen, kept it in a safe place, and Cadell had known where that was. Which would be to assume a great deal, including that Slingsby had been murdered intentionally and that Wallace had conspired with Cadell to that end because Slingsby resembled Albert Cole.

How did Cadell know a ruffian like Wallace?

He quickened his pace, striding along the footpath between the crowds of shoppers, clerks and errand boys and sightseers. He must go and talk to Wallace again, before he stood trial and was in all probability executed. Why had he not said he had moved the body when Tellman questioned him before? It would hardly make any difference to his sentence to plead that it had been a fight rather than a deliberate attack. He would be hanged either way.

Or did he expect to come up before Dunraithe White . . . and believe he would be acquitted? Was that why White was a victim?

And why kill anyone to have Balantyne suspected? Why was the blackmail over the Abyssinian affair not enough? What extra was wanted from Balantyne more than the others?

Pitt found himself almost running, and he hailed a cab with

waving arms, shouting at the driver as he leapt in, "Newgate Prison!" He felt the cab thrust forward, throwing him against the seat.

But by the time he reached Newgate he had changed his mind. He leaned forward and rapped on the cab wall, raising his voice.

"Sorry! Forget about Newgate. Take me to Shoreditch."

The driver grunted something unintelligible, which, considering its nature, may have been as well, and changed direction abruptly.

Pitt began in the public house where Tellman had said Wallace and Slingsby had started their quarrel, then progressed to the regular denizens of the immediate area. He had to part with a good few coins to assist memory and goodwill, and he ended the day with nothing which would have served as proof in a court, but he was quite certain in his own mind that Wallace could have come back within half an hour of the murder and taken the body of Slingsby. Certainly the body had disappeared within that time. There was no knowledge or indication that anyone else had moved it, and opinion seemed to be that it had been Wallace's problem and he had dealt with it. They had supposed it would be into the river, but that was only because it was the most obvious thing to do. Taking a cart and carrying the body to Bedford Square would be too outlandish, and utterly pointless, to have occurred to them.

The best and final thing to do was to see if anyone had lent, or had stolen from them, such a vehicle.

With a little more generosity and a certain number of threats and promises, he succeeded in discovering that one Obadiah Smith had indeed had his vegetable cart removed without his permission, so he claimed, and to his great inconvenience. It had been returned in the morning.

He left Shoreditch elated. It was hardly worth going to Newgate. Wallace would probably deny it, but Pitt was now convinced that Wallace had murdered Slingsby with the quite deliberate intention of moving his body and placing it on Balantyne's doorstep, with the snuffbox in his pocket, and the receipt for the socks, perhaps obtained by Wallace himself, pretending to be Cole. And this had been done on Cadell's instructions. It would be very satisfying to see Wallace's face when he heard that Cadell was dead and could not possibly rescue him.

But why Slingsby and not the real Cole? Where was Cole now? Was Tellman having any success in finding him?

However, when Tellman reported to Pitt that evening, within twenty minutes of Pitt's arriving home himself, he had nothing to offer at all. They sat around the kitchen table in deep gloom. Charlotte had made a large pot of tea, and Gracie had abandoned even pretending to be peeling potatoes or cutting the strings off the beans. She was not going to be occupied in such things when there were really important matters to talk about.

"Nobody has any idea," Tellman said defensively. "He could have gone anywhere. If he had any family, no one heard him mention them. They could be in Wales, for all anyone knew. Or Scotland."

"Army records would know where he came from," Pitt pointed out.

Tellman flushed. He was furious with himself because he had not thought of that.

"Well, if someone were arter 'im, 'e wouldn't go back there, would 'e?" Gracie said defensively. "If we can work that out, mebbe they could too . . . stands ter reason, don't it?" She looked from Pitt to Tellman and back again. " 'E'd a' gorn somewhere as nob'dy knows 'im. I would."

"Why would anybody be after him?" Pitt asked. "He didn't do anything, or know anything, so far as we can tell."

"Well, w'y else would 'e scarper?" she asked reasonably. "Goin' by wot you said, 'e 'ad a decent job an' a good place. Yer don't jus' up an' leave things like that, less yer got summink better or there's someb'dy arter yer."

"Bit chancy, wasn't it?" Tellman said reluctantly, flashing Gracie a look of gratitude, and obviously unwilling to slight the favor by criticizing her logic, but driven to it by necessity. "Someone we don't know of went after Cole, just the day

307

before poor Slingsby gets done in by someone who wants to pretend he's Cole?"

"That's it!" Pitt banged his fist on the table. Suddenly it was obvious. "They went after Cole first. They tried to kill him, but somehow they failed. He got away. Perhaps he was a better soldier than they realized, experienced in hand-to-hand fighting," he said eagerly. "He escaped, but he knew they'd come after him again, perhaps a knife in the back next time, or a shot. So he took to his heels and disappeared . . . anywhere. It doesn't matter where . . . just out of London, to a place they'd never think of looking." He turned to Gracie. "As you said, they know his military record, that's why they wanted him, so the last place he'd go would be back to anywhere he had a connection with." He stared around the table. "That's why we can't find Cole . . . and I daresay we never will."

"So they found someone who looked like him," Charlotte took up the train of reasoning. "They had the snuffbox anyway, and they either stole the sock receipt or had one made up."

"Had it made up," Tellman put in. "Easy enough. Go and buy three pairs. Get yourself noticed. Say something about being a soldier, the importance of keeping your feet right. The shop clerk remembered all that, but not much about his face."

"Who is 'they'?" Charlotte asked with a little shake of her head, a sharp return from logic to emotion. "Cadell . . . if it has to be . . . and who else? Ernest Wallace? Why?" She bit her lip, and her expression betrayed her disbelief. "I still can't accept that." She looked from Pitt to Tellman. "You haven't found any reason why he should suddenly need money, or connected him to any plot to invest in Africa or anywhere else. Aunt Vespasia says he just wasn't that sort of person."

Pitt sighed. He reached his hand across the table and put it over hers.

"Of course she doesn't want to think so, but what is the alternative?"

"That someone else is guilty," she answered, her voice

without the certainty she would have liked. "And he killed himself . . . because . . . I don't know. He was so worn down by the blackmail he hadn't the strength to go on."

"And confessed," Pitt said gently, "knowing what that would do to his family? To Theodosia? And they have grown-up children, a son and two daughters. Have you seen what Lyndon Remus and the other newspapers have made of the scandal? Poor Gordon-Cumming pales beside it."

"Then he could never have done it," she said desperately. "He must have been murdered."

"By whom?" he asked. "No one came or went but the family servants, and the entrances were observed all the time."

She took her hand away, fists clenched. "Well, I still refuse to believe it. There's something we don't know. . . ."

"There's a lot of things we don't know," he said dryly. He ticked them off on his fingers. "We don't know why Cadell wanted or needed money, or even if that was the purpose of the blackmail. We don't know why he chose specifically the other members of the orphanage committee of the Jessop Club. There must have been dozens of other men he knew as well, and could have created a web of fear around, built on imagination and misinterpretation. We certainly don't know how he ever made the acquaintance of Ernest Wallace or why he trusted him."

"We don't know why Wallace lied to protect him and is still lying," Tellman added.

"Yes, we do," Pitt answered. "At least, we can deduce it. He is in Newgate and doesn't know that Cadell is dead. He must be assuming that Cadell will twist the knife in Dunraithe White, and Wallace will be acquitted. He also doesn't know that White has just resigned from the bench."

"Then tell him," Charlotte retorted. "That may concentrate his mind wonderfully. Show him he is completely alone. He has been let down on every side. Cadell has escaped, in a fashion, and left him to hang . . . alone."

"Don't make no difference whether you 'ang alone or

together," Gracie said with disgust. "Don't suppose it feels no different. 'E killed Slingsby, so 'e'll 'ang any which way."

Pitt rose to his feet. "I'll still go and see him."

Charlotte's eyes widened. "Now? It's half past six."

"I'll be back by nine," he promised, walking to the door. "I have to speak to him."

Pitt hated visiting prisons. The walls closed in on him with the cold gray misery of countless angry and wasted lives. Hopelessness seemed to seep from the stones, and his footsteps echoed behind the warder's like multiple treads, as if he were preceded and followed by unseen inmates, ghosts who would never escape.

Ernest Wallace would be tried in a week or two. He was brought into the small room where Pitt waited for him. He looked small and tight, and beneath his smug expression there remained a lifelong anger that was bone-deep. He glanced at Pitt, but there was no visible fear in his eyes. It seemed to amuse him that Pitt had come all the way to Newgate to see him. He sat down at the other side of the bare wooden table without being asked. The warder, a barrel-chested man with a disinterested face, stood by the door. Whatever these two were going to say, he had heard it all before.

"Where did you go after you had fought with Slingsby?" Pitt began, almost conversationally.

If Wallace was surprised he hid it well. "Don' remember," he answered. "Wot's it matter nah?"

"What did you fight about?"

"I told yer, least I told the other rozzer, 'baht summink wot 'e took orff me as e'd no right ter. I tried ter get it back orff 'im, an 'e laid inter me. I fought 'im . . . natural. I've a right ter save me own life." He said that with some satisfaction, meeting Pitt's eyes squarely.

Pitt had thought he expected the blackmailer to influence the trial and get him acquitted, at least of murder. Now, in the fetid room with its smell of despair, he was certain of it.

310

"And when you saw that you had killed him, you just fled?" Pitt said aloud.

"Wot?"

"You ran away."

"Yeah. Well, I didn't think as any rozzer'd believe me. An' I were right, weren't I? Or I wouldn't be here now, lookin' at a charge o' murder." He said it with considerable self-justification. "Yer'd a' seen as I were defendin' meself from a geezer wot were bigger'n me, an' got a right temper on 'im." He almost smiled.

"Is Albert Cole dead too?" Pitt said suddenly.

Wallace kept his face straight, but he could not prevent the ebb of color from his skin, and his hands twitched involuntarily where he had laid them with a deliberate show of ease on the tabletop.

" 'Oo?"

"Albert Cole." Pitt smiled. "The man Slingsby looked like and was mistaken for when we found him. He had a receipt belonging to Cole in his pocket."

Wallace grinned. "Oh, yeah! Yer made a right mess o' that, din't yer."

"It was the receipt that did it," Pitt explained. "And the lawyer from Lincoln's Inn who identified him. And of course Cole is missing."

Wallace affected surprise. "Is 'e? Well, I never. Life's full o' funny little things like that . . . i'n't it?" He was enjoying himself, and he wanted Pitt to know it.

Pitt waited patiently.

"Yes, it is," he agreed. "You see, I think you can't tell me where you went after you killed Slingsby because you came back, within minutes, and loaded his body into a vegetable cart you'd 'borrowed' after dark. You took it to Bedford Square and left it on General Balantyne's doorstep, exactly as you were told to do."

Wallace was tense, his shoulder muscles locked, the sinews in his thin neck standing out, but his eyes did not waver from Pitt's.

"Do yer? Well, yer can't prove it, so it don' make no

311

difference. I says as I killed 'im 'cos 'e came at me, an' scarpered arterwards 'cos I were scared as no rozzer'd believe me." His voice descended into mockery. "An' I'm real sorry abaht that, me lud. I won't never make a mistake like that again."

"Talking about judges," Pitt observed steadily, "Mr. Dunraithe White has resigned from the bench."

Wallace looked mystified.

"Am I supposed ter know wot yer talkin' abaht?"

Pitt was shaken, but he concealed it. "Perhaps not. I thought you might come up before him."

"Well if 'e i'n't a judge no more, I won't, will I? Stands ter reason."

Pitt dropped the blow he had been waiting for.

"And another thing you might not have heard, being in here . . . Leo Cadell is dead."

Wallace sat motionless.

"Committed suicide," Pitt added, "after confessing to blackmail."

Wallace's eyes widened. "Blackmail?" he said with what Pitt would have sworn was surprise.

"Yes. He's dead."

"Yeah . . . yer said. So is that all?" He looked at Pitt with wide eyes, untroubled, his lips still smiling, not the fixed and awful grin of a man whose last hope has slipped away, but the satisfaction of someone supremely confident, even if he had heard some news which he did not completely understand.

It was Pitt who was thrown into confusion. Reason and hope disappeared from his grasp.

Wallace saw it, and his smile widened, reaching his eyes.

Pitt was suddenly furious, aching to be able to hit him. He rose to his feet and told the warder he was finished before he betrayed his defeat even more. He walked out of the gray suffocation of Newgate totally perplexed.

He arrived home in Keppel Street still just as confused, and if possible even angrier, but now with himself rather than only with Wallace.

"What's wrong?" Charlotte demanded as soon as he was

312

in the kitchen. They must all have heard his footsteps coming down the passage from the front door, and were sitting around the table staring at him expectantly. He had not even bothered to take his boots off. He sat down, and automatically Gracie poured him a mug of tea.

"I told him I believed he had come back and moved the body to Bedford Square," he answered. "And I could see it shook him."

Tellman nodded with satisfaction.

"And I told him Dunraithe White had resigned," Pitt went on. "And it meant nothing to him at all."

"I don't suppose he knew his name," Charlotte explained. "Just that there was a judge in the blackmailer's power."

"And then I told him Cadell was dead," Pitt finished, looking at their expectant faces. "He didn't give a damn."

"What?" Tellman was incredulous, his jaw dropping.

"He must have," Charlotte said abruptly. "He must have known Cadell. It can't have been all done by letter." Her eyes widened. "Or are you saying it wasn't Cadell after all?"

"I don't know what I'm saying," he admitted. "Except that I still don't understand it."

There were several minutes of silence. The kettle whistled on the hob, gathering shrillness, and Gracie got up to move it over.

Pitt sipped his tea gratefully. He had not realized how thirsty he was, or how keen to get the taste of prison air out of his mouth.

Charlotte looked apologetic, and very faintly pink.

"General Balantyne was worried about the funds for the orphanage at Kew . . ." she said tentatively.

"I've been out there," Pitt answered wearily. "I've been over the books with a fine-toothed comb. Every penny is accounted for, and I've seen the children. They are healthy, well clothed and well fed. Anyway, Balantyne thought there was too little money given them, not too much."

"That's a turn up," Gracie said dryly. "I never 'card of an orphanage afore wot 'ad enough money, let alone too much. An' come ter that, I never 'eard o' one wot fed an' clothed its

313

kids proper. Beggin' yer pardon, Mr. Pitt, but I think you was took in. It were likely the master's own kids as yer saw, not the orphans."

"No, it wasn't," Pitt said wearily. "I saw upwards of twenty children."

"Twenty?" Gracie was incredulous.

"At least. More like twenty-five," he assured her.

"In an orphanage?"

"Yes."

" 'Ow big's this orphanage, then? Couple o' cottages, is it?"

"No, of course not. It's a very large house, dozen bedrooms or more, originally, I should think."

Gracie looked at him with weary patience. "Then you was took proper. 'Ouse that size they'd 'ave an 'undred kids at least. Ten to a room, countin' little ones. Big ones ter look arter 'em."

"There were nothing like that many." He thought back on the clear, light rooms he had seen, admittedly only two or three of them, but he had chosen them at random, and Horsfall had been willing enough to show him everywhere he wished to go.

"Then w'ere was the rest o' them?" Gracie asked.

"There were no more," Pitt replied, frowning. "And the money was about right for that number, to feed and clothe and pay for the fuel and keeping of the house."

"Can't a' bin much, then," Gracie said dismissively. "Yer can feed an orphan kid, fer a few pence a day, on bread an' taters and gravy. Clothe 'em in 'and-me-downs and stuff wot's bin unpicked an' remade. Get a pile fer a shillin' down Seven Dials way. Same wif boots. An' w'en yer places kids, which in't often, like as not they leave their clothes be'ind. An o' course w'en they grows out o' them, someone else grows inter 'em."

"What are you suggesting?" Charlotte turned to her, her eyes wide and dark in the dying light. The gas was flickering yellow on the wall.

"Maybe they are good at placing children?" Tellman said.

314

"If they give them a little education they could go into trades, be useful?"

"You live in a dream, you do," Gracie said, shaking her head. "Nobody places orphans that fast. 'Oo wants extra mouths ter feed these days? 'Less they're workin'."

"They were little children," Pitt put in. "Those ones I saw were as young as three or four years old, most of them."

Gracie's eyes were full of pity and anger. "Yer think kids o' three or four can't work? 'Course they can. Work 'ard, some o' them poor little bleeders. An' don't answer back nor run away. Too scared. Nothin' ter run ter. Work 'em till they either grow up or die."

"They weren't working," Pitt said slowly. "They were happy, and healthy, playing."

"Till they get placed," Gracie answered him. "There's good money in that. Sell an 'ealthy kid fer quite a bit . . . specially if yer got a reg'lar supply, like."

Charlotte used a word that would have appalled her mother, breathing it out in a sigh of horror.

Tellman regarded Gracie with dismay.

"How do you know that?" he demanded.

"I know wot 'appens ter kids wot's got no one ter take 'em in," she said bleakly. " 'Appened ter one o' me friends, down the street. 'Er ma got killed an' 'er Pa got topped. 'Er an' 'er bruvvers got sent ter an orphanage. I went ter see 'er, year arter. She were gorn ter pick oakum, an' 'er bruvvers gorn up north ter the mines."

Charlotte put her hands up to her face. "Does Aunt Vespasia have to know, Thomas? She couldn't bear it. It would break her heart to know that Cadell did such a thing."

"I don't even know if it's true yet," he answered. But it was a prevarication. In his heart he was certain. This was a secret worth committing blackmail to hide. This was why Brandon Balantyne had been singled out for the most powerful threat, even destruction, if possible. He had been asking too many questions. After the Devil's Acre, he was one man who might be very difficult to silence. This was why all the members of

315

the orphanage committee were victims. There was nothing random or opportunistic about it.

Charlotte did not bother to argue; she knew Pitt too well. Tellman and Gracie both sat silently.

"Tomorrow," Pitt said. "Tomorrow we'll go out to Kew."

Pitt and Tellman reached the orphanage at mid-morning. It was a hot, still day, already oppressive at ten o'clock as they climbed the slight hill towards the large house.

Tellman screwed up his face against the light and stared at it, unconsciously thinning his lips. Pitt knew Gracie's words were sharp and hurting in the sergeant's mind. He drew in his breath as if to speak, and then said nothing after all. They approached the front door in silence.

It was opened by a girl of about eleven, plain-faced and straight-haired.

"Yes sir?" she asked.

"We would like to see Mr. Horsfall," Pitt said bluntly, allowing no opportunity for refusal.

A small boy ran down the hall, making a noise in imitation of a galloping horse, and another followed him, laughing. They both disappeared into a passageway at right angles to the one that led from the door, and there was a squeal from somewhere beyond.

Pitt felt the anger boil up inside him, perhaps pointlessly. Maybe Gracie was wrong? There was far too much money for the few children he had seen, but perhaps there were more somewhere else? Perhaps Horsfall really did find homes for them? Perhaps there was a dearth of orphans at the moment, and many childless families?

"Now, if you please," he added as the girl looked doubtful.

"Yes sir," she said obediently, and pulled the door wider. "If yer'll wait in the sittin' room I'll fetch 'im for yer." She showed them to the same homely room Pitt had seen before, and they heard her feet clatter along the wooden corridor as she went about her errand. They remained standing, too tense to sit.

316

"Don't suppose he'll run, do you?" Tellman said dubiously.

Pitt had thought of it, but Horsfall had no reason to fear anything now. "If he were going to, he'd have gone when Cadell shot himself," he said aloud.

"Suppose he knows?" Tellman pursed his lips, frowning. "If he does, why is he still here? Does he inherit the orphanage? Where does the money go anyway? Why share it with Cadell in the first place? Do you suppose this is Cadell's house?"

Those thoughts had occurred to Pitt also, and others that troubled him even more. At the back of his mind was the complacent expression in Wallace's face when Pitt had told him Dunraithe White had resigned from the bench, and even when he had said that Cadell was dead.

Wallace's impassivity about White could have either of two explanations. He did not know of White's involvement, and therefore his resignation held no meaning for Wallace, or he knew the blackmailer would not allow White to resign. He would let him know that if he did, he would exercise his threat and ruin him anyway.

Then why had he not been shattered to learn of Cadell's death? That removed every chance for him of escape from the noose.

There could be only one answer . . . it was not Cadell he was depending upon.

Either Cadell had an accomplice . . . which would explain why Horsfall was still there, or it was not Cadell who was the blackmailer, but someone else.

Tellman was watching Pitt, waiting for him to speak.

It could not be Guy Stanley. He would not have ruined himself, not so completely. Neither did Pitt believe it was Balantyne. He had never even considered that it could be Cornwallis. That left White and Tannifer.

He looked up at Tellman. "Where was Dunraithe White when Cadell was shot?"

"You mean, you don't think he shot himself?" Tellman seized on the change of wording instantly.

"I don't know," Pitt replied. He shoved his hands hard into

his pockets, leaning against the wall and staring back at Tellman.

"No one else was there," Tellman pointed out. "You said so yourself."

"Wallace believes the blackmailer is still alive, and he knows Cadell is dead," Pitt argued. "What about Tannifer?"

"I don't know." Tellman shook his head. He moved restlessly about the room. "But he can't have been at Cadell's house, or he'd have been seen."

There was no further time to pursue it because at that moment the door opened and Horsfall came in looking blankly from one to the other of them.

"Good morning, gentlemen. What can I do for you this time?"

His smug unconcern infuriated Pitt, the more so for his own inner confusion. Something essential was still eluding him, and he was bitterly aware of it.

"Good morning," he said grimly, his body tight and his jaw clenched. "How many children have you here at present, Mr. Horsfall?"

Horsfall looked startled. "Why . . . about fifteen, I think." He shot a look at Tellman, and then swallowed. "We have been very fortunate in placing several . . . lately."

"Good!" Pitt said. "Where?"

"What?"

"Where?" Pitt repeated a little more loudly.

"I don't understand. . . ." He was still only mildly uncomfortable.

"Where have you placed them, Mr. Horsfall?"

Tellman moved to the door, as if to cut off Horsfall's retreat.

"Er . . . you mean the exact addresses? I should have to look it up. Is there something amiss? Has someone proved unsatisfactory?"

"Unsatisfactory? What an odd word to use of a child," Pitt said coldly. "Sounds more like placing a servant."

Horsfall swallowed again. He eased his shoulders up and down, as if to relax tense muscles.

"Yes . . . silly of me," he agreed. "But I feel responsible

318

for our children. Sometimes people expect better behavior than . . . than young people are capable of. New surroundings . . . strange . . . new people . . . not all children respond well. They become used to us here, of course, used to our ways." He was talking a little too quickly. "Don't always understand change . . . even if it is change for their good. . . ."

"I know." Pitt's voice was like ice. "I have children myself, Mr. Horsfall."

"Oh . . ." Horsfall paled. He licked his lips. Pitt had said nothing threatening, but the look in his eyes was enough to warn of savage dislike. "Well . . . what is the problem, Mr. . . . er . . . ?"

"Where were these children placed?" Pitt repeated the original question.

Horsfall was clenching and unclenching his hands.

"I told you . . . I should have to look it up. I don't have a good memory for the details of addresses . . . large numbers of . . . addresses."

"Approximately . . ." Pitt insisted.

"Oh . . . well . . . Lincolnshire, yes; Spalding. And several . . . as far north as Durham . . . yes."

"And Nottinghamshire?" Pitt suggested.

Horsfall's eyebrows rose. "Why, yes. Nottinghamshire too."

"How about Wales?" Pitt went on. "South Wales. Lot of mines in South Wales."

Horsfall was white, a sheen of sweat on his face. "M-mines?"

"Yes. Children are useful in lots of places . . . in mines, up chimneys, in factories, cleaning out corners adults can't get into, especially small children, young . . . thin. Even three- and four-year-olds can be taught to pick rags, pick oakum, send them out into the fields to work. All sorts of crops need taking up . . . by hand . . . little hands are as good as big ones and don't need paying . . . not if you've bought them. . . ."

"That's . . ." Horsfall swallowed and choked.

"Slavery," Pitt finished for him.

"You can't . . . you can't prove that. . . ." Horsfall gasped. His face was running with sweat.

"Oh, I'm sure I can." Pitt smiled, showing his teeth.

Horsfall ran his hands over his brow.

"Do you know a man named Ernest Wallace?" Pitt asked, changing the subject suddenly. "Small, wiry, very bad temper indeed."

Horsfall's deliberation was plain in his expression. He could not judge whether acknowledgment or denial was going to make his situation worse.

Pitt watched him without the slightest pity.

Tellman did not move.

"I . . . er . . ." Horsfall hesitated.

"You can't afford to lie to me," Pitt warned.

"Well . . ." Horsfall licked his lips. "He may have done the occasional odd job around the . . . garden . . . for us. Yes . . . yes, he did. Wallace . . . yes." He stared at Pitt as at some dangerous animal.

"Where does the money go?" Pitt switched back to the original line of questioning.

"M-m-money?" Horsfall stammered.

Pitt moved forward half a step.

"I don't know!" Horsfall's voice rose as if he had been physically threatened. "I only take my pay. I don't know where it goes."

"You know where you send it," Tellman said bitterly. He was shorter and narrower than Horsfall, but there was such a rage in his voice that the bigger man quailed.

"Show me!" Pitt commanded.

"I-I don't have . . . books!" Horsfall protested, raising his hands as if to ward off a blow.

Pitt was unimpressed. "You have accounts of some kind. Either you have a master who takes the money from you one way or another, or else you haven't, and you are responsible for it all. . . ." He did not need to continue. Horsfall was shaking his head and waving his hands in denial. "Is this house yours?" Pitt pressed.

"No. Of course not. It belongs to the orphanage."

"And the profits from selling the children?"

"Well . . . I wouldn't use terms like that. . . ." Horsfall sputtered.

"Slavery, Mr. Horsfall—the selling of human beings—is illegal in this country. You can be charged as an accomplice or all by yourself, as you like," Pitt answered. "Where does the money go?"

"I'll-I'll show you." Horsfall surrendered. "I only do what I'm told."

Pitt looked at him with complete disgust and followed him out of the room to find the notes he kept of his transactions. He read them all and added them up. Over the space of eight years it amounted to tens of thousands of pounds. But there were no names to prove in whose pockets it had ended.

The local police arrested Horsfall and placed someone in temporary charge of the orphanage. Pitt and Tellman set out on their way back to London, traveling on the ferry, glad of the bright air and the sounds of the busy river.

"He should swing," Tellman said between his teeth. "That blackmailing swine won't get him off."

"I'll be damned if he'll get Wallace off either," Pitt retorted.

Tellman stared straight ahead of him up the river towards the Battersea Bridge. A pleasure boat passed them going the other way, people waving, ribbons and streamers bright in the wind. He did not seem to see it. "If it isn't Cadell, then it's got to be White or Tannifer." He looked at Pitt's bulging pockets. "We've got enough paper there to work out where the money went."

It took them a day and a half of painstaking, minute unraveling of buying and selling, of finding the names behind the names, all accomplished with savage deliberation, but by four o'clock in the afternoon, two days after their return from the orphanage, they could prove that the trail led to Sigmund Tannifer.

Tellman stood with the last piece of paper in his hand and swore viciously. "What'll he get?" he said fiercely. "He's sold little children to labor in the mines like they were animals.

Some of them'll never see the light of day again." His voice caught with his emotion. "But we can't prove he knew what Horsfall was doing. He'll deny it. Say it was rents or something, surplus from other properties. He blackmailed innocent men and near drove them mad with fear . . . enough to make Cadell shoot himself and White resign . . . but we can't prove that either. We'd have to show that he threatened to expose them, and that would only ruin them just like he said he would. We'd be doing it for him." He swore again, his fists clenched white, his eyes blazing. He was demanding an answer from Pitt, expecting him to solve the injustice somehow.

"It wasn't even blackmail," Pitt said with a shrug. "He didn't ask for anything. He would have . . . their silence over the orphanage, if they had ever found out . . . but it never came to that."

"We've got to get him for something!" Tellman's voice rose to a shout, his fist gripping the air.

"Let's go and arrest him for taking the proceeds of Horsfall's business," Pitt answered. "No jury will believe he thought that it was profits from the kitchen garden."

"That doesn't matter a damn," Tellman said bitterly.

"Oh, I don't know." Pitt pulled a face. "I think that officious little newspaper writer, Remus, could make a good story out of it."

Tellman stared at him. "He couldn't know . . . could he?"

"He could if I told him," Pitt responded.

"We can't prove that Tannifer knew what Horsfall did."

"I don't think that will bother Remus too much. . . ."

Tellman's eyes widened. "You would tell him?"

"I don't know. But I should enjoy letting Tannifer think I would."

Tellman laughed, but it was an unhappy, mirthless sound.

Sigmund Tannifer received them in the ornate withdrawing room without the slightest indication in his smooth features that there was anything amiss or that he could be concerned over any matter but Pitt's progress in concluding his case. He looked at Parthenope, who was standing beside

322

his chair, her vivid face for once completely at peace, reflecting none of the anxiety that had so disturbed her on Pitt's previous visits.

"Good of you to come, Superintendent," Tannifer said, pointing to the chairs where Pitt and Tellman could be seated. "Miserable end to the matter. I admit, I never imagined Cadell could be so . . . I am at a loss for words. . . ."

"Vicious . . . cruel . . . utterly sadistic," Parthenope supplied for him, her voice shaking and her eyes filled with anger and burning contempt. "I am so sorry for Mrs. Cadell; my heart aches for her. What could be more terrible than to discover the man you have loved, have been married to all your adult life and have given your loyalty and your trust . . . is a total blackguard?" Her whole slender body shook with the force of her emotions.

Tellman glanced at Pitt, and away again.

"My dear," Tannifer said soothingly, "you cannot bear the ills of the world. Theodosia Cadell will recover, in time. There is nothing you can do for her."

"I know there isn't," she said desperately. "That's what makes it so awful. If I could help . . ."

"I was quite shocked when I returned the day after his death and read the news," Tannifer went on, looking at Pitt. "I admit, I would have believed it of almost anyone before him. Still . . . he deceived us all."

"Returned from where?" Pitt asked, irrationally disappointed. He already knew no one had been to Cadell's house. What had he hoped for?

"Paris," Tannifer replied, leaning back a little in his wide chair, his hands folded comfortably. "I went over in the steamer the day before. Exhausting. But banking is an international business. Why do you ask?"

"Only interest," Pitt replied. Suddenly all his anger returned in a wave, almost choking him. "And did you deposit money in a French bank?"

Tannifer's eyes widened. "I did, as a matter of fact. Is it of interest to you, Superintendent?" He was at ease, bland, sure of himself.

329

"Is that where the money ends up from the orphanage, in a French bank?" Pitt said icily.

Tannifer did not move. His expression did not change, but his voice was oddly different in timbre.

"Money from the orphanage? I don't understand you."

"The orphanage at Kew which is supported by the committee of the Jessop Club," Pitt explained elaborately. "All of whose members were victims of the blackmailer."

Tannifer stared back at him. "Were they? You never mentioned the names of the other victims."

"Yes . . . Cornwallis, Stanley, White, Cadell, Balantyne and you," Pitt answered him gravely, ice in his voice. "Balantyne especially. That's why the corpse was left on his doorstep, to terrify him, possibly have him arrested for murder. Of course, that is why Wallace tried to kill Albert Cole to begin with, only Cole fought back and escaped." His eyes did not move from Tannifer's. "Then he thought of the excellent idea of using Slingsby, whom he knew, and who resembled Cole so much. He bought the socks himself, spinning a yarn so the clerk would remember him and identify him as Cole, and put the receipt on Slingsby's body. And Balantyne's snuffbox too, of course."

"Ingenious . . ." Tannifer was watching Pitt closely. He opened his mouth as if to lick his lips, then changed his mind.

"Wasn't it," Pitt agreed, not even allowing his eyes to flicker. "If any of the committee had taken up Balantyne's anxiety over the amount of money put into the orphanage, for what was actually very few children indeed, then the blackmail threat would have silenced them."

Parthenope was staring at Pitt, her fair brows drawn into a frown, her mouth pinched.

"Why did it matter that there was too much money and very few children, Superintendent?" she asked. "Surely only too little would be cause for concern? Why would Mr. Cadell want that kept silent? I don't understand."

"The answer was not easy to find." He spoke now to her, not to Tannifer. "You see, the committee put money into the orphanage, and a great many orphans were sent there from all

324

over London. But it also made a huge profit, tens of thousands of pounds, over the years because the children didn't stay there very long." He looked at her puzzled face, the wild emotions in it, and felt a moment's misgiving. But his anger was white-hot. "You see, they were sold to work in factories and mills and mines, especially mines, where they can crawl into spaces grown men cannot. . . ."

She gasped, her face bloodless, her voice choking.

"I'm sorry," Pitt apologized. "I'm sorry you had to know that, Mrs. Tannifer. But the proceeds from this trade are what has finished this beautiful house and bought the silk gown you are wearing."

"It can't be!" Her words were torn from her in a kind of shout.

Pitt took the papers from the orphanage out of his pockets and held them up.

Parthenope swung around to Tannifer, her eyes beseeching, filled with terror.

"My dear, they were East End orphans for the most part," he said reasonably. "Perfectly used to hard conditions. They were not children of people like us. They would have had to work wherever they were. At least this way they won't starve."

She stood frozen.

"Parthenope!" There was impatience in his tone. "Please have a sense of proportion, my dear, and of the realities of life. This situation is something you know nothing about. You really have no idea—"

Her voice was harsh, a travesty of its previous beauty.

"Leo Cadell was innocent!" There was agony in her cry.

"He was innocent of blackmail, yes," he conceded. "But nothing was ever asked for, except worthless trinkets." He looked at her with exasperation. "But I presume he must have been guilty of using his wife's beauty to advance his career, which is pretty disturbing, because he shot himself when he feared exposure. Guilt does some strange things."

Her face was racked with emotions so deep it was a white,

325

contorted mask, terrible, painful to see. "You know what he was accused of."

"You had better go and lie down," Tannifer said more gently, his cheeks a little red. "I'll call your maid. I'll be up to see you as soon as I have dealt with Pitt and . . ." He gestured at Tellman. "Whatever his name is."

"No!" She staggered back, then turned and fled from the room, leaving the door swinging behind her.

Tannifer looked back at Pitt. "You really are unnecessarily clumsy, Superintendent. You might have spared my wife that sort of description." He glanced down at the papers in Pitt's hand. "If you think you have something with which to charge me, come back when I have my legal representative present, and we'll discuss the matter. Now, I must go to my wife and see if I can help her to understand this business. She is rather naive as to worldly things, idealistic, as women sometimes are." And without waiting for Pitt to answer, he strode from the room and into the hall.

Tellman glanced at Pitt, all his fury and frustration in his eyes, challenging, demanding some justice.

Pitt moved towards the door.

Before he reached it a shot rang out, a single sharp explosion, and then a thud.

Pitt lurched forward and almost tripped into the hall, Tellman at his shoulder.

Parthenope stood on the stairs with a dueling pistol in her hands, her arms rigid out in front of her, her back straight, her head high.

Sigmund Tannifer lay on the tiled floor below her, blood oozing from the hole in his forehead between his wide-open eyes, his face filled with amazement and disbelief.

Tellman went over to him, but examination was pointless. He had to be dead.

Parthenope dropped the pistol, and it clattered down the steps. She stared at Pitt.

"I loved him," she said quite steadily. "I would have done anything to defend him. I did . . . anything . . . everything. I dressed up as the gardener's boy and killed Leo Cadell be-

326

cause I thought he was blackmailing Sigmund and would ruin him for something he didn't do. I knew where to find him. I wrote the suicide note on our own stationery, just like the blackmail letters Sigmund received . . . wrote himself." She started to laugh, and then to choke, gasping for breath.

Pitt took a step towards her.

She unfroze. Her whole body was shaking in agonizing grief for love and life and honor lost. She reached behind her waist to the back of her skirt, and her hand came forward holding the other pistol, the pair to the one on the floor at Pitt's feet.

"No!" Pitt shouted, stumbling forward.

But quite calmly now, as if his cry had steadied her, she put both hands on the pistol, lifted it to her mouth and pulled the trigger.

The shot rang out.

He caught her as she pitched forward, holding her in his arms. She was so slight there seemed hardly any weight to her for so much passion. There was nothing he could do. She was already dead. The betrayal, the grief and the unbearable guilt were ended.

He bent and picked her up to carry her, unheeding of the blood, or the pointlessness of being gentle now. She had been a woman who had loved fiercely and blindly, giving her whole heart to a man who had defiled her dreams, and she had broken herself to protect something which had never existed.

He held her tenderly, as if she had been able to know what he felt, as if some kind of pity mattered even now.

He stepped over Tannifer, and Tellman held open the withdrawing room door for him, his face white, his head bowed.

A CONVERSATION
WITH ANNE PERRY

Q. Anne, why did you decide, when you first began writing the Charlotte and Thomas Pitt series, to set your novels in Victorian England?

A. I did not choose the Victorian period with intent. I had been writing nonmystery novels set in many periods, without success. My first mystery, and first book which sold, was *The Cater Street Hangman.* Believe me, nothing makes you love a period like acceptance!

Now I love it for its atmosphere, contrasts between wealth and poverty, what seems to be and what is, for its glamour and squalor, and for the fact that it is largely before the use of science in detection. It is also a mirror of our own time close enough to be valid, and far enough away to be bearable. I get immense pleasure from the manners which are so much subtler than ours, and therefore fun to write about. Romance can legitimately go on for ages.

Q. How much research have you had to do—in the past and on a continuing basis—to ensure that your novels are historically accurate? Do you enjoy the research?

A. To begin with I had to research a great deal. Now I hope I know the period well enough to write most of the book with only minor checking, except for whichever subject I have chosen that is unusual to that book. For example, photography, the workings of the Victorian theatre, 1890s spiritualism, and so on.

Q. Now that you have two long-running series—the Pitt mysteries as well as the more recent William Monk novels—you write two complete books a year. How do you organize your writing time?

A. I love working. I usually begin around nine A.M., break for half an hour's lunch, work again until five P.M. or six P.M., have supper, and often go back for an hour or three in the evening. Monday to Saturday. No one is driving me to this. I do it from choice.

I plan a book in considerable detail long before I start Chapter One, etc. I brainstorm with my assistant, who picks all the holes she can, and then we mend them (I hope). Usually a full single space, legal page per chapter—twelve or thirteen chapters. That may be done up to a year before I start. I like to have two or three in hand.

Q. Do you have a favorite character in your novels?

A. A favorite character? Whomever I am working on at the time. Of all of them, if I have to choose—possibly Great-aunt Vespasia.

Q. In the Monk series, the protagonist is plagued by a faulty memory—sometimes inopportunely faulty. Do you plan to have Monk fully regain his memory, or will he always be troubled by partial amnesia?

A. No, Monk is not going to regain all his memory. Two reasons: I believe it is medically unlikely, and I have far too much pleasure dealing him his past a card at a time to spoil it by dealing the cards all at once. Then I could not spring any surprises.

Q. Some of your novels are being adapted for television. Please tell us about that. And how do you feel about your creations being interpreted by flesh-and-blood actors?

A. I am delighted to say that *The Cater Street Hangman* has been filmed for TV, as a pilot for a series, we hope. In the United

States it played on the A&E network. I think they have done a superb job, everyone involved, but particularly the casting director, who could have taken the actors out of my imagination and given them flesh. The physical appearances are all exactly as I would have wished, but far more important, the spirit is there. I am totally delighted. It is a most extraordinary thrill to see what has been inside your head become real in front of you.

Q. You also write short fiction, notably a story in Ballantine's Canine Crimes *anthology. For you, does the writing process change when you turn to the shorter form?*

A. I enjoy writing short stories, from the totally light and, I hope, funny stories like "Daisy and the Archaeologists" in *Canine Crimes*, through to the dark and tragic mystery, such as the one called "Heroes," set in the trenches of World War One. Yes, the writing process has to be tighter, the plot cannot be fudged at all, and there is little time to set an atmosphere. But drama does not change, nor does dialogue or character—and perhaps not mystery either. You still need a crime, some detection, and an honest resolution.

Q. In your spare time, what writers do you *read?*

A. Whom do I read? I have just been rereading a little Dante, a lot of poetry, sometimes fantasy, and am about to start a book given me today about religious versus humanist ethics.

I also enjoy all sorts of mysteries, particularly present-day American—as far from my own as possible!